Chivalry at its finest . . .

"The Traveller"
By Lynn Kurland,
USA TODAY BESTSELLING AUTHOR OF *MY HEART STOOD STILL*

A bedraggled knight makes a solemn vow to protect, defend,
and rescue any and all maidens in distress—
even those from Manhattan . . .

"The Minstrel"
By Patricia Potter,
USA TODAY BESTSELLING AUTHOR OF *THE PERFECT FAMILY*

A vow to marry for love transforms a marquis into
a minstrel who must sing for his supper—
and for a woman whose heart is true . . .

"The Bachelor Knight"
By Deborah Simmons,
USA TODAY BESTSELLING AUTHOR OF *MY LORD DEBURGH*

A forgotten vow comes back to haunt
the greatest knight in all the land,
when a fair maiden asks for *his* hand in marriage . . .

"The Siege"
By Glynnis Campbell,
AUTHOR OF *MY CHAMPION*

Trapped underground with his unwilling betrothed,
a determined knight vows to free her—body and soul . . .

A Knight's Vow

Lynn Kurland
Patricia Potter
Deborah Simmons
and
Glynnis Campbell

JOVE BOOKS, NEW YORK

This is a work of fiction. Names, characters, places, and incidents are either the product of the author's imagination or are used fictitiously, and any resemblance to actual persons, living or dead, business establishments, events, or locales is entirely coincidental.

A KNIGHT'S VOW

A Jove Book / published by arrangement with
the authors

PRINTING HISTORY
Jove edition / September 2001

Visit our website at
www.penguinputnam.com

ISBN: 0-515-13151-2

A JOVE BOOK®
Jove Books are published by The Berkley Publishing Group,
a division of Penguin Putnam Inc.,
375 Hudson Street, New York, New York 10014.
JOVE and the "J" design
are trademarks belonging to Penguin Putnam Inc.

PRINTED IN THE UNITED STATES OF AMERICA

10 9 8 7 6 5 4 3 2 1

Contents

The
Traveller

✝

Lynn Kurland

Once upon a time there was a knight who made a vow, a solemn vow given with all his heart and soul to protect . . .

one

A nearly deserted chapel near the Scottish border, 1299

The air inside the small chapel was thick with portents, omens, and a goodly amount of dust. The latter caused the resident priest to double over with hacking that came close to rendering him quite unfit for his duties. He straightened finally with a great creaking noise, then coughed gingerly a time or two to test the workings of his frail frame. Finding it not unequal to his present business, he took a deep, wheezing breath and continued.

"Ah, let me think a moment," he said, scratching his stubbled cheek, "um . . . a vow . . . ah, a *solemn* vow to protect—"

"Aye, aye," the knight standing before him said impatiently, picking a nit or two off his tabard and noting the threadbare patches. Damned seamstresses.

"And defend women of all stations—"

The knight grunted in grudging assent. All women save seamstresses, perhaps.

"And champion children—"

The knight turned a baleful eye on the nearest child he could see—his squire, no less—who was currently rummaging about behind the altar. The old priest was concentrating so hard on remembering what he was trying to say that he apparently didn't realize what mischief the boy was combining. The squire popped up from behind the stones with a triumphant smile, holding aloft a loaf of bread in one hand and a jug of drink in the other.

"Excuse me for but a moment, Father," the knight said politely. He strode around to relieve the lad of his burdens, then booted him strongly on the backside. The boy went scampering off with a curse. Not as foul a curse as it likely could have been, though. The lad had no illusions about not receiving his share of the spoils. He scuttled to the back of the crumbling chapel and huddled near the knight's gear. The knight tucked the bread under one arm, the bottle under the other and went to stand in front of the friar yet again.

"Now," he said shortly, "let us be about this sorry business. I've an assault to mount, and I need your blessing."

The priest chewed upon toothless gums. "Let us see, my lord," he said, fumbling nervously with his robes and apparently searching his aging mind for further promises to bind upon the hapless man before him. "Um . . . women . . . um . . . children . . . er—"

"Nuisances, both," the knight muttered.

"Hoisting of swords and such," the priest said, looking upward for a bit of inspiration.

"Aye, aye," the man said, wondering if hoisting his sword with a man of the cloth skewered thereon would count as a breach of the vow he was making. He forbore, however. He had need of whatever help he could obtain. His inheritance hung in the balance.

"Ah," the priest said suddenly, springing to life as if he'd been pierced by St. George's sainted blade itself. "Aye, one last thing is needful."

The knight felt himself chill at the sudden fire that burned brightly in the priest's eyes. He hardly dared speculate on what it might mean for him. Even so, he was no coward, so he pressed forward.

"And that would be?" the knight asked, steeling himself for the worst.

The priest's words spewed forth in a great rush. "The most important thing of all, something that no honorable knight would think to go into battle without, aye, likely the most fitting vow a man of a chivalrous nature would take upon himself . . ."

The knight flinched. The saints preserve him.

"A vow to protect—"

Never a pleasant word.

"Defend—"

Even worse.

"And rescue—"

The knight closed his eyes and began a prayer of his own.

"Any and all maidens in distress, but preferably a maiden in the greatest of distress . . ."

And then Sir William de Piaget, rebellious son of the useless, never-take-a-vow-upon-pain-of-death Hubert of Artane, grandson of the illustrious Phillip of Artane and great-grandson of the legendary Robin of Artane, knew he was in deep trouble, for no lad from Artane—save his sire, of course—had ever made a vow he hadn't kept. It would be as impossible for William to break his word as it would be to take his own life.

But the thought of a possible maiden in distress, added to his other problems, was almost enough to induce him to consider both.

Once upon a time there was a knight who made a vow, a solemn vow given with all his heart and soul to protect women of all stations, champion children, defend and rescue any and all maidens in distress, but preferably one in the greatest of distress . . .

two

❧

Julianna Nelson stared glumly at the selections facing her at the counter. What she wanted was a DoveBar with dark chocolate firmly encasing chocolate ice cream that would leave her twitching till about 2 A.M. But in her continuing and eternal quest to remove ten pounds from her thighs, she had decided that the pleasures of the cocoa bean were no longer hers.

Damn it anyway.

"I'll take the carob-covered raisins," she said with a sigh.

"Excellent choice," the salesgirl said. "I'll throw in a few carob-covered carrot slices as well. They're well chilled," she said with a bright smile. "You'll love 'em."

Julianna could imagine many things she might feel toward them, but she suspected love would not be on that list.

"Anything to drink?"

Julianna looked hopefully for some sort of cola dispenser, but she saw nothing but a blender and what looked remarkably like lawn clippings in the bowl next to it, so she shook her head no. Quickly. Before the girl decided to puree any of that grass into something resembling a beverage.

Julianna took her purchases, hoisted her bag onto her shoulder and shuffled gloomily toward an empty table near the window. Actually, all the tables were empty, but she hoped that at least there she might soak in a few UV rays to cheer herself up. She sat, tried a carrot, tried not to gag, and looked around for something to take her mind off what she was trying to ingest.

Ah, her mail. She'd grabbed it on her way out that morning for another ugly day of job hunting. She'd made it through two interviews before stopping for sustenance. Unfortunately, there wasn't much call for her kind of specialty in New York these days. Her prospects were grim and her savings account balance even grimmer. She'd have to do something, and soon, if she intended to eat again. It was tempting to indulge in a far-fetched wish that a knight in shining armor might come to rescue her from her plight. That was certainly more appealing than the alternatives.

Going home wasn't an option. She'd have to listen to her father lecture her on the idiocy of having gotten two advanced degrees in Ancient Languages while dabbling in cartooning and lapidary arts. She'd have to yet again explain her fascination with all things old, with things that made her laugh, and with sparkling things that went around her wrists and dangled from her ears—and why she had no desire to teach any of the above.

Her mother would look at her reproachfully and ask when she planned on settling down and producing a few grandchildren. Then she would face the inevitable comparisons between her and her sisters. No, home was not the place for her right now.

Siblings? Well, there was always her older sister's offer of a couch, but that came with let-me-set-you-up strings attached and Julianna didn't want to be set up. If she couldn't manage to land a decent job, how was she supposed to land a decent guy—even if he came as a fix-up? No, far better that she get her life together, then look for a man.

She could only hope that when she managed the former, she wouldn't be too old to attempt the latter.

She sighed, indulged in carob-covered raisins, and pulled out her mail. Bills, bills, and catalogs she could never afford to order from. She gathered up the lot to pitch in the trash when something slipped out, falling onto the table with a substantial *plop*. Julianna looked at the return address and blinked in surprise.

All right, so she wasn't completely surprised. The letter was from a college roommate she hadn't seen in years, but it was, after all, not entirely unsolicited. Julianna had written her old roommate in care of that roommate's publisher, but she'd only half expected a response. That she'd actually run across Elizabeth again was something of a miracle.

She'd been intending to use some scraped-together money for a nice, highbrow piece of ancient poetry when she'd seen a book just lying on a chair in her favorite bookstore. She'd picked it up and almost put it back down again. Romance wasn't her thing, but she'd flipped back to look at the author photo just to see what kind of yahoo wrote the stuff. Her surprise was complete when Elizabeth Smith's face stared back at her.

Elizabeth's bio had said she was married and living in Scotland. Julianna wasn't very good at keeping up with old friends, but she'd found herself turning over a new leaf. She had taken the plunge and written. It had seemed like a good thing to do at the time, though she hadn't really expected anything to come of it.

Now as she read her old friend's letter, she realized that maybe that small effort on her part might have been one of the best decisions she'd ever made.

There was the usual business about home and family (husband, son and another child on the way), and a dismissive line or two about what was apparently a very successful career. But it was the very last of the letter that had Julianna sitting up straighter in her chair.

You mentioned you were changing jobs. If you have some free time, why don't you come to Scotland? We have plenty of room in the keep, and you'd be amazed at what Jamie's land can do toward healing all sorts of hurts. You can stay as long as you like. Who knows, you might even find yourself never wanting to leave.

But I have to warn you now, you'll need to be careful where you go. I know you'll have a hard time believing this, and I probably shouldn't be putting it in writing, but there are several places near our home that require care while roaming over.

Julianna frowned. And just what was that supposed to mean? Would she be thrown in jail for trampling clumps of heather or annoying delicately constitutioned sheep?

You have to be careful in England, too, or so we've found. I'm sending you a map. If you come straight here and don't stray off the beaten path, you should be okay. In case you get lost, though, be careful. Like I said, you never know what kinds of unexpected travel you might be doing thanks to an innocent patch of grass.

Julianna flipped to the last page and looked at the map Elizabeth had drawn. She recognized England's shape. There were several Xs drawn here and there. Julianna peered more closely and saw that beside each was a little label written in Elizabeth's clear hand.

Chaucer's England.

Revolutionary France.

Trip to the Picts.

Julianna laughed. She couldn't help it. Either Elizabeth was trying to cheer her up with a little make-believe, or she had smelled too much pure air and lost her mind. Julianna suspected that perhaps it was the former. Elizabeth had always been able to make her laugh, had always thought Julianna's forays into cartoonland were brilliant and had worn every piece of jewelry Julianna had made her—even when the metal had been of considerably iffy quality.

And now an invitation to visit. Julianna looked out the window and felt a strange hope begin to bloom in her heart. Scotland in the spring. Could there be a more lovely place to try to right what was wrong in her heart? She mentally counted the meager contents of her savings account. If she found a cheap fare, didn't eat much en route (or afterward), and mooched off Elizabeth while she was there, she might actually manage it. Besides, who knew what kind of contacts she might make? Maybe she'd run into someone who had a need for a little Old English translation, or help with his Anglo-Saxon, or had some Roman inscriptions he was just dying to learn to read. She had skills. She was just trying to use them in the wrong place.

Julianna folded the letter up and had almost tucked it away in her purse when she noticed a very small postscript.

By the way, watch out for Gramercy Park as well. That place is a minefield. Fell asleep on a bench there once and wound up practically on another planet. Love, E.

Julianna revisited her earlier opinion of her friend's mental state. It was obvious Elizabeth had lost her mind and was now mixing fantasy with reality. The book Elizabeth had written had been a time-travel where the heroine had fallen asleep on a park bench and woken up in medieval Scotland, but that had been pure fiction as far as Julianna had been concerned. Obviously, Elizabeth was starting to take herself way too seriously.

Well, the very least she could do as a friend was to hurry over and bring the girl to her senses. Surely she could deplete the rest of her meager funds on such a mission of mercy and not feel guilty about it.

Julianna shoved her carob delights into her high-capacity black shoulder bag, hoisted it and left the shop. Too bad such Gramercy-Park transporting wasn't possible. It would have saved on plane fare.

She paused outside Rockefeller Center and contemplated her next two appointments with placement agencies.

A dead-end job or a trip to Gramercy Park?

A painful afternoon trying to justify her skills, or an afternoon in the sunshine on a park bench, willing herself across the ocean?

It took her all of two minutes to decide before she turned and jaywalked across the street—communicating to the angry cabbies in the multilingual hand gestures all true New Yorkers instinctively knew—then stopped in at Godiva's to charge a very expensive box of assorted truffles. That necessity seen to, she then headed toward the subway that would drop her near Gramercy Park. What the hell. If she was going to lose her mind, her savings and all possibilities of food and rent money in one afternoon, she might as well be fat, happy and relaxed while she did it.

Once she'd reached the park, she concentrated on finding a likely bench. All were occupied with various sorts of people she had no desire to get to know better.

And then she came upon The Bench.

She looked at it and had the strangest tingle go down her spine. It could have been from the volume of bird poop adorning it, but then again, it could have been something else. Julianna looked down at her one good suit, a black Donna Karan number that had cost her an enormous amount of money but was practically guaranteed to get her taken seriously in any number of employment situations. She wondered how hard it would be for the dry cleaner to remove bird droppings from the back.

Expensively hard, she decided. No sense in adding any unnecessary expenses to her venture. She looked around for something to use as cleaning tools. She plucked a couple of leaves off the tree overhanging the bench, made herself a relatively clean place and turned to back into the seat. She heard what sounded like a shotgun go off over her head and sat down in surprise. Her surprise doubled when she felt herself sit in something remarkably squishy. Before she had a chance to wonder what it had been, the same explosive sound came from just above her head. She realized that the same bird had deposited a second, and hopefully final, load onto her shoulder.

She had no need to ask what she had just sat in.

The bird chirped once and flew off, apparently feeling much better.

Julianna was suddenly very grateful for a warm day, as it was a certainty she wouldn't be going anywhere until after dark now. She probably could have covered herself up with the shawl she'd stuffed in her bag that morning, but that would have meant more dry cleaning and she suspected what she now had already was going to cost her a fortune. So she turned her mind to more interesting things, namely discovering just what lay inside that five-pound assortment of Godiva she'd just purchased. She sniffed, selected, nibbled, then began her work of focusing on getting herself zapped over to Scotland without having to resort to forking out plane fare. She savored the chocolate and fantasized about fields of heather and handsome, bekilted Scotsmen.

Time passed.

She contemplated getting up and going for a drink, but then she might have lost her place on The Bench and that she couldn't have.

The afternoon waned.

A bathroom was starting to sound mighty nice as well, but that would have meant facing the general public and Julianna did still have her pride. She could only imagine the looks she would get in her doo-doo-bedecked silk suit.

Twilight fell.

It was starting to get cold. The park, she found, was suddenly quite empty. She pulled her feet up onto the bench and hugged her knees. A strange mist came up from the ground and surrounded her. Now, if it had been just any odd mist, she would have chalked it up to a sudden cloud of cannabis wafting her way from behind a bush, but it was more than that. Much more. There was a chill and a definite sense of Something Being Up.

Julianna grabbed her bag and began to wonder if Elizabeth's book had been more autobiographical than she'd admitted. Then again, hadn't Elizabeth warned Julianna about the park?

"Oh, man," she whispered, squeezing her eyes shut and hoping her sudden sense of vertigo was due to four truffles of superior strength and quality. "Man, oh, man."

A stiff breeze full of mist blew over her suddenly. She opened her eyes and saw a boy standing in front of her, possibly the filthiest, scrawniest-looking teenager she had ever seen. His eyes widened and he yelped and ran off before she could yelp and run off herself.

And then she realized something else.

She wasn't sitting on a park bench anymore.

She started to hiccup.

She should have paid more attention to Elizabeth's postscript. She'd been cocky. She'd been pooped on. There had been red flags aplenty, but she'd ignored them. Maybe she deserved what she was getting.

And now, here she sat in a location of indeterminate origin, listening to what sounded remarkably like cursing coming her way—Old Norman French cursing, mixed in liberally with a few of those Middle English swear words she was just certain no one had ever really used.

She closed her eyes tight, clutched her bag to her chest and tried to smother her hiccups. Maybe if she sang a cheerful song her reality would return to normal. Yes, that was the ticket. She latched on to the first thing that came to mind.

"It's the story . . . of a lovely lady . . ."

three

❦

" 'Tis the *sorriest* tale I've ever heard," William growled at his squire. "A woman did you say?"

"Sittin' all alone," the boy nodded, his eyes huge in his face. "Rockin' and singin' as if she's a mad thing."

"Sitting where?" William demanded.

"Where you intends to scale the wall, my lord, else I wouldn't have troubled you."

William grunted. At least he'd trained Peter that well. He looked skyward, cursed, then shook his head. The bloody venture had been doomed from the start. And now a mad creature to dispatch before he could be about his business. For all he knew, she had alerted the keep's inhabitants to his intentions already.

The siege was not going as he had planned. Apparently his sire—the same fool who had absconded with William's keep—had removed his lips from the ale spigot long enough to see to a defense. Twelve men only, and some of them less than able, but 'twas still a dozen against one. Or one and a bit, if you were to count Peter in the bargain, though how a cast-aside bastard child rescued from village streets could be much aid against trained men, William surely didn't know.

For the first time he found himself regretting not having acquired a few guardsmen over the years. Aye, and he should have held on to much more of the gold he'd acquired from his forays into the French tournament circuit. Unfortunately, he'd never thought to want home and hearth, so what had been the need for bags of gold that called out to any and all ruffians? William had preferred to travel lightly, live riotously, and remain free of the clutches of thieves and desperate heiresses both. No men to feed had seemed like a good thing at the time, but now he began to wonder if he might have been better served to have retained a few men-at-arms to aid him in his ventures.

Not that he'd ever suspected he would have any ventures—not of this sort anyway. Being the second son of a completely useless second son, he had known he would have little, if anything, come his way. His grandsire had been generous enough to have seen him sent to squire. Phillip had also equipped William with a bright new sword and fine destrier upon his having earned his spurs. For those things alone, William had been damned grateful. He surely hadn't expected anything else.

It had caught him completely by surprise to have a missive find him in France telling him that he had an inheritance—albeit a less-than-perfect one—in England and would he please return to claim it? William had known of his grandsire's passing, but hadn't been able to return to see him laid to rest. The tidings of his prize in England had come from his uncle. William had been surprised at the gift but even more surprised that the keep hadn't gone to his father or his brother first.

Then again, his father and brother were fools, which both his uncle and his grandsire had known very well. Appreciating his uncle's good judgment, William had been more than happy to see to a bit of said uncle's business before taking up his residence.

He had then expected to make his way north and find a hot fire and drinkable wine waiting for him. He hadn't expected to find his father in possession of his inheritance.

Damn the useless fool.

So, now he was faced with the unenviable task of trying to wrest his home from underneath his sire before his sire depleted what poor sustenance remained in the larder and impregnated what minimal number of serving wenches might be found inside.

"The woman, my lord," Peter reminded him.

And if that weren't task enough, now he had a mad-woman to contend with?

"Aye, aye," William grumbled. "Show me the way, lad. Mayhap she can hoist a sword. We'll put her to use."

But he cursed fluently and vigorously as he tromped after his squire. The mist was formidable and it wasn't until they were fair crashing into the wall surrounding the keep that William realized where they were.

Well, 'twas a woman, to be sure. Daft as a duck, no less. She was rocking and singing just as Peter had warned, with her eyes scrunched up tight and a sack of some kind clutched firmly to her chest. William found the words of her song unintelligible and the tune nothing short of irritating.

"Will you cease?" he whispered sharply. "Will you bring the barbarians from the north down upon us with that foul noise?"

The woman opened her eyes and then closed them again just as quickly. Her teeth began to chatter, which did nothing to improve the rendition of her lays.

William looked up and saw the glint of something directly above the woman's head. He shoved Peter back, then leaped forward and hauled the woman to her feet.

And then, as if he'd been trying to maul her instead of rescue her, the ungrateful wench hauled back and clouted him with the sack she had been clinging to.

William stumbled backward and clutched the abused side of his head as he tried to regain the sense she had fair knocked from him. He blinked a time or two and eyed the heavy black sack with disfavor.

A movement above assured him there was yet something else unfriendly afoot. He reached out to jerk the woman away from certain danger only to find she was rearing back for another swing. He backed away instinctively, then watched in horror as the contents of a large pot were poured down upon the hapless wench—half expecting to find her screaming from being drenched in boiling oil.

Hearty laughter from above turned his suspicions in another direction. As did the sudden cessation of all movement and sound from the madwoman in front of him.

William leaned forward and sniffed. Then he put his hand
to his nose to save it further abuse and looked at the former
contents of the keep's cesspit which now adorned the
woman standing before him. Apparently all was not well at
Redesburn's supper table. William shook his head in sympathy.

And as he did so, an unwelcome memory assaulted him.

. . . *vow to protect, defend, and rescue any and all maidens in distress . . .*

The priest's gleefully spoken words echoed through
William's poor mind, making him wonder what in hell's
name he'd been thinking to visit a priest in the first place.
And to have given his word? By the saints, he'd been just
as daft as the creature before him!

He looked at her narrowly. Surely this one didn't qualify
as one he should rescue. He spent a moment or two working that out only to find himself assaulted by yet another
annoying thought.

Chivalry is never convenient.

William pursed his lips. That had been his grandsire's favorite saying. And as his grandsire had already given him
so much—including all his gear, his morals, and enough of
the Artane blood that the gift of swordplay ran true in
him—William supposed he had little choice but to heed the
words and rescue the damned woman.

Mayhap it would rain and rid her of some of her stench.

William cursed heartily, grasped the woman by the hand
that clutched her sack so she would leave off with clouting
him with it, and dragged her after him. At least she had
ceased with her singing. William found himself grateful for
that small respite.

He stomped back to his camp, cursing all the way. What
was he to do with the wench now that he'd rescued her? He
needed his mind focused on the task at hand, not fretting
over furnishing soft surroundings for a woman. The stench
of cesspit leavings wafted past him again, and he decided
that the first thing to do was rid her of that. Even if she
could keep herself from singing, she would give away their
position by her smell alone.

William paused at his hastily made camp and consid-

ered. This was not a place he'd intended to inhabit for
long—surely not long enough to see to the comfort of a
woman. They could make no fire, lest it give away his position, and there was nothing to use for a shelter. He sighed
and rolled his eyes heavenward. Why couldn't things have
been simple?

Retreat.

What a nasty word that was.

It appeared he had no choice. He looked at Peter.
"Gather our gear. We'll go back to the chapel."

Peter apparently found the idea to his liking, for he
wasted no time in doing as commanded. William wondered
if there had been perhaps more sustenance behind the altar
than he'd noticed. He saddled his mount, then looked at the
woman he'd left standing a pace or two behind him. She
was watching him with what he could only deem horror.

"What?" he demanded. "Have you never cast eyes on a
poor knight before?"

Her eyes were huge in her face. She shook her head
slowly.

At least she wasn't completely witless. But that she
should think so little of him, his threadbare tabard and
patched cloak aside, rankled. He drew himself up.

"I am lord of that keep," he said, pointing back toward
his absconded-with castle. "I was attempting to retake it
when you distracted me from my purpose."

She looked neither impressed nor contrite. Indeed, she
looked to be on the verge of breaking into song again.
William reached for her bag, intending to hold it for her
whilst she mounted his horse. She held it away immediately, her eyes taking on a feverish light.

"What have you therein?" he asked in annoyance. "Sacred relics?"

"W-what?" she managed.

Ah, so she was at least capable of a response, useless
though it might have been. William looked at her with a
fresh eye. Perhaps she wasn't as daft as she seemed. And
then he looked at her truly and wondered why he'd been so
distracted by the disasters around him that he hadn't seen
what he was facing. He ignored the refuse in her hair and on

her clothes and noticed, for the first time, just how
strangely she was dressed.

All in black, she was, as if she'd been a demon sent
straight from Hell. Her skirts—if that's what they could be
deemed—fell just to her knees in the manner of the Scots.
Below that, her legs were as black as her skirts, but with
big, gaping patches of white. William bent and examined
and found that her legs were covered by hose, but of a
flimsy kind of cloth he'd never before seen.

And then there were her shoes. They had likely been
white at one time and perhaps would be nearly so again
once they were clean. They were laced with colored string
of some kind and adorned with shiny beads. The beads directly over her toes were yellow with marks that greatly resembled a smiling face.

Miraculous and nothing but. William straightened and
looked at the woman again. Perhaps she was a saint come
back to life, or an angel come to aid him in his quest. For
all he knew, aiding her might in turn be what aided him—

He found himself suddenly on his back thanks to a great
wallop on the head. He shook his head and struggled to
clear his vision. His lurched to his feet and swayed for a
moment or two.

"She went that way," Peter said wisely, pointing to the
south.

William tossed Peter onto their packhorse, then swung
up onto his own mount. It took him only minutes to catch
the woman, and by that time, his temper had fair overcome
him.

"Stop, you fiendish wench!" he bellowed.

The woman turned to look at him without ceasing her
flight and that was her mistake. She tripped and went
sprawling. William winced at the unmistakable sound of
skull against something unyielding. He pulled up his mount
and jumped down.

Damnation, this was all he needed to make his miserable
life complete. He scooped the wench up in his arms, tossed
her over his horse's withers and mounted. Now he had no
choice but to make for the church again. Perhaps he would

leave her there and return to see to his business. Aye, that would count as rescuing, wouldn't it?

He studiously ignored the fact that foisting her off on an unwilling priest might not fulfill the defending and protecting portions of his vow.

Vows, he thought with disgust.

He should have known where they would lead.

four

❧

Julianna came to with a roaring headache. She didn't dare open her eyes, on the off chance the pain might choose to intensify. Good grief, what had happened to her? Had she been assaulted by thugs? Robbed? Mugged while innocently savoring chocolate on a park bench?

She wrinkled her nose at the smell that seemed to be all around her. Maybe she'd sat in bird poop so long that it was starting to take on an odor she hadn't known it could. Well, no sense in putting off the inevitable any longer. She would have to open her eyes, get up and go home. Maybe it was still dark outside and she would only be gaped at by night-people on the subway. It could have been worse.

She opened her eyes.

Oh. It *was* worse.

There, not five feet from her, was a man—a man she unfortunately recognized all too well. Damn, she thought she'd dreamed him. But there he was, with his little scrawny helper, starting to go through her purse.

"Hey," she croaked. "Stop that."

The man looked up calmly, as if he felt no guilt at rifling through her things. He held her chocolate in one large hand. Julianna watched in horror as he prepared to toss her box of truffles over his shoulder.

"That's Godiva, you idiot," she gasped, lurching forward.

He said one word very sharply. Julianna quickly ran through her mental New Jersey–synonym finder and came up with a blank. Searching back into the unused portions of her overeducated brain, she came up with an obscure word that sounded remarkably like what the man had just barked at her.

Poison.

"Heavens no," she said. "Chocolate." She held her head between her hands and crawled over to the man on her knees. She kept one hand in place to keep her head from spinning off her shoulders and groped for her things. She shoved what little he'd gotten around to investigating back into her purse and snatched the golden treasure from his hands. "It might be the last of it I can afford." She inched her way back to the wall she'd been apparently sleeping against and clutched her bag to her chest. No sense in letting it out of her sight again.

It took a moment or two for her head to clear, and when it did, she wished it hadn't. Maybe she had a concussion. Maybe her headache was causing hallucinations. Maybe she was losing her mind.

Well, whatever the case really was, one thing was for sure: She wasn't in Gramercy Park anymore.

She suspected she might not even be in Manhattan anymore.

Maybe there'd been more to Elizabeth's map than met the eye.

She looked around her. She was in a ramshackle old stone church. It still had a roof and walls, but there were plants growing where they shouldn't be and all sorts of nestlike items loitering inside that she was just sure housed animals of dubious origin. She looked to her right and saw an altar adorned with what she could only assume was an unconscious priest. She was worried he might be dead until he suddenly gave a great snort, then began to snore.

Okay, you might have found something like that in Jersey.

But that didn't account for the guy facing her who continued to demand "Who are you?" and "Whence hail you?" in a language that sounded remarkably like Middle English. When those very intelligible words gave way to what resembled Norman French to a frightening degree and a litany of curses she could only half understand, she began to think that even Jersey couldn't produce something quite this strange.

Then there was the chain mail to consider. A student of medieval languages didn't learn the words without learning a great deal about the history. His gear looked late 13th century. Maybe early 14th if he'd been poor and had to use hand-me-downs. But his sword was very bright and no doubt very sharp. She looked to her left and found two large horses standing just inside the front door of the church.

Hollywood movie set?

She had her doubts.

By the way, watch out for Gramercy Park. That place is a minefield. Fell asleep on a bench there once and wound up practically on another planet.

Elizabeth's words came back to her mind with uncomfortable clarity. *Another planet* was just a figure of speech, wasn't it? She hadn't landed on some kind of *Star Trek* world where life was perpetually stuck in the Middle Ages, had she?

". . . and to be sure, I only made the vow to assure myself of success," the man was saying as he eyed her with distinct disfavor.

Julianna had been watching his lips move; she realized only then that he'd been using them to form words.

"I'll need all of that I can have," he continued with a grumble, "for removing his sorry arse from my keep will be a difficult task even if he can scarce hoist a sword to save his neck."

Julianna felt as if she'd been dumped suddenly into a foreign country where the babbling going on around her had suddenly begun to resemble the language she'd been diligently studying. Only, she was beginning to wonder if her brief semester exchange at Cambridge had been enough to get her American professors' accents out of her ears. Then it struck her that she was listening to a man gripe at her in Norman French and curse the teenager sitting next to him in Middle English—and it was then she began to be firmly convinced that she was losing her mind.

"'Tis his father's sorry arse he speaks of," the teenager supplied cheerfully. "Stole his—"

The kid ducked a friendly, if pointed, cuff to his ear and fell silent. Julianna looked at the man and latched on to the one word she thought she could repeat without screaming.

"Vow?" she asked hoarsely.

"Aye, pox rot you," the man replied curtly.

She blinked at him.

He cursed. "To rescue and defend any and all maidens in distress—"

"Protect," the priest supplied in a weak voice, then began to cough, which precipitated an abrupt slide off the altar. He landed with another cough and a snort. He shifted around, made himself comfortable, then almost immediately began to snore again.

The man threw the man of the rotting cloth a dark look, then returned his unfriendly gaze to her. "Now, for the last time, what is your name? Whence hail you?"

Julianna took a deep breath. It was just all too unreal. She couldn't believe what she was hearing. She didn't want to believe what she was smelling. Her every molecule of common sense didn't want to come to the conclusion that seemed most obvious.

Time travel.

It wasn't possible.

Was it?

She looked at the man and smiled weakly. What the hell. Might as well try out the truth on him and see how he reacted. Maybe she would exhaust his stores of Norman French, and he would give up the game and admit it had all been an elaborate hoax. He'd show her to the showers, beg her forgiveness for pulling her leg so hard and long, and then offer her a job with his reenactment society.

Or maybe he wouldn't do any of those things. Maybe he wouldn't believe her, he'd think she was a witch, and try to burn her at the stake. Because no matter what her common sense said, she was almost certain she wasn't in Manhattan anymore. Though her forays into the lands south of the city had been few, she was almost certain that not even Jersey could cough up scenery like this. The one thing she was sure of was that the man she was going to have to get help from didn't exactly look like he headed up the local Welcome Wagon.

"Your name," he repeated.

"Name," she agreed with a croak. "Julianna Nelson. I'm from New York." She was certain her accent was far from perfect, but she hoped she was managing to get her words in the right places and get her meaning across. "Manhattan," she clarified.

"Manhattan?" he repeated. He shook his head with a frown. "'Tis unfamiliar to me."

"That ain't the half of it, buddy," she said under her breath.

Then she took a deep breath—and wished she hadn't. Memories flooded back, as did the strong suspicion that she'd had the contents of a Porta Potti dumped on her. She started to hiccup. It always happened to her when she got really stressed. It was unpleasant during job interviews; now it was just downright annoying—probably because every time she sucked in air involuntarily, she wasn't quite sure what else she was sucking in off her clothes.

"Water," she asked. *"Hic-hic."*

"Hic-hic?" He looked at her as if she'd lost her mind, but another round of violent hiccups apparently cleared up the mystery for him. He frowned. "There is a stream—"

"Yes." She nodded. "Where?"

He rose, eyeing her bag once more, but apparently her smell was enough to keep him at bay. He kept his distance enthusiastically as he led her out the front of the chapel and a small distance away. He pointed to the small trickle, then folded his arms over his chest and waited.

Julianna took a big drink, praying the water wasn't polluted enough to kill her. It didn't stop her hiccups, but it slowed them down enough that she could turn her mind to others things—namely a bit of a bath. Never mind that it was raining enough to soak her through to the skin. Never mind that there wasn't enough current for a good wash and that a good wash would likely have given her pneumonia. She wanted her clothes off, her hair clean and she wanted to do it in peace. She looked at her unwilling host.

"Go," she said pointedly. No sense in muddying up the communication flow with words that didn't need to be there.

"Nay."

"Privacy," she attempted, with another hiccup.

He looked at her blankly.

"I want to be alone," she said, in her best Garbo imitation.

That only served to force his eyebrows up below his ragged bangs. He put his hand on his sword.

"My vow," he said, as if the very words left a bad taste in his mouth. "I will protect you. 'Tis my knightly duty."

"You could—*hic*—turn your back."

"I might miss an assailant."

Great, a lecher with scruples. Julianna considered her alternative, which was to smell like a sewer for the foreseeable future, then turned her back on her uneager protector and took stock. She set her bag aside, then took off her shoes and tried to discreetly pull down her nylons. They were almost a total loss, though she supposed holes were better than completely bare legs, so she put them in a pile to wash. She took off her jacket and wondered if a good dunking in a cold stream would violate the dry-clean-only dictum on the tag. There appeared to be no other choice. Her skirt followed, adorned as it was by bird poop and other unmentionable substances. Her blouse only had minor damage, so she started with that first, ignoring the fact that she was kneeling in the mud with her back to a man, wearing only her slip.

She'd had better days.

She also could have wished for much firmer thighs as she leaned over and dunked her head into the water. The touch of the icy stream sent her headache into another dimension entirely, and she thought she just might faint. Before she could truly give in to the impulse, she felt strong hands on her arms, holding her back from a complete tumble into the stream bed. An ungentle hand washed her hair for her, then wrung the water out with an expert twist or two. Julianna soon found herself back on her feet, squinting up at a man substantially taller and broader than she, who apparently wasn't bothered by a little rain. She wiped the water out of her eyes, took as good a look as her pounding head would allow and realized, with a start, that while her rescuer might have been grumpy, he was extraordinarily good looking.

His hair was dark as sin—and as the thought ran through her mind, she realized that she had perhaps read one too many of Elizabeth's romances. Since she'd only read one, perhaps even that had been too much for her. Too bad she didn't write them. The man in front of her would have been good hero material. He had an amazing pair of light gray eyes, a chiseled jaw and sculpted cheekbones. Yessir, she would definitely have to tell Elizabeth about him the first chance she got.

She also suspected shoulders and arms that looked that substantial even in chain mail didn't come from a desk job. He made her feel fragile. She sensed that, miraculously, the extra ten pounds on her thighs were melting into insignificance.

"Can you stand?" he asked.

"Um-hmm," she said, unable to suppress the start of a smile. She noticed, quite suddenly, that her hiccups had gone the way of her common sense. Well, if she had to get thrown back into some alternate reality, or off into some rustic land that time had forgotten, this was certainly the way to go. "Thank you."

He grunted. "Damned vow."

But his grumbling didn't stop him from dumping all her clothes into the stream and swishing them around in a particularly manly fashion—quickly and not very carefully. Julianna would have protested his less-than-gentle treatment of her two-month-salary suit, but then again, she wasn't having to wash it and watching her rescuer do her laundry was wrenching another smile from someplace very tender inside her.

He had all her dripping things in one great paw, and then he turned purposely toward her bag.

And her smile faded abruptly.

She dove for it just as he did and for the second time in recent memory she felt as if she'd dashed her head against a rock. She straightened, rubbing her head only to find him doing the same thing. She scowled at him, received a scowl in return, then found herself beginning to sway. She really had to stop abusing her skull or she'd be in serious trouble. She watched the ground beginning to come toward her and closed her eyes in self-defense. Great, all that washing up and now she was going to get all muddy again.

She soon found herself, however, not on the ground but held up on her feet by a pair of very strong hands.

With her bag firmly clutched to her chest, of course. Not

even a potential slide into unconsciousness was enough to make her let go when Godiva was at stake.

"I'll carry that," he announced, looking at the bag purposefully.

Couldn't he think about anything else? "You won't," she stated with equal firmness.

"I'll not maul your sacred relics."

She looked up at him skeptically. She'd seen him starting to look through her bag with the methodical impartiality of an NYPD veteran. His apparent lack of respect for her comfort food was enough to forbid him any further access. Who knew what else he might choose to discard?

He sighed, rolled his eyes heavenward and, before she could squeak out a protest, swooped her up into his arms and was striding back toward the crumbling church, her clothes and shoes grasped carelessly in one hand.

"Oh, my," she said, putting her hand to her heart in a Southern Belle gesture she had never before used in her life.

Dire circumstances brought out the best in a woman, apparently.

He grumbled something at her, and it took a moment or two for her to work it out. When she did, she started to laugh.

Chivalry is never convenient.

He looked at her, seemingly startled, then frowned and continued on his way. Julianna found herself deposited back where she'd started. Her clothes hit the floor next to her. She stood, shivering, and watched as the man fetched a blanket from his gear. He came over to her with an easy gait and draped the blanket around her shoulders.

"Oh," she said, nonplussed. "Thank you."

He grunted, then turned and nudged his dozing companion with his foot.

"Up, Peter," he said. "Keep watch. No fire, understood?"

"But, my lord, where go—"

"To sleep, child. You'll manage for an hour or two."

The boy named Peter gulped, then jumped to his feet. He accepted the man's sword with scrawny, quaking arms and a great shiver. Julianna watched as the knight—and she could hardly call him anything else after watching him draw that medieval broadsword with the big fat red gem winking like blood in the hilt—turned his back on them both and went to the other side of the chapel. He rolled up in his cloak and soon was still. Whether he slept or not, she couldn't have said.

One thing was for certain: He wasn't about to answer any of her questions. And she had plenty of questions. Such as where was she really? Why was everyone currently speaking languages that were popular eight hundred years in the past? Why were there horses defecating not twenty feet away and no one thought it was weird?

That didn't begin to address how she was going to get out of where she was and back to where she should have been. She looked at William's back and decided that he wasn't going to be of any use on any of those problems at present.

She looked to her right. The priest had propped himself up with his back against the altar and was drooling as he dreamed.

That left the scrawny kid in front of her, who looked at her as if she'd just been released from an insane asylum. Great. Bad enough that he thought she was crazy. Worse yet that he was holding the sword.

The only bright spot was that he did look hungry. Maybe it was time for a serious foray into the depths of her bag. Surely there would be something there to sway a teenager. She could hold lunch in her hand and use it as a bribe for information.

She sat down as gracefully and as modestly as she could, keeping her eyes on the unstable-looking sword bearer. She wondered what would possibly entertain the kid. She had her Godiva, of course, but she had the feeling that would be wasted on him. If his boss thought it was poison, he probably would too.

Okay, so chocolate was out. She contemplated the contents of her bag. Scarf, Dick Francis mystery, dog-eared copy of *The Canterbury Tales* for long subway rides, and dire-dire-emergency bottle of pop she *never* touched. For all she knew, it might save her life one day. She had her Day-Timer with its special section of games for those bored in meetings, and a pair of Cole Haan pumps that never touched anything rougher than Berber carpet. There was her sketchbook and a pencil case full of colored pencils. Oh, and what she'd purchased at the health-food store. She suspected carob-covered carrots were not the way to this kid's heart, but it was the best she had, so she would make do.

She pulled out the crinkly bag, held it in her hand and looked Peter in the eye.

"Now, Peter," she said in the don't-give-me-any-crap voice she reserved for civil servants and the super of her building, "I have a few questions for you. . . ."

five
❧

$\mathcal{T}$ wo days later, William stood at the edge of the forest, stared off into the mist surrounding his seized castle and cursed his current straits. He should have been inside his keep with a warm fire near his toes and a bottle of something drinkable and sweet at his elbow. And he would have been, and two days ago at that, had events not conspired so strongly against him. Now look at him—out in the rain, staring stupidly at his quarry and finding himself without a strategy.

He sighed and leaned back against a tree. His hope of surprise was gone. Even though he stood in the shadows of a goodly bit of forest, he suspected he was being marked. No doubt Hubert's men had enlightened him at great length and with great merriment about the events at the wall two nights earlier.

William sincerely hoped his sire had laughed long and well. It would be the last thing he'd find to laugh over for some time to come. For even though Hubert was a drunkard and a fool, he couldn't have been fool enough to believe a little refuse would keep William from taking back what was rightfully his.

Of course, that was before William had found himself saddled with a woman who likely couldn't fend for herself if she'd been left inside a secured hall with a larder full to overflowing and two score of the finest mercenaries as guardsmen.

William cursed heartily, though it provided him with little

satisfaction. For the first time in his life, he found himself forced to care not only for someone else's, but for his own sweet neck as well, and that was a sorry state of affairs indeed. His value as a warrior had always come from his total disregard for his own safety. He had dared where others had shrunk back in fear. He'd forged ahead where others had hesitated. He'd thrown himself into the heat of battle with abandon where others had stopped to consider the cost. Such had won him a fiercesome reputation and enough gold to see himself fed, wined and wenched to his satisfaction whenever he pleased.

Should any of the victims of his former ruthlessness have been witness to his current state, though, they likely would have laughed themselves ill. William of Artane, callous executor of war, hesitating because of a woman.

Pitiful.

He pushed himself away from the tree and gave himself a good shake. What did he care for a woman who had no business roaming about by herself—and just where was Manhattan, anyway?—and likely deserved whatever fate she met? He was a warrior, by St. George's foul sword, and his business was before him in the keep, not behind him in the chapel.

He looked over said keep with a critical eye. The wall was crumbling in places, but sturdy enough to still keep out most assailants. William felt sure he would be pleased by that fact when he was viewing those walls from a different vantage point. The hall itself was small, but perfectly adequate for a minor lord such as himself—at least what he could tell of it from just being able to see the top of it. He hoped to find it defensible on closer inspection.

But how to take back his inheritance? He stroked his chin thoughtfully. Perhaps he should merely plant himself on the road up to the gate and challenge his father's men to come and meet him one by one. He could dispatch a dozen men, assuming none of them stuck a bolt through him first.

But what if those were men beholden to the keep and not to his sire? He would be killing his own potential guardsmen.

He chewed on that for a bit, then contemplated another idea. He could strip down to his hose, a tunic and a leather jerkin and simply slip over the wall at a vulnerable place, sneak inside the keep and put his father to the sword before anyone was the wiser. He'd done it before with great success.

It was, however, a very dangerous idea.

"Damn woman," he muttered, then turned and melted back into the woods. What did he care what happened to the wench? The priest had been addled when he'd bound that into the vow. How could William possibly be held to such a thing, especially in light of what kind of creature he'd stumbled upon?

He walked swiftly back to the chapel, but still it took him a goodly while to get there. By the time he reached the crumbling building, he was cross, soaked to the skin, and wondering what had possessed him to ever have come to the chapel in the first place.

Never discount aid from Above.

William wished his grandsire were there before him, for he would have given him some pointed thoughts on the matter. How could any wench be thought of as help from a celestial source? Aye, 'twas a pity Phillip was no longer alive. William would have retaken his keep, then returned to Artane and dumped his wench of questionable origin off on his grandsire, just to see how she would have changed his mind.

William took a deep breath to stifle what would no doubt have been a sigh of epic proportions, then slipped inside the door of the chapel. He gave his horse a pat, then looked around him to see what sort of madness Julianna was combining today.

He would have cursed, but he was too busy losing his breath. Damn the woman. Was it not enough that she had befouled his plans? Did she also have to render him dumb and faint in the head as well? If he'd had any idea just what had lain beneath the cesspit refuse, he never would have rescued her.

He wondered absently if he could truly be held to his vow if the maiden in question was of the ilk of wench that could completely distract a man from his manly duties. Perhaps he would question the priest more closely on that—but later. Now 'twas much more satisfying to look at the wench in question and give in to a few well-earned, silent grumbles.

She was sitting on the floor playing—ah, if he could but

remember the last time he'd had leisure for a game!—something called checkers with his squire whilst the priest looked on. The game was something she'd unearthed from her sacred relic sack. William was itching to get a more thorough look at the sack's contents, but apparently he'd been too free with her belongings the first night, for no other look had been offered to him. Peter, however, seemed to suffer from no such ban, for he was allowed to paw liberally through Julianna's gear.

That was the first thing that set William's teeth on edge.

The second was the woman who, after cleaning up a bit, had turned out to be not so much beautiful as striking—and would that someone had struck him on the head before he'd rescued her! He hadn't paid much heed to her whilst she'd bathed that first evening, apart from saving her yet again from another disaster by stopping her from tumbling face first into the stream. He certainly hadn't thought of her as he'd taken a well-deserved rest. More unfortunate was he that he'd awoken soon after to find the arresting woman hiccuping fiercely as she tried to make sense of his squire's babbles. William hadn't been able to take his eyes from her, despite his best intentions.

She'd been offering Peter something from the palm of her hand as if he were a whipped pup who needed to be taught to trust again. And damn the lad if he hadn't succumbed fully. Even the priest had stopped making signs to ward off evil long enough to sample something from Julianna's golden box of poison. Godiva. Hah. What sort of foodstuffs was that?

The third thing that he found to be more of a distraction than he would have liked was the matter of her origins. Manhattan? He'd never heard of such a place, and he'd seen a goodly amount of villages in his travels. Not only that, how had she found herself without kin or servants, sitting against his wall dressed in clothing he had surely never seen the like of before?

Perhaps these were mysteries he should see to before he ground his teeth to powder.

And perhaps *then* he might have the peace he needed for planning his assault.

William stepped out of the shadows and crossed over the broken stone floor. Perhaps when he was lord of his own keep, he would see this chapel restored as well. Despite its distance from the keep, it could be made useful. To be sure he would need all the blessings he could get.

He stopped a handful of paces from his unstable wench and looked down at her. Well, at least today there was no sign of hiccups, nor of those foolish songs she seemed to spout without warning.

Nor was there any acknowledgment of his presence. William almost opened his mouth to chastise her for her lack of respect, but found himself distracted by the substantial amount of curling hair that fell down far past her shoulders. It was tangled and lovely, and he found himself tempted to put aside his cares for a moment and take his fingers to it that he might put it to rights.

And where such a damned foolish impulse had come from he couldn't have said, but he was powerfully tempted to put his hand to his forehead and see if he burned with a sudden fever.

Perhaps Julianna's madness was catching.

Then she lifted her face up and looked at him. And he knew that not only was he feverish, he was fast losing whatever paltry wits remained him.

Striking.

Aye, she was that. Her eyes were a blue of such painful vividness, he could scarce look in them. Her skin was fair and smooth, and her face was of a shape to be so pleasing, it was all he could do not to cup it in his hands and kiss a mouth that surely seemed fashioned for just such a thing. But beautiful? Nay, he could not say that about her.

Yet he suspected he would be hard-pressed to forget the sight of her.

She turned her attentions back to the game, and William felt his head clear. He glared at the priest and cleared his throat. The priest leaped immediately to his feet and began bobbing respectfully.

William waved the man away and concentrated his energies on the two still sitting. Peter seemed to feel the heat of his master's gaze still somewhat compelling, because he looked up with only a minor hesitation.

"My lord?" he said.

"On your feet, you ungrateful wretch," William growled.

Peter cast one last, longing look at his game before he crawled to his feet and vacated his place. William sat down with a grunt and looked at Julianna. "You will," he said without preamble, "show me your sacred relics."

Her mouth worked a moment or two, and he greatly feared another attack of hiccups. Then she seemed to gather herself together.

And then she shook her head.

William frowned. He was not accustomed to being contradicted. "You will—"

"I want to know the date first," Julianna interrupted firmly. "The year."

"The year?" he repeated in surprise. By the saints, perhaps she was further gone than he'd feared.

"The year," she said, pulling her bag into her lap. "Peter didn't know, and your priest is convinced it is 1250."

Twelve-fifty? William shook his head. Daft soul.

Julianna carefully put her checkers game into the bag as well.

William frowned. She was supposed to be pulling things out, not putting them away. Ah, well, it didn't look as if he'd have his look until he satisfied her demented curiosity.

"'Tis the Year of Our Lord, 1299," he said with a sigh. "A year from the world coming to an end, though I don't believe that foolishness." He looked at her to see if she agreed.

She was looking at him as if *he* were the one who was daft.

"The Year of Our Lord's Grace, 1299," he repeated firmly. "The same as it was yesterday and the day before. And as it will be tomorrow—"

A horrendous rending sound echoed in the chapel. He was on his feet, crouched with his sword drawn almost before he knew he intended to do such.

He looked about quickly, but saw nothing. His squire and the priest had flung themselves behind the altar. Julianna was staring at him as if he'd just confirmed her worst fears. Then she slowly held up her bag.

"Zipper," she said.

He lowered his sword slowly. "Zipper?"

She pulled on something and the sound rang out again,

only more faintly this time. William sank to his knees, gaping at the sack. By the saints, there was more to this business of carrying sacred relics than he'd expected.

Then another thought occurred to him. Perhaps 'twas the burden of transporting those relics that had wrought the foul work upon her senses. She was, after all, merely a woman and likely not equal to the stamina required for such a thing. Had her obligation to her relics driven her mad?

That was somehow a far sight more comforting than believing she'd arrived in her current state on her own.

"I want to go home," she whispered.

That was the other thing that puzzled him. Her language was understood well enough, though 'twas spoken a bit strangely. But her habit of throwing in words he could not divine was frankly quite disconcerting.

"You want to go home," he said, immediately deciding that he had no time for such a journey. He had a keep to recover and after it was recovered, he would likely be spending all his time trying to keep it recovered. Besides, his vow only called for rescuing and defending. It didn't call for providing an escort back to wherever she'd come from.

"I'm not really sure how I got here—if here is really a place anyway and not some wacky medieval reenactment boot camp—"

He paused and considered. How had she come to be sitting against his wall with nothing but her relic sack to guard her? Was she a nun? A saint?

". . . I'm just not up to this," she was saying, beginning to hiccup again. "I don't—*hic*—like to camp, I hate to wear nylons—*hic-hic*—and I think I'm allergic to your damned horses—*hic*—"

William greatly suspected that saints did not swear. He was almost certain they didn't hiccup in such a ferocious manner.

"Not even sit—*hic*—com songs are working for me!" she exclaimed, glaring at him as if all that was amiss in her life was directly attributable to him.

A madwoman, he decided with finality. But one possessing sacred relics that he was almost certain would aid him in his task.

'Twas a certainty they couldn't hurt.

"I really want to go home," she said, shutting her eyes as if even the very thought of such a thing pained her.

"I will help," William lied, deciding that whatever he had to say, he would say if it would get him a look inside her bag.

She opened her eyes and stared at him as if he'd just saved her from being tossed into a fiery furnace.

"You will?" she whispered.

His conscience pricked him fiercely, and it was with a great effort that he ignored it. The woman was daft. Surely that made his vow of no effect.

Didn't it?

He gritted his teeth. "Aye, I will," he said, fully intending never to do the like.

Her look of gratitude was almost his undoing. But he hardened his heart, reminded himself that she was daft and he wasn't really responsible for her; then steeled himself for a look at things that would no doubt provide him with his heart's desire.

Never mind that she was striking. Or that she accorded him trust he surely didn't deserve. She was a madwoman and he wasn't answerable for her fate.

Or so he told himself.

six
❦

Backwoods? Rural? Julianna was fast coming to the conclusion that there wasn't a rustic word in any of the languages she knew that described the yokel-like condition of the crew she was facing.

Could it have something to do with the current date?

Twelve-ninety-nine. She'd finally resigned herself to the truth of it. How could she deny it, given the circumstances? Take the reactions, for instance, to her little show-and-tell of the contents of her bag. Spiked heels had left knight, teenager and priest falling back in horror. Day-Timer with pencils had left them gaping in slack-mouthed astonishment. A Mickey Mouse Pez dispenser had left the priest crossing himself, William scratching his head, and Peter holding out his hand for candy.

Teenage boys acted like teenage boys no matter the year, she supposed.

She had turned to literature to see what sort of reaction that would get. She peeked over the top of her book to see three belly-laughing yahoos. No offense to the Screen Actors Guild, but she had her doubts it had many members who could read *The Canterbury Tales* in the original language, much less guffaw over their contents.

William had definitely loosened up the longer she'd read. He now managed to contain his mirth long enough to sit up, wipe the tears from his eyes and cough a time or two.

"By the saints, Julianna," he said, "you're a fine spinner of tales. Can you do another?"

"I didn't spin them," she said, turning the book so he could see it. "I'm just reading what's written here."

"Bah," he said, waving a hand benevolently. "Women cannot read. But you needn't fear we'll think less of your words just because they come from your head."

"I can too read," she said tartly, "and what I'm reading is what's written on this page. Here. Look for yourself."

She watched his face still at the sight of the book shoved at him, and she knew in an instant that he couldn't decipher what was written there. She brought the book back in her lap without hesitation, though why she wanted to save him embarrassment of admitting his illiteracy she couldn't have said. It wasn't as if he'd done all that much for her.

Besides washing her hair, that was.

"Where did *you* learn to read?" William asked, as if her own possible qualifications were too ridiculous to contemplate.

"I learned in school. Then at university," she answered. "Cambridge here in England, University of Indiana at home."

"Cambridge," William said, looking at her skeptically. "Do they allow women to study there?"

Julianna wished suddenly she were sitting back on The Bench in Gramercy Park covered with bird poop. She wished she were sitting in a lousy interview trying to justify the fact that she was fluent in Latin, Norman French, and various forms of English instead of listening to a happy combination of all three being spewed at her from three directions in a decrepit church in the middle of the Middle Ages.

She wondered if this sort of situation could be considered a dire, *dire* emergency. When she felt her breath begin to quicken and knew that another round of serious hiccups was on the way, she decided quickly that it could. She reached into her bag, dug around in its depths and pulled out her don't-drink-until-absolutely-necessary cola. Without a pause, she twisted the top of the plastic bottle, sniffed quickly to appreciate the fine bouquet of escaping gases she didn't want to identify, then pulled the top completely off, put the bottle mouth to her lips and took an enormous swig of nirvana.

Odd how she'd forgotten that carbonation burned like whiskey.

She coughed, her eyes watered madly, and she soon found herself being slapped on the back by what felt like half a dozen baseball bats.

Her drink was ripped from her clutching hands, and William's face came into view not six inches from hers.

"What do you?" he bellowed. "Think you to poison yourself truly this time?"

Julianna held up her hand to stop him from trying to beat any more oxygen into her lungs, coughed another time or two, and gasped out her most pressing need.

"Give it back," she wheezed. "It's my last one."

"And none too soon, I'd say," William said, eyeing the bottle with disfavor. "Where did you come by this foul drink?"

"I brought it with me."

He resumed his seat, keeping her final vestige of cola-ized civilization firmly clutched in his hand, and lifted one eyebrow as he looked at her.

"Brought it with you from where?" he asked.

Well, there was no time like the present to explain the future.

"I brought it," she said without hesitating, "from the year 2001."

William blinked at her, Peter's mouth hung open and the priest began to cross himself again.

These were not good signs.

Then all three suddenly relaxed and smiled indulgently as if they'd orchestrated it. They looked at each other.

"Womanly weakness," the priest offered.

"Daft as a duck," Peter said wisely.

"Too much learning," William concluded. "And ill aftereffects of her misfortune at the bailey wall." He turned and looked at her. "Think you the refuse seeped into your head and fouled your thoughts?"

"No, I—"

"A pity we've no surgeon," he said, frowning suddenly. "He could look at your head and see if any holes there are leaking."

"I don't have any leaks in my head!" She held up her Day-

Timer. "What about this? What about the shoes? Good grief, what about *me*? How did I get out here in the middle of nowhere just out of the blue?"

"Aye, how did you?" Peter piped up. He caught William's frown and ducked his head. " 'Tis a fair question, my lord."

"It matters not," the priest said, rubbing his gnarled hands together. "She's a maiden fair in need of a rescue. 'Tis his duty to see to her."

"He has not the time," Peter said, turning a disgruntled look on the priest. "She's befouled his plans. No offense, my lady," he said, throwing her an apologetic look. "But you did. My lord was nigh onto recovering his keep when we found you sitting against the wall, and what was he to do?"

"Couldn't leave her," the priest said, shaking his head. "Against his vow."

Peter snorted. "What has his vow served him, old man?"

"What would you know of it, young pup?" the priest said, smacking his toothless gums together energetically.

"I knows plenty," Peter replied hotly. "More than you, I'd say."

"You know nothing," the priest said.

The argument only escalated from there. Julianna looked at William, curious as to when he intended to stop things only to find him flipping thoughtfully through the pages of her Day-Timer. He fingered the metal rings, idly flicked the plastic placeholder, then gave a closer look to the pouch full of pens and pencils. Then he looked up at her suddenly, and she saw the unmistakable signs of someone coming to a conclusion.

Silently he rose to his feet, hauled her to hers, then scooped up her bag. Without asking her opinion, he kept her hand in his and led her from the chapel. Julianna had to jog to keep up with him as he strode off into the woods. He walked for perhaps a quarter of an hour before he stopped in a little clearing, dropped her hand and turned to face her. But he said nothing.

Julianna started to get uncomfortable. There was still plenty of daylight left in spite of the clouds, and she had no trouble seeing the expressions that passed over her rescuer's beautiful face. Curiosity, puzzlement, but mostly skepticism.

"Are you a demon?" he asked suddenly.

She blinked. "Me? Of course not."

"Hmmm," he said thoughtfully. "I suspected that might not be the truth of it. Your visage is too pleasing for that."

"Well," she said, finding herself beginning to blush in the way she generally did when she tripped on the sidewalk in front of construction workers, "thank you."

"An angel then?"

Apparently he wasn't interested in lingering over compliments. Julianna smiled weakly. "Do I look like an angel?"

She knew she was fishing, but she could hardly help herself. But then, as she found herself being pinned in place by those pale gray eyes, she realized she was way out of her league with this guy. She'd only meant to wring another compliment from him. She hadn't meant to have herself raked over by a frank perusal that left her wishing she had something besides the muddy ground to sit down on. Whatever else she could find to say about the man, she had to admit that he certainly could leave a girl feeling as if she had no secrets with just a look.

"You, lady," he said at length, "look nothing like any angel I've ever seen."

"Have you seen many?" she asked, wondering why her voice had suddenly acquired such a breathy quality. Well, at least she wasn't breaking into a debilitating round of hiccups.

"I've seen my share," he said.

Sure you have, she meant to say, but he had taken a step or two closer to her, lifted the hand that wasn't still clutching her Day-Timer and reached out to touch her hair. If she hadn't wanted to sit down before, she was almost overpowered by the desire now. She just wasn't sure at all that her knees would hold her up much longer.

"Hair in such disobedient disarray?" he mused, tucking a lock of errant hair behind her ear.

Julianna made a mental note to cancel that appointment she had to get her hair straightened. Suddenly, all the frustration of years of fighting with it vanished. Hell, it was *good* hair.

"Eyes that fair pierce my soul?" he continued, looking down at her gravely.

Bag the green contact idea, as well. Blue eyes were a *very* good thing.

"Nay, lady," he said quietly, "you are no angel. What you are, I do not know. But I do know that now I've seen you, I could never forget you."

Julianna knew her mouth was hanging open very unattractively, but what could she do? One of the most handsome men she had ever seen was giving her the compliments of her life—never mind that he was carrying a sword, wearing her purse and clutching her Day-Timer as if he meant to do damage with it—and looking as if he might kiss her at any moment. She wasn't drooling and she wasn't hiccuping. Life was good.

William slid his hand under her hair, and Julianna felt a shiver go through her. She watched as he lowered his head and knew that a moment of truth was upon her. He was going to kiss her, and she suspected it was going to be the kiss of a lifetime. His lips were a half inch from hers. She closed her eyes and hoped she wouldn't embarrass herself by melting at his feet.

Then he froze.

"Are you a saint?" he asked.

Julianna jerked her eyes open—it was a supreme effort to do so—and blinked at him. "Huh?"

"A saint?" he asked urgently. "Damnation, what am I thinking!"

She grabbed him before he could pull too far away. "I'm not a saint," she said. "Really. Now, where were we?"

"I cannot kiss a saint," he said, looking faintly horrified.

"I told you, I'm no saint. Honestly."

But he had already pulled his hand out from under her hair. It was, however, still resting on her shoulder, which, to her mind, was a very positive thing.

"I suppose not," he said slowly. "After all, saints do not swear."

"Damn straight."

"Or have such problems with their breathing."

If she could have produced a hiccup right then, she would have. It figured the one time she wanted them, she couldn't get them. "You're so right," she said encouragingly.

"There is, however, your sacred relic sack to consider."

"It's just stuff. I wouldn't worry about it."

"And this, what did you call it?" he asked, holding up her book.

"Day-Timer," she said, searching desperately for something to get him back on track. "But look at my hair. Any saint you know have hair like this?"

He looked but, disappointingly, didn't touch. "Nay," he admitted slowly.

"Eyes?" she said, opening them wide for his inspection. "Baby blues like this?"

He shook his head slowly, the slightest of smiles crossing his face. "Nay, my lady, I've seen none like them."

"There you go then. I'm not a demon, an angel or a saint. Now that we've got that settled . . ." she trailed off meaningfully.

He kept his fingers on her shoulder and reached up with his thumb to touch her jaw. He smiled a half smile at her. "But, if you're none of those things, then who *are* you?"

"I'm just Julianna," she said simply. *Now kiss me, you big lug, and let's see if that doesn't give me new purpose in life.*

"Do you know," he said conversationally, as if tracing lazy circles on her cheek and jaw wasn't the most incredibly distracting thing a man could do to a woman he'd come very near to kissing into incoherence, "that once I fancied you were a saint come to aid me in my quest?"

"Did you now?" she wheezed.

"And I hoped that something in your sack would be just what I needed to liberate my keep from my sire's vile clutches."

"Sorry," she managed. "Unless you'd like to clobber them with my Cole Haans—um, the shoes with the spikes," she clarified.

He continued to stroke. "I can think of no other being but a saint who would appear from nowhere, without kin or husband. You haven't any gear as well."

"It's a long story."

He looked at her in silence for a moment or two.

Then he began to frown. Julianna watched the doubt develop in his face, and she had no idea how to stave it off.

"I do not believe," he said finally, "that the Future could spit out one of its own and land her at my keep. In spite of what you carry in your sack."

Julianna swallowed with more difficulty than she would have liked. He might have still been caressing her face, but somehow the skepticism in his expression had turned to something very unyielding. She wondered if this was the expression his victims were treated to before he put them to the sword.

"You can," she managed with as much sincerity as she could, "believe what you like, but it doesn't change the truth of it."

"It makes no sense."

"I know."

He pursed his lips. "'Tis that bloody vow I made. I think I've conjured you up because of it. I *never* should have let that daft priest bind me to any rescues."

"Well," she said, feeling a little flat all of a sudden, "you don't have to keep it."

He jerked back as if she'd slapped him. "Not keep my vow? My honor rests upon it!"

"Oh," she said, "well, then. But why did you make it in the first place?"

"'Tis a very long tale," he said, stepping away from her and fumbling with her bag. He managed to get the zipper open, her Day-Timer inside, and the zipper closed again with only a minor shiver or two. He looked at her and shook his head. "You may be no demon, my lady, but your gear is passing strange."

"It's—"

"Future gear," he finished for her. "Aye, aye, I know."

"Tell me about your castle," she said, aiming for a distraction. All right, so she'd lost out on the kiss of a lifetime. She'd never get close to having another one if he kept looking at her like she'd just slithered up from Hell for a visit.

"I was in France," he began, "leading a very pleasant, if purposeless existence, when I received word from my uncle, Henry of Artane—Have you heard of him?"

She shook her head.

"Ah, well, perhaps Manhattan is a little more primitive than I suspected—"

Julianna watched as he took her hand in his and turned her back toward the chapel. It was such an ordinary thing, holding hands with a man. Yet, somehow, the feeling of his warm, calloused hand holding hers was possibly the most singularly amazing thing she'd ever felt.

"He bid me come back to England to claim an inheritance my grandsire had left me," William continued. "It should have gone to my sire first, of course, but he being the wastrel he is, could not possibly have held it. The saints only know where my older brother is, but I suspect that he's currently loitering beneath a dripping ale spigot. That left only me. I suspect that when my father learned of my uncle's intentions, he was passing furious."

Julianna looked up at him as he talked and wondered with even more amazement how it was that she was walking through the woods, holding hands with a man who spoke Norman French as easily as if it had been his first language— which it was. And when he apparently wasn't sure she understood something, he would repeat it in Middle English, just as easily as you pleased.

She was suddenly very grateful for all those hours spent studying. Who would have thought it would have become so necessary to her survival?

"Of course, the keep wasn't promised to be in perfect condition. I daresay, though, that 'twas the best my grandsire could have in good conscience offered me. He had six sons, you see, and that many more grandsons, as well as girl children, so there is only so much land to go around, never mind his great wealth. I felt fortunate to have been offered anything at all."

Fiefs, peasants, swords and inheritances. Julianna listened, shook her head and wondered just how in the world she was supposed to fit into all this. Or was she? Was she supposed to try to get back home?

"I suspect that my grandsire felt that if I had some land under my feet, I might turn my mind to other things, namely getting myself a wife and an heir—"

That brought her out of her reverie. "You're engaged?" she demanded. "Betrothed?"

"Betrothed? Saints, nay." Then he looked at her sharply. "You?"

"No," she said. She wanted to believe he looked relieved at that fact. But why should she care? She wanted a good job, travel and life in the fast lane. What could possibly be appealing about a man, a home and a family?

Besides just about everything?

She considered. If she found herself making a home and family with this man, she could use all her language skills. She could probably even use her metalworking skills. She certainly didn't see a blacksmith hanging around as part of William's entourage. She'd made jewelry before. Couldn't she parlay that into a little sword-making?

Now, the cartooning was a bust, but she could live with that, couldn't she? Then again maybe she could start her own newspaper with spoofings of the current monarch taking up serious front-page space. Roasting the monarch could possibly lead to a roasting of oneself so she was back to cartooning being a bust.

". . . Of course, I was very surprised to find my own gates barred against me, and my sire no doubt reclining upon his sorry arse in my chair. I had just made my vow—for vow-making is very much a part of my family, you see—and was preparing to scale the wall when I happened upon you."

"Looking less than my best."

"Aye, my lady, you were passing pungent." He sighed. "Now you have my poor tale and see why I thought perhaps you had come to aid me."

"I wish I could," she said.

He gave her a little smile. "It matters not. I can see to it myself."

"What will you do?"

"Well, I had thought to climb over the wall in the night and murder my sire before he was the wiser, then rout out his men before the whole keep was awake and had raised arms against me."

"Sounds dangerous," she said breathlessly.

He shrugged. "I've done it before with great success."

That thought was enough to push her over the edge. To think he had done something that perilous and could discuss it so casually was astounding. So she made the only response she could.

"*Hic,*" she said. "*Hic-hic.*"

"Ah, by the saints," he said with a half laugh. "I can see how you feel about that."

"Sorry—*hic-hic.*"

"'Tis in the past, Julianna." He sighed and dragged his free hand through his hair. "Saints, but I cannot think of it now. 'Tis a pity, though, for it made me a good warrior."

"Climbing over—*hic*—walls?"

He shook his head. "Nay, lady. Having no one to care for but myself."

"What's changed?" she asked. "Find someone recently?"

And then she clapped her hand over her mouth on the pretense of trying to stop her hiccups. In reality, it was the only way she could stop the words that seemed to be spewing out of her mouth without her permission.

William stopped and turned to look at her.

She found, suddenly, that the words had ceased to flow as quickly as they'd started to. Even her hiccups disappeared. A silence fell until all she could hear was the call of the occasional bird and a bit of wind blowing gently through the trees. But she couldn't look to see where the wind was blowing or what birds were carrying on their sporadic conversations. All she could do was look at the man in front of her: a medieval knight with a sword at his side and her bag over his shoulder who was looking at her with an intensity that left her weak.

"Aye," he said at length. "I have."

"Really," she managed. "Who? Peter?"

He shook his head.

"The priest?"

He shook his head again, and damn him if he didn't reach out, slide his hand under her hair again and move closer to her. Julianna swallowed with a gulp. She wanted to get a definitive answer out of him, but she found herself becoming quite distracted by his hand tangling gently in her hair. It was a most mesmerizing feeling, and she found herself absorbed by it—and the sheer amazement that she'd actually found someone who was single, handsome and gallant. Never mind that he was in the wrong century entirely.

He smiled down at her, and she thought the sheer wattage of that smile might just start up her unfortunate reaction again. But before she could catch her breath to make any kind of hiccuping noise, he bent his head and kissed her.

Heck, who needed to breathe?

"Perhaps," he said at length, when he lifted his mouth from hers, "our good priest had more sense than I suspected in the wording of his vow."

"Were you supposed to rescue a maiden in distress?" she asked, wondering if he would notice if she started to fan herself. Who knew that kissing out in the rain could generate such internal heat?

"Aye, I was."

"And rescue her from dragons?" she added, wondering in addition if he could feel her knees becoming wobbly.

"There was nothing about dragons. I suspect the only foul thing I will be rescuing you from is the foodstuffs and drink in your sack." He smiled down at her. "Let me be about the reclaiming of my hall, then we'll see to a decent meal or two."

All right, so it wasn't a proposal. It was an invitation to dinner, and who knew where that might lead? Besides, Julianna was starting to wonder about the advisability of living on bottled water and carob-covered fruits and vegetables. The sooner William got on with his little project, the better as far as she was concerned.

"I have a stun gun you could use," she offered.

"How does it go about its work?"

"You poke someone with it and it leaves them senseless and drooling."

"So does my sword," he said. "Let us go back. I'll manage well enough on my own."

Maybe it was for the best. For all she knew, William would point the thing the wrong way and there he'd be, senseless and drooling, and then she and Peter would be the ones trying to pick up his sword and do damage with it.

"So," she said, as they walked back to the hall, "what's next?"

"I daresay I have little choice but to climb over the wall and murder him in his bed."

She stopped still. "You said you weren't—"

He bent his head and kissed her again so quickly, she didn't see it coming. And when he stopped and simply looked down at her, she found she just couldn't say anything at all.

"I'll return," he said.

"But—"

"I'll return, Julianna. I vow it with my life."

Great. She had just hooked herself up with a medieval knight bent on murder and mayhem. Her mother would have fainted dead away at the thought.

She wondered in passing how Elizabeth would have reacted to the news: *Oh, by the way, on my way to your castle, I paused in the Middle Ages and found myself being rescued by a knight. A very handsome, attentive, manly knight . . .*

She very much suspected Elizabeth wouldn't have been surprised. But she wondered what Elizabeth's advice would have been. Stay in the past, or try to get home? Hmmm, ask a complete romantic if she should fall in love, or go back home and look for a dead-end job?

Julianna wondered absently if she could survive the rest of her life without a flush toilet.

Or with a man who thought nothing of risking his life in the seemingly riskiest of ways. Well, if she was going to be any good at this time period, she would just have to suck it up and trust him. She took a deep breath.

"All right," she said, lifting her chin. "Do what you have to."

"You'll be here when I return?"

It was on the tip of her tongue to say *Where else would I go,* but she stopped herself just in time.

She took another breath. The pond was deep and she had no idea what was lurking on the bottom, but there was no sense in not jumping in with both feet.

"I'll be here." She paused. "And that's my choice."

He smiled again, and she wondered why in the world he didn't have a line a mile long of girls waiting for that look. Then again, maybe he didn't show it to very many people.

"Have you ever had a girlfriend?" she asked.

"Women?" He looked dumbfounded. "Dozens."

"Why didn't you marry any of them?"

He laughed and shook his head. "By the saints, lady, you have no fear of me, do you? That isn't a question many would dare ask."

She only waited. If he had some major flaw, it was best she know about it now.

"I'm not overly wealthy," he said, looking amused. "I have too many scars from battle. Or perhaps 'tis I was waiting for the Future to spew you back at me. Does that satisfy?"

Before she could find any good response to that, he had kissed her again and then was leading her back to the chapel, still shaking his head and smiling.

What else could she do but the same?

seven

William stood in the shadows of the trees and looked at the keep before him. He realized with wry amusement that he'd stood in the same place the day before, staring in much the same way, but with far different thoughts. He'd wanted his keep, to be certain, but he'd been driven to action by thoughts of the manly comforts of a warm fire, a well-manned garrison, and lists for his pleasure.

Odd how the passage of a single day could change a heart so.

He still wanted his keep, of course, and lists for himself and his garrison, but added to that was the thought of hearth and home for a wife and children—one wife in particular, that is.

He eased back into the forest and made his way silently around the perimeter of the castle, making a mental note to clear more trees when the keep was finally his. 'Twas far too easy for an enemy to hide himself in such substantial growth, even if William found himself obliged a time or two to crawl on his belly to take advantage of the cover of smaller bushes and things.

He crept around to the back of the keep and waited for a goodly while to make certain there was no stray guard haunting the walls. He saw no movement, but that didn't satisfy him. He had a very good reason to keep himself alive, and he suspected that reason would be passing angry with him if he left her stranded with Peter and the priest. He tightened the strap that bound his sword to his back and felt himself begin to smile in spite of the seriousness of his situation. By the saints, the woman was fascinating. Not only was she looking more beautiful to him by the heartbeat, but she could read.

Perhaps she had learned that in the Future as well.

By the saints, he could scarce fathom such a thing as a body traveling from another time. But he could fathom her in his bed, next to him at supper and bearing him a dozen children with riotous hair and eyes so blue they would hurt a man to look in them.

And if he could hope for the latter, perhaps he could believe the former.

All of which left him where he was at present—preparing to scale his own walls and rid his keep of his unwelcome and certainly uninvited guests so he could proceed with the rest of his life.

He sighed deeply and steeled himself for what was to come. It would have been easier with a ladder, or a rope for that matter, but those things came with the price of possible discovery, which he was unwilling to pay. He would have to find what finger- and toeholds he could, and pray his eyes had told him true that such things actually existed on the scarred outer walls. He had exceptionally strong hands, which was a boon, and his boots were worn clear through to the toes, which was also a boon at present. And he'd scaled less inviting walls than this with no more than his own poor form as his only aid.

So, taking advantage of the last bit of darkness before dawn, he slipped from shadow to shadow and approached the wall.

It was easier than he'd dared hope, which left him cursing silently at the sorry state of his keep's outer defenses. He would have to see to them at his earliest opportunity. Until he had sufficient men to guard those walls, they would need to be an unassailable shield.

He slithered over the wall and dropped into a crouch on the parapet. His heart raced at the sight of a guardsman he'd narrowly avoided knocking off. The man turned and died before he had the chance to shout a warning. William did not slay him gladly, for he very much suspected that if the men had a choice between him and his sire, they would choose him. But he couldn't allow himself to be discovered, not when the first difficulty had been overcome so quickly.

He pushed the body close to the wall, that it might not be noticed right off, then inspected the inner bailey. From what he could see, his uncle hadn't done justice to the sorry condition of things. The buildings were falling down and the courtyard was covered with piles of what he was sure would eventually reveal themselves to be refuse and waste. He shuddered to think what the inside of the keep would look like.

But 'twas his, this pile of stones, and he would have it—gladly.

He looked up at the sky and was surprised to find that night was waning. Obviously he'd spent more time pondering than he should have. Well, there was naught to be done about it but proceed as quickly as he dared before dawn. Given what he'd observed over the past few days, there weren't all that many souls to be rising and working, but a rooster crowed whether its master willed it or not. 'Twas best he was about his business whilst he still had some cover of darkness to aid him.

He clouted another man into insensibility as he made his way along the walls toward the steps that slid down into the courtyard, but he saw no other man and heard no shout of warning.

There was something rather unsettling about that, on the whole.

He looked for a way into the keep, but saw none but the hall door. It left him with little choice but to enter thereby. He took a final look about the bailey, saw no movement coming even from the poor huts scattered here and there, then began his assault. He hugged the side of the hall and made his way carefully.

No one stopped him.

The hall doors were open, and he walked inside as if he had every right to. The smell alone almost knocked him flat. Once his eyes had ceased to burn from the smokey interior and a few of his wits had returned to him, he noticed something else odd.

There were no men sleeping on the floor.

If he hadn't been unnerved before, he was now.

He knew he had no choice but to search the keep and there was no better place to start than the kitchen. He made his way there carefully. The stench of that place was worse, if possible, than the rest of the hall. There was only a pair of scrawny lads there, sleeping on the floor, apparently quite overcome with weariness. William retreated silently.

He made his way back into the great hall, found a stairwell and climbed it to the upper floor of the keep. He crept down the passageway and peered into a large solar and a small chamber. Both were devoid of all but the most rude and rough bits of furniture. Aside from a single, drunken knight sprawled in a passageway, William found no other bodies.

And then a most unsettling thought occurred to him.

Had he been anticipated?

And then an even more unsettling thought occurred to him.

What if his father was now encircling the chapel with his men?

William thumped back down the stairs, ran through the empty great hall, threw open the doors and crossed the empty courtyard. He was not stopped, saw no soul, and that only added to his fear. By the saints, if he had left Julianna behind in danger when he'd thought the danger was in front of him. . . .

It was only when he reached the gates that he found himself skidding to a halt. He gaped at the sight in front of him and realized just how seriously he'd miscalculated his father's deviousness. He was, quite frankly, amazed that the man had stopped downing his ale long enough to conceive a plan this foul. William felt the point of his sword falling downward until it was stopped by the dirt at his feet.

Ah, by the saints, he hadn't planned for this.

"Look you what I found outside my walls," Hubert drawled. "Three little ruffians bent on mayhem."

William looked at Julianna as she stood next to his father with her glorious hair caught firmly in the bastard's hand. She looked at him, then closed her eyes and winced as Hubert tightened his fist.

Peter and the priest were being held by others of his sire's guard. Even his horses had become prisoners.

"We came to help ye, my lord," Peter squeaked, then he was cuffed into silence.

"He needs all of that he can have," Hubert sneered. "Why Artane thought you could hold this land is beyond me."

William looked at his father and could scarce believe he'd been sired by the fool. William put his shoulders back. His character had been shaped by his grandsire and his uncles and they were the finest of men. Their blood also ran through his veins. Not for the first time, he was very glad his father had departed Artane after William's birth and left him behind in his grandsire's care.

Hubert gestured negligently to one of his men. "Kill him," he said.

William watched a crossbow be lifted, and he cursed. He'd known it. Hadn't he known it? The one thing he could not possibly defend against and that was what he faced. He wondered fleetingly if he could possibly dodge the bolt.

What would become of Julianna otherwise?

The man took aim.

A movement startled William. He looked to Julianna to find that she had elbowed his father full in the nose. The man released her with a howl and clutched his face. Then Julianna prodded the bowman with something held in her hand. He screamed, then fell to the ground, senseless and drooling.

"Stun gun," she said proudly.

Then Hubert struck her full across the face and sent her sprawling on the ground.

William roared. He cut down five of his father's men before they knew what he intended. The remaining five threw down their weapons and backed away. William would have been pleased with himself, and with the hasty release of his squire and priest, but he turned his attentions back to his sire and caught an unobstructed vision of his lady who was now back on her feet.

With his father's knife to her throat.

"It would seem," his father said tightly, "that I have something you want."

William stabbed his sword into the dirt at his feet and placed both hands on the hilt.

"You cannot win, Father," William said, his chest heaving. "Release her."

"Choose," Hubert returned. "The wench or the keep."

William wouldn't have been more surprised if his father had reached out and clouted him on the nose. "But—"

"Choose!" his father shouted. "The wench or the keep! I'll not be left with naught for all my trouble!"

William considered the odds of slaying his father before his sire slew Julianna, but knew almost immediately that such a thing was beyond possibility. He'd already made good use of his own knife by burying it to the hilt in a fallen knight's eye. He could retrieve his sword and heave it at his sire, true, but 'twould be just his luck that his father would use Julianna as a shield.

Julianna shifted with her stun gun in her hand, and William stepped forward instinctively.

"Nay," he said, shaking his head.

"Do not," his sire commanded, pressing the blade more firmly against her neck. A small trickle of red crept down her throat. Julianna lowered her arm, closed her eyes, and swallowed convulsively.

William closed his eyes briefly and saw in his mind the pitiful pile of stones behind him. It was his birthright, a legacy he could pass down to his children, a final gesture of love from a man he had loved with all his heart. It meant security, steadiness, a place of his own—all the things he had never had the whole of his adult life.

Then he opened his eyes and looked at the woman held captive in his father's foul embrace. She had opened her eyes and was now looking at him with absolutely no expression on her face. That alone told him that she was trying very hard not to force him into a decision.

Then she hiccuped.

It came close to slitting her throat for her.

"Daft wench," his father muttered, shifting the blade in his hand.

William smiled in spite of himself and, as he did, he realized the truth of the matter. His home was before him. In truth, if he'd wanted a pile of stones of his own, wouldn't he have found one by now? Apparently he was destined to go about without ties.

Save for the one he intended to make with the woman standing before him now hiccuping madly.

Nay, there had been little need for thought. If the choice was between Julianna or the crumbling wreck behind him, there was no choice to be made.

"Take it," William said, jerking his head toward the hall. "Take your blade from my lady's neck and seek out your comforts within. But remove your steel carefully, Father. You'd not like your death otherwise."

Hubert looked at him narrowly. "Your word that the hall 'tis mine?"

"Aye," William said simply.

"Vow it."

"Oh, by the saints," William said in disgust. "Take the bloody pile of stones. I'll not trouble you further for it. Give it to your other son. If you can find him to foist it upon after you've had done with it."

"Rolfe is a fine—"

"Drunkard and a fool," William finished for him. "Aye, his life is a fitting legacy for your own. I'm certain he'll be quite happy to see what you have for him."

"I *never* would have given it to you," Hubert snarled.

William shrugged. His elder brother was no doubt lying in some deserted corner of a village, reeking of wine and whatever else he had found to imbibe. The only thing that would have surprised William would have been to find his brother alive and well. Nay, Hubert would not find him to gift him anything.

"Vow it," Hubert repeated stubbornly. "Vow you'll leave me in peace and never return."

William inclined his head. "I vow that I'll leave you in peace and never return. Now, release my lady."

Hubert looked to be considering something foul. William looked at his father dispassionately and shook his head.

"I wouldn't."

His father shifted—the first sign of nervousness William had seen in him.

"Think you I can kill with my sword alone?" William

asked pleasantly. "I assure you, Father, that my time spent in the company of honorless mercenaries was not wasted. I can call to mind half a dozen ways to end your life—very painfully, I might add—without putting my hand to my sword."

"You gave me your word you'd leave me be," Hubert said, but there was a quaver in his voice.

"Aye, if my lady comes into my arms unharmed," William said calmly, as if he had an indefinite amount of time to discuss the matter—and as if his heart wasn't beating in his throat with the force of a dozen heavy fists. By the saints, all it would take was the slightest pressure and her throat would be cut. Her bloody hiccups were nigh onto seeing to that by themselves. Her lifeblood would spill from her and there wouldn't be a revenge vile enough to remedy that.

Hubert considered. Then he lifted his knife away. Before William could move, he shoved Julianna toward William. She stumbled and fell facedown in the dirt at William's feet.

But at least she was free. William pulled her up and into his arms. He couldn't look at her. He'd just traded his inheritance for her and he damn well didn't want to see revulsion on her face. He looked at Peter.

"There's another horse inside the gates. Fetch it."

"But—" Hubert protested.

"Payment for your unchivalrous treatment of your future daughter," William said pointedly. "Unless you'd care to haggle more?"

"You said you'd leave me be!"

"I will. And I'll also take your best nag before I leave. Consider yourself fortunate. I could have taken much more."

"Honorless whoreson," Hubert spat.

That stung, but William let it pass. "My vow was to leave you be. I daresay you wouldn't be qualified to judge how I honor that."

Peter returned with a horse that William suspected wouldn't last the se'nnight, but at least it would carry the priest. William threw Peter up onto the packhorse, tossed the priest onto the feeble nag, then led his trembling lady over to his own mount and helped her up into the saddle. He looked once more at the hall that was no longer his, then at his sire.

And then he looked up at the woman with the riotous hair and striking blue eyes and found himself smiling in spite of his attempts to stifle it.

"Well?" he asked.

"Hell of a trade," she said hoarsely.

William laughed as he swung up behind her. He looked at his sire and gestured to the keep.

"'Tis yours, Father. May you live long to enjoy it."

Hubert glared at him, but tromped inside the gates just the same. His five remaining guardsmen followed him none-too-eagerly. Well, the man he'd left senseless on the wall would wake up soon enough, as well as the drunkard in the passageway, and perhaps they could cheer their fellows. William felt a weight come off his shoulders and he whistled cheerfully as he turned his horse south. Perhaps binding himself to a hall was truly not for him.

"Where are we going, my lord?" Peter asked.

"I've no idea," William said pleasantly.

He had several destinations in mind, but none of them would be reached that day, so what was the point in worrying about it? They would ride for a while, then he would give thought to where he might take his lady.

"I'm—*hic*—sorry," she whispered.

"Nay," he said, shaking his head. "Do not be. 'Twas a fair trade."

She took several deep breaths and, miracle of miracles, her breathing returned to normal. She relaxed in his arms.

"I probably should have stayed at the chapel," she offered.

"Aye, well, perhaps that is true."

"I thought you might need some help."

He suspected that now was not the time to point out that he was the trained warrior, not she. She was trembling in his arms, and he supposed that she either felt badly for his loss or realized how close she had come to death. He could scarce chide her for her act, especially when it had been conceived as a means to aid him.

"'Twas a generous gesture," he said.

"I never meant for you to lose your keep."

"I gained my lady in its place." He paused. "Where is your sacred relic sack?"

"Strapped to your horse."

"Well, see?" he said. "You've your dowry to offer me, as well as your fetching self. What else could I want?"

She twisted to look up at him. "You want me?"

He smiled dryly. "I just traded my birthright for you. What does that tell you?"

"Was that a proposal of marriage?"

He laughed softly. "I'll give you a proper one when I've decided where we'll go."

"Oh," she said, "I kind of liked being haggled over with your father's knife at my throat. Really. What more could a girl want when it comes to romance?"

He wrapped his arms around her and held on, amazed at how comforting it was to do the like. He'd made the right choice. What was a pile of stones when compared to a woman whom he thought might just learn to love him in time?

He found himself turning toward the east and realized he was heading toward Artane. It was home enough for the present. He could wed her there properly, then perhaps they would decide what to do.

He smiled, because he simply couldn't help himself.

eight

Julianna had learned, after three days of slow travel, how to sleep in manly arms on the back of a horse. Riding a horse was not a skill she had ever planned on having, but apparently it was something she was going to have to add to her repertoire. When in Rome—rather, when in medieval England . . .

They'd elected to rise in the middle of the previous night and get going. She hadn't been all that excited by the idea, but when William had promised her a soft bed instead of lumpy ground if they hurried, she'd quickly found more enthusiasm for the idea. She'd just as quickly fallen asleep in the saddle, propped up against William's chest.

The lightening of the sky had woken her—that and a healthy poke from her quasi-fiancé. She'd opened her eyes.

And fought a healthy round of hiccups.

It was a castle, and what a castle. It looked horrendously medieval, in mint condition and—distressingly enough—inhabited. She'd seen a few inhabited castles during her tenure in England as a student, but they'd been updated with things like electricity, AGA stoves and indoor plumbing. There had usually been cars parked out in front and some sort of accommodations for touristy visits. Villages had consisted of quaint brick houses, nicely paved streets and hospitable B&Bs.

Not open sewers, huts made from straw and inhabitants who looked as if they had never taken a bath in their lives.

The very functional drawbridge was down and a continual

stream of humanity crossed over it either on foot or horse-back. Julianna felt incredibly conspicuous in her Keds and Donna Karan suit. William removed his cloak from his shoulders and draped it over the front of her. It didn't, however, cover her shoes.

"Better?" he asked.

"Oh, sure," she agreed. "It'll keep me warm until they stoke up the fire to burn me at the stake."

He only snorted out a little laugh and expertly avoided trampling a peasant boy or two who were scuffling near the guard tower.

They dismounted in the courtyard. Julianna found that she could do nothing but clutch William's hand and gape at her surroundings. Her purse found itself hoisted over his shoulder for safekeeping, and she found herself being led up steps into what she could only assume was the great hall. Maybe she wasn't much of a judge in such matters, but it looked as if whoever owned this place was incredibly rich.

"You grew up here?" she managed as he opened the door for her.

He looked down at her with an amused smile. "Aye. Does that surprise you?"

"Your family must have buckets of money."

"And my grandsire had several sons and a pair of daughters. Gold doesn't last long with so many children to see to."

She paused before they went inside and looked at the man who had not only saved her life, but had practically proposed as well. She wondered if he resented the wealth, since he certainly didn't have very much of it himself. And now he had even less, thanks to her.

"I'm sorry about your castle," she said.

He waved aside her words. "I've told you—how many times now?—that I feel myself well rid of the place. 'Twas a generous gesture on my grandsire's part, and I daresay he knew I was grateful. But there is more to life than a pile of stones."

"But—"

"It would have taken a great deal of work to have made it habitable, Julianna."

"Well, remodeling is hell," she agreed.

He kissed her briefly. "We'll rest here for a few days, then see where our fancy takes us." He smiled encouragingly. "We'll find someplace that suits. And you'll not starve. I haven't fed you very well as of yet, but I promise I'll do better. For now, my uncle sets a fine table and we'll eat our fill."

And that seemed to be all he wanted to say on the matter. Not that he would have had a chance for much more talking because Julianna found herself swept up into activity that was almost annoying in its intensity after days out in the boonies.

To think she had once enjoyed the bustle of New York City.

William's uncle descended upon them with smiles and hearty hugs, closely followed by his wife and so many of William's cousins and other assorted family that Julianna gave up trying to keep names straight. What she did understand was the offer of clean clothes. She worried, as the women prepared to abscond with her to places unknown, that she might not be quick enough on her feet to come up with a decent explanation about her origins, but William solved it for her. He put one arm around her and the other around his aunt and spoke in a low voice.

"Julianna is from Manhattan," he began.

"Where?" his aunt queried.

"A little place that would likely seem very strange to us. They have different forms of dress and the like, and she's very tender about it all. You'll take care of her, won't you, and not hurt her feelings?" he finished, looking at his aunt with a devastating smile.

At least Julianna was devastated by his smile. Apparently his aunt wasn't immune to his charms either.

"Of course, love," she said promptly.

Julianna looked at him openmouthed, but he only winked at her and sauntered away.

"What a lovely pair of shoes," his aunt remarked kindly.

Julianna gulped and managed an inarticulate sort of response she sincerely hoped passed as a thank-you.

A short while later she found herself in a room where she was washed, coiffed and perfumed by a handful of women she'd never seen before. She was then dressed in clothes that were made on the fly by a handful of very speedy seamstresses. Her shoes were examined closely, then cleaned expertly. The beads were lovingly and thoroughly buffed to a brilliant shine. Julianna modeled her new outfit, then looked down at her feet and burst out laughing.

If any of her professors could have seen her, dressed in medieval finery with Keds on her feet, they would have swooned.

No one else seemed to find it strange though, so she turned her attentions to other things—namely a little nap. She had eaten heartily during her morning of beauty so when she was offered a bed, she took off her gown without a second thought, crawled under the sheets in her sliplike shift and promptly passed out.

She woke to find it was morning again, and she was surrounded by women bent on foofing her up for some kind of shindig.

"What's going on?" she asked sleepily as she was dragged out of bed.

William's cousins all laughed. "Your marriage, of course," they all said together.

She was dressed, her hair was braided and done up in some sort of medieval headgear, and she was hustled to the chapel almost before she was awake enough to realize it.

The place was packed.

What she wanted was to sit down and take stock of the situation.

She spent the rest of the day wanting to sit down and take stock of the situation.

But by the time she actually managed to get a grip on the events of the day, it was evening, and she was in Artane's tower room facing her husband who looked much less bewildered than she felt. She looked down at the simple gold ring that he had apparently given her at some point during the wedding ceremony. She looked up at him.

"Did you propose to me yet?" she asked, scratching her head.

"I believe, my lady," he said gravely, "that 'tis too late for that. I fear I've already wed you."

"And I said yes."

"That was the word you gasped out when I pinched you, aye," he said, a twinkle coming into his eye.

"Well," she said with a frown, "I don't remember much of it."

"Then let me remind you. We met before our beloved priest who demanded a recounting of all we would bring to the union. You offered—"

"My sacred relic sack."

"Aye, and my family was most impressed with the sheer weight of it. I brought myself—"

She looked at him narrowly. "And quite a bit else if memory serves." She pointed a finger at him. "You said you were poor."

"Well, I'm less poor this evening than I was this morning," he said with a snort. "My uncle was passing, and stubbornly, generous."

"Of course you didn't have any gold stashed in his castle either," she said pointedly.

He shrugged. "I wasn't completely without a thought for the future. I could have set aside more, I suppose, but I never planned to need it. My cache certainly wasn't enough to make me rich. But my uncle's gift of several dozen knight's fees . . ."

"That was a nice thing for him to do."

"Aye, and it will likely get us murdered on the side of the road," he said with a grimace.

"Cheer up," she said. "It could be worse."

He looked at her silently for a moment or two, then smiled. "Aye. I could have passed on my grandsire's gift and never come back to England. I could have never gone to Redesburn. And look you what I would have missed."

She smiled weakly. "And I would still be sitting against that wall, covered in various forms of, well—"

"Aye," he agreed. "That."

She stood there and looked at him. He returned her gaze steadily. Julianna wiped her hands on her dress. It wasn't as if she hadn't thought about doing, well, *it* before. She had. Lots. She'd just never really had the right guy and the right time in the right place.

She put her shoulders back. All that had changed. She was now married to a gorgeous man who apparently liked her well enough to give up his inheritance for her. His future plans certainly seemed to include her in a big way.

He was waiting.

Julianna held up her bag. "What do you want first, me or my dowry?"

"Your dowry."

Her smile faltered. "Oh," she said. She held out her bag. "Here, then."

He took it and set it down behind him. "That's done, then. Now I'll have you."

"Oh," she said, feeling quite a bit better.

He held out his hands and she put hers into them. He pulled her a step closer, then smiled down at her. Julianna watched the candlelight flickering over his face and wondered why she hadn't done more things by candlelight when she'd had the choice. It was a very soft, gentle light. She suspected it was something she could learn to appreciate very much.

"May I say something?" William said. "In all seriousness?"

Oh, great. Was he going to tell her that along with the "minor" amount of gold he'd managed to send home for safekeeping, he had a mistress or two tucked away as well?

"Yes?" she asked sharply.

He clasped his hands behind his back and looked at her solemnly. "I hope," he began slowly, "I hope that in time you will, if nothing else, become fond of me." He took a deep breath. "Nay, that isn't what I mean. I hope that in time, you will come to love me."

Then he shut his mouth and looked at her in silence.

"That's it?" she asked, incredulous.

"Aye," he said stiffly. "Unless the thought—"

"I thought you were going to tell me you had a mistress!"

He looked at her with an expression of complete bewilderment. "I just wed you. Why would I keep a mistress?"

"You tell me."

"I'm telling you that I have fond feelings for you," he said, sounding as if those feelings were about to take a hike out the door. "Feelings that I am quite certain will only increase with time. And I hoped," he added with a scowl, "that you might feel the same way."

Julianna felt many things, but most overwhelming of which was surprise that she found herself standing in the tower room of a castle, married to a man she had known not quite a week, and happier than she'd ever been in her life—even when faced with a dwindling stash of junk food and no possibility of indoor plumbing in the near future.

So she took a step forward, put her arms around her medieval knight and snuggled against his chest. His arms went immediately around her in a sure embrace. Julianna sighed happily.

"Well?" His voice rumbled deeply in his chest.

"Yes," she said. "I think it's more than possible." She pulled back only far enough to look up at him. "I think it's unavoidable."

He bent his head and kissed her softly. "Then let me make you mine in truth. With any luck at all, that will endear me to you and start us on the proper path."

"You don't want to look in my bag first?"

He shook her head with a smile. "Later. I've the true prize in my arms and no desire to relinquish it. The other will keep."

How could she argue with that?

And she found that along with being an exceptional swordsman, her husband was an exceptional lover.

She was very grateful she'd had such a good night's sleep the night before.

Julianna opened her eyes and realized that it was morning. She realized then that it had been the cold that had awakened her. Odd how one grew accustomed to the warmth of a husband in such short order.

Odder still how one grew accustomed to other things as well in such short order.

The thought of that made her blush and she was grateful the candle that burned on the table probably wouldn't give her away. Who would have thought it? If she'd known that's what she'd been missing, she might have indulged a little sooner.

Then again, perhaps it all had to do with the man she had married.

She turned that thought over in her head for some time—coming quite easily to the conclusion that William and a ring on her finger had made all the difference—then she tried to get up. She clenched her teeth to keep from groaning from the protests of sore muscles.

"Are you unwell?"

The deep voice startled her and she sat up with a squeak.

"'Tis only me, Julianna," William said, sounding amused. He was sitting at the table, but turned to look at her. "Who else?"

"Who else indeed," she muttered as she gingerly got to her feet and pulled a blanket off the bed. She wrapped it around her and went round the end of the bed to stand next to her husband. He was holding her copy of *The Canterbury Tales* and fondling it with what she could only term reverence. "Find anything interesting?" she asked, noting the contents of her bag littering the table.

He shivered. "Interesting, nay. Unsettling, aye."

"I told you the truth."

He looked up at her, then put his arm around her waist and hugged her. "Aye, and more the fool am I for not having believed you at first."

"It's a lot to take in."

He dropped his arm and bowed his head. "Aye. It is."

She had the sinking feeling that maybe he was beginning to have serious regrets. She contemplated going back to bed and trying to reawaken after William had dealt with things, but that would have been cowardly and she wasn't a coward. Or, not much of one, anyway.

No, she wasn't and it didn't matter if she'd just decided that a medieval kind of gal should have a medieval sense of courage. William was, literally, all she had in the world and she wasn't going to let something as stupid as his discomfort come between them.

"All right," she said, kneeling down next to him, "talk. I can't guess what you're thinking and I'm not going to try. If you have regrets, you'd better tell me now."

"Me?" he said, looking at her with an expression of surprise. "Rather you should have them, I'm thinking."

"Me?" she asked in much the same tone. "Why would I have regrets?"

He held up a sportswear catalog. "Look at this," he demanded. "Look at what you've given up for me."

"That?" she asked with a half laugh. "William, there's more to life than clothes."

He blinked, silently. Then he smiled a bit ruefully. "I suppose there is. But Julianna, these marvels—"

"Mean nothing if I had to trade you to have them," she finished. She smiled up at him. "I'm passing fond of you, you know. You're well worth trading my birthright for."

He kissed her and she was almost certain she felt the tension ease out of him.

"I feared," he whispered against her mouth, "that you would wake and regret having given yourself to me. Especially when I understood what you had given up."

She didn't want to tell him that he didn't understand the half of it, so she merely nodded and let him kiss the socks off her. If she'd had socks on, that was. Soon she didn't even have on a blanket, and she was just sure she soon wasn't going to be able to walk anymore.

"Will you read to me?" he asked much later as he snuggled happily next to her in bed with her Chaucer in his hands. "These stories are passing amusing."

She smiled at him and touched his cheek. "I could teach you to read them yourself."

"There is no use in it. The priest here at Artane tried to teach me, but without success. My father, on one of his rare visits to see if I lived still, said I was too feebleminded to manage the feat."

"Your father is an ass."

He smiled briefly. "Aye, I suppose so."

"What was the problem?"

"I couldn't fathom the letters," he said. "They moved about and turned themselves around until I wept in frustration. So I conceded the battle and turned my energies to other things."

"It's probably dyslexia," she ventured, hoping she was

right. "The same thing happens to me with my numbers. Half the time they're not in the same place I left them when I go back to read them again. It's very confusing."

He leaned up on one elbow and looked at her in astonishment. "Nay," he breathed. "For you too?"

She took a deep breath. She didn't want to promise him something she couldn't deliver, but maybe with enough time, she could help him. And after all, she had all the time in the world and not a lot of distractions.

"I think you can learn to read," she said slowly. "But it wouldn't be easy."

He looked as if she'd just come down from heaven and given him his heart's desire. The terrible hope on his face almost brought tears to her eyes.

"Think you?" he whispered.

"Anything's possible," she said quietly.

He lifted one eyebrow as he looked at her, then smiled. "I suppose, lady, that you are proof enough of that. But for now, read me another tale or two and I'll be content."

She took the book and opened it only to have something fall from the pages. She unfolded it.

It was Elizabeth's map.

"What is this?" he asked.

"It's what got me into trouble in the first place," she said dryly. "My friend drew me a map of England. According to her, these places are spots where if you stand on them, you can travel through time."

"And you stood on one of these?" he asked, tracing the outline of the island.

"Nope. I sat on a bench in a park. It's the same idea though."

"Tell me what they say," he urged.

"Well, I guess they're all to different centuries. The Picts—those were the ancestors of the Scots up north. Vikings—"

"Aye, I know them," he said with a shudder. "Unpleasant lot."

"Pirates in the seventeenth century, Jousts in the Middle Ages—"

"A fine destination," he noted.

"And this one . . . here . . ." She squinted to make out the words—and when she thought she might have the faintest idea what they said, she sat bolt upright. She scrambled out of bed and practically leaped to the table.

William soon came up behind her, wrapped a blanket around her, and peered over her shoulder. "What does it say?"

She pulled the candle toward her and held the paper behind it where she could see the words clearly. "It says," she began, squinting to make out Elizabeth's tiny writing, " 'Return to Scotland of the Future.' And there's a note at the bottom that says 'Good from Any Century.' "

"By all the saints," he breathed. "Think you 'tis true?"

She could hardly breathe. To think that she might be able to get home. To think the possibility existed and she'd had the answer in her bag all the time. She turned her head to look at him.

"I can't imagine why Elizabeth would be lying."

"Julianna!" he exclaimed suddenly.

She looked back at the map and screeched.

The paper was on fire.

William yanked the map away, tossed it on the table and beat the flames out.

"Crap, crap, crap," she said, hopping up and down. "Did I ruin it?"

He looked at her with a rueful smile. "Came close, I'd say. You tell me what's gone."

She took the map and noticed that Trip to the Picts was nothing but a black curl, as was any reference to Vikings.

"We weren't interested in those anyway," she said, holding the map well away from the flame and peering at it closely. "It's okay," she said with relief. "There the little circle is, right there. Now, if we just had any idea where *there* was."

And then she realized what she was saying.

She had just married a medieval knight and committed herself to a life with him. Even contemplating returning home was something she couldn't allow herself to do.

Unless he wanted to come along.

She looked up at him to find him studying her with a thoughtful expression.

"What?" she asked.

He smiled faintly. "I'm wondering if we're considering a like foolish notion."

"A little jaunt to the future?"

He nodded, then shook his head. "I cannot believe I'm even considering it. It seems passing improbable."

She sighed. "It's probably a really silly idea anyway—"

"But one worth considering," he finished. "What think you of a walk on the shore? I've always done my best thinking there."

"Is there a possibility of breakfast first?"

"I think, my lady, that too many days of subsisting on your future food has shown you what a foul work it has wrought upon you. Aye, we'll have something edible before we go."

He took the map from her, folded it carefully and placed it back between the pages of the book. "We'll keep this with us at all times as well. No sense in losing it before we've had a chance to try it."

"William, we don't have to—"

"Don't you wish to go home?"

It had become altogether too possible for her taste. She couldn't move. She couldn't shake her head or nod or even breathe for that matter. There was only one thought that seemed to be clear in the swirling mist of possibilities. She looked at William and smiled.

"My home is with you."

"See?" he said with satisfaction. "I told you that you might become fond of me in time."

She put her arms around him and hugged him. "How right you were."

"Clothes, food, then the shore," he said, kissing the top of her head and disentangling himself from her arms. "We'll have clearer heads for thinking there."

Julianna dressed in her medieval clothing and tried not to let her thoughts run amok. Somehow, though, she just couldn't stop them. It was one thing to be stuck in the past and be resigned to it. It was another thing entirely to think that perhaps there was a way back to the future.

Then again, perhaps she had already made her choice. She'd married a man centuries in the past with every intention of staying with him. A little piece of paper wasn't going to change that.

But what if it were true?

She could hardly bear the thought of it.

nine

Wﬁilliam walked down the passageway to his uncle's solar, trying not to think about what the man's reaction would be to the question William had to put to him. He paused before the door, clutched the rolled map in his hand, then knocked.

"Enter."

William cast a look heavenward before he blew out his breath and entered his uncle's chamber.

Henry looked up from his table upon which was spread a variety of sheaves of paper. He smiled. "You left your bride so soon, nephew?"

"She begged me for a rest."

Henry laughed heartily. "No doubt, lad. Well, now that your labors have obviously been properly accomplished, what other mischief are you combining?"

William pulled up a stool and sat facing his uncle. He realized, with a start, that he'd done the same thing scores of times before, except it had been his grandsire sitting opposite him. He found the memory surprisingly hard to face.

"You too?" Henry asked wistfully. "I can call to mind countless times when I sat in council with my sire exactly thusly."

William cleared his throat roughly. "Perhaps 'tis unmanly to miss him."

"He was as much your sire as he was mine," Henry said simply.

"Aye, he was." William fingered Julianna's map for several moments in silence until he thought he might be able to speak without an embarrassing display of emotion. "And I am grateful for it," he managed finally. "He made a man out of me."

Henry drummed his fingers thoughtfully on the table. "He would have agreed with your choice, I think."

"My choice?"

"To trade that crumbling holding for your lady. Though I wonder what it is you'll do now. Castles are, as you know, bloody expensive to build and man."

William snorted. "You gave me enough gold to at least see to outer walls. Perhaps a tent would serve as the hall."

" 'Twas the very least I could do," Henry said. "Now, how is it you intend to proceed? Will you wait out your sire, or retake your keep despite your vow?"

William took a deep breath, then looked his uncle full in the face. "Neither."

Henry blinked. "Neither?"

"I would like Peter to have it after Hubert is dead."

Henry's jaw slid down. "Your squire? And where is it you intend to be?"

"I'm going to Manhattan with Julianna."

"And just where is Manhattan?" Henry asked. "I've tried to puzzle it out in my head, but I cannot seem to place it. On the continent?"

" 'Tis a small island," William said, thinking about the geography lesson Julianna had given him earlier that morning in the sand. Manhattan was an island indeed, though one his uncle never had and never would clap eyes on.

The saints pity him for a fool that he thought he actually might himself.

But that didn't stop him from bringing out his map and spreading it out before his uncle.

"Ignore the words," William said. " 'Tis a jest from someone Julianna knows. But I would know about this mark here." He pointed to the red circle. "I think it lies near Falconberg. What think you?"

Henry studied the map in silence for a great amount of

time. William suspected his uncle was mentally judging William's own wits—or lack thereof.

"'Return to Scotland of the Future,'" Henry mused. "'Good from Any Century.'" He looked up at William. "A jest?"

"A poor one."

"Who is your wife, William?"

"No one who needs to be drawn and quartered, uncle."

Henry seemed to consider, then he smiled briefly. "As you say. Now, you intend to travel to this small red marking?"

"Aye."

"And do what once you're there?"

"What do you think, uncle?"

"I think 'tis madness, William."

"Likely so."

"You needn't give up your keep, nephew."

William took a deep breath. "Keep my priest, if you will, and my squire. If I get word to you that I've found another place to call mine, send them to me. If not, please let the priest live out his remaining years here. And give Redesburn to Peter."

Henry looked at him, then shook his head with pursed lips. "I think too much traveling has given you fanciful ideas, lad, but it will be as you wish. And aye, I would say this is close to Falconberg. You know how things are there?"

"Nay. Should I?"

"Be aware that 'tis those of Brackwald ilk who hold it."

"Wasn't there a fire there once?"

"Aye, a mighty one and it killed the last of the Falconberg line. The younger Brackwald lad rebuilt the hall. 'Twas rumored his elder brother was the one to set the fire and perished thereafter with a knife in his back for the deed. The saints only know who put it there. I suspect, however, that you can count on a decent bite at the board and perhaps even a bed if you ask nicely."

"Thank you, uncle."

"When are you planning to leave?"

William smiled and stretched. "In another day or two. You've a fine goosefeather mattress in that tower chamber, my lord, and I'm loath to leave it."

"And I do set a fine table."

"Aye, that as well." William rose. "Thank you, my lord. For everything."

Henry waved aside his words. "Nothing I wouldn't have done for a brother."

If sitting on his favorite stool hadn't come near to unmanning him, hearing that certainly did. William left before his uncle could see his tears.

They left a month later. William tried to convince himself that they needed to depart sooner, but he couldn't manage it. He spent hours walking the paths he'd walked in his youth, reliving moments spent with his grandsire, storing up in his heart the sights, smells and sounds of his home.

Ofttimes Julianna came with him on his little rambles, but just as often she stayed behind. In such cases, he found her almost without fail in the company of his aunt, bludgeoning the woman with questions. His aunt answered everything with endless patience. William had laughed behind his hand the first time he'd seen the two women at it. He half suspected his aunt feared she would drive Julianna off some hidden precipice into madness if she did not humor her. If she thought there was aught amiss with his lady, she said nothing of it. And on the morn of their leave-taking, she presented Julianna with a satchel full of womanly things—from cuttings from her garden to all manner of threads, needles and cloth.

Julianna, likely much to his aunt's relief, accepted all in stunned, grateful silence.

They traveled in relative luxury, with a horse each and a packhorse loaded up with as much gear as Henry had been able to force on them. Not being sure where their travels would take them, William had accepted all and ignored his discomfort over the charity. He was too old for such quantities of gifts, but for all he'd known, that would be what sustained them for quite some time.

Well, that and the bags of gold hanging from his saddle that clanked like hammers on anvil with each fall of hoof.

And so William had kept a crossbow loaded and loose in his hands as they traveled, certain their wealth would be a beacon to any and all ruffians in the countryside. Adding to his unease was Julianna stopping them several times, telling him that she was certain she'd heard someone traveling behind them.

William had heard nothing, though, so he passed it off as her preoccupation with his aunt's gifts, which she delved into every chance she got.

It took them well over a fortnight to reach Falconberg. They hadn't traveled with haste, and William wondered if Julianna's reluctance mirrored his.

What if the map was wrong?

"Is this it, do you think?"

His lady wife's voice startled him out of his reverie. He looked at her and smiled grimly.

"Falconberg? Aye, but I think we won't trouble the lord for a bed. He'll send someone to see who we are, no doubt, and we'll give him what answers he wants. But I've no mind to find myself inside walls this eve." He unloaded his crossbow and hooked it over his saddlebag. "Let us find a place to camp and see if we can look as harmless as possible."

She nodded and reined in her horse.

Then she froze.

"William, look."

He followed her gesture, then felt the hairs on the back of his neck stand up of their own accord.

There, not ten paces before them, was a circle. A faery ring was what some folk called it. The circle of flowers bloomed eagerly, as if it wanted nothing more to invite the hapless soul within its bounds.

"By the saints," he managed in a choked voice.

"Do you still want to go?"

He swallowed with difficulty. "Aye."

"Then let's do it now," she said, dismounting. "I think we need to hurry."

Her urgency became his. He dismounted as well and led both his horse and the packhorse into the circle. Julianna followed him. Her horse had scarce placed all four feet inside the circle when he heard the crack of a twig.

And then the sound of something far more lethal.

He turned instinctively at the sound of a crossbow bolt

being pulled back into place. Likely one of Falconberg scouts—

He froze at the sight that greeted him.

"Good morrow to you, son."

William wondered absently if he would have the time to slip the dagger from his belt, flip it so he grasped it by the blade with his fingertips, then fling it into his father's eye before the fool squeezed the trigger and sent the bolt flying home.

Hubert smiled in triumph. "Did you think I would simply fade into oblivion?"

A body could hope. William glared at the man who had sired him. "You have your keep. Isn't that enough?"

"Ah," Hubert said, looking at Julianna briefly, then back at William, "but I have no lady to share it with."

"Find your own," William said, slipping his other dagger down from inside his sleeve. "You'll not have mine."

"Won't I?" Hubert mused. "I suppose we'll soon see—"

And with that, Hubert released the crossbow bolt.

And at the same moment, William sent his blade hurling toward his sire.

"No!" Julianna said, and, to William's complete horror, threw herself in front of him.

"Julianna, nay!" he cried out, trying to jerk her back. He set her aside, then looked down at his chest, fully expecting to see an arrow protruding from between his ribs. He wondered, absently, why there was no pain. Perhaps that was a gift for the dying. . . .

Then he realized something quite astonishing.

There was no bolt.

He looked up.

His father was gone as well.

"Oh, my goodness."

William turned his attentions to his wife, wondering if he might find the arrow lodged somewhere in her precious form. But she was standing on her feet with apparent ease. Her eyes were huge in her face, those beloved eyes of vivid blue, as she looked around them.

"The trees," she whispered. "Look at the trees."

"Julianna," he began.

"Look at the forest," she insisted.

William scowled. There were several things that were of much greater importance than observing the forest around them, such as finding out where his father had hidden himself and why neither of them was bleeding from a life-threatening wound.

Then he understood the words she had spoken.

Forest?

He looked down. They were still standing in the midst of a faery ring, but the trees surrounding them were far different than they had been but a moment before. Gone were the shorter, leafier trees. In their place were tall, close-set evergreens that cast the glade into deep shadow.

William gaped at his wife. "Think you we're in Scotland . . . ?"

"I don't know what else to think."

William looked around him, searching the shadows for his father. But the man was nowhere to be seen. Nor was the knife that William had flung at his sire.

He suspected this was not a mystery that would be easily solved.

"Let us mount up," he said, handing her the reins and giving her a leg up. He swung up onto his own horse. Wherever they were, and whoever might or might not be following them, they would no doubt be served well by removing themselves from an open glade. "We should keep watch for my sire."

"I don't think he'll be following us."

"Don't you?" William asked. "What would stop him?"

She smiled weakly. "He's a nasty person?"

"Then only saintly souls are allowed to skip about the centuries as if in a dance?"

"One could hope."

"One could hope my blade found home in his chest. I daresay, my love, that such will be the only way he remains behind."

Which meant he would be keeping watch for a goodly while, until he was satisfied.

But for the moment, what he did know was that he'd been

spared, for whatever the reason. He wouldn't be caught unawares again.

He led the way along a path that seemed to be unnaturally well-trod, past a large pond and into a castle courtyard.

There were strangely formed wagons with shiny wheels and enclosed with brilliantly colored coverings standing in front of the hall door.

"Cars," Julianna breathed.

Well, an explanation was definitely in order, but perhaps later, after they'd discovered where they were truly and if the inhabitants were friend or foe.

Julianna slid off her horse near the hall door. William was hard-pressed to tie up their horses to a post and catch her before she'd ascended the three flat steps. He managed to catch her hand before she knocked. He drew his sword, pulled her behind him and gave her a pointed look. She rolled her eyes and sighed. But she stepped behind him willingly enough.

He turned his attentions to his current task and banged on the door sharply with the hilt of his sword.

The occupants weren't expecting visitors, if the lack of haste employed in opening the door was any indication.

A young man pulled the door open, drinking deeply from some kind of long, white box. He finished, dragged his sleeve across his mouth and looked at them with great indifference.

"Yeah?"

"Who is lord of this keep?" William demanded. "I'll speak with him immediately."

"And you would be?" the other asked.

William eyed him narrowly. The lad was doing irreparable damage to the peasant's English, but perhaps he was a servant and knew no better. Though with the way he slouched against the doorframe as if he hadn't any cares, William feared he hadn't yet hit upon the boy's identity. Perhaps this was the steward and he was accustomed to men banging on the doors, demanding to see his master. William knew there was no fault to be found with his own appearance. He could thank his uncle for replacing his threadbare garments. Whoever this young pup was, he should have been more impressed. William resheathed his sword with a flourish and put his shoulders back.

"I am William of Artane," he said slowly and distinctly, as if that very utterance should cause all within hearing to back up a pace. "And I demand to know where I am."

"William—" Julianna poked him in the back.

"And in what year," William added for good measure.

"William—"

"Julianna, I can see to this on my own."

"Julianna?"

William looked back at the keeper of the door and was surprised to see a flicker of emotion cross his face.

"Julianna Nelson?" the young man asked.

"Julianna de Piaget," William corrected, but before he could elaborate on that, his wife had popped out from behind his back and was blathering on in the same horrific butchering of the peasant's English the lad had used.

He found, however, that if he concentrated very hard, he could understand most of what was said. That, at least, gave him some small measure of comfort. Perhaps 'twas true he couldn't read. He did, however, have an ear for different tongues. He suspected it might serve him very well.

The lad was holding out his hand. "Zachary Smith. Elizabeth's brother."

Julianna took his hand and William snatched his wife's hand away just as quickly. He threw Zachary Smith a glare. How dare the wretch take liberties with his bride!

"All right," the young man said, carefully backing up so they could enter. "No problem. Come on in."

"Where is Elizabeth?" Julianna asked.

"She and Jamie are away for a week or so. It's just me. Alone. Again."

Elizabeth was Julianna's friend and the maker of the magical map. William suspected he would eventually thank her for the like. First he would have to see if the Future agreed with him, for though he'd had no direct answer to his question, even he possessed wits enough to know that if he was looking at Elizabeth MacLeod's brother, he'd come to Julianna's time in truth.

The saints preserve him.

"This is the deal."

William stiffened when he found himself being stared at so pointedly by young Zachary Smith.

"No swords down the toilets. No phone calls without supervision. No standing in front of an open fridge taking a bite out of everything inside. And the remote is mine in the evenings."

William had no idea what idiocy the lad was babbling, so he dismissed it and began to look about him.

There was a very adequate fireplace with several comfortable chairs set before it. William nodded with satisfaction. That, at least, he found to his liking. He strode out into the hall and looked about him. No rushes, but the floor was passing clean and had a pleasant smell. He turned to his left and walked into what he assumed might be the kitchens.

And then he froze in place.

Several enormous boxes made from materials he'd never before seen in his life stared back at him in a forbidding, unyielding way.

Zachary Smith pushed past him and walked to one of the boxes. William found he couldn't even hold out a hand to stop the lad.

"Fridge," Zachary said, wrestling with one of the shiny beasts and opening its belly. "Not much food, of course, because no one's gone shopping. But you can scrape the mold off—"

William looked at his wife and very carefully swallowed. It served him not at all, but he hoped it looked like a manly swallow and not the one of a body about to fall to his knees and weep.

And then bless his sweet lady if she didn't put her arms around him and soothe him in the very comforting French he'd grown to manhood speaking.

"Let's go have a nap," she said.

He knew that word. It was a word from her Future, but one he had grown heartily fond of in the past month.

"We'll put it all to rights later," she added.

"Think you?" he whispered against her hair.

"I do."

William took a deep breath, stepped back and stiffened his spine. "As you say. First, I must see to our mounts and bring in our gear. Then you may lead on to where we might nap in peace."

He had, after all, put his foot to this path and there was little hope of turning back. He was not one to walk away from a battle and if the Future wanted to wage one against him, it wouldn't come away victorious.

He only hoped the fridge was the least of the marvels he would be called upon to endure.

Once upon a time there was a knight who made a vow, a solemn vow given with all his heart and soul to protect women of all stations, champion children, defend, and rescue any and all maidens in distress, but preferably one in the greatest of distress.

And when he found such a maiden, he vowed to rescue her from dragons, sweep her up into his arms and carry her off to his castle near the sea where he would wed her and make yet another vow to . . .

ten

Julianna tapped her pencil against her chin. "'... make yet another vow to ... love, honor and cherish ...'"

She scratched that out and scowled. Much too modern. She'd have to pick her husband's brain for what had actually been said during their wedding ceremony. All she could remember of it was having him poke her when it was time for her to agree to be his.

She wondered what William would say when she told him he was going to be starring in the children's book she'd decided to write.

Scotland was, apparently, very conducive to thoughts of creating books.

She looked around her and had to shake her head over her surroundings. Who would have thought that such an innocent wish to come to Scotland would have resulted in this?

She herself was snuggled up in a comfortable chair in what Zachary called Jamie's thinking room with her sketchbook in her lap. Her husband sat next to her in the largest chair in the room, looking incredibly knightlike in borrowed jeans with his sword across his lap. She smiled and contemplated the house rules he'd broken already—and only seventy-two hours into his visit.

His sword had indeed gone down the toilet to test its mettle—the toilet's not his sword's—and many other places it definitely shouldn't have gone. Only Zachary's quickness had saved William from electrocuting himself.

A very angry, sleepy man in Venezuela had been the recipient of William's first random, long distance phone call.

The only up side to the refrigerator doors having been left open was that William had pretty much cleaned out the contents first. Luckily there hadn't been much to throw away.

And now the battle for the remote.

Zachary had, obviously, lost.

Apparently he wasn't up to Artane standards of swordplay.

She looked at Elizabeth's younger brother and wondered at his calm in the face of the storm he'd faced over the past three days. Maybe William wasn't the first to have found refuge in James MacLeod's modern castle. Zachary seemed to find nothing odd about the strangled noises of horror, delight, and amazement that her husband was currently making as he watched TV. When William gurgled out a particularly hairraising oath at the scantily clad women on an underwear commercial, Zachary only yawned, stretched and got to his feet.

"Anyone want dinner?" he asked.

William perked up immediately. "Dinner?"

Zachary nodded. "We have a deep freeze. Lots of frozen pizzas in there." He patted his stomach affectionately. "Combination. Pepperoni. Sausage. Very tasty."

Julianna suspected Zachary was a from-the-box connoisseur, given what he'd cooked up for them so far. But since she hadn't had to do the cooking herself, she had no complaints.

"I'll help," William said, heaving himself to his feet. He sheathed his sword with a flourish, then looked at Julianna. "You rest and work on your drawings. I'll come fetch you when we've laid the table."

Zachary looked at her beseechingly, but she only smiled. William in the kitchen was a rather frightening prospect. She scanned him for potential life-threatening current conductors, but except for his sword, apparently all metal had been left in their bedroom. He was much more likely to investigate small electrical gadgets with a knife than he was that huge blade, so she supposed he was safe enough. She waved at Zachary as he was summarily dragged from the room.

Julianna leaned back against the chair and sighed deeply. She could hardly believe that it was almost two months ago that she'd been miserable in the city, pounding the pavement for a job and ducking fix-up offers from well-meaning relatives and friends. She would definitely have to thank Elizabeth for taking care of the latter. Not that her employment situation was any better, but at least now she had some use for her language skills.

Zachary had told her to make herself at home, that they could stay as long as they liked. He'd found them clothes and kept them fed. He'd given them the guestroom. He'd also been very matter-of-fact about William taking his time to adjust. She had wondered if this wasn't the first time he'd gone through this.

Of course, that didn't solve their long-term problems of what to do and where to go—and how to get there. Her passport was at home and William didn't have one. Zachary had assured her his brother Alex had dubious connections that would see to all that in time. But even if he could and they could get back into the States, what would they do there? She couldn't imagine William rattling around her four-hundred-square-foot apartment while she worked in the restaurant industry because she couldn't find a job that took advantage of her particular skills.

She looked down at her sketchbook. Her doodles would make a very interesting children's book, but she suspected that wouldn't keep them fed.

William was an exceptional knight, but she suspected that that wouldn't keep them fed either.

She looked thoughtfully at the television and blinked at the commercial for bus tours of strings of castles and notable residences. Maybe they could hire themselves out as tour guides. She wondered if Artane could possibly exist in any kind of form resembling what she'd seen not a week ago, and if the current earl had any need for anyone to explain how things had been in the Middle Ages.

Not that either of them could admit firsthand knowledge of that, of course.

But the idea was somehow very tantalizing. Maybe she and William could start their own reenactment society. They could lure unwary travelers into the wild and convince the hapless souls that they had actually traveled back in time.

What an incredible thought.

She wondered, however, about William's potential opposition to the idea. With the way he seemed to be taking to Zachary Smith's diet, she might never get him away from boxed food again.

Well, she'd have to approach him later. For the moment, she would take his advice and rest. It would give her ample time to contemplate the wonders of modern food, the miracle of hot running water, and the delight of a luscious down comforter to snuggle under at night.

With a man she had found seven hundred years in the past.

And that thought brought her up out of her chair. She followed her nose down to the kitchen. She leaned against the doorframe and smiled at the sight that greeted her eyes. Zachary was reading the pizza box out loud to her husband, pausing every now and again to explain where the ingredients had come from. Julianna shook her head in wonder at how quickly her husband was picking up Zachary's words—and his American accent. His gift for language was nothing short of astonishing.

Something inside her eased, something she hadn't even realized was anxious. If William could adapt this easily, then they would make it. She hadn't really realized until that moment how desperately she'd wanted that.

William turned and looked at her and the welcoming smile on his face made her realize that perhaps his wish that she would love him might be coming true much sooner than he'd anticipated.

"What have you drawn?" he asked.

She shrugged. "Just doodles."

"Might I see?"

She opened her sketchbook and handed it to him.

"A fine dragon, my lady. And a formidable knight. What are these scribbles here?"

"The story."

He smiled at her. "And how does it end?"

She smiled back. "With a vow."

"A very original idea."

She laughed. "A little too close to reality?"

"That depends on how well your drawings resemble my sweet visage."

"I'll do my best."

"I've no doubt you will. Now, will you have some of these foodstuffs? The combination flavor looks to be a true marvel of modern pizza creation."

How could she resist the man? She laughed as she turned and wrapped her arms around him. She hugged him tightly, then leaned up and whispered three words in his ear.

"Do you?" he said, pulling back in surprise.

"Aye," she said, finding suddenly that the reality of such a simple expression of affection had brought tears to her eyes.

"In truth?" he asked quietly.

"I vow it."

He swung her up in his arms before she knew what he intended. She managed to keep her sketchbook from sliding south.

"No pizza?" Zachary asked.

"My lady just told me she loved me," William said, heading toward the doorway of the kitchen. "Food can wait."

"Wow," she said with a laugh. "You must like me."

"Love, Julianna," he said, not breaking stride. "I love you."

"Do you?" she asked wistfully.

"I vow it."

And with William of Artane, there was no greater guarantee. To think it had taken traveling through time to find him.

She wondered if that bench in Gramercy Park could be bronzed without inviting countless questions as to why.

Then she found that her husband required all her attention, so she gave up thinking about things that didn't matter and concentrated on the one person who did.

And when he asked her to promise that she would always do the like, she did the only thing she could.

She did belong, after all, to a vow-making family now.

Turn the page for a special excerpt from

My Heart Stood Still

by Lynn Kurland

coming from Berkley in October, 2001

The Border
Fall, 1382

They had betrayed her with a promise of the sea.

Go with the Englishman, and he will show you the strand, her half-brother had said. *Father has traded you to make an ally, but you'll have a keep on the shore as your recompense,* her half-sister had said.

Trust us, they had said.

Liars both.

The woman stood in a cold guard's chamber and stared out the small slit of a window before her. The only thing she could see was darkness, but perhaps that was a boon. It obscured the bleak, endless stretches of land that surrounded the keep in which she found herself captive—land seemingly so far removed from the sea she wondered if the villagers even knew that such a thing existed. 'Twas almost a certainty she would never see the like now.

She was tempted to weep, but she knew it would serve her nothing, so she forbore. After all, she was a MacLeod and MacLeods did not weep with fear.

Despite how desperately she wanted to do so.

That she found herself in straits terrible enough to warrant tears was difficult to believe. Was it possible that just a fortnight ago the Englishman had come to her home? She'd stirred herself only long enough to determine that he held no interest for her, then thoroughly ignored him. 'Twas odd to see an Englishman so far north, true, but her father often had men from many foreign places at their keep. She'd had much to occupy her and had paid little heed to one more fool loitering at the supper table.

A pity she hadn't, for the next thing she'd known, she'd been given to the Englishman in trade for a debt her wandering, gambling, whoring stepbrother had owed him. That her father would think so little of her that he would send her off with a stranger didn't surprise her. That a stranger would take her as payment for such a staggering debt surprised her very much indeed. What value she had to him, she couldn't imagine.

Perhaps she should have refused to go. She would have, had she supposed she had had any choice. But she'd been but one lone woman in a press of half-siblings who hated her, with a father who had forgotten she existed until that moment when he'd needed her. The whole lot had no doubt been rejoicing that they would soon be well rid of her. Defying them all had been unthinkable.

Besides, she had contented herself with their promises of a keep by the sea.

More the fool was she for having believed them.

August, 2001
Maine

Thomas MacLeod McKinnon was a man with a problem.

Not that problems bothered him usually. He generally viewed them as challenges to be solved, heights to be summitted, obstacles to be climbed over and outdone. That was before. This was now, and his current problem was the sight before him.

There were, and he couldn't really call them anything else, mouse ears poking up from behind his rhododendron.

He blinked, drew his hand over his eyes for good measure, then looked again.

Now the ears were gone.

He shifted his last sack of American junk food to his other arm, then crossed his porch to look more closely at the bush in question. He bent down and studied it, trying to judge what the angle of his vision had been a moment before and how such an angle might set a particular configuration of leaves into an earlike pattern. He pitted all his skills of observation and his considerable stores of logic and ingenuity against the problem. After several minutes of effort, he came to a simple conclusion:

He was losing his mind.

"Okay," he said aloud. "There are plenty of reasons for this."

The rhododendron didn't offer any opinions on what those reasons might be.

It would have been something he could have dismissed rather easily if it had been the only sighting. Unfortunately, he'd just about run off the road on his way home from the store thanks to the same delusion. He'd been innocently driving along when he'd glanced in his rearview mirror and seen those same black orbs attached to a beanie hat floating quietly in midair in his backseat.

All right, so he was driving an old Wagoneer that hadn't been washed all that often. It hauled stuff for him and that's all he cared about. It was possible, he supposed, that some dust particles left over from his last trip to the dump had coagulated into a beanie-and-mouse-ear configuration. It was possible that the sun had reflected off something else and cast a shadow where you wouldn't have thought one should be.

It was also possible that his first conclusion was right and his mind was really starting to go.

He turned away and let himself into his house before he did anything else stupid, like discuss his hallucinations further with a plant. He dropped his keys on the entry hall table and walked back to his kitchen. Could an ultra-unhealthy meal of eggs, spicy sausage and extremely processed cheese spread cure delusionary states? He wasn't sure, but he was willing to try.

He emptied his groceries out onto the counter, pulled out a frying pan and dumped the sausage into it. He turned the burner up to high and listened with satisfaction to the sound of saturated fat sizzling happily. This was the life for him. Uncomplicated. Unfettered. Uncluttered by visions of things that belonged in theme park gift shops.

Thomas tilted the pan to roll the sausages to one side, then cracked a handful of eggs into the freed-up space. With what the immediate future held in store for him, who knew when he might get a decent meal again?

He turned the heat down then began to walk around the kitchen, looking out the windows at the sea rolling ceaselessly against the shore and enjoying the smell of a late breakfast filling his kitchen. The more he prowled through the kitchen, though, the more unsettled he began to feel. He supposed it had a great deal to do with the fact that he was standing in a house he'd built with his own two hands, yet he planned to leave it behind and spend a year in a strange, foreign land.

The
Minstrel

✝

Patricia Potter

Prologue

❦

England
1485

Duncan, the Marquis of Worthington, rode like all the hounds in hell pursued him.

He'd thought that this trip to northern England would be a triumphant one. He had won back the estates taken by Edward during his Yorkist reign. Duncan's father had died defending the castle, and his mother and all her servants had been driven out.

Now the estates had been returned by Henry Tudor. Duncan had sent his men ahead to see that the castle was vacated by the Yorkist supporters. He didn't really care how the eviction took place, although he had told Gilbert to treat the womenfolk gently. His mother, once more the Dowager Countess of Worthington, would disapprove if he did otherwise, and his mother was the one person on the earth he did not want to disappoint. She was a great and gentle woman.

Then there were the vows he'd taken to protect and defend women.

Not that there was much honor left in England after such a long civil war.

He'd then planned to ride to the side of his mother, who was living at St. Anne's Convent, and take her in comfort to their restored holdings. But before he could leave the king's side, a messenger had arrived. His mother was dying of consumption. If he wished to see her, he could no longer tarry at the court of Henry VI. He had, after all, received what he wanted: the Worthington title and estates.

He'd left the next day with only Rhys, the captain of his guard and trusted friend, and each had exhausted three horses to arrive in two days. . . .

He looked ahead. *Not far now.* By the saints, he would arrive by moonset. He tightened his legs around his mount, urging it to greater speed. He'd bought the gelding in a village along the way, when his second horse started to slow.

The animal increased its stride and Duncan saw the outlines of the stark stone building of the convent. But though the building itself was bleak, the gardens around were lovingly tended by the nuns.

His mother had been happy enough there. She was deeply devout and had always loved gardens. She had, in fact, been at her happiest kneeling in God's earth. He had sent her what he could during the years, though he himself had been unable to return.

Duncan had not seen her in seven years, and it pained him that he had not provided better for her. Nay, more than pained. Agony sliced through him. He had seen so much blood and hardship in the past decade. He thought he had steeled himself against emotion. But now it thundered through him. *I must not be too late.*

They arrived at the entrance and Duncan rang the bell at the gate. He paced impatiently until a small window in the gate opened.

"I've come to see the Dowager Countess of Worthington." The habit-clad woman hesitated. "You are her son?"

"Aye."

The stone gate opened. "She has been waiting for you."

He breathed easier. "She still lives then?"

"Come with me," the woman said without directly answering his question. She bowed her head and led him through gardens of herbs and flowers to the stone edifice. She opened it without anymore words, then led him to a small room.

He saw a small slight woman lying on little more than a cot. There was little else: a small table, a stool and a cross that hung above the bed. The entire space was cold and bare, and the ache in his heart deepened. He should not have left her here. He should have found some way . . .

A Sister sitting on a stool beside his mother rose silently and disappeared out the door. He went over to the cot and knelt by its side. "Mother," he said.

His mother's once blond hair was now white. Her face was pale, but her blue eyes burned fiercely. She held out her hand. "My son," she murmured. "I prayed . . ."

"We have our lands back," he said, wanting to comfort in some small way.

Judith, once said to be the loveliest woman in northern England, smiled, then lapsed into a fit of coughing. He touched her cheek and felt its heat. He took a cup of water on the table and held it to her mouth. She swallowed slowly, with obvious pain, but her eyes never left him.

"I'll take you home," he said.

She shook her head. "This is home. The Sisters have been kind, and I have peace now. I am ready to go to our Father."

"Nay," he said, as if he could, indeed, hold death at bay.

"He granted my wish by bringing you . . . here to me," she whispered, her voice dropping. "I wanted to see you." She hesitated. "Have you wed, Duncan?"

"Nay," he said softly. "I have been . . . busy."

"You are the last, Duncan. And, God help me, my favorite. Your brothers . . . gone. Your father . . ." Her fingers dug into his. "I wanted to tell you, to ask you . . ." She started to cough again and he felt helpless. His suddenly clumsy fingers offered the cup again, and he saw blood on its edges.

She looked fragile, as if she would drift away from him any moment. He didn't know if he could bear that. He wanted to give her so much. She'd never had much at Worthington. His father had been a brutal man who had gotten her with child year after year. Two died in her womb. Another three died before their first birthdays. Only two had lived past fifteen, and one of those—his older brother—died for the Lancaster cause.

"What can I do, Mother?"

"Swear to . . . me," she said. "Swear to me you will **marry** for love. Protect her. Take care of her." She smiled weakly. "Love her, for there is no greater joy in life."

He was stunned to silence. He had never seen a tender word exchanged between his mother and father. His mother had been obedient and had busied herself with her gardens, particularly after Duncan and his brother had been sent away to be trained in arms.

Had they—his mother and father—ever been in love? He didn't think so. It had been an arranged marriage. She had brought land to his father, and he had given protection to her family. A sudden thought hit him. Had she loved someone else?

"Duncan." Her voice was weaker, as if her words were pulling her lifeblood from her. "Your oath?"

He didn't believe in love. It was naught but a myth. A whimsey.

His hands tightened around her almost lifeless one. He wanted to give her his strength. Her gaze, bright with fever, bore into his. "Your vow."

Duncan nodded. "I vow," he said, watching as she closed her eyes and one last soft breath escaped her lips.

one
❧

Making a vow was bloody well easier than keeping it.

Duncan looked about the great hall, already a disaster from the last occupant's indifference, and saw only greed.

They had been coming nonstop, these neighboring families, all with marriageable daughters. They had knocked on his door, expecting hospitality ever since he'd made the mistake of letting it be known that he was looking for a bride.

The hopefuls came in every size and weight, of cheerful and fearful countenance, of sensible and foolish temperaments, of plain and beauteous visages, of great dowries, and not-so-great dowries but aspirations nonetheless.

Mostly he saw greed.

There was one shy but fetching lass who had attracted him, but she trembled every time he neared. He overheard her telling her father that his scarred face and reputation terrified her. He didn't want a terrified bride and had no idea how to calm her fears.

None made his heart sing. If, indeed, hearts did sing. He doubted it, but he had made a vow to his mother, and he was bloody well going to try to fulfill it. He had never broken a knightly vow in his life; and he didn't intend to start with one he made to the only person who had ever loved him.

He sat at the table and fought the loneliness and the futility of his vow. 'Twould be far better to just take a bride as others did: to gain land, men at arms, wealth. There was, he thought, no such thing as true love. It was an invention of the minstrels and troubadours, of storytellers and ballad writers.

But still he had made that blasted vow. . . .

A young woman leaned over, offering a cup while exposing some of her endowments. He had a whiff of perfume that nearly knocked him off the chair. Her father, a neighboring earl, grinned foolishly. A little earlier he had stopped Duncan in the hall and said he would exceed any other dowry.

He was, Duncan knew, a former supporter of the Yorkist cause and probably feared retribution from the new Lancaster king. He was only interested in selling his daughter to save himself and his estates. But, then, so were the other hopeful fathers who accompanied wives with anxious expressions.

A minstrel entered the hall and stood, awaiting Duncan's nod. Duncan had hired the wandering gypsy as his hall filled. It wasn't hospitality. It was for his own sake. A distraction from the mayhem his hall had become.

He should never have told the priest about his mother's request. Duncan was sure that was the source of all his uninvited company.

The minstrel, a gypsy who had appeared just days ago, started to play, the sound of his lute drowned by the increasingly loud voices. But in fleeting moments, the sound drifted over to him and Duncan knew the voice was good. Not as fine as Rhys's, though. For a moment he thought back to those lulls between battles both in England and on the continent. Rhys had the Welsh love of music, and he'd taught Duncan how to play. They'd done so privately, Duncan not wanting to be thought soft by his men. But his soul had grabbed at it, like a drowning man reached for a branch to save himself. With the exception of his mother, who had been a gentle but distant figure, he'd known little but training and war for more years than he wanted to remember.

He wished he were playing that lute, rather than feeling the fool sitting amidst a ruinous manor beset by the oddest assortment of prospective brides he'd ever seen.

Lucifer's horns, but he'd rather face a hostile army. At least he knew the proper responses there.

His attention ran back down the table to his current guests. They included three barons, two earls and one marquis, all of whom wanted to improve their lot. Among them were seven marriageable daughters. And this was the second lot.

Blasted rules of hospitality. He would like to toss all of them out, but then in this political atmosphere, one needed all the allies one could find. Insulting daughters was not the way to win them.

A flash of brilliance suddenly struck him. A messenger from the king. A summons to the court. Of course, the court would be every bit as bad as this situation. The word most likely had traveled far and wide, and he would be deluged there, too, by prospective in-laws who would see little but his purse. And his status as a favorite of the new king. God knew he had fought for him long enough.

He wondered whether any woman would want him for himself, and not his wealth. Whether he could find a gentle soul who would not tremble at his reputation.

The earl on his left asked him to tell the company of the Battle of Bosworth, the one that saw the death of one king and placed a crown on another. It was a transparent attempt to give Duncan a chance to boast. Boasting was the last thing he wanted to do. He was sick of battle, of the noise and the smoke and the smells. He wanted to forget—not remember—the dead men who would never go home and the maimed ones who'd lost any chance of a decent life.

Shades of Lucifer, he wanted peace. Peace with a woman who didn't fear him or desire his wealth.

His eyes went to the minstrel again and a thought tickled his mind. He could play a passable song on the lute and the viele. He could even sing. He only knew songs of war and battle, but surely they would be in demand.

Days—even weeks—of being invisible was an irresistible thought. He could take measure of the young ladies without fearing they wanted him for all the wrong reasons.

He had been gone more than ten years. Only those in the immediate area would recognize him. If he traveled north . . .

The more he thought about it, the more appealing the idea. He even smiled. Twenty faces smiled back at him. Not one, he judged, with sincerity.

Only Rhys was to be trusted. He and the men who had fought for the Tudor cause for so many years. Rhys could stay and take care of the estates, particularly the cleaning of the castle He wanted them in good condition when he brought home a bride. One that wanted him for himself. If, indeed, such a person existed.

ℒady ℒynet Hampton of Clenden stared at her father. "You cannot mean it."

George, the Earl of Clenden, drew himself up to his full height, the one indication of his determination. He usually slouched, stammered, and shambled his way across a room. He was lovably incompetent at almost everything. Well-meaning but ineffectual. Lynet had always wrapped him around her finger.

But not this time. "You have two sisters, gel, who want husbands. None of them can wed until you do. It is time for you to make a decision."

"They can marry. . . . I can stay and take care of you."

He looked at her glassily, and she knew he had taken courage from brandy. "Your mother says they cannot wed until you do. You are ruining their chances, my girl."

"There is no one . . ."

"That is why I am inviting three men who have asked to call upon you. By the end of the fortnight, you will choose one." He blinked rapidly. "And you will be charming and spend time with each of them. You will not steal away."

She wanted to defy him. She probably would have, had she not known how much it would hurt him. As resentful as she was at his edict, she knew he wanted only the best for her, and he'd been ill lately. She knew he was determined because he believed it the best for her.

"Who did you invite?" she asked.

"The Viscount Wickham, Lord Manfield and the Earl of Kellum," he said, obviously encouraged by her question. "They are all young," he added hopefully.

She knew Wickham and Kellum. Wickham was in his early twenties, an attractive but callow fellow who thought of nothing other than hunting, unfortunately more for the sport than for the food. Kellum, on the other hand, liked little but himself. He was always preening in the steel mirror.

She didn't even want to think of the third.

Why couldn't everyone just let her alone with her music and books? She would be entirely happy that way. She didn't want a marriage built on necessity, like that of her parents. Her mother was a scold, and her father ignored his wife as much as possible. They suffered each other and nothing more.

She did not want to go through her life like that. But neither did she want to wound her father.

"Papa, what if I don't find someone I can abide?" She didn't even think of love as a possibility.

He looked profoundly unhappy. "Then your mother says you should be sent to a convent." He took her hand. "I must have an heir, my daughter. I have not been feeling well, and . . ."

And she was the oldest daughter of three. There were no sons.

"I will try," she agreed, not knowing what else to do.

He beamed. "I knew you would. They are fine men. All of them."

A lump formed in her throat. She knew she and her sisters were a disappointment. He'd tried not to show it, but the odd wistful observation about this young man or another gave him away. And Lynet knew she was her father's favorite. She loved her two younger sisters, but neither of them had ever had a moment's serious thought.

"I really will try," she said again. And she would. She would put away her lute and her dreams and do her duty.

Rhys regarded Duncan with horror. "You are daft, my lord."

Rhys was the only person who would so address him. He had the right, since he'd saved Duncan's life more than once. It mattered naught that Duncan had done the same for Rhys.

"You yourself told me I would make a good troubadour."

"I was flattering you."

"Then you believe I could fail?"

"Aye."

"And that I cannot play the viele?"

"Aye," Rhys insisted determinedly. "You know naught but

battle songs. You know nothing of the songs young ladies desire."

"You can teach me."

"This is madness, my lord. You cannot ride alone. You have too many enemies."

"No one will recognize a simple gypsy minstrel."

"They may not recognize who you are, but they certainly will know *what* you are. You wear arrogance like a cloak."

"You forget the time I was a spy."

"And I had to rescue you when you insulted a general."

Duncan drew up to his formidable height. "He deserved to be insulted," he said defensively. "In fact, he was too stupid to even know he was being insulted."

"You do not make a good servant."

Duncan decided to ignore the observation. "I want to borrow your lute and viele."

"Nay."

"You are my liege man. What is yours is mine."

"Really, my lord?" Rhys said with unimpressed boredom.

"Saints be saved, Rhys, do you not want me to fulfill my vow?"

Rhys regarded him solemnly for a moment. "I think it would be a very fine thing if you find a bride. But I don't think you will find an honest one with dishonest tactics."

"Do you think I can find one here? Is there one here that you would see as my wife?"

Rhys grinned. "In truth, I do not. So I will loan you my lute. You can find your own viele. I need mine to lure my own maid." His smile faded. "But if you do not return in a fortnight, I will come after you."

"I need no nursemaid," Duncan said gruffly, though in truth he appreciated the man's loyalty.

"We will see about that. When do you plan to leave?"

"In the morning. I can no longer stand this company."

"If you wed, you will be expected to host not only this company but the king."

"Ah Rhys, you always remind me of such unpleasant truths."

"The price of wealth and prestige, my lord. You had best get used to it."

"'Tis worse than battle, I think," Duncan said. "I have no talent for politics."

"You regained your land. I think you have a fine talent for politics."

The thought did not please Duncan. The idea of freedom did.

"I see your mind is decided," Rhys said. "I know you well enough not to argue further. But mayhap you should learn a few more songs."

"Nay, I know enough," Duncan said, "and if I do not leave in the morn, I will go mad and toss out everyone."

The gleam in Rhys's eyes disconcerted Duncan. He dismissed it. He'd seldom failed at anything, and surely he could be as good as the man who had performed tonight. No one listened anyway.

His new profession would begin tomorrow.

two
❧

To his chagrin, Duncan discovered he was *not* a very competent minstrel. For one who had always excelled at whatever task he'd undertaken, it was bitter medicine to swallow.

He didn't know what had gone wrong. He had planned so carefully. He had borrowed worn clothes from Rhys and others. He had prepared a repertoire. He had even practiced. He had set forth with high expectations of success if not acclaim.

But how did one entertain when no one would listen? When they drank and laughed and exchanged lies?

Oh, for sure, his playing was competent enough, said his temporary employers. But he had a tendency to glower at the audience and his repertoire consisted mostly of mayhem and battles.

He was depressing, he was told. Did he have no love songs? No amusing riddles? No one could dance to his somber music. No one wanted to look longingly into another's eyes when minstrels sang of death and destruction.

Well, *merde*, that was what he knew.

He'd not lasted long enough anywhere to measure the worth of the ladies of the household. He'd already been dismissed from three households. And with unseemly haste, especially from the last one.

He should have listened to Rhys. He could always go back and admit defeat, but such admissions did not come easily to him. How could he learn a more pleasing counte-

nance with a scar running over part of his face? He'd tried
to explain that it came from a displeased lord.

The lord of the manor—a minor baron, by God—said he
completely understood why Duncan received the scar.
"'Twas obviously a dissatisfied employer," he'd asserted. It
had taken all of Duncan's will not to seize his sword and
give a scar himself. But then word would travel about the
warrior minstrel, and no one would hire him.

Yet he wasn't ready to surrender.

He gathered his meager belongings and the nag he'd
found along the way. Someone had been beating the beast,
and he'd bought it with the coin he'd brought along. By the
saints, it had been the sorriest piece of horseflesh he'd ever
seen but, with a few days of good food, was already looking
better.

He decided to walk. He was in far better shape than the
nag. He had heard from other musicians that there might be
a temporary position some fifty miles north. An earl was
holding a house party that would last a fortnight or more.

Mayhap in that fifty miles, he could practice smiling.

The thought brought a glowering frown to his face.

A plague on bloody vows.

Lynet sneaked out of her room in the early morning hours.
She'd appropriated hose from the clothes her father meant
for the poor box and shortened them to fit her legs. She also
found an old, worn tunic months ago. A cap covered her
long hair which she had twisted on top of her head.

She'd promised her father to see to the guests, but none
would be up until midday. They had supped and drank late
into the night.

Stealing a few hours before her father and the guests
awakened would do no harm. She would be back before her
father knew.

The suitors had already been here three days, and she was
ready to go daft. One—Viscount Wickham—was handsome
and attentive; but he had pinched her last night and had
kicked one of the dogs. She could never marry anyone who
kicked a dog.

The second, Lord Manfield, was far more pleasant; but
he obviously had eyes only for her younger sister. Lynet had
seen them whispering and giggling together. To accept him
would be deeply hurtful to Evelyn.

The third—Robert, Earl of Kellum—had expressed an
opinion that educated women were the devil's work, and that
producing heirs was a woman's only function.

Lute in hand, she made her way down the steps. A certain
peace had fallen on this part of England after so many years
of civil war, and there were few guards. Even these, she suspected, would be asleep after the night of revelry.

Several servants, however, were lighting fires in the hall
and kitchen. She easily slipped past them and hurried over
to the stable. The stable lad, whose business it was to stay
awake to unsaddle and saddle horses, was nowhere to be
seen. She couldn't handle a large saddle, and she didn't want
one in any event, much preferring the close ride of bareback.
She put a bridle on her mare and led the horse to a mounting
block and mounted, wrapping her legs around Bridie's sides.

She leaned down. "I've missed you," she whispered. Bridie tossed her head and then pranced out the door toward the
postern. William, the guard posted at the gate, was accustomed to her morning rides. She knew he would say nothing
unless asked directly, and she planned to return before anyone did. In any event, her father was a lax master. He had
few retainers, and paid them poorly, especially since the un-
easy peace had come to England. As a result they tended to
make their own rules.

She smiled at William as she rode through the postern
gate and ducked to avoid a falling stone. The walls, along
with the castle, needed substantial repairs, but, as her father
often moaned, all his money had to go for the marriage portions. He could only hope to find a generous son-in-law.

At that dismaying thought, she urged her mare into a trot,
then a canter. She had a favorite spot, a pool formed by a
stream meandering down from the hills. Although near a
road, it was protected by a stand of oak trees, and the water
rippled with gold during the first hours after dawn.

Lynet knew she couldn't stay long. She had to get back
before the castle awakened or her prospective grooms would

be outraged by her riding like a lad and alone at that. That indiscretion would break her pledge to her father. She had promised to try her best, and she meant to keep her word.

She slipped down from Bridie and tied the reins to a tree. She'd looped a rope around her neck for the lute and now she slipped it off and found a dry spot to sit. She wanted to watch the sun touch the water and turn it to liquid gold. Most of all, she wanted peace.

Mayhap, she thought, a nunnery would be preferable to marriage. But then she probably couldn't have a horse. She most certainly wouldn't be able to ride one like a lad and race across the countryside. God, she thought, had surely blinked his eyes when he'd made her a female.

She fingered a tune on her lute. She would have much preferred the harp, but that was far too large to bring. She'd played it last night for the guests, at least for the few who listened, but her suitors had paid scant attention. They'd been far more interested in the food and drink.

She hummed along with the lute, then sang a French song of a woman who loses her soldier love. For some odd reason, most of the songs she knew were French, as if the English had lost their talent for song during the long civil war. She could barely remember when England hadn't been at war, since friends became enemies, then allies, then enemies again. There had been no demand then for marriage because no one knew when an alliance might mean losing a head. The Hampton family had survived relatively untouched because there had been no sons, and her father had been too old to fight. They'd declared their loyalty to which ever party was in power in northern England.

Peace. What a rare state.

She finished her song and played something of her own devising, closing her eyes and enjoying the warm morning breeze as her fingers plucked the strings.

How in the Holy Mother's name could she choose between the three suitors? None stirred her heart, but mayhap no man ever would. Was love just a myth?

Her fingers stilled as she was suddenly aware of a silence. It had not been there several moments earlier. No trill of birds. No chattering of squirrels nor the rustling of branches as they scampered across the trees.

Fear filtered through her consciousness. She had heard no one approach, but she knew she was no longer alone. Summoning her courage, she opened her eyes.

They found a pair of legs.

Her eyes moved up. And up. And up.

"I did not . . . hear you approach, sir," she said as her gaze reached his face. By the saints, he was tall. Her gaze lingered on his face. It was strong, even arrogant. A scar ran across his forehead, and his face was all planes and angles. His eyes were unusual: a silvery blue. Cold and piercing. She shivered in spite of the warmth of the morning sun.

Her gaze hesitated at his mouth. His lips had an odd crook to them that gave him a quizzical look that broke some of the severity of the face. Still, it was a forbidding visage.

She lowered her eyes. His clothes were rough. He wore a patched dark doublet over a plain cambric shirt. Well-formed legs were covered with worn hose. A workman's clothes, but carried like a lord.

"Lad, I did not mean to startle you, but by the saints you have a fine voice." His voice was gruff. Deep. Rumbling.

She knew she probably should go. She should be cautious. England was still a dangerous place. Men forced from their homes had become outlaws. Poachers hunted the woods despite the threat of hanging and would do anything not to be caught.

And yet . . .

He thought her a lad. A young one whose voice had not yet changed. Dressed in obviously ill-cut clothes. No threat to a very large stranger.

She lowered her eyes to the ground. "Thank you, sir," she said.

"Would you play something else for me?"

"I cannot," she said. "My master will be looking for me."

She did not look up, but she knew his gaze was boring into her. It sent heat rushing through her.

She wanted to get up but feared that if he received too good a look he would realize she was a woman. And her mare, which was grazing behind some trees, would certainly not be ridden by a servant.

Lynet could not help but look up, though, and she saw his own mount, a swayback pitiable excuse for a horse that showed a lack of attention and care. The stranger would most certainly prefer her Bridie.

How could she make him leave?

She tried not to look at the scar across his forehead, nor his russet-colored hair that was shorter than fashion. A soldier's scar. A soldier's hair. A soldier's stance.

"The lord patrols these lands fer poachers," she said, trying to make her English far less fine than she usually spoke. "He will hang you fer sure."

"And what about you?" he asked, amusement lighting those hard eyes. "Does he also hang horse thieves?"

He had already seen Bridie. She decided to bluster her way through. "I am exercising her," she said with dignity.

"So I see," he said. "The lord allows lads barely out of swaddling to exercise fine animals."

"I am a good rider."

"And a good musician, and I have need of some lessons." He fumbled at a pouch at his waist and tossed her a gold coin. "I will pay for a lesson."

She automatically caught the coin. A shilling. Any servant would be impressed. But how was it that he tossed it out so easily, as if it meant nothing to him "I cannot," she said again. "I will be missed, and beaten," she added for good measure, trying to make her voice sound far lower than it was.

His frown deepened. He started to say something, then halted as if he thought better of it.

"I must go," she said again, but her legs did not seem to want to move.

"Will you meet me here tomorrow then?" he asked.

"But why?" she asked, unable to hold the question in her throat.

He stood silent for a moment as if weighing whether to reply. Then he sighed. "I wish to better myself and become a minstrel. I know a few songs but not enough."

"You have money to throw away," she countered. "Why then would you need a position?"

" 'Tis the last of my pay. The army has been disbanded," he admitted with a wry twist of those intriguing lips. "I am looking for a steady occupation. Some of my comrades said I have a passable voice, but it seems they may be the only ones to think so. I have already been dismissed thrice."

"Why?" Lynet asked, curious why a man with a starving horse and a patched doublet would have such a coin to throw at a servant.

"I know only songs of war, not of pleasure," he said. "And they say my countenance is . . . too severe."

She could believe that. He had not smiled once, although amusement had touched his eyes for a brief second.

Her head said no. Her heart said otherwise. He was no brigand, only a man seeking to better himself. Mayhap he had a family. . . .

She looked back at the stream. Time had run away. She had to leave before her absence was noted. And she sensed he would not let her go without a promise to return. Was a promise made under duress not a promise at all?

"Aye," she said.

His eyes judged her. Then he nodded. He leaned down and took her hand to help her up. She came up fast. Never had she experienced the kind of strength that made her feel as light as a feather. But his hand did not let her go. Instead, he gazed down at it, his fingers running over the hand that was soft except for the calluses formed by playing the harp. Then his eyes widened as his gaze moved to her face again.

His hand reached out and plucked the cap from her head. The cloth caught a ringlet that fell down around her face. It then fell to her breasts. They were small and had been disguised by the shirt and loose tunic, but they were noticeable when she stood. "Merde, you're a female."

Lynet's eyes met his. They were like a wolf's, the same silver-blue she had seen in a pup she'd once rescued after its mother had been killed. She tried to pull away but his hand did not let hers go. She felt warmth course through her fingers, up her arm and through her veins.

"Who are you?"

"Just a servant," she said.

"In a lad's clothes?"

"They belong to my brother. I am safer from trespassers as a lad," she retorted with a very unservant-like snort. "I am not so likely to be accosted."

"Why is your brother not providing escort?"

She crossed her fingers and lied. "He is dead, sir."

A silence prevailed. At least she had stopped his questions.

"Do you swear to come back on the morn?" he asked after what he apparently decided was a respectful pause.

She turned the gold coin in her fingers. "Will you have another coin then?"

"Yes. And gratitude." His grumbling assent told her he was not used to offering gratitude.

The air grew even warmer between them. There was a kind of expectancy she'd never felt before. He waited, patiently, but she suspected that it did not come easily to him. She would have thought otherwise for both a soldier and a minstrel.

"I will try to come in the morning. At sunrise," she said.

He nodded, taking it as his due. She didn't understand that either.

"Where will you stay?"

He shrugged. "Under the skies."

"It will rain tonight."

"I've been rained upon before."

She wanted to tell him to go to Clenden for warmth and shelter. Her father never turned anyone away, much to the disgust of her mother. But if she did that, he would discover who she was and likely tell someone that she had been alone in the woods. Men did not keep secrets well. Then her father would know she had disobeyed and would likely put a guard on her.

So, instead, she nodded.

"If you do not come, I will hunt for you," he said. "You have my coin."

She turned the shilling once more in her hand, then tossed it back to him. "No, I do not. Use it to feed your poor horse. The neglect is shameful."

Before he could say more or gather his wits, she turned and ran through the trees. He started after her, only to see her grab the reins of the horse he'd seen earlier. Before he could reach her, she'd used a fallen log to mount and was racing away.

three

❧

What servant cared more for a nag than for a gold coin?

It humbled him. And shamed him, although the horse's condition was none of his doing and, in truth, the beast's lot had improved considerably in his company.

He thought about following her, but he knew his nag couldn't keep up with hers, nor did he wish to scare her away. He could only hope she returned.

He wondered who she was. She said she had a master, which meant she was a servant of some kind. But what kind of servant was given leave to ride a fine mount like the one she had, even to exercise her?

The daughter of a stable man? That was a possibility. It would explain her riding ability. But what explained her skill with a lute?

He wondered how she would look with her hair flowing down her back. Underneath the cap, it had been the color of bronze, a rich gold-red, and her eyes were indeed unique. A gold-flecked gray-green that had widened with anxiety when her gaze met his. She had been ready to bolt, and yet there had been courage there too.

He was making too much of it. She was a servant. She was most likely bound to the land or to the house. And except for the hair and eyes, she was no beauty. Her mouth was too wide, her chin too sharp.

But her voice was like that of a songbird, sweet and pure.

Her songs actually had a melody to them, unlike his own toneless strumming. If she would but instruct him for a day or so, he felt sure he could continue his quest with no one suspecting he was not as he presented himself. He would do something fine for her, in return. He would buy her freedom and make it possible for her to go wherever she wished.

In the meantime, though, he would have to find a place to camp. She had warned him that trespassers were not welcomed, and he did not want to be turned away from this household. He'd been told there were three daughters of marriageable age, and he wanted to look them over in his own way and at his own leisure.

He turned to the white horse that so obviously had been responsible for the censure in her voice. "Come on, nag," he said, tossing in his hand the coin she had thrown back to him. "Let us see if we cannot find you some decent feed."

He turned and started walking back to the last village, the one where he'd learned about the festive activities planned at Clenden. He wanted the horse to look improved on the morrow when he met with her again.

If she appeared.

She was too late. Her father's men were up, and so was the stable lad.

At least she saw none of her suitors in the courtyard. She doubted whether they would recognize her riding in as the lad. Her hair was tucked back under the cap and she lay on the mare's neck as she cantered inside, trying not to look at the faces of her father's guard.

Young Selwyn ran to take the horse. "The lord has been asking after you," he said.

"What did you tell him?"

"That I knew nothing, mistress, but he noted that your mare was missing."

By the furies, her father would pick this one day to rise early. "He did not blame you?"

"No, my lady," he said, but his forehead was knotted with worry. He needed this position, such as it was, and she knew it. He was the sole support of his mother, who had been widowed when a horse had kicked her husband in the head.

"I will let him know I spirited her out when you were busy getting feed."

"You had best go in through the kitchen," he said. "Mayhap you can make the stairs without anyone seeing you."

"My thanks," she said. She left the mare in his good hands. She disliked doing that; she would rather rub the horse down with her own two hands. But she may have tested her father too well.

Oddly enough, after this strange morning, a nunnery held less interest than it had before.

As she tried to slide through the kitchens without anyone seeing her, she thought again about the stranger in the woods. She had no doubt he had told it truthfully when he said he had been a soldier. He looked like a soldier. She'd seen enough quartered at Clenden to know the type.

He had cool eyes that missed little, and the scar above the left eye branded him a warrior. He also had the alertness she'd seen in soldiers—the gaze that never quite stopped roaming as if seeking danger around every corner. Such a man would have difficulty settling down to a sedentary life, or even a peaceful one as a minstrel. And yet he'd seemed determined to do just that.

She simply could not imagine a love ballad coming from the mouth that had frowned so.

But his plea had been so earnest.

She made it to her room without encountering her father or any of their guests. She said a brief thank-you to the saints. Her maid, Willa, was waiting for her, her face crinkled with worry.

"Your father is looking for you," she said. "One of the young men has made an offer."

"Did he now?" Lynet asked, biting her lip. All of a sudden, she compared each of them to the stranger in the woods. How quickly she'd lost her fear of him. He had been so large, so . . . severe in visage, and yet . . .

She was being silly. He was nothing but a wandering would-be musician, a man trying to survive by his wits.

Do you swear to come back in the morn?

She swallowed hard. How could she go out again? If one of her suitors knew she was meeting a man in the woods, her reputation would be destroyed forever.

Lynet turned her mind from the stranger and tried to concentrate on what her maid had just said. One had made an offer.

"Which one?" she asked.

"Your father did not say."

She thought about the three again. Which did she wish was the one? Of course, if the marriage portion was large enough, she knew she could have any one of them. Her father had been cagey about that, however. To his credit, he had hoped for a son-in-law who truly cared for her.

Her mind roved over the candidates. She had not been impressed by any of them and now, after this morning's odd encounter, even less so. Even the handsome Wickham was pale and puny next to the would-be minstrel. His eyes had none of the depth and complexity, nor was his walk as powerfully graceful.

She swallowed hard as Willa helped her into a shift and corset. She hated corsets and usually did not wear them, but this morning she would have to placate her father and would dress to please him if not the rest of the household. She had promised not to disgrace him. She chose a gown that made her eyes greener.

Willa brushed her hair, parted it and left it to flow down her back. Her face was still rosy from her morning adventure.

"You look lovely, my lady," Willa said. "There is a sparkle to yer eyes. Is there one of the young lords that you fancy?"

Lynet looked closer into the mirror. Did she see a sparkle there?

Nay. It was just Willa's imagination. There was nothing to cause such a reaction.

She rose, steeling herself for the coming interview. She wondered just how much her father was willing to pay for a son-in-law. It seemed as if she were being bought and sold. The groom gave her a dower which, of course, he controlled; and her father gave her husband a marriage portion, which he could use in any way. It was, she thought, most unfair to her.

She had to admit her father had given her time to choose a

husband. She was nineteen when most girls married at fourteen or fifteen. Her sisters were now sixteen and fifteen and complaining bitterly about their unmarried status. But she had so wanted to marry for love.

Love grew between married people, her father contended, but she had not seen it grow between her parents. They tolerated each other. She had wanted so much more. She had wanted a love that jongleurs and minstrels celebrated. 'Twas foolish, she knew. But still, she had hoped . . .

Now all she had was the songs.

Her father was waiting for her in the oriel behind the great hall. It was a small room lined with a large fireplace and many books, her father being a scholar by nature. She and her sisters had been fortunate in that he was advanced in his thinking and believed women should be educated as men were in Latin and philosophy and history. Her sisters had cared little about such subjects but she had been an avid student, which is why, she knew, she was his favorite and why he'd allowed her to wait so long for marriage.

But now he had need of an heir. He could wait no longer, and she suspected he had investigated the three suitors before inviting them and found them to be of good reputation.

He stood next to a fire now. "You left the castle," he said. "And in a lad's clothing and without a guard."

She lowered her head. "You know how much I love to ride in the morning."

"It is dangerous, Daughter. There are many soldiers prowling about now that so many have been dismissed. It is not safe and it is not . . . the way of a lady."

"I went early enough that . . . none would be awake."

"I want your promise you will not go again without a guard."

Her promise. Her sworn oath to the stranger. How could she make one that would nullify the other?

She tried to avoid the question. "Willa said you wished to talk to me about an . . . offer?"

He frowned as if he knew exactly what she intended, but her question had the effect she wanted.

"Kellum," he said with satisfaction. Of all of them, Kellum was most highly placed.

"He does not approve of educated women." she said.

His frown deepened. "He did not say that to me."

"He did to me. You would not want all your teaching to be for naught."

He looked decidedly uncomfortable. "I will talk to him about that. But," he added hopefully, "he is a fine-looking man and would produce handsome children."

"And ignorant ones," she said.

"Is there one of the others you prefer?" he asked, an anxious look on his face.

"Wickham kicked one of your dogs."

Her father looked more distressed. He could not abide cruelty to animals. "And Manfield?" he said with almost desperation.

"I think he prefers Evelyn."

Her father's eyes cleared. She had said nothing bad about him. "That is because you have not given him a chance. You are always disappearing and Evelyn is always here."

"I will make a bargain with you," she said.

He looked at her suspiciously.

"There are no brigands out at dawn," she said. "They are sleeping after committing their nefarious deeds." She didn't know whether that was true or not, but it sounded logical. "I promise I will choose a husband within the week if I can enjoy what freedom I have."

Her father looked at her warily. "I suspect you would go anyway," he said.

"I may not be able to do so again after a wedding," she said.

"You will not let anyone see you?"

"Nay, and you know the servants will not talk."

"You have them under your spell, right enough," he grumbled. "They pay more attention to you than to your mother or me."

She said nothing. Just waited. It was not much of a bargain for herself, but then she knew her father was determined in this matter of marriage. And at least she could fulfill the vow to the stranger.

Her father mumbled a moment or two, then nodded his head. "Mind you, let no one see you or . . ."

"I will not," she said. "And I will be careful."

A look of resignation settled on his face. "Be careful, too, that your mother does not know."

"She will not."

He looked at her for a long moment. "I want nothing more than for you to be happy, my daughter, but there is a duty to family, to your sisters, to your mother. There must be an heir."

Lynet knew that. She knew how much her father had longed for an heir all these years. She had been selfish. She had wanted perfection when there was no perfection in the world. She had wanted her heart stolen, but there was no thief with honor.

She nodded.

"A bargain then, Daughter? Any of these three men would make a suitable husband, and if not one of them then you must tell me who."

"A bargain, Father," she assured him.

He did something he had never done before. He placed a hand alongside her cheek for the barest of a moment, then dropped it and turned away. He'd never expressed physical affection before. A gruff "well done" had been his highest praise.

A week. She had a week to fulfill her vow to choose a husband. Mayhap it was not a vow at all since it had been made under a certain quiet duress. But something in her heart told her she must honor it.

She knew it was something she had to do.

Would she return? She had thrown his coin back to him.

He found himself pacing near the pool even before dawn. His old nag stood not far from him, her head hanging down to eat the rich green grass even after stuffing herself with oats last night.

He wanted the lessons, he'd told himself. And yet it hadn't been the music that echoed in his mind, but the fine, stubborn face as she'd thrown his coin back at him. It had been a unique experience, a curious disdain.

What manner of a woman was she?

Duncan thought about the color of her eyes, the gray moss

green that was filled with a ready intelligence. A woman masquerading as a boy. It was preposterous. Mayhap she had been a figment of his imagination. Or a spirit of some kind.

He had been here since the wee hours of morning, ignoring the winds that cooled the warmth of yesterday. He took Rhys's lute and sat where she had sat, and played one of the songs he knew. It was a French song about the Crusades. There was nothing gentle about it.

He finished it and suddenly knew he was not alone. He had lived by instincts these past ten years and yet he had heard nothing—not the whinny of a horse or a footfall. By the saints, but he was slipping.

"You have a good touch," a soft voice said. He turned where he sat and saw her standing underneath a large oak. He didn't see her horse.

"You came," he said, somewhat stupidly.

"I said I would."

"I feared I had frightened you."

"I'm not easily frightened."

She was wearing the same clothes she'd worn yesterday. He wondered now how he had ever mistaken her for a lad, even though once more her hair was hidden beneath a cap.

"I did not hear you."

"You should not hear someone when you are playing. You should be listening to the music."

"I doubt there was much musical about it. I've been told I am heavy-handed."

"Whoever told you that knew little. 'Tis your choice of songs that is heavy-handed."

He stood then, towering over her, though she was tall for a woman. "Your master? Does he know about me?"

"He knows naught other than I'm exercising his horse."

"To which house are you bound?"

"I thought you wanted to know about songs," she said, turning way.

"I do. Do not go, mistress." He couldn't remember when last he had pleaded with anyone, man or woman.

"No more questions," she said.

He nodded and handed her the lute. Her own hands were empty.

Her fingers fondled it, ran lightly over the fine wood and tested the strings. He thought they sounded far better under her touch than his. " 'Tis a fine instrument," she said after a moment. Now there was a question in her voice; the lute was far too fine for a common soldier.

"A friend . . . wanted me to have it."

Her face immediately clouded and he realized she'd concluded that his friend had died. How was he to explain his friend was at Worthington, trying to straighten the keep for an intended bride?

"Teach me a few songs," he commanded, forgetting that he was a supplicant, a gypsy wanderer, not a marquis used to having commands immediately obeyed.

The startled look in her eyes told him he had made a mistake. He continued awkwardly, "I also need a few more lessons in . . ."

"Humility," she finished.

He couldn't stop the small smile he knew was forming. "Humility," he confirmed.

"A smile helps, too," she suggested.

"I've been told I am not very accomplished at that either," he admitted wryly.

"It is really not that hard."

"Is it not, mistress?"

"Can you not think of something fine? Like a sunrise? Or a pool like this one? Or a sunset?"

Her face had lit as if that very sun was shining on it. He had never seen anyone who took such joy in simple things. To him, those images held different meanings. A sunrise meant a new battle, sunset the coming of night and danger, and water had to be crossed usually at the most inopportune time.

But he did look up and consider her words. The rising sun sprinkled the water and trees with drops of brilliance, and he felt it against his face, warming him.

Or was it the woman who warmed him?

Was she a woman? In the boy's clothing, she'd looked no more than twelve or thirteen. But when her cap had fallen yesterday and her hair floated around her face like a halo, she'd looked very much a woman.

He told himself not to think such things. She must be in

service. He was enough of a lord to know that men of his rank did not marry servants. King Henry would not be pleased, and Henry's favor meant a great deal to him. It meant keeping his holdings. And, quite possibly, his head.

"You are looking at me, my lord, not the fine things to inspire you."

"You do not think you can inspire someone?" he asked.

Her face turned a rose color. "Oh, no, my lord. I know I am plain."

He wanted to reach over and touch her face, to see whether it was truly as smooth as it looked. He wanted to pluck off the ridiculous cap and let the hair flow again. He wanted to tempt a smile from her face and see whether she was really as pretty as he thought she might be.

He could do none of those things. He had always honored women, as his mother had taught him. He'd tried to be fair and honest even with the women he paid for favors. And he knew from the stirring in his loins that if he touched her now he might well not be able to stop.

Duncan knew nothing about her, not whether she had a man of her own. He could not imagine that she did not. Her voice alone would be a siren's song. And yet she obviously did not believe herself attractive.

He shook such thoughts from his mind. He knew how unwise it would be to love—and marry—a commoner. The king would most certainly disapprove. Henry Tudor had himself, in fact, wanted to find a wife for Duncan, wanted to engineer an alliance with a Yorkist family. For Duncan to take a servant as wife would be a direct insult to the crown. He had pledged to marry for love, but he knew with all the knowledge of his thirty-two years that it had to be a woman of the nobility.

Why was he even thinking such thoughts? A chance encounter. A few lessons. Then he would be on his way.

Why then had she haunted his sleep last night and made him eager for the dawn?

His gaze met hers, and the throbbing inside him grew stronger. A catch in his heart stunned him.

Those eyes were so clear, so full of lively intelligence. So probing.

He tried again to dismiss all these observations. "Where should we start?"

"Mayhap with a smile," she said with a small one of her own. It lit her face, just as he expected. It also lit something inside him.

"You must learn to give it freely," she added, watching him carefully. "No one wants to listen to a dour minstrel."

"They do not?"

"Nay. They want to feel happy. Now try," she commanded.

She looked so serious, so dedicated to the task at hand. He knew when the side of his mouth started moving in an upward direction. Now, how long had it been since that had happened? Not since so many battles and deaths had hardened his heart, encasing it like a band of steel.

"That is better," she judged, "but mayhap a little wider."

Mischief sparkled in her eyes, and his heart took a sudden leap.

She took in hand her own lute, which had been strung around her back. "Follow me," she said.

She started to play a wistful sounding tune, and he took up his own instrument and tried to follow her fingers. Despite the quality of the lute, the sound his fingers made did not have the light, magical sound of hers.

"Gently," she said. "Just barely touch the strings. Do not attack them."

In minutes, his fingers moved as lightly as hers. She stopped and listened to him, tilting her head in a way he found altogether too beguiling. Her mouth stretched into a quizzical smile. "Where did you learn to play?"

"A comrade. A Welshman."

"Did he ever smile?"

"All the time."

"Could you not have learned that from him."

"I did not think I was so . . . inept."

She threw back her head and laughed. No mockery. Just gentle amusement. An amusement she invited him to share with her. "I cannot believe you feel . . . inept often."

He frowned. Unfortunately he *had* been inept too many times. He had been arrogant and sure he was right. He had endangered his guardsmen more times than he wanted to remember. He'd had to learn caution.

Her face bent over the lute. "This is a song by Bernard de Ventadour, a protégé of Eleanor of Aquitaine," she said.

The words flowed over him. "When I hear in the wood the song of birds which brings sweetness to my heart . . ."

A month ago he would have laughed at such sentimentality. Now he heard the birds in his heart as well as in the trees. Both seemed to be singing along with her. The morning was brighter than any he had ever seen, the sky bluer and the sun warmer. Every one of his senses was heightened.

He hummed along with her, and she turned to him. "You sing the words."

He had not objected to singing songs of war. He hesitated, though, at singing songs about birds and love and flowers. It was not manly.

But she had an expectant look on her face.

Rhys had said he had a pleasant enough voice. But then Rhys was a friend, and his critics along this particular journey had been many and insulting. He'd wanted to take his sword to some of them. After all, they had been talking so loudly and drinking so much, how could they know whether he was an adequate musician or not?

He wasn't sure he wanted to find out.

"I will go if you do not try," she said.

He had a memory for words and music. Her threat was enough to prompt him to start the song. If he made a fool of himself, it would be no more than he had done in the last three halls. God help him if any remembered that lone musician. He had thought only of the moment, not the future. He cringed at the thought of confronting one of his erstwhile employers at court.

He strummed the strings of the lute, and his voice drifted across the river. He did not look at her. He did not want to see the same scorn he had seen on other faces. In truth, he was about ready to take his poor excuse of a horse and head back home.

He looked at her. No disgust in her eyes. No disappointment. Instead, her eyes regarded him with a certain wonder.

No one had ever looked like that at him before. Certainly no woman. No fear. No awe. No greed.

He suddenly wished he was the man he was pretending to be. A man free of responsibilities, of duties . . .

He stopped suddenly. He reached out and touched her face. His fingers caressed her skin. It *was* as soft as it looked. Soft and ever so seductive.

Her eyes widened, the gold flecks more evident in the gray-green depths. He traced a path along her cheekbone. Then, unable to help himself, he leaned toward her and his lips met hers in a whisper-light kiss.

Her lips responded for the slightest measure of time, then he felt a shiver run through her. Before he could move, she was on her feet, backing away. He reached out his hand to her. "I do not wish to frighten you."

She took another step back. "Nay, you did not. But, but . . ." she stammered, "you must not . . ."

"Why must I not? Are you promised?"

"Yes," she said.

Against all reason, his heart plummeted. He should have known. She'd been kind to a stranger, nothing more. He bowed formally. "I am most sorry, mistress. I did not intend to offend you."

"I must go," she said.

"I must needs more lessons."

"A smile," she said. "That is all you need."

But he needed a great deal more and knew it.

"Meet me here tomorrow." It was a command rather than a question. "One more time."

She looked startled.

Finally, she nodded and turned.

"Your name?" he asked.

But she was gone, speeding through the trees. He knew if he went after her, she might never return. She had gifted him with her time. But it was on her terms.

He'd never been good at accepting another's terms.

Now he knew he must. Or he might never see her again.

That was a thought he could *not* accept.

four

❧

Lynet knew she could not return to her special place in the woods.

Her world changed the moment he had touched her. It was as if she'd been branded. Except the pain was an exquisite pain. No man had ever touched her so intimately before. She had not expected the tremors it caused, nor the heat that coursed through her.

She had not expected that it would turn the world upside down.

And *he* had done that.

Just his very appearance had started her world swirling, then the sound of his strong—yet uncertain—voice had deepened the longing within her. She had not recognized it before. She had thought herself content. At least until her father had decreed marriage.

She knew nothing of him except he was a soldier. And she hated violence. Her family had lived on the sword's edge these past decades, balancing between loyalties to the red rose and the white rose. Neighbors who had made the wrong choices had lost their lands. And their heads.

She had lingered much too long. She'd allowed herself to be drawn into his spell. She always considered herself practical and yet she found herself doing extremely impractical things. She should never have come here this morning. She should never have let him touch her.

Her body felt different, just because of that one caress.

It felt alive.

And it terrified her.

She had made promises.

Any feelings for the stranger, she assured herself, were only a lie, a reaction to her father's ultimatum. But she knew if she had stayed, she would have succumbed to his touch, to the magic that somehow wove around them.

He was a soldier and a wanderer. Mayhap he even had a family tucked away somewhere. Most certainly a woman. There was a certainty about him, an air of authority that placed him above the common soldier, at least those she had seen accommodated at Clenden. And he'd been clean, his body smelling like soap and leather.

He was different from anyone she had ever met. She did not even know his name, ever though they had shared quiet moments both yesterday morn and this one. In truth, she had never before enjoyed a man's company as she did with her would-be troubadour. Whimsically, she thought about the names he might go by. John, most likely. That was the most common name.

But he was anything but common. Gareth, mayhap, or Banning. Bryce. All those names conjured images of strength.

She neared the castle and knew once again she was late, too late, she suspected, to slip in unnoticed on her fine horse. For a moment she thought about going back and exchanging her mare for the stranger's nag, but then there would be a search for Bridie and the stranger would most likely be hanged. He probably would be anyway, if he remained lurking about. He had obviously disregarded her warnings.

And yet he'd seemed to step out of nowhere yesterday morning. Like a ghost.

He was no ghost. A ghost didn't burn skin where he touched, nor did he smell of woods and soap and leather. He didn't play the lute and sing in a pleasantly deep voice. A ghost didn't make a heart thump harder. At least not pleasantly.

By the saints, but she was sounding like a woman in a poem, not a flesh and blood person with obligations.

She went into the woods on the fringe of the castle and tied her horse there. She could slip unnoticed into the bailey, and

Selwyn could fetch the mare later. At least she hoped she could slip by unnoticed. It would be a disaster if she ran into any of the visiting lords. She reached the gate and knocked on it. William peered out at her, then let her in.

Lynet smiled at him as she went through the gate.

"Yer horse, my lady?"

"Selwyn will fetch him. I lost track of time and thought it easier to come in this way."

William nodded his agreement. It would be his hide as well as hers if the lord knew he had been letting her ride every morning. In return, she'd often slipped him pastries from the kitchen and even some of the castle's finer wine instead of the coarse ale usually provided the soldiers.

And then she saw Robert, Earl of Kellum. He was mounted with several other men, including Manfield and Wickham. She glimpsed the huntsman and several dogs running excitedly beside him. A hunting party. Her father was not with them, but that was not surprising. His gout made it difficult for him to mount and ride.

Grateful that no one noticed a small lad, she ducked behind the kitchen that was located in the lower bailey, separate from the main building. She hoped they would not see Bridie. Or the stranger. Dear saints in heaven. *The stranger.* She had to reach him before they did and tell him to leave the forest. The dogs would undoubtedly pick up his scent, and he could be seized as a trespasser or, worse, poacher.

He could hang.

She waited until the hunting party thundered out of the gates. Then she ran over to William. "I must leave again," she said. "Selwyn is busy and there is no one to fetch Bridie."

William hesitated. "Wha' should I say if my lord asks if you have left?"

"Tell him I said I had his permission," she said. "I should not want you to get in trouble."

He gave a long, resigned sigh.

But he opened the gate. She ran out. She could no longer see the horsemen.

Her heart pounded. Could she reach the stranger in time?

*   *   *

Duncan knew he should leave. He had no reason to remain by the sparkling stream and the pool it formed. No reason at all. Yet he was loath to go. He could still hear the music, still see the slow, delighted smile on his companion's face as he'd hummed along with her. The grass was bent where she had sat, and her music still echoed in the woods.

She might well be a sorceress, if he believed in such things. She was like a wood sprite, a fairy, appearing out of nowhere. He'd almost followed her this time but feared, if he did, she might disappear forever and not return.

Why had he not persisted in obtaining her name?

He'd been bewitched. That was the only explanation. He'd never been at a loss before. He couldn't remember a time when he hadn't been in control. But after a few moments with this young woman, he'd been reduced to a stammering schoolboy.

Even now he didn't wish to move.

The sound of baying hounds shattered the peace. He moved then. He did not want to be caught here. If so, he would have to reveal his identity if he weren't hanged immediately. Even then, he doubted anyone would believe him. A marquis disguised as a wandering gypsy?

Even if he could convince someone, the results could still be disastrous. The story would travel throughout England. The Marquis of Worthington traveling as a poor, inept minstrel. He would become a laughingstock and all of England would think him mad. He would be considered daft at best, a lunatic at worse. He wouldn't blame Henry for taking back the estates.

He went over to the nag. She certainly couldn't outrun hounds, but he might have a small surprise for them. He had not anticipated this exactly, but he always carried a portion of mustard with him. It was used by many households to disguise the taste of salted meats and spoiled poultry. He hadn't known where he would be staying or what he would be eating, and mustard concealed any number of sins.

He looked in his saddlebags and found the pouch. He sprinkled it over the area, then mounted and guided the horse into the water. It was shallow though swift. The mustard would distract the hounds, the water would then mask any lingering scent. He couldn't go downstream toward the road. The hounds were coming from that direction. He would have to go upstream, follow the hill. He turned his horse toward the hills and tightened his thighs to speed her up. The horse moved into an awkward trot, kicking water up his hose and ill-fitting shoes. He made the crest of the hill just in time. He heard the triumphant bay of the dogs, then confused yapping.

He smiled to himself and slowed the horse, but continued to put distance between himself and the other riders.

£ynet had been prepared to throw herself upon the stranger to save him. She'd been convinced he would be apprehended by now, and she would have to reveal herself. It would be humiliating, and she knew it could ruin her. Admitting she knew a vagabond musician, had even met with him alone, would destroy any chance of a good marriage. She would, no doubt, be sent to that nunnery her father had threatened.

But if she saved a life, it would be well worth it.

Her father was tolerant and treated his tenants better than most. But he did not tolerate poaching. He had turned others over to the sheriff for the crime, particularly in the last few years when thieves seemed to be everywhere. The by-product of a civil war, her father said, and good people could not tolerate it.

She didn't know how the stranger was supporting himself, or eating. He had had the one coin, but his horse was as pitiable as any she'd ever seen. It must have been his last coin, and he'd been desperate enough to make a living that he had offered it to her. Therefore, he might well have been poaching.

She heard the baying stop, and then the confused yipping and barking that meant the hounds had lost the trail of whatever—or whoever—they were following. She turned, then considered what she'd heard. The animals had been on the trail of a quarry. She knew that. What stopped them?

Had they found him? Or had they merely been outfoxed by their quarry?

She decided to circle around the riders, then follow the

stream through the hills. If she found him, she would make
sure he was safe. She would give him the locket she wore underneath her tunic. The locket had been a rare gift from her father, but was not a life more important?

It was made of gold and would be worth something to him.
She would convince him to leave.

She met the creek far above the riders. She knew if the
hounds had lost the scent he must have come this way. The
riders, she hoped, would give up on this particular quarry and
look for something else. Not that they would find much. This
entire area had been well hunted by troops during the civil
war. First the Yorks, then the Lancasters.

She hoped her father was not worried about her. If he were,
she doubted whether he would openly search for her. He
would not want anyone to believe her a disobedient daughter,
who might also be a disobedient wife. She had wished many
times that she had been the son he'd had wanted so desperately, both for his sake and her own. She could not even imagine the freedom of being a man.

Like the minstrel. He could go anywhere he wished. Envy
filled her mind.

She watched the sides of the creek, looking for signs of a
rider emerging from its bank. She was so intent on the ground
that she nearly fell from the saddle when another rider appeared.

She saw the thin white legs of the nag first, then her gaze
moved upward. The saddle was worn, but he sat it easily. She
had not seen him on horseback before, and she realized immediately that he was not unused to it. He sat in the saddle
like a man born to it.

His cap was pulled down over his eyes and his lips had a
wry twist to them. "I thought I outwitted them," he said.

"You did. But *I* knew you were there, and they didn't know
what the dogs were after."

"Why did you come back?"

To save you? As she looked at him, she suddenly realized
how foolish that was. Even on the swayback mare, he looked
every part the lord. He looked at ease, even, mayhap, a little
amused. Nothing at all like a man being hunted.

"I . . . was afraid for you."

Something changed in his eyes. He moved his horse toward her and reached out a hand to take hers. "I . . . have been a soldier for ten years," he said. "I've fought in Europe, and I've fought too many of my countrymen. I know well how to look after myself."

Lynet suddenly felt foolish. And yet fear had burned inside her.

"And no young woman," he continued, "has ever worried about me before." There was something oddly poignant about the words, about the sudden discordant vulnerability she thought flashed through his eyes. Tension leapt between them, filling the air with expectancy. She felt the throb of her heartbeat grow stronger. The sound reverberated through her body.

She started to back her horse away. His touch was like a torch against her skin. The air seemed to still.

"I will go then," she said, knowing that every moment she stayed would make it that much harder to meet him again. The thought of never seeing him again was unbearable.

"What is your name, mistress?"

She hesitated. Everyone in the nearby village knew her. And "Lynet" was not that common a name. "Mary," she said.

"Mary," he said slowly, as if folding his tongue around it.

"And you?" she asked.

"I go by many names, Mary," he replied, once more saying the name as if it were something very tasty.

"It is unfair to talk in riddles," she chastised him.

"Call me Robin then," he said.

"I must get back," she said, aware now that the sun was straight above. If nothing else, she must return before the hunters did. The last thing she wished was to meet them.

"You still owe me a lesson," he said.

He had been an apt student. He knew enough now to hold a musician's post while learning more songs.

If only he would smile more.

She looked back up at his face. He was smiling now. At least, it was a half smile. It was quite hard to tell the way his lips had those little crooks in them. But his eyes looked softer than they had before, more approachable. She wanted to stay and see exactly how approachable they could be. She wanted to sit with him and hear his adventures and ask him about foreign lands.

Most of all she wanted to feel the touch of that callused hand on hers again.

She wanted it so badly that it terrified her. "I must go," she said again.

He maneuvered his horse in front of her. "Not unless you promise to meet me again."

She tried to move around him, but the horse he rode was quicker than she thought possible.

"I will be beaten," she said desperately.

"And I will kill whoever might attempt to do that," her minstrel said in a very unminstrel way. In fact, she felt a shiver down her back. *He meant it.*

"All right then," she said. "But up here. There is a cave just beyond those branches." She pointed to a huge oak that grew crookedly on the side of the hill. "There."

"At dawn?"

"Aye."

"I will comb the countryside if you do not come," he said with a frown.

She believed it too. "Please, I must go now."

He turned his horse so she could get by.

"My thanks," he said, "for worrying about me."

His voice was humble, and her chest suddenly ached. *No young woman has ever worried about me before.*

What would he do when he discovered who it was that so worried about him? Would he believe himself only an amusement?

Why had she not told him in the beginning? Because then he would have gone. She would not have had this one last adventure.

And what price might they both have to pay for it?

five
❦

Dawn could not come too early for Duncan.

He had left the creek and had ridden into the village. There he had again found an inn for himself and some feed for the mare. He made what he hoped were discrete queries about a maid named Mary.

Everyone regarded him suspiciously until he offered to trade a meal for entertainment and gossip from other parts. The offer was readily accepted. He remembered what Mary had told him, had tried a smile and lightened his fingers. It did not seem to help. Drunken conversation drowned out nearly every sound, but nonetheless he had established the fact that he was, for better or worse, a minstrel, an entertainer. He hoped the word would drift to Clenden.

After he put down the lute, he found conversation far easier. He was a wanderer and must have news to share. What was happening in the countryside? Had he been to London? Had he seen the new king? Had he heard of new taxes?

He answered as well as he could. He did not say he had fought with the Lancasters. This was northern England and most of the loyalties here had been with Edward and Richard of York. Regional hostilities, he knew, would exist for a long time. Too many nobles had been attainted, too many estates taken. There were already whispers of another rebellion to remove Henry Tudor.

But Duncan knew the country was weary of war and that

Henry was aware of the conspirators. He would not tolerate their activities for long.

He said none of this. Instead, he spoke of court gossip, marriages and new alliances. Many would have heard of such, even if they had not oft supped with the king.

"We ha' a bride here, too," said one man whose tongue loosened as he drank. "'Tis said the earl's oldest daughter will wed. 'Twill mean a fine celebration.

Clenden was where he had been headed before his encounter with the forest maid. He'd heard there were to be guests, and guests usually meant employment for musicians, hopefully not just a night or two. He'd wanted to stay places long enough to learn about the ladies in the household.

But he had delayed his visit upon meeting his lady of the woods. He feared that were he to leave, he may never see her again.

Could she possibly be in service at Clenden?

"There are two more daughters to wed," another man said. "The earl was cursed with females and no son."

Two unwed daughters.

"They be beauties, too," said another. "Too bad about the eldest. She be plain. But the marriage settlement will be high."

Duncan listened idly. He knew he should be paying more attention. This was, after all, the reason for his journey. But he had no interest in noble ladies at the moment. He could only think of a young girl dressed as a lad who rode as well as any man.

He also wondered whether this journey had really been to find a bride, as much as it had been a quest for freedom. Freedom from responsibilities, from taking men into battle. He couldn't remember a time when he wasn't aware that everything he did could result in someone's death. In truth, he had made a vow to his mother, but he'd seized upon it as an excuse to be someone else for one small period of time, someone who could wander as he wished, befriend whom he wished. He'd wanted to escape the constraints of his rank.

He knew he would not have much longer to steal these hours. Henry Tudor would expect a wife and he would expect taxes. He would also expect him to be rebuild Worthington.

Loyalty from a king usually lasted only as long as the useful-
ness of the subject did. Duncan had no illusions about that.

He emptied his tankard of poor ale and pushed back his
chair. He had already announced that he would sleep in the
woods since he was using his last coin to feed his horse. He
was regarded as a madman at that pronouncement, but he said
he had a long distance to go and it was a small enough price
for transportation.

The innkeeper told him he would be welcome to a free
meal the next night, if he would sing again. It was the first
time that he had been asked back, and he felt a jolt of pleasure at being accomplished at something other than killing.
He nodded, then left.

An hour later he was at the cave his lady had pointed out
earlier in the day. It was deep and he was protected from the
wind. He built a small fire.

Five, six hours before dawn. He could barely believe how
anxious he was, how worried that she would not come. He
had learned nothing about her, had no way of finding her.

He considered riding into Clenden as he had first intended
rather than skulking about in the woods and being taken for a
thief or poacher. But what if he was turned away before finding her? Then he would have no excuse to linger.

Other than a plain dirk, he had no weapons. No one would
believe him a lord. More likely he would be considered a lunatic. And that would not be far from the truth.

Merde, what was he doing? Mooning over a servant girl,
who was probably already pledged to another, when he should
be about finding a wife. One that would be acceptable to King
Henry. Otherwise, what would happen to his estates?

He had fought ten years to restore the properties to his
family. He had been too late to bring his mother back home,
but he was not going to let his ancestral home go. He owed it
to his forebearers—and to his future children.

Fool. Still, he didn't move. She had probably risked everything for him, taking her master's horse yet again. He should
do something for her. If only he knew who she was.

For one of the few times in his life, he did not see a straight
line to an objective. He had never liked subterfuge, but the

moment he'd embarked on this folly, he'd buried himself in it. He should just walk away.

But then he would never see her again. The thought filled him with quiet despair. Another morning at least. Just one more morning.

Mary. It was a quiet name. A tranquil name. But it did not quite fit her. She had fire in her eyes. Curiosity. She would be no tame wife for a man.

He realized suddenly he wanted no tame wife.

Unable to sleep with his mind filled with images of her, he took the lute and strummed it.

Lynet knew she would meet him the next morning. Still, she knew she was risking everything, including her father's respect and love. Yet she could no more stay away from the cave on the morrow than she could keep the first rays of sun from touching the earth at dawn.

All the way back home, she could think of nothing but him despite the danger for both of them. She managed to return before the hunters and slip through the empty bailey up to her room.

Willa was waiting for her. "My lady? Your father has been asking for you." Her voice was full of curiosity.

Lynet trusted her completely, and she knew she would need help in the morning. It was time to confide in someone. "I have been helping a troubadour improve his craft," she said.

Willa's eyes opened wide. "A troubadour, my lady?"

Lynet nodded. "And I might need your help in the morning."

"Is he handsome?"

Lynet mulled that question. He wasn't. And yet he was fiercely attractive. Or just attractive in a fierce way. She was babbling in her mind.

Willa giggled. "I see he is, my lady."

"I am just helping him learn a few songs, Willa," Lynet insisted. "He is a soldier who was discharged. He is looking for a new occupation." Unfortunately her face felt hot, and she knew it must be scarlet.

Willa looked at her knowingly. She was a born romantic, and her eyes were twinkling. "Good," she said.

"It is not good at all. He means nothing to me. I am just . . ."

"Helping," Willa finished with a grin. "What can I do to help, my lady?"

"You can visit your sick mother tomorrow," she said.

"But she . . ." Willa stopped suddenly. "Oh. Of course I must."

"I will tell Selwyn to have a very gentle horse ready for you in the morning, and I feel a bit faint. The monthlies. I believe I will stay in my room most of tomorrow."

Willa's eyes gleamed with adventure. "Before I leave, I will bring you chocolate and tell everyone you are not to be disturbed."

"It could be dangerous for you."

"Poof," Willa said. "I am just happy to see your face light like that."

"I will have to chose a husband soon." It was as much a reminder to herself as to Willa.

"All the more reason to have an adventure," Willa said.

Lynet knew that Willa had had a few amorous adventures herself, and she had always envied the maid her freedom. *She* could marry the man she loved. *She* was not restrained by rank and family loyalty.

They discussed the details of tomorrow's switch, then Willa helped her dress. Her father, Willa said, had asked about her but he'd had a bad day with the gout and had been too miserable to worry about her.

Lynet went to her father's room. She had selected a gown that was her father's favorite and that drew a smile from him. "You look very well, Daughter," he said. "Robert will be pleased." He hesitated, then added, "Have you considered his offer?"

"It would not be fair to the others," she said primly.

He sighed. "I will expect you to choose one," he said.

"I know."

"I do not feel well enough to go to supper," he said. "You go along and entertain them." He looked old and frightened. Her heart contracted. Though he was not a man who showed affection, he had taught her to read, had given her the means to take her own adventures through books. He had allowed her to ride, or at least had not forbade it. She owed him much. She leaned over and kissed him, seeing the pleased surprise in his eyes.

Then she left the room and steeled herself for the evening ahead.

Lynet tried to be pleasant at the evening meal. She smiled, asked pleasantly about the hunt and praised their skills when told they had killed some pheasant. Robert, Earl of Kellum, grumbled about lazy dogs that went crazy when they were tracking some animal.

She'd smiled her best smile. "The dogs are usually very good at finding their quarry," she said.

Robert frowned. "Could have been a poacher," he said. "There were a number of tracks but your huntmaster couldn't tell what was new and what was old."

Or mayhap chose not to, she thought. The huntsman was old, and he had been sorely tried these past few days by the guests. "I go there on occasion," she said. "They probably belonged to me. And I doubt whether it was a poacher," she said. "The poor know they can get food from Clenden. It was probably nothing but a cagey fox."

His expression cleared at the explanation. "Will you take a moment of air with me, my lady?"

She knew what he'd wanted. He wanted to know whether she favored his suit. She looked up at him, at the face that was far more handsome than her minstrel. But there was none of the character that was etched in the other's face, no crinkles around the eyes that spoke of having experienced more than wealth.

But she'd had no reason to refuse him. "Yes," she said.

They walked for several moments. She felt it hard to believe how ill at ease she was with her father's guests, and how completely comfortable she had been with the wanderer. But then she'd always been ill at ease with her father's friends. They were loud and boisterous and talked of little but war.

"Your father said the decision is yours," he said, a note of disapproval creeping into his voice. "I am hoping you favor my suit."

"Why?" she asked, really wanting to know. "Why would you wish to wed me?"

"It would be a good alliance, my lady. For both of us. My family has a long history of siring sons. It does not have wealth. Your father needs an heir, and my estates need the marriage portion after years of war." He hesitated. "He also needs our friendship. Your father tried to be neutral but to the Tudor that means he is an enemy. Mine favored the Lancasters. He needs us."

A business and political arrangement. Nothing more. And an emphasis on sons. She knew what that meant, and her soul shriveled at the thought of bedding with Robert.

At least, he did not pretend. And yet it seemed so cold. Not one word of affection, not one fond look. She shivered. It would be the same with the other two, she knew. The reasons might vary some small bit, but the motive would be the same. The other two would marry her, too, whether they wished it or not. Their families' needs transcended the myth of love. She felt cold and empty.

Robert leaned down and kissed her. It was a rough kiss, almost brutal with no hint of gentleness. "I will care for you, my lady," he said when he released her. "You will want for nothing." Except love. Except tenderness.

"I am aware of the honor you offer me," she said, her face stinging from the roughness of his skin. "But my father told the others he would give me a fortnight to choose. It would be unfair . . ."

"I can offer more than the other two," he said. "We have the Tudor's trust, and we breed boys."

As if she were a horse or cow. "I have made a promise to my father. I cannot break it," she said.

He smiled, and she realized that he considered that her consent. Pride, she thought, would not allow him to believe otherwise. "I will wait for your decision then, my lady," he said.

He turned and guided her back inside. He had apparently achieved what he wanted. At least he had demonstrated a readiness to wed her, she thought, which was more than the other two had done.

Why could she think of naught but russet hair and silver-blue eyes?

She turned to say good eve to him, but he was already headed for the wine. His mission apparently had been accomplished.

Tomorrow, she would see her musician for the last time. She would suggest that he leave Clenden because the company was leaving and the earl would not be in need of a minstrel. He would fare better farther north.

She did not think she could bear the possibility of Robin coming to Clenden. Would he be silent if he knew she had lied to him? Would he blurt out something unwise? She could well believe that her father or suitors might kill him if they thought he had trifled with her.

Lynet did not sleep that night. Instead she rose before dawn. Willa, who slept on a cot in an anteroom, woke with her. Lynet slipped into one of Willa's dresses, promising a new one in return. She did not want to meet the minstrel in a lad's clothes. But neither could she wear any of her own gowns. He would know immediately she was not what she had said she was, and she wanted no barrier between them.

Lynet had already told Selwyn to have Sadie, an older, very quiet mare saddled for Willa who was to see her mother. Willa would first, however, tell the cook that her mistress had the monthly vapors and did not wish to be disturbed. Willa would then exchange places with her and stay in Lynet's bed.

As soon as Willa completed that errand, Lynet took Willa's cloak and slipped out the door and down the quiet halls; only the servants in the kitchen were awake. The horse was saddled. Selwyn, no doubt, had gone back to bed. She led the animal to the mounting block. She saw Selwyn then, and knew he recognized her. She put a finger to her lips, and he nodded. He gave her a hand up, then slipped away.

In minutes she was free.

Would he be there? Part of her prayed he would be. Another more practical side knew she should hope he was not.

Duncan's horse neighed and arched its head. Duncan stood and went to the mouth of the cave. He had shaved in the cold water of the stream, but he felt unkempt. He also felt like a young untried boy meeting his first young love.

Then she rode up, this time on an older horse that moved slowly. Still, it looked fat and well kept.

He went over to her and offered her his hand. She was riding in a man's saddle, her cloak nearly covering her, but as she threw a leg over the horse, he saw a flash of leg as her gown pulled up.

He caught her as she slid down from the horse, and she was closer to him than ever before. Only a whisper of a breath separated them. She looked up at him, her eyes intense and wondering and . . . searching.

His hand came up and the tips of his fingers touched her cheek, just as they had the day before. His fingers caressed the sweet curves of her face, and he was amazed that the gesture was so intimate, so wondrous. His breath caught in his throat. He'd never wanted anything as much as to lean down and kiss her. Not just a brief touch of their lips, but a deep, full, possessive kiss. He felt her tremble in his arms, and his heart jerked.

His right hand moved from her cheek to the hood of the cloak, slipping it down from her hair, and his fingers moved the pins that held it in place. Ringlets of dark hair fell around her face. They felt like silk to his rough fingers.

He pulled her tighter against him, feeling the slenderness of her body against his. The trembling of her body slowed. Stopped. Then she looked up at him again with those lovely gray-green eyes.

He bent down and his lips met hers. It was a soft, searching touch, an inevitable kind of kiss that was as natural as stars appearing at night. Waves of tenderness cascaded through his body, and he realized they had been building over the past few days. There was also a new excitement, an exhilaration at touching her, of feeling her skin against his, and, most of all, of feeling her trust. He felt alive for the first time in years, truly alive. Every nerve end jerked with sensations, and yet he restrained himself as he never had before.

She obviously did not feel the same restraint. He felt her reaching up on tiptoes, her body fitting into his, and her lips responding as no woman had before. Her lips opened instinctively to him, and he felt the warmth of her hands as they went around his neck, fingers playing against his skin.

His kiss deepened, became almost frantic with need. Honey and fire. Sweetness and pain. He had not realized how easily they went together. His blood was like currents of liquid fire, searing every nerve. Their bodies melded together, separated only by the cloth of their garments, but that seemed small barrier.

Duncan had never before experienced such a conflagration of desire. He forced himself to step back. He knew from her kiss that was both shy and eager and that she was a virgin. He could not take that from her, and he knew if he did not stop now he could never stop. He had never wanted anything—anyone—as much as he wanted her.

"Ah, mistress," he said in a voice he knew was ragged. "We cannot."

Her eyes looked glazed as she stared at him. Glazed and beautiful. He had not noticed before how lovely she was. But now she stood in the brisk, cold air, dark hair framing cheeks that were rosy with cold—or heat—her lips slightly swollen from the kiss. He thought he had never seen a more beautiful woman. Or desirable one.

And never one less suitable.

Henry would not approve.

To bloody hell with Henry.

six
❧

Lynet's heartbeat accelerated. She had never been so close to a man before. She felt his body change, harden. Waves of forbidden but delectable sensations ran through her. She responded by snuggling even more closely into the curve of his body.

He touched her cheek and that one gentle gesture ignited fires everywhere inside her. His kiss was tinder to those flames. She suddenly was filled with a wanting so strong and so deep that she could not move.

"Mary," he whispered and for a moment the name broke the spell. *Mary.* The name of someone else. A maiden without responsibilities. She closed her eyes, wishing she was indeed that person. Robin would be accessible then, even though he was quite obviously a wanderer with no roots.

His finger fit under her chin, turning it upward until she had to look at him. She opened her eyes.

His own silver-blue eyes were like blue fire, the hottest part of the flame. The odd twist in his lips was even more noticeable, turning up one side quizzically. "Are you a sprite who appears only to me?"

She did not want questions, and she seized upon his fancy. She only smiled.

"Then I must discover on my own whether you are flesh and blood," he said. With a rough groan, he embraced her again. His lips pressed against hers recklessly, this time with a hard passion that stole her breath. Tenderness faded into something that was all need.

Lynet instinctively opened her mouth. His tongue thrust inside, then gentled as his lips had minutes ago. It slid across her tongue, then seduced the corners of her mouth, almost dancing as he aroused complex, shuddering reactions that roiled through her.

She snuggled even more firmly against him, and her body felt a wicked sweet heat as her blood seemed to slow and simmer.

She heard a whimper deep down in her own throat. Since the first moment she'd met him, something had happened to her senses. Now she was awash in sensations she knew could ruin them both. Yet, she couldn't push away. A few more moments . . .

A few . . .

Robin's mouth pulled away, but she felt his rasping breath against her neck as he scattered butterfly-light kisses along her cheek, then down her neck. His hands moved provocatively along her back. The combination of gentleness and barely restrained passion was intoxicating.

Drugging and seductive . . . and, strangely enough, comforting. She had the oddest sense of belonging in his arms.

But she could never belong here. Never. She had a duty to her family. And Robin? He had not spoken of love.

And if he knew who she was truly?

She suddenly wrenched her mouth from his and forced herself to take one small step back.

She tried to take another one, but his hand caught her wrist. It was like an iron band.

"I will not let you run away again," he said. "Not until I know where to find you."

She bent her head. "I cannot say."

"At least now I know you are no sprite. Or fairy."

Her fingers clenched into a fist. Otherwise she might lift one hand and touch his face as he had touched hers. "I know not what you mean."

"A sprite does not kiss that way."

"And have you kissed that many sprites?" She desperately wanted the conversation to go in another direction. She lifted her eyes to meet his. She wondered whether her face was as flushed as it felt.

He smiled wryly. "Ah, you have me there. I have scant experience in such things," he replied as humor crept into his voice. It was disarming. It was . . . irresistible.

"If you have any, you have an advantage over me then, sir," she said.

"No, I think not," he said, his fingers rubbing hers. "I have no advantage. Sprite or no, you have bewitched me. I fear if I let you go, I will never see you again." He hesitated, then added, "No one in the village has heard of a Mary who rides horses like Diana and has a father who works with horses."

"You have been asking about me?" Apprehension made her stiffen.

His gaze bore into hers. "Is there a reason I should not?"

She lowered her gaze. "My reputation. Is that not reason enough?"

"I was very clear that I owed the young lady a coin, for she helped me when I needed it. I wanted to thank her. I said nothing that would harm you."

Not knowingly. But the color of her eyes was unusual. If he had bandied about a description . . .

His eyes were questioning her now. "Tell me where you live," he said. "Is it Clenden?"

She shook her head. Dear saints in heaven, what had she done? All she needed was for him to ride up to Clenden and describe a maid he'd been meeting in the woods. His life might well be forfeit.

"You must not look for me," she said.

"I do not think I can do that."

"You must. You must promise me now."

"Why?"

"I . . . am bespoken." It was only a small lie. She would be betrothed by the end of the week. "My betrothed would . . . feel it necessary to try to kill you."

"You believe he can do that?"

"No," she said softly, eyeing the strength of his shoulders, the confidence with which he carried himself. He could well defend himself. But it would be her father who would go after him, and her father was no match for him. It would be her father who died. And then Robin would be hunted. And killed. Robin could defend himself but not against large numbers.

Robin. Her father. She could not bear being the cause of either's death.

"You do not love him," he stated as if it were a fact.

"Yes . . ."

"No," he insisted.

"I do," she said stubbornly, even though she knew her eyes must belie the statement. She could not take her gaze from him, from the determination in the clenched jaw, the burning fire in his eyes. She could not even move away.

"You are lovely," he said unexpectedly. "I envy him."

"I am plain," she protested. She'd always known that. No one said so, of course. Not in so many words, but they had always praised the beauty of her sisters and rarely did the same with her. Her mirror, made of polished steel, reflected a very ordinary face.

"Only to a blind man," he said as his hand took hers and brought it to his mouth. "He must be a poor suitor indeed if he has not told you that you have hair the color of a copper sun and eyes that reflect all the wondrous colors of nature."

She was stunned by the words. And the gesture. It was one made often by courtiers, but Robin was no courtier, though he sometimes spoke as well as one. By his own words, he was a soldier trying to better himself.

Flustered, she retreated to her question. "Do you vow you will not ask questions about me?"

"I do not make vows lightly, mistress," he replied, well remembering the last one given, the one he'd made to his mother. "And that is not one I'm sure I can keep."

"What others have you made?"

That I would marry for love. That vow was heading him straight toward disaster. "That I would be loyal to the king." If only those two vows did not conflict.

"Have you seen him?" she asked. "Some say he will ruin the country."

Duncan chose his words carefully. Clenden was in northern England which had been mostly loyal to the Yorkist cause. "He has issued ordinances protecting the rights of civilians. He seems a fair enough man." He took her hand and guided her to a dry spot. "But you have not yet told me where I can find you."

"I cannot," she said miserably.

Tell her. Tell her who you are. But the moment he did, all would change. They would no longer be two strangers of equal rank who reveled in one another's company. Would she be awed? Appalled at his lies? His subterfuge? Would she think he was only toying with her?

He was not ready to break the magic of these moments.

But neither was he willing to let her go this time without learning more about her. Or how she came to speak so well. Or play and sing so finely. Had she been a lady's maid or mayhap a by-blow of some important man? And yet she had said her father was a groom. No explanation made sense.

Impulsively, he held out his hand. "Come with me," he said. He could not remember when last time he had been impulsive. Not even this journey to find a bride had been impulsive. It had been calculated, carefully planned with an immediate objective in mind.

Asking a servant girl to run off with him *was* impulsive. And marriage could be disastrous—for both of them. Henry Tudor had made his wishes clear. Anyone violating them did so at their peril. And that of the people they loved.

Did he love her?

Or was it the sun and the stream and the sense of freedom he was feeling for the first time in his life?

He looked at her and his heart pounded harder. His breath caught in his throat. She made the sun seem brighter. He wanted to touch her. Not just with lust, though he would be lying if he said nay to that. But he also wanted to just . . . feel the softness of her cheeks, the silkiness of her hair. He wanted to hear her sing, and he wanted the warmth that her nearness raised in him.

Love? What did *he* know of love?

The silence echoed through the forest, a pause that was full of electricity.

Then she released his hand and her fingers did what his had moments ago. They explored his face, caressing the scar near his eye. It was as if silk was being drawn across his face, and yet there was heat, too.

His heart shifted inside him. Turned. Skipped.

"Will you?" he asked again, holding his breath, wanting with all his will for her to say "aye." No questions. No reservations.

Instead, she looked bewildered. "Where . . ."

"Do you trust me?" He heard the intensity in his voice. The need to have her trust was overwhelming. Even though he'd done nothing to deserve it.

He saw her swallow hard. Her small hand tightened in his. "I would not have come had I not."

"Would you leave here? Now? With me?"

It was unfair. He knew it was. For all she knew he was a penniless, inept minstrel; a soldier whose skills were no longer required; a wanderer who had no home to offer, no security. He did not know exactly what she had now. Her dress was worn but was of good quality. She had access to fine horses. She spoke well.

Why would she choose a wanderer? But he needed to know that she would choose him for himself alone, not the wealth he could bring her. In truth, he might have little if he displeased Henry with his choice. By the saints, but he wanted to be chosen for himself.

He did not know what to expect. He saw from the emotions in her eyes that she wanted to go with him. There had been a sudden jump of joy in her eyes. But it had faded as quickly as it had come.

Instead, she moved another step back. "I cannot."

"Does your betrothed offer more?" The question came from confusion, from the hordes of women who had lusted over his fortune but not him.

"It is not that," she said. "It is honor. I have made promises."

Duncan had no answer for that. Honor had always meant everything to him. How could he ask anyone else to forfeit it?

She had turned away as she said the words and now his fingers turned her face back toward him. Tears shimmered in her eyes.

He thought about his options. He'd always thought about his options. He had done it for years during a civil war and as a mercenary in Europe. He could reveal who he was. He could shove aside any suitor. He had the rank. He had the power.

That wasn't what he wanted. He'd wanted someone to come to him with her free will, with no reservations.

He wanted what he could not have. He knew that now. He would continue his journey. Surely he could find a noble lady with no entanglements. The problem was that he did not want a noble lady. He wanted his lady of the woods.

"Robin?"

Her soft voice seemed to float across the short distance between them. Her fingers tightened in his.

The name was foreign to him. It even took him a moment to remember that he had given it to her. She talked about honor. He wondered whether she would think he had honor if he revealed who he really was.

He dropped her hand. Mayhap he would wait another day. A day or more. Mayhap then he would know in truth. He might know what to do.

He turned away from her, but not before Lynet saw the vulnerability in eyes she expected rarely had any.

She wanted to reach her hand out to him. She wanted to say yes. She wanted to tell him she would go anywhere with him, but she feared it would mean his death. Her father would do anything to get her back. He had been indulgent in many ways, but he would never be indulgent with his honor. He had asked three potential suitors to his home. If she were now to run off with a roving minstrel, she would destroy his reputation forever. And his honor.

He would avenge that. He would have to, or see his power ripped from him. He had balanced his loyalties carefully during the civil war. He needed the goodwill of the men he'd invited as potential sons-in-law. For her to leave with an itinerant musician would be a great insult.

But how she wanted that. She wanted it with all her heart and soul.

She had read the romances of *The Castellan of Coucy* and *Aucassin and Nicolette*. In the latter, Nicolette, a captive maiden without lands, falls in love with the son of a nobleman. She was imprisoned, but finally escaped with her love and joined him in many adventures. She even traveled as a minstrel in her efforts to rejoin him when they were separated again.

Could it not be the other away around? Could not the daughter of a nobleman run off with a minstrel? Or was love just a fancy, told by minstrels and jongleurs to entertain? She had seen little happiness between her parents and had wondered whether true love existed. She had hoped, but never believed. She'd certainly never expected it.

Now, as she looked in the minstrel's eyes, she realized it did exist. Three days, and her world had changed. And having tasted it, she must let it go. She would have memories though. And that was more than she had thought to have.

"I cannot go," she said again, trying to convince herself as much as him. She tried a smile. "I expect you will find a position soon. There is an estate a day's ride from here. I heard some soldiers talking. There is a hunting party. They will be in need of minstrels."

"You want me to go?"

"No. But I cannot continue to . . . disappear, and you are at risk here."

"I can go to Clenden."

Her throat grew tight and horror ran through her, cooling the warmth that was like warm molasses. Robin would discover who she was. He would think she had played him for a fool; or worse, he would say something to someone.

"Everyone is leaving," she said, trying to make her voice indifferent. "There is no longer a need for minstrels."

He raised an eyebrow. The left side of those crooked lips twisted upward. "You know this?" he stated quizzically.

"Everyone knows."

"I hear there is going to be a wedding. The oldest daughter. Surely there would be a need for more musicians. Unless," he added, "you think I am not accomplished enough."

She felt herself pale. Had her father already broadcast news? Or had Robert? He had been sure enough of himself. If such gossip had already spread, then . . .

Her silence seemed to tell him what he asked. He gave her a rare wry smile. "You do not think I can sing."

"No," she said, "but I was told . . . the wedding is months away. There is no . . . need."

Duncan watched her carefully. She was lying. He could see it in the way her face had paled. Her gaze wouldn't meet his. But why?

He stood awkwardly, not quite knowing what to do. She was obviously trying to rid herself of him. And yet her eyes sent a different message altogether. There was fear, confusion. Need. Yearning. The kind of yearning—he suspected—that echoed in him. He had more than thirty years and he'd never felt like this before. He had the terrible feeling that he never would again.

Was there indeed only one true mate for every man?

He could just grab her and carry her away. But there would be no honor in that. Not even love. Might never overcame that particular emotion. It was the one, he speculated, that had to be returned in full measure. It could not be forced.

He stepped away from her. He took his lute from his pack and strummed a song that she had taught him. Had it sounded this sad before? He thought not. He sought a way to keep her with him. "If you believe me still so ill-prepared, will you teach me more songs?"

Her gaze met his. "One more lesson. Will you then leave?"

"Is that your wish?"

"Yes," she said defiantly, chin high. And yet it trembled slightly. She really was a very poor liar. She wanted him as much as he wanted her, yet something was keeping her from admitting it.

But he knew he would learn nothing else by direct questions. If he continued with them, he feared he would never see her again. So he merely nodded and said, "I am grateful."

She suddenly smiled, a relieved and spontaneous smile. No more personal questions. No more questions she couldn't answer. What was she hiding? A secret deeper than his own? "It is easy to teach you anything," she said. "You have a talent."

"You do not have to leave soon?"

"Not until noon."

"You have a lenient master. Or father." He was probing again, but she merely smiled.

"I did not bring my own lute," she said.

He went back to her and gave her his. Her hands ran over the strings. "This is very fine," she said. "You said a friend gave it to you?"

"Aye. A Welshman."

Her eyes questioned him. Wales was known for its wildness. And the wildness of its people.

When he did not elaborate, she strummed the strings and sang a song of a love that could not be. One lover died, then the other killed herself.

"That is not very cheerful," he noted.

Her eyes, when she looked up at him, were wistful. "Do you believe people die for love? Or is it a myth?"

He had always scoffed at the thought before, but now . . .

"I would not know, mistress."

"Have you ever loved anyone?" Her eyes studied him as her fingers continued to play the lute.

"Yes," he said.

"And you left her?"

"No."

Frustration crept into her eyes. "Will you tell me about her."

"I do not know much about her," he said. "She appears as if by magic and leaves the same way."

Surprise crossed her face, then it slowly reddened. "You must not jest that way."

"I do not jest, mistress. I have already asked you to go away with me."

"But you never said where, sir. You seem to enjoy your . . . freedom."

"My home is south of here. It is modest enough."

"You have never been wed?"

"I have been fighting these last ten years, some of them on the continent. There was no time for love."

She placed the lute next to her and touched his scar again, her fingers running over the ridges. "How did this happen?"

"Carelessness."

"I do not like to think of you being hurt." The feeling in her voice made him ache almost unbearably. There had been few people who cared about his health.

"It was nothing."

She took one of his hands in hers and studied it, the calluses formed by years of using a sword. Training. Killing. By the saints he was weary of it all. He wanted peace. And this woman represented peace.

He needed that. Most of all, he knew, he needed *her.* He did not care about her position or her rank. She had a tranquillity that would win over whoever she met. Even Henry. He had fought ten years for the Tudors. The king could not deny him this. But then he knew the king's fury when someone defied his wishes. He'd wanted a wife for Duncan, but he'd wanted one that would solidify his power. He'd wanted a valuable alliance.

If Henry opposed a marriage to a commoner, then he might well lose his estates and be forced into exile once again.

But did she want him? Did she feel the same?

If he had to leave England, would she leave her country, her family? Was it even fair to declare his intentions and ask before making sure of his position with Henry?

Her eyes seemed to say so, but did she . . . want him enough, love him enough to risk everything for him? Were the minstrels and jongleurs right? Was there such a thing as mutual love?

His hand went up to her face again, touching it with infinite tenderness. His fingers explored her face, seeking to know her thoughts, her very soul. Who was she, this maid of the forest? A siren who could change a man's path and fill him with a longing that he'd never known before?

Her eyes widened, then seemed to plead with him. Wide and wondering and full of mystery.

The air between them was expectant with questions unanswered and yet neither was ready to shatter the magic that had wrapped around them. There was a silent intensity, a rare understanding that he knew would vanish if he questioned any longer.

Duncan leaned down and kissed her again. It was a mistake. The kiss became hungry, desperate, her lips as eager and needy as his. He tried to smother the growing ache in himself, to hide his agonizing need, but he could not, especially not as her body leaned against his, all the hesitant shyness fading.

His hands touched her back and moved with seductive practice. He felt her tremble again, then his kiss deepened and the fire between them ignited once more, this time with an appetite and greed he could no longer control. And, he knew instantly, neither could she.

An elemental force bound them now, and it was impossible to contain.

Even had he wanted to.

His hands moved up and down her back, causing her body to move into his, and his lips broke away from hers and went to the nape of her neck. He nuzzled it, feeling every movement of her body as it reacted to his hands, to his mouth. His body was responding in the same elemental manner, growing hard under his garments.

She cried out and his mouth moved from the back of her neck to her lips again, claiming them with a raw need while one hand played with the back of her neck, fingers running over her skin with breeze-light teasing. Hunger was nuanced. Needy yet almost achingly gentle. His fingers went to the ties of her gown and were fumbling with them when he heard the first noise behind him. He heard a profanity, footsteps rushing at him, and then there was pain.

And darkness.

seven

$\mathcal{T}$he men appeared so suddenly and the blow fell so un-expectedly, Lynet could not react quickly enough. A scream died in her throat as her minstrel fell over. She barely reacted swiftly enough to stop the blade that was about to drop on him.

She threw herself over him. "No," she said.

Robert, the Earl of Kellum, stared at her, then lowered the sword. "We heard you cry out." He looked at the prostrate form on the ground. "I'll kill him."

"Nay," she said. "He was not attacking me. He has done nothing." Her hands touched the bleeding wound on his head from the blow of a mailed fist.

"Who is he?" Kellum demanded, his facial expression full of disbelief.

"An honest man—a soldier—who has done no harm to anyone," she said, knowing as she did that she was destroying herself and quite possibly her father. But she could not let Robin be killed for her own careless actions.

"Your father told me you were a virgin, a woman above re-proach," Kellum said with disgust. "And I find you rolling in the grass with a . . . commoner." He had put his dirk in its sheath, but his hand was still on its hilt, and she could see he was barely controlling his rage. She had not yet accepted him, and still he was acting the betrayed husband. His brown eyes were dark with fury, his lips bent with contempt.

She had no excuses to make. Her gown was half off, her

hair laced with leaves, and she knew her lips were swollen. Any excuse she might attempt would place blame on Robin and most certainly bring about his death.

"There is no blame but my own," she said as she stood, positioning herself over the unconscious minstrel.

His eyes bore into her. "I will leave in the morrow," he said. "My offer, of course, no longer stands. Even your marriage portion could not . . . make marriage palatable with a . . ."

He stopped himself with obvious effort, but he did not have to finish. Five men, including one of her other suitors, stood watching with varying expressions on their faces.

Lord Manfield stepped up, his eyes sympathetic. He was, she knew, the one her sister wanted. And if his eyes were any test of the soul, he wanted her sister too. He knelt next to Robin. "Not a fatal blow," he said.

"He must be the trespasser we've been seeking," Kellum said. "A poacher, most likely. We will take him back to Clenden. Her father can decide his fate."

Lynet looked down at her minstrel. The bleeding had stopped, but he had not moved. Her father would be furious, but he was a fair man. He would not seek the man's death for her own indiscretion. It meant, though, that her father would send her to a convent. He would have no choice. She'd disgraced the family name.

The thought of never seeing Robin again was devastating. She'd hoped she could avoid a loveless marriage. She'd preferred a tranquil life either at home or in a convent. But that was before she'd known the joy—the exquisite pleasure—of being with Robin. Before irresistible urges had occurred inside her body. The sensations lingered. New and intoxicating and wonderful.

But dangerous. Very dangerous feelings for someone like her. And Robin.

"Let him go," she said.

"Nay, my lady. I think not. Your father should be made aware of your . . . conduct. And this . . . knave's. I believe Lord Clenden would want to know this man has been skulking around, seducing his daughter."

She stood tall. Her eyes met his. "The man is twice the man you are, Robert. He did not avoid the king's service."

The slur appeared not to bother him. "It depends which king you are talking about, my lady. Is he York? Or Lancaster?"

A trap. She knew it instantly. He could use her answer against her. And her father.

Manfield faced Kellum. "Enough," he said. "This man needs care. And I do not care for your attitude toward Lady Lynet. She has not accepted you. She owes you nothing."

Gratitude surged through her. Her sister was fortunate.

"Thank you," she said.

His face softened. "One cannot choose whom they love," he said, his glance going to Kellum, then returning to the man still lying on the ground. "And often for good reason. But I do think it wise to take this man to Clenden. He needs attention."

Kellum grunted with disgust. He kicked away the lute on the ground, and Lynet reached down to rescue it. It was obviously Robin's only possession of any value.

Robin moved slightly and groaned.

Kellum signaled for the accompanying men in arms to take him, but Manfield pushed them aside and stooped down again. He shook the minstrel once, then twice. Another slight groan but his eyes did not open. He turned to Lynet. "What is his name?"

"Robin."

Kellum's eyes narrowed. "Robin what?"

Lynet could not answer, and the silence was damning. Not only was she cavorting with a commoner, she did not even know his full name.

"Mayhap our host can solve this mystery at Clenden," Kellum said. "I for one do not intend to waste more time there. Do as you wish." He strode away toward the trees and then and only then, did Lynet see the horses there. How could they both have missed the approaching horses and men?

Then she remembered that magical moment when nothing existed in the world but Robin and herself, and the feelings flooding them. How could that have happened?

She heard Kellum riding away, two men with him. Waiting with her was Manfield, the Clenden huntsman and one of

Clenden's retainers. Both were looking at her with concern. Both were friends. But even through the concern, she couldn't help see their shock.

Her conduct had been outrageous.

But mayhap she could convince them to take them into the village.

Manfield seemed to read her mind. "Kellum will be telling his version, my lady. You should be there to tell your father your own."

Lynet's fingers touched Robin's face, then his thick hair. What would be best? All she wanted was to make him safe. To protect him. It was a strange feeling and one she doubted he would appreciate. There had been such assuredness to him. Confidence. Even an odd grace that seemed to belie what he was.

Would he be better in the village? But there was no physician, certainly none as competent as her own two hands. Why did he not wake? Or his eyes open? If they took him to the village, he may or may not receive the care he needed. And her father would still find him. "We will take him to Clenden," she said.

It took two men to put him on a horse. She took his lute and mounted her own mare as he was secured to the heavy saddle.

They turned toward Clenden. Her heart pounded as she realized what she would face. And Robin. But nothing mattered if he lived. And her own memories would sustain her. They would have to.

Duncan woke in a dark, damp place. His head seemed to explode. His eyes could barely make out the ridges of the stone walls through a small piece of light filtering in through a window.

As he moved, pain rolled over him like thunder during a storm. He tried to stand but his legs would not hold him. He touched his cheek and felt the stiffness of new bristle and the sticky moisture of seeping blood.

He tried to remember the last hours. Then panic seized him. And fear.

He didn't know where he was.

More importantly, he could not remember how he got here.

*L*ynet had never seen such disappointment, such grief touch her father's face. Even worse was the bewilderment. How could his daughter do something like this?

Her mother's countenance was, as always, cold. But Lynet saw the glitter of rage there.

"You will go to Holy Cross Convent at Wyckford tomorrow," she said. "You have ruined this family. You have destroyed your sisters' futures. You may even have sentenced your father to death. He needed the good favor of the Lancasters. Now we have no hope of it."

Lynet ignored her mother. She couldn't remember the last time her mother had touched her or sung a lullaby to her or showed any interest other than disdain. Lynet had always felt she was a threat to her mother's beauty, to her eternal quest for youth. And she knew her mother had wanted sons, not daughters. The three of them represented failure.

"I want to know that he will be tended, then set free with his belongings," she said.

"He seduced you," her father thundered. "I can have him hanged for poaching, for . . . touching you."

"I am still a virgin, Father. And he did nothing I did not want," Lynet said. "I would tell a court that."

"Not if he does not live," her mother said. "No one will blame us if . . . he dies of his injuries."

Lynet knew her father had the power of life and death, and now the anger to use it. She did not recognize the fond, indulgent parent she had loved.

"I will do anything . . ."

"You can do nothing now, Daughter," her father said. "Kellum and Wickham have left, and no doubt will spread this tale throughout England. Manfield has not, but he has asked for your sister's hand. Ordinarily I would refuse until you were wed, but now . . . I must admire the young man for his offer at this time."

She swallowed hard. She had hurt her sisters' chances at a good marriage. Manfield may have asked for Evelyn's hand, but would his family countenance it? "Papa, please . . . take care of him. He did not know who I was, and he did nothing but ask for my help. He believed I was but a servant and still he was kind. I know I have disappointed . . . and dishonored you, but I must be sure that . . . the stranger is tended and released."

"I cannot promise that," her father said. "He seduced you. He is probably a thief as well."

"He is a musician, and kind," she said. "Please allow me to see him. Then I will do whatever you wish. And gladly."

He looked at her with sad eyes. "Nay, you will go to Holy Cross tomorrow, and you will stay in your room until you leave." The grief in him was palpable. "Did you not think of your sisters? Your mother?"

She thought she saw a glint of tears in his eyes as he turned away. She was dismissed, and she knew there would be no reprieve. She knew him that well.

She would find a way, though. She had to find a way to see Robin and set him free. Then she could go willingly into a life of prayer.

He fought frustration. Bits and pieces of half-formed pictures moved around in a head that ached almost beyond endurance. He tried to hold them there, but they were as fleeting as the small flashes of light that came through the hole in his door. *Think.* Why was he here? A face flashed in his memory. A shy smile. Green eyes.

But the harder he tried, the more facts escaped him. He looked down at his clothes: a linen shirt, jerkin and hose. Worn. Even coarse. Unfamiliar for some reason. He was used to something else. He knew it.

Merde, but his head hurt. And he was thirsty. Ever so thirsty. Where was he, and why?

The door creaked open, and someone entered. A woman holding a basket. For a moment his heart seemed to skip, then returned to normal as he saw more of a well-endowed young woman. The door closed behind her.

"My lady asked me to tend you," she said, placing her burden on the floor. She was young and buxom. She wore no cap, and her flame-colored hair was tied back by a ribbon.

"Do I . . . know you?"

She looked at him curiously. "No. I am Lady Lynet's maid."

"Lady Lynet?" He knew from her face he should know who she meant. But the name carried no familiarity.

She was already busy. She had brought a pitcher of water and a cup. She poured water into the cup and offered some to him. He drank thirstily.

When he'd slaked his thirst, he handed it back to her. "My thanks," he said.

Her eyes were curious in the dim light. "My lady wants to know how you fare."

"I do . . . not remember what happened."

"You were struck on the head."

"Why?"

She colored. It was obvious even in a dim cell. "You remember nothing of my mistress?"

"Just . . . fleeting images. Does she have green eyes?"

She smiled. "Aye, and she said you are a minstrel."

A minstrel. He tried to think. That did not sound right.

The young woman dipped a cloth into the water and wiped the blood from his head. Then placed a poultice against it. "My lady told me how to make this," she said. Then she hesitated and added, "They are sending her away tomorrow." She blinked back a tear.

He knew suddenly it was because of him. Thoughts that had fluttered around began to come together. But the name made no sense. "Mary?" he asked as the name suddenly popped into his head.

She looked confused. "My mistress is Lynet. She is the daughter of the Earl of Clenden."

Clenden. The pieces started to come together. Not completely, but one at a time.

He went back to what had been said. "She is leaving?" *Who?*

"Aye. Her father is sending her to Holy Cross because she was found with you."

"Mary?"

"Lady Lynet," she insisted again. "She would not let them slay you. She asked me to tell you she is sorry that you were injured."

All of a sudden, everything fell into place. The clothes he wore were not his. He was Duncan, Marquis of Worthington. And the forest maid . . .

Bloody hell! Why had he not guessed before? He had known she was well spoken. And how many servant girls could ride as she rode? His lady of the woods was a lady in fact as well as in conduct.

"Sent away?"

"Her father said she has disgraced the family. No man will accept her now."

"She did not defend herself?"

She shook her head. "One of the men invited here as a prospective husband found you together. I am told she stood between you and a blade." She shuddered at the thought and tears came to her eyes. "They tried to blame you but she would not let them. And now she is being sent to a convent."

There was no other man. For a moment, joy flooded him even as he realized that they both had been at cross purposes.

It was daft and impossible and ironic. And now she was going to be sent to a convent, and he was locked in someone's blasted dungeon. No one would believe him. And he did not have time to send for Rhys. Well, he had made this mess, and it was up to him to solve it. With some help.

He also knew he had indeed found a woman who wanted him for himself. Someone brave enough to sacrifice herself and her future for a humble minstrel.

The question was whether she would forgive him for his own masquerade. Hers made sense. Having found herself face-to-face with a stranger, she was protecting herself. His reason was far more devious.

"What is your name?" he asked. "And how long have you served your mistress?"

"Willa, and I have served her nearly all our lives."

He thought for a moment, then asked, "Is there a way to see your mistress before she goes?"

"She is locked in her room."

"It is important."

Her eyes met his. "I will do what I can."

"Some wine for the guards, mayhap?"

"My lady has already thought of that," she said, "but my lord has threatened their lives if she disappears."

"Is he so formidable?"

"Nay," she said. "He is usually the most kind of masters, but he is very angry. He had invited prospective husbands for her this fortnight, and she had promised to make a selection. The one who . . . discovered the two of you has already left. My lord believes she has ruined the family."

"Who were the prospective husbands?" he asked.

"The Earl of Kellum, Lord Manfield and Viscount Wickham," she said.

"Did she favor any?"

She shook her head, then her face colored again. "Only you, sir."

"Did she tell you that?"

"She did not have to."

His eyes met hers in the dim light. "Will you help us, Willa?"

He saw fear flicker across her face, then she straightened. She smiled, a slow smile that lit her face. "Yes."

"Even at the risk of your own life?"

"My lady would die in a convent. She has so much . . . life."

"She does," he said, "and you will come with us."

"Come with you?"

"I would not take her away from such a loyal friend," he said.

"But you . . ."

"I have friends. I can take care of her. Of both of you." He knew that if he said more, she would thank him a madman and would refuse to help at all.

"I will try," she said.

The door opened with a clatter and Willa jumped away. A large, burly man entered. "You must go before the captain comes," he said.

"I will bring some food later," she said to the guard. "You have not even given him water."

"He was unconscious," the guard replied defiantly. "And the earl gave no such orders."

"Do you not think for yourself, John?" she said, and the guard's face reddened. Duncan realized that the guard was smitten with the maid.

"You can bring it," he said after a moment.

She smiled. "You are a good man, John," she said as she gave Duncan a wink and went through the door.

That smile again. She had the same courage as her mistress. She would be a fine addition to Worthington. Mayhap Rhys . . .

The door clanged shut, and he was left alone again, the ringing still loud in his head. Tonight. If nothing went wrong, he would be riding away with a woman he truly loved.

If it did, he might not see the morning, nor might she ever again know freedom.

For now he would have to wait. It would, he knew, be the longest wait in his life.

eight

❧

Willa and Lynet whispered together, knowing a guard stood outside Lynet's room. Though the door was a heavy oak, the gravity of the upcoming evening and its dangers lowered their voices.

Their hands clenched together, in anticipation and fear and in friendship. After tonight, it seemed unlikely they would see each other again. There would be no more delay in dispatching Lynet to the convent.

"Thank you," she said to Willa. "Thank you for being my friend."

Willa turned red. Her eyes misted. "I will miss you, my lady."

"And I you." Lynet went to a box that sat on a chest and took out several pieces of jewelry, including a necklace of pearls and another of amethysts. She held them out. "Take these, Willa. Sew them in your dress. Sell them if you are ever in need. I will also give you a note saying I have gifted you with them. No one can ever accuse you then of taking them."

Willa's hands trembled as they held them. "It is too much."

"There will never be 'too much' for such loyalty," Lynet replied with a break in her voice. Willa was risking her own life. "I will not let you leave the room without them. And," she added sadly, "I will not be needing them."

"You can take them," Willa said. "You can escape and use the funds yourself. You can meet your Robin later."

"I cannot dishonor my father any more than I have," Lynet said. "I cannot deepen the shame for my sisters."

She made her tone determined. She had to be determined. She had already done so much damage to her family and to Robin. To everyone she loved. All for a few fanciful hours. And that's all they were, she told herself. A few moments of magic that could never last, could never really be real.

"Go now," she said, knowing that she could not be resolute much longer. Oh, how she wanted that magic. The gentleness of his fingers, the branding of his lips. Her chest ached almost unbearably as she wondered whether she could ever quench the burning, untamed yearning inside herself.

Willa tucked the jewels inside the bodice of her gown. "I will keep them for you, my lady," she said as she opened the door, and nothing else could be said without being overheard. "I will bring your supper later."

The rest of the day passed by slowly. Lynet spent most of the day at the window, looking down at the bailey below, envying the freedom of the men riding in and out. Would she ever have the freedom again to ride free, to wander in the woods, to sing?

She fought waves of quiet despair. The only comfort was knowing—hoping—that Robin would be freed. He, at least, could still have life.

She would not cry. She had memories now. Memories she had not had before.

She did not move as the sun sank below the horizon and shadows turned the green hills dark. A few stars appeared, but most were hidden by clouds skittering across the sky. She prayed for rain. Rain would justify a full cloak. Rain would also erase the tracks of a fleeing rider.

How long now? Willa was going to wait until late in the evening, when the guards would already be sleepy.

They had talked about trying to drug the wine, but neither had any access to a potion that would be safe enough. The wine itself would have to accomplish their aim. Would John take it?

Probably. Her father had never been a feared master. He

seldom disciplined his people, a failure for which her mother often took him to task. But he hated personal conflict. He usually just turned away from it and pretended nothing happened. That he had not done so this time showed how very angry—and disappointed—he was.

She knotted her fingers together. Another hour. *Dear Mother in heaven . . .* How could she bear it when every minute seemed a day?

The floor of the cell was damp and cold. Duncan had slept in worse places and had always been able to sleep. Not now.

Willa had promised to return. Would she? Would she be allowed? And Lynet? He tasted the sound on his tongue, and he liked it. He had liked "Mary," too, but it had never seemed to fit her. "Lynet" did. It had a grace that she had never quite been able to hide.

And now? He'd been caught in his own trap. He did not even have his own ring, the Worthington seal, with him. He had thought it might give him away. Now he wished he had not been so cautious. Nor so clever.

How much of his adventure had been a true attempt to fulfill the vow to his mother, and how much his wish to escape responsibilities even for a short time? He had commanded soldiers since he was nineteen, and he could not remember a carefree day until a week ago.

And now someone else—someone he knew now he loved—was paying for those moments. Others might also pay, including the young maid.

But if he had not indulged himself in fancy, in whimsy, he might never have met Mary. *No, Lynet.* Even if he had met her, he may never have seen the wood sprite beneath the lady, the gentleness and passion under a lady's manners and breeding. He wanted to think he might, but in truth would she have seen "Robin" under a soldier's uniform and his fierce reputation? Or would she have been repelled by it?

Now, though, he might well have spoiled everything. If only he could get her to Worthington, then they could work out the whole blasted mess. Her family would be pleased. How could they not with a match such as he would propose?

His rank and properties far exceeded those of any of the men Willa had mentioned.

But first he had to get out of here.

His head still pounded, though it no longer bled. He was hungry, but he'd been hungry before. The most surprising of his wounds was his heart. It ached for her in ways he had never thought a heart could feel. When his mother had asked for his vow, he had thought love would be a comfortable, calming accommodation. He had never believed the poets and minstrels. He had never thought it could be an all-consuming thing that burned even as it refreshed, that it could make him forget even ordinary caution, that it could turn the sky to sapphire instead of blue and the breeze to perfume, and sprinkle the water with gold. He had never held such thoughts before, had not seen the world through eyes that enhanced rather than saw it coldly and logically.

His feet had never been so light, nor had a song been in his soul. Which was, he thought wryly, why he'd been such a miserable failure as a musician. But had he taken the song from Lynet in return? The thought was excruciating.

He heard footfalls again. Voices through the door. Willa's voice, seductive this time. He moved closer.

"You can leave it with me," Duncan heard the guard say.

"I must see him to report back to my mistress," she said. "And I have also brought something for you." Her voice was lower than he remembered. It held a promise.

A key turned in the lock of his cell, and a basket was thrust inside. Duncan had only a moment to see Willa's face—and a faded blue wool cloak—before it closed again. He took the basket and started to eat the bread even as he listened.

He heard Willa laugh. "It is fine wine, John. It was my mistress's and she sent it to you for allowing the minstrel some food."

"Just a small sip then," the guard's voice said.

"A sip only," Willa agreed.

Duncan listened as time rolled on, and the guard obviously took a second sip, then a third. The man's voice roughened, and Duncan heard him plead, "A kiss, Willa."

Duncan closed his eyes and tried not to listen. He wondered why Willa was doing this. He knew, though, that he would find a way to reward her.

After a few more murmured pleas for more than a kiss and teasing protests from Willa, he heard her say, "I will get some more wine, John, and then . . ."

There was a protest, then steps hurrying away.

Duncan finished the last of the bread, then looked out of the small barred window. The guard, sprawled across the chair, had a tankard tipped upward. His eyes were turned toward the corridor where Willa had disappeared. Several minutes later, the tankard clashed on the floor. The man barely moved at the sound.

Duncan's hands balled into fists. Was Lynet going to come down? If not, he would find her. By the saints, he would find her.

He paced the room restlessly. Then he went back to the door and waited.

It seemed forever before he heard steps again. He peered again through the barred window of the door.

A blue cloak, this time the hood over the head. The walk seemed different from Willa's but the form was the same. Heavier than Lynet's, more buxom.

Willa again. Disappointment crashed down on him, even though he knew why she was there. His freedom. But Lynet had not chosen to come. Not chosen or was not able.

The figure stooped next to the guard. Loud snoring noises continued.

Fingers took something from the belt around the guard's tunic, then the hooded figure came to the door and fitted the key into the lock. It did not work for a moment. She tried again and finally, with a rasp, the lock turned and the door opened.

He stood and stared for a moment. Although the hood covered the upper part of her face, a lock of bronze hair tumbled alongside her face. From the candles impaled in the hallway, he could see the soft gray-green of her eyes.

"Mary," he said with the slightest hint of a smile. "Or is it my lady?"

The air, already heavy, thickened with strong emotion as her gray-green eyes looked shadowed, tired, wistful. Even through the dim light, though, he saw a sudden response to him. Her eyes seemed to light. "Robin. Are you . . . well?"

Her hand went to the side of his head. He knew from past injuries it must be ugly. The rest of him was none too pretty either. He had several days' beard and his hair was lank and damp with sweat. Still, her hand clasped around his when he held it out. "I prayed you would come," he said.

The light faded from her eyes. "You must go. Now."

He gave her a bow. "It *is* my lady?"

"I did not mean to lie to you," she whispered. "But if I told you who I was, I feared you would go."

"I think not," he replied, bringing her hand to his mouth. "Will you come with me now?"

"I lied to you," she said.

"Sometimes there is reason to lie," he replied.

"No," she said in a broken voice. "There is never a reason good enough. I might have brought ruin upon you. You must leave now, and I cannot go."

"Because I am not a lord . . ."

She took his hand and kissed it. "Because it could well mean your death, and I cannot do that."

"I should make that decision."

"There are others too," she added, and he saw a tear hover at the side of her left eye. "My father. My sisters. Even my mother. They will all suffer. I cannot let that happen."

"Will spending your life in a convent help that?"

She looked up at him. "Willa . . . should not have told you."

"Willa is a good friend."

She smiled. "She is. And nothing must happen to her. She is in my room now pretending to be me. I could not leave her there."

He studied her. "You have grown some."

"A layer of clothes," she said. "And now you must hurry before the guard changes."

"That will not be until dawn." The fingers of one hand continued its clasp of hers. Those of his other hand touched her face, caressing it. "My wood sprite," he said, his heart beating so loudly he thought she must hear it. "You are beautiful. And gallant."

She turned around abruptly. His hand dropped from her face, but the other caught her arm and kept her from fleeing. "What if I were a lord?" he asked. "One more important than those fops who care of nothing but money?"

A faint smile appeared on her lips. "I am not impressed with lords. 'Tis one reason I . . . care for you. You have earned everything. It gives you character I do not see in others."

A knot of uncertainty twisted his stomach. He had thought his true identity would solve all their problems. He'd even thought, mayhap, that she would fall immediately into his arms. Now he wondered whether revealing his identity would make things a great deal worse.

"If I promise to take care of everyone . . . ?"

"You cannot promise such a thing. My father did not support the Yorkists but neither did he support the Tudors. Many have already lost their lands. The men he . . . chose for me have ties to Lancaster. The only way I can . . . lessen the insult to them is to enter the convent."

"You would not be able to ride. And sing."

For a moment, despair seemed to cloud her eyes. Then she seemed to will it away. "I will be content. You must go. A friend has a horse saddled and waiting outside the walls just inside the forest. You can leave by the postern. Willa has offered some wine there too. They should be asleep."

He leaned down, brushing her lips with his.

Her face tilted upward and her arms went around him just as his surrounded her. His kiss roughened, stirred by a bittersweet emotion he could not define. Instead of backing away, her mouth, her tongue, met his with equally fierce need. He was a fool for lingering, and yet he could not leave.

Lynet knew she should go. And make him go. But one last kiss, one last remembrance of something bright and shining and wonderful. Every moment was dangerous for him, and yet . . . she rejoiced in the fact that he knew it and still he stayed. The fact that she had lied to him had not mattered. She'd feared he would hate her for the lie and for putting his life at risk.

She should have known better. He feared nothing, and that fact terrified *her*.

She felt the barely restrained passion in his large body. She felt it in herself. A wildness, a yearning that made her want to go with him. That she could not gave rise to wave after wave of despair. And yet she knew she could not let him see it.

Instead, she met him desire for desire, need for need. Her lips didn't yield to his, they challenged his. She stood on tiptoe, her arms tightening around his neck, feeling the roughness of his face, the hard tense muscles in his arms and chest.

Anguish, deep and bleeding, sliced through her like a knife. Her fingers stroked the back of his neck, seeking his warmth, compulsively needing to touch him. She knew she should make him go, but just a moment more. A moment that would have to last a lifetime.

His tongue entered her mouth, and she felt sensations she had never known before. Her body strained against his in primal need as she met caress with caress, hunger with hunger. How could love be so agonizingly painful?

Then she heard a stirring behind them, and so apparently did he. His lips left hers, and his gaze went to the guard. He left her, and she felt an immediate loss. She watched as he picked up the guard easily, his strength so long hidden under the minstrel's clothing evident. He put the man in the cell, then turned to her. "We should tie him."

She leaned down and pulled up her gown and tried to tear a piece from her chemise. It wouldn't tear.

He grinned at her, then reached for the guard's knife and in seconds had several pieces of cloth. Quickly, he tied the guard's hands behind him, then gagged him. He did it with such efficiency of movement, she knew he had done it before. He was, she realized suddenly, no ordinary soldier. He did everything with an assurance and confidence that came from command. She'd been around soldiers enough to know that. Why had she not realized it before?

Her heart pounding, she watched as he closed and locked the door, then took her arm with his hand. "Who are you?"

"We must go," he whispered, his hand still holding hers.

But she stood her ground stubbornly. She had played a role. Had he? "Who are you?" she asked again.

"Does it matter?"

"It must," she said brokenly. "Lives . . ."

"No one will be hurt," he said. "I swear." He looked into her eyes. "I have never broken a vow," he said, his silver-blue eyes boring into her. "Do you believe me?"

The world stilled in that moment. Her gaze met his. Intensity reigned there. Questions. Hope even.

It was the hope that reached her. The vulnerability she had seen before. And yet there was confidence too. A confidence she believed.

No one will be hurt.

She didn't know who he was, or what he was. But she did believe him. She didn't even question that belief.

She slowly nodded.

"A pen and ink," he said. "Can you get them for me?"

Her mind still swimming with emotion and her body still reacting to his, she nodded.

"I will wait here," he said.

She hesitated a moment, reluctant to leave, afraid that her confidence would falter if she did, then she took one of the candles impaled on a vertical spike along the wall, and quickly sped to the oriel off the great hall where her father kept books. It was a measure of the fact that her father did not consider the minstrel a threat that there was but one man on guard.

She took the quill and ink, and two pieces of parchment. She wrote a brief note of her own, saying she had tricked Willa, that she loved her father. She hesitated, then left it on his desk. She was committed now.

When she returned, Robin was pacing. She saw the tension in his body, and she was struck again at how much he seemed to have changed in the past few hours. No longer was he the whimsical vagabond musician. No longer did amusement sparkle in his eyes.

He took the paper and ink and wrote quickly. No common soldier here. Few commoners could read or write.

"What are you saying?"

He looked up. "That I will keep you safe and that no one else is to be blamed." He hesitated, then added, "And I am inviting him to a wedding." He suddenly dropped to his knees. "Will you marry me?"

She looked down at him. He did not look comfortable on

his knees. She knew immediately it was no common position for him. He was asking her to trust him. Asking for her faith. Asking her to believe him. And in him.

No one will be hurt.

She swallowed hard. She had never reached out to anyone before. She had never really trusted. Doubts still nagged at her.

"There is but one horse. My father will come after us. He will . . . kill you."

"Trust me," he said again.

To the depth of her soul, she did. God help her, but she did. "Yes," she said simply.

A smile such as she had never seen before crossed his face. It was blinding. "I love you," he said.

She didn't have to tell him the same. She knew her face did it for her.

He placed the note carefully on the table where the guard had sat, then together they quickly moved along the corridor to the kitchen, then out a door. Staying in the shadows, she led him to the postern. The guard, as she expected, was asleep.

She opened the gate. He took her hand again and once through they ran together toward the wood. Great billowing clouds shrouded the moon and stars, and she knew they were virtually invisible.

They reached the horse. It was a strong, swift one, and he gave her a boost, then swung up behind her with the ease of a born horseman. She leaned against him, feeling his strength, taking courage from it as they first walked, then trotted toward the road.

The breeze was stiff, the sky still black. As they left the woods, rain began to fall. His arms tightened around her, and the last of her doubts faded. For better or for worse, she had given over her life to him.

She half turned and her right hand touched his face. "Where are we going?"

He chuckled. "I was wondering when you would ask. Home, my love. To Worthington."

"And is your name truly Robin?"

"Nay, it is Duncan, Marquis of Worthington, and you will be the Countess of Worthington."

A marquis!

Mary and Robin.

She leaned back against him and started to laugh.

Then she heard the rumble of his laughter behind her. Joy bubbled up inside, joy and wonder and contentment. Everything *would* be all right. Her father would be overjoyed at such a union. She didn't know why the masquerade. Perhaps the same as hers. A few moments of being ordinary, of being wanted for oneself and not a title or money or position. They had years to find out. To explore and explain.

To love.

She looked upward. Rain still splashed around them but she started to see the first early glow of dawn. Her lord, Robin—nay, Duncan—gathered her closer in his arms and turned the horse toward the rising sun.

Home. They were going home.

Epilogue

✦

Worthington

$\mathcal{T}$he wedding was to be magnificent.

Even Henry Tudor--the new king--was at Worthington to attend the ceremony. He had made his pleasure known that one of his favorite, and most loyal, lords had chosen a wife, and had chosen—to his mind—well. He'd welcomed an alliance with the north counties.

His gift was a pair of white horses.

He had arrived two days ago, a month after sending the horses. He'd erupted into laughter as he heard about the unconventional courtship. "Worthington never does anything the easy way," he'd said. "You are a good match for him, Lady Lynet."

Lynet visited the stable, and the matched horses, on the morning of the ceremony. She had worked with Duncan's staff for more than a month making the manor presentable, and now she needed a few moments of peace before standing in front of the king, her family and scores of important guests to say her vows.

She knew she should return to her chamber. Her sisters were probably waiting there to help her dress. They had been in residence since soon after that first initial visit by her father.

She would never forget the shock in his eyes when he learned that the contents of Duncan's note were true. He had ridden through the gates of Worthington accompanied by an ill-equipped group of men. He'd been raging. Until, that is, he'd discovered that the man he'd come to punish was one of the most feared and respected lords in the realm.

Until he heard that the dowry for his daughter totaled more than all the lands he owned.

Until he heard Duncan's offer to help with the marriage portions of Lynet's sisters.

Until he saw the way, he said, that his daughter's eyes sparkled.

And until he learned of Henry Tudor's blessing upon the union.

The latter was enough to quiet any rumors about his daughter and now he basked in the newfound prestige among his neighbors. He had arrived just two days ago with his almost speechless wife who preened and fussed over Lynet as she never had before . . .

One of the nearby horses nickered lightly and she smiled. She didn't have to turn around. It was the nag her minstrel had ridden into Clenden. But the mare was no longer a nag. She was sleek and well-fed and a favorite of the household.

"My future wife," Duncan said, placing a kiss on her neck. "I thought I would find you here."

"You should not be here, my lord. They say seeing your wife on her wedding day will bring bad luck. Willa will be horrified."

"Seeing you will never bring me bad luck. It brought me the best good fortune in my life."

She turned and looked up at him. How had she ever not known he was a man of honor.

"Even with my mother?" she said wryly.

"She gave birth to you, my love. I can admire her for that alone."

She reached up her hand. Her fingers caressed the severity of his face. The glow in his eyes softened it, though.

And in a few hours he would be hers. Totally and absolutely hers.

Her Robin. Her minstrel.

Her love.

His fingers caught hers, and brought them to his lips. "Are you ready, my wood sprite?"

"Aye, my minstrel," she said, a chuckle erupting deep in her throat. "Now and forever."

"I will compose a song for this occasion," he said, laughter dancing in his eyes.

She looked heavenward, except there was only a roof.

"You said forever," he reminded her.

"So I did," she replied, tightening her fingers now intertwined with his as they turned toward the great hall . . . and soon the priest. But as she met his eyes and saw the love in them, she knew they would not need a song. It was already in their hearts.

The
Bachelor Knight

Deborah Simmons

one

"My lord! My lord!"
Heedless of the shout, Sir Berenger Brewere stood staring off into the distant hills, lost in thought. The peaks were too far away, he mused, and hardly steep, but still taller than the lands around him. With that thought, Beren swung his gaze across his demesne, feeling a curious mixture of pride and longing. There were no mountains here, no rocky crags, only gently rolling slopes. *But all of it is mine.*

"Sir Brewere!" The use of his surname roused Beren at last, and he turned slowly to cover his lapse. How many years would it take him to recognize his own title? King Edward had bestowed upon him the barony and fiefdom for services rendered during the war in Wales, and Beren lived like a lord. Why could he not answer as one?

Beren sighed, turning away from the heights to the young squire who shouted to him so eagerly. Now what had sent the boy racing to find him? he wondered. A call to arms? A visit from the king? Farman, a youth Beren had plucked from obscurity, was far too easily excited. Whatever it was, no doubt Beren must now set aside his half-formed plans to view the distant hills more closely and attend to some business of knighthood, whether it be war or justice that commanded his attention.

Farman halted before him, a bit breathless after his run from the castle to the grassy slope where Beren waited. "'Tis a messenger, my lord, bidding you away!"

'Twas from the king then, Beren thought. In years past, he had served other lords, but now he was vassal to none except Edward himself.

"A summons to court?" Beren asked. He was not certain where the king was in residence, but he knew the spot likely would be overrun by fools and greedy, jealous courtiers—a situation he little liked. However, Beren hid his distaste from his squire as he began to stride back toward the castle that bespoke his allegiance, if not to the court, to Edward himself.

"Nay!" answered Farman wide-eyed. "'Tis a summons, aright, but not from the king. 'Tis a demand that you go at once to a place called Brandeth, at the behest of someone called St. Leger."

For a moment, Farman, and all around Beren, faded away at the mention of his old patron, Clement St. Leger. He drew in a harsh breath. *Brandeth.* 'Twas a name he had not considered in years, though he had begun his life there.

"Lest you refuse, the messenger, a bold fellow indeed," Farman commented in an outraged tone, "reminds you of your oath. 'Recall to him his vow,'" Farman recited. "And then he left, without even waiting upon you, my lord!"

Stirred from his thoughts by Farman's indignation, Beren glanced down to see that the youth was practically in a froth that anyone, let alone a mere messenger, should fail to make the proper obeisance to Sir Berenger Brewere, knight of the realm, holder of vast lands, baron to the king. Beren smiled, for he did not take himself quite as seriously as his squire.

Farman eyed him quizzically. "'Tis a jest, then, my lord?" he asked.

Beren's smile faded. "Nay, 'tis no jest, but a duty I am bound to fulfill," he answered. As if pausing his pace might mire him once more in memory, Beren walked swiftly now, the squire hurrying to keep up with him.

"But who is this St. Leger? Some foreign king? I have heard naught of him," Farman replied.

"That does not make him less," Beren said, a bit sharply. The squire was becoming too full of himself, too accustomed to visits of the mighty and royal to recall that a man was measured neither by his fame nor his bloodlines.

"But why should *you*, the greatest knight in the land, have to wait upon *him*?" Farman asked, stubbornly insistent upon his master's importance.

Beren halted, his eyes drawn to the distant peaks and beyond to that which he could not see: tall cliffs and crashing surf and a castle set amongst them. He murmured an answer, half to his squire and half to himself, "Because I swore an oath, and a knight's vow is broken only by death."

Ever alert, Beren had noted the changes in the lands around him, the seabirds on the wing and the tang in the air that spoke of the ocean. Old feelings stirred, unwelcome, making him irresolute for the first time in many a year, and he faltered for a moment before urging his destrier on.

He could not ignore the summons, though he had been tempted to send a messenger ahead to inquire about it. After all, he had many demands upon his time, including those of his own demesne, his obligations to the king and the courts of justice, and the people within his domain. Yet now he must leave all to be off on an errand the purpose of which he knew not.

And well Beren disliked approaching any situation without sufficient information. He had not become this successful by being unprepared. So he approached the holding with the wariness of a battle-hardened soldier, suspecting that things at Brandeth must truly be dire for Clement to call upon him after all this time. But no sign did he see of siege or trouble of any kind, only the stark beauty of the cliffs.

Here, at last, were heights, rising from rocky stretches of beach into the very clouds, and Beren felt his heart pounding in an old, nearly forgotten rhythm. His first thought was that he had stayed away too long, his second that he never should have returned. Tearing his gaze away from the tall faces of stone, he looked to the road ahead, avoiding distraction, until he turned round the last outcropping and saw Brandeth.

Beren sucked in a harsh breath. He remembered it rising out of the natural wall behind it as if carved from the very elements, a vast and impenetrable defense, but now the castle appeared dwarfed by its surroundings, so much so that for a moment Beren wondered whether some part had been lost to war or fire. It was only after much contemplation that he realized the place was the same, while he had changed. The keep that had once loomed so large within his vision had been dwarfed by the higher towers and sprawling walls of his own demesne, as well as others he had seen in endless travels.

Brandeth now appeared small and isolated, little more than an old-fashioned square keep with outbuildings surrounding it in haphazard fashion. Quelling whatever feelings threatening to erupt at that discovery, Beren studied the area carefully, intent not upon reminiscence, but appraisal. Still, nothing appeared amiss, and lifting a hand, he sent his train forward along the path through the village.

Spilling out from the foot of Brandeth, the hamlet looked peaceful and prosperous, though tiny to Beren's jaded eyes. They passed through it quickly, climbing the rough track meant to keep invaders away, and at the castle gate, they halted, surveying the area carefully before continuing into the bailey, though there were enough men-at-arms to defend themselves against attack.

Clement had not come out to meet him, which could be a sign that he would not defer to his old squire, and Beren frowned at the slight before he told himself that the lord might simply be ill. That could explain his absence, but what of the summons itself? Why send for Beren after all these years? His mouth tightened in frustration, for he could provide no answers.

Outside the keep, Beren was greeted enthusiastically by a young man whom he did not know, which was both a relief and an annoyance. He was not eager to see anyone who would recognize him, but he could tell that Farman, ignorant of his master's history here, was disappointed by the lack of pomp and ceremony and cheers to which they had become accustomed. Only Beren knew how unlikely the people of Brandeth were to welcome him in such a fashion. And even should they be so inclined, this was not a rich holding and could ill afford tournaments and such, a realization that somehow pained Beren.

He pushed the sensation aside, grunting in displeasure as the past loomed up before him. Ever since receiving the summons, he had felt it, the reason he didn't want to be here, why he was relieved that no one who remembered exactly who and what he was came to greet him. Pride, one of a knight's sins, was plaguing him, and no doubt, he would be tested more before this visit was over.

Hardening in his resolve, Beren took a handful of men and strode inside the hall, prepared to face his first demon. He stood tall, his gaze sweeping the room that immediately fell into quiet. Again, he was surprised by the size, so much less than he remembered, but he was also impressed by the aspect. Although smaller than he recalled, the space was cleaner than his own hall; and though little furniture was about, the walls were painted and covered with colorful tapestries that drew the eye.

Lest he pause too long in reluctant admiration, Beren dragged his attention away, letting it roam over the few people who stood by, until it rested upon Hubard, the old bailiff. Wrinkled and stooped, the white-haired retainer posed no danger to anyone. Why, then, did Beren feel sorely set upon as the man moved toward him? He stiffened, his body tensed, his hand unwittingly settled upon the hilt of his sword, but Hubard only bowed low, as befitting Beren's new stature. Then, to Beren's amazement, the old man began to weep.

Startled, Beren stepped forward, uncertain how to react until the bailiff lifted shining eyes to him once more. "Look at you! Just look at you, the greatest knight in all the land," Hubard said, shaking his head, while servants and residents crowded close, whispering in hushed voices. "Clement would be so proud."

Would be? Beren barely had a chance to note that peculiar choice of words when silence fell upon the hall once more. He glanced up to see a woman, slender and blond and beautiful, as fair as the palest rose, the finest jewel, the clouds that rimmed the highest peaks. It was only after his heart began a fierce thundering in his chest that Beren recognized her as Guenivere, Clement's daughter.

"Welcome, Sir Brewere," she said, the title stiff and formal on her lips. "Thank you for coming."

The past that Beren sought to avoid rose up to meet him, and unprepared as he was, he lashed out at this unexpected vision of his former patron's daughter, little changed and yet wholly different. "Where is Clement?" he demanded.

"My father is dead," Guenivere answered, and a spasm of pain marred her lovely face, only to be quickly masked. When had she learned to dissemble? Beren wondered. When had she begun to hold herself so distant? Like a bright star, beautiful and yet untouchable. But then, hadn't she always been far out of his reach? The thought burned within him, as did her next words.

" 'Twas I who summoned you," she said.

"You? Why for?" Beren asked, angry that he had been dragged across the country for what? A woman's whim? His own torment?

Guenivere eyed him somberly as he tried to reign in his temper. Beren told himself that she knew him not, that her pause in no way reflected his response, and yet her pale blue eyes seemed, as always, to hold the wisdom of the ages and insight into all things, including himself. Beren decided it was merely a trick of the light, but her gaze held his, steady, unyielding, and he felt the flow of her strength, tender in its woman's guise, yet hard as steel.

"You once vowed to serve this family always and above all others," she said. "Do you not remember?"

Beren's jaw tightened. Of course, he remembered. His oath had brought him to this pass, though it was little to his liking.

"Now has come the time of my need. Will you refuse me?" Guenivere asked, her luminous eyes clear and questioning.

Beren stared at her dumbly, shying away from the expectation there, the accusation implicit in the blue depths. But there was no need for rumination. He could give no answer except one. Drawing a deep breath, he dropped upon one knee at her feet and bowed his head. "What is it you require of me, lady?" he asked, his voice suddenly hoarse, his throat thick.

The hall seemed even more silent than before, as if all those about them strained to hear or held their breath in anticipation. Beren felt as though the moment dragged on endlessly while he knelt before her, the past closing in on him, whether he willed it or no. It constricted his chest, choking him, and for a moment he struggled for air. Then he heard her voice, soft and deliberate.

"I would ask that you marry me," Guenivere said.

At her words, Beren's head jerked upward, to be followed quickly by his body as he rose to his feet in shocked confusion. Had he heard aright, or was his mind, burdened by the weight of memory playing tricks upon him? He stared at her, his breath coming harshly, his heart thundering. "Why?" he demanded.

Unmoved by his obvious agitation, Guenivere answered him calmly, as if they were discussing the weather, not this incredible proposition. "Because my father is dead," she replied. "I need a husband, else the lands that I own will be forfeit. My neighbors are clamoring to add Brandeth to their holdings, and I would be married to one of my own choosing."

"Are you a widow then?" Beren asked, his thoughts a mad jumble.

"I have never married, Beren. Why would you think so?" Guenivere countered, a sharp edge to her voice for the first time since she had appeared before him, cool and remote.

He felt like a blabbering fool, rather than a knight and a warrior of some standing. "I had heard that you were betrothed some years ago and assumed . . ." Aware that he sounded like an idiot, Beren didn't finish the sentence. Instead, he cleared his throat, lest his next words come out a desperate croak. "Why me?"

Guenivere glanced away, whether by chance or because she was unable to meet his gaze, Beren knew not. "Because you are so strong and powerful that none will dispute your claim and because you own far greater properties, you will not concern yourself with one tiny demesne." She turned to look at him directly once more. "I can maintain my heritage and protect my people, as I have these past few years during my father's illness."

Beren wasn't sure just what he had expected as an answer, but it wasn't this cold calculation. The past yawned before him now, a dreadful abyss before which he teetered, and he stepped back to take a deep, sustaining breath. Right now he couldn't afford distractions; this was too important. So, push-

ing aside all else, he tried to concentrate on the here and now,
no matter how strange it might seem.

The king had long accused him of playing the bachelor
knight when he had more than enough money and lands to
take a wife. And lately Beren even had considered the
prospect, with the idea of allying himself with one of the other
large landowners. A union with a tiny, inconsequential baron-
age such as this one was not what Edward had in mind, Beren
was certain. And yet, how could he refuse?

His knight's oath bound him to protect and defend all
women in distress, and Beren had gone one step further. On
one bleak morning long ago when Clement had girded him as
a knight, he had added a vow of his own. In heartfelt gratitude, Beren had pledged his sword to the St. Legers for all
time. He had sworn to die for them, gladly. Now how could
he refuse to do any less?

"Very well, Guenivere," Beren said, acutely aware of the
sound of her name upon his lips, spoken aloud for the first
time in his life. "I will marry you."

Either Guenivere was very sure of herself or very sure of
him, for Beren soon found that all was in preparation for their
nuptials. A priest appeared at once to perform the ceremony,
so as to avoid any questions of validity, and Beren wondered
if the haste was so he wouldn't have time enough to change
his mind. More likely, Guenivere didn't want to be able to
change her mind, he thought ruefully.

In truth, Beren was glad of the speed, for he did not care to
think too much upon what was happening. He was tired after
the days of travel, weary in both body and spirit to find himself back at his journey's beginning, and unwilling to exam-
ine too closely the sudden and bizarre turn of events.

Beren told himself that he had no choice except to marry
Guenivere, that his oath was what bound him, and that it was
the only reason he had agreed to the union. But at the edges
of his mind the past loomed, mocking his feeble attempts to
explain away his actions so easily.

The wedding itself took on an unreal aspect, and Beren
went through the motions like one in a dream. It was only

when he took Guenivere's hand in his that he was jolted to full awareness, for the touch of her fingers, soft yet firm, sent a rush of heat spreading through him, startling in its intensity. Long-buried feelings flooded him, and he didn't know whether to weep with the strength of them or bellow his denial.

Because he could do naught else, Beren added this new promise of marriage to his previous vow. Yet, when he spoke, it was with a conviction born of more than duty, his chest suddenly tight with some unnamed emotion. Bidden to kiss his bride, he hesitated, stunned at the very thought. When he did not move, Guenivere leaned up and brushed his cheek, in a cool, bloodless action that chilled him. Then it was over, and the feasting began.

As Guenivere called for the celebration, Beren stared numbly after her, adrift once more. He felt like he had fought in one too many tournaments, smote so long and hard with sword and lance that his head rang from it. Drawing a harsh breath, he tried to recover himself, ruthlessly pushing aside all thoughts of other, earlier times in this hall.

Yet, how could he? Among the figures of his own men, eager for the coming food and drink, Beren saw some familiar faces. Most appeared content, happy even, but did some eye him with disapproval? If so, how could he blame them?

Restless, Beren stalked past the revelers as ale and wine began flowing freely, but there was nowhere else to go in the small space. He paused near the tall doors, now thrown open wide in welcome, and halted there, staring out into the setting sun, but even that sight tugged at his memory, and he swore soft and low.

Although he considered going outside, the thought of old haunts stayed him, and Beren turned his head away. Noticing a movement out of the corner of his eye, he swung round to see a servant boy carrying too much wood upon his back. Anger surged inside of him, as well as something else, deeper and more stirring. "Who bade you bend yourself under such weight?" Beren demanded.

"No one, my lord," the boy answered, eyes wide with fear. Or was it loathing?

"Tell me, for I am your lord now," Beren said, though the words seemed to stick in his throat.

"N-no one, I swear! I was just trying to save myself another trip," the youth said. His innocent reply flustered Beren. With a grunt, he sent the boy about his business, only to find another nearby servant eyeing him, obviously curious about his odd behavior. Beren drew a deep breath. He had reacted overmuch in this instance, but he knew all too well the backbreaking toil of one not born to the manor.

With that thought, the past crowded in on him again, and since he could go nowhere to escape it, he searched for what little comfort he could find. At last, he found Guenivere in the throng, his gaze touching upon her long, blond tresses with a kind of awe. Warmth, unbidden and long denied, seeped into him, driving away all the years of toil and war and proving of himself, almost as if they had never been. Dangerous thoughts, Beren acknowledged, with a frown. Some knights were enamored of tender emotions, and some even wrote poetry, but not working knights, not men who had to make their own ways in the world.

So Beren held at bay the tide of memory that threatened to engulf him, watching her now with new eyes, more calculating and less dewy with youth. And what he saw was a woman full-grown, past her girlhood, but possessing a rare beauty that was only enhanced by time. Why had she not married? What had Clement been thinking to leave his heritage in such disarray? Beren frowned once more. Guenivere said he had been ill. Perhaps he had not been thinking clearly.

Beren found it hard to concentrate himself as he watched her. She moved with an easy grace, as regal as her namesake, but with an open demeanor that encouraged small gifts from the children in the hall. Beren saw her bend down to receive a flower and give a kiss of thanks, and it seemed as though the path he had climbed for so long was shifting, altering the life he had led in some irrevocable fashion. He felt light-headed, like he was falling, dropping from dizzying heights. Or had he merely returned to the ground where he belonged?

Refusing to acknowledge such fancies, Beren held himself tall and straight and apart, as befitting the knight he was, surveying all about him in the long habit of a warrior warily assessing his surroundings. And as the evening wore on, Beren decided that he had good cause to be cautious. Indeed, he studied his bride with growing concern, for although she seemed to greet castle residents and servants and villeins alike with cordiality, she did not extend the same consideration to one of her guests, namely *her husband*. Even his own men were obviously entranced by the lady of Brandeth, and she did not hold them at a distance, but she stayed away from Beren.

At one point, he thought perhaps it was his own lingering on the edges of the gathering that caused his ostracism, and so he entered the fray, inching closer to Guenivere, only to see her slip away. It was not obvious to the casual observer, perhaps, but Beren could hardly ignore it. And his temper, barely leashed since his arrival here, began to tug at his restraint.

What was she about? At her command, he had married her. Did she intend to shut him out of her life, now and always? Immediately, old doubts and suspicions swamped him. Had she taken his name to protect her interests, while disdaining him as too ill-bred and lowborn to be her true consort? Beren's mouth tightened into a hard line. She was wrong, if she thought to dismiss him so easily.

She might be using him, but he would be her husband, for that was part of the bargain. Did she think to wed him and send him on his way? Did she not realize what happened between husband and wife?

Although Beren had not allowed himself to consider all the ramifications of his nuptials, his reaction to that acknowledgment was swift and sure. His body grew hard, his braies tightening around him, at the very thought of bedding Guenivere. Tonight. *Every night.* He drew in a harsh, unsteady breath and tried to master himself, for obviously his bride was not quite as eager as he.

Did she think to cuckold him? Beren's blood boiled. He had vowed to serve this family, but not to that extent, not to his own disgrace. And did he not deserve an heir? Why should he tender his hard-won lands back to the crown? Although he had rarely thought about passing on his holdings, now the vague idea became a very real possibility. And Beren was surprised at his own reaction as a fierce yearning shook him to the core. Suddenly, he wanted a son, and not just with anyone, but with this woman.

The notion of Guenivere round with his child sent heat surging through him again, but it was not simply lust that affected him. Pride and hope and long-forgotten dreams pressed in upon him, constricting his chest. For a moment, Beren dared not breathe, so precious was the vision, but before long, he exhaled harshly, dismissing his fantasy. For how would such an idyll come to pass when his bride wanted naught to do with him?

Anger gave him more power than helpless desire, so Beren seized upon it, searching the throng for Guenivere once more. However, the crowd was thinning out now as villagers left and servants took away cups and food, and he did not readily see her. A few of his knights lingered near the hearth, toasting their liege, but few ladies still graced the room.

Then, abruptly, Beren felt a prickle on the back of his neck that roused all his awareness. He turned slowly, to find not Guenivere, but something else for which he had been searching this hall: an unfriendly face. It was Crispin, an older knight who had long served at Brandeth and made no effort to hide his displeasure at the sight of Beren.

They stared at each other across the space of tiles. Then, deliberately, Beren stepped forward, seeking out his old nemesis. Memories of jeers taunted him, but he ignored them, focusing on the here and now, where he would judge the knight anew.

"Well, Crispin?" he asked. "Have you no congratulations for me?"

The elder man nodded curtly. "Of course, . . . my lord," he said, but his mouth was drawn into a sort of sneer that made his disapproval clear. Here, at last, was someone who did not want to see Guenivere wed to a man such as Beren. The two continued to face each other, Beren well aware of the other man's enmity. It was not a new sensation, but he was an adult now, grown beyond the sting of words. Wasn't he?

"You have done well for yourself, considering your origins," Crispin said. "But 'twould be perhaps better had you rested on your laurels at Edward's side, rather than return here."

"And why is that?" Beren asked.

"You may find that things are not unchanged here."

Beren affected a smile. "But that is to my advantage, is it not?" he asked, alluding to his own differing circumstances.

Crispin flushed, but did not retreat. "You may think that you have all you ever desired, Berenger, but I doubt that your *wife* shares those sentiments." The claim was too close to Beren's own suspicions for comfort. Perhaps Crispin sensed his weakness, for the man pressed his attack. "Indeed. 'Tis not the usual wedding night, is it, when the bride retires alone?" he asked, with a smirk.

Beren's temper flared. He was tempted to have done with this mockery of civility and challenge his old rival, but two things stopped him: consideration for Guenivere and Crispin himself. The man was no longer young, and whatever dreams he had once nurtured were long gone. He remained as he had always been, a bachelor knight with no lands or men of his own, serving a small demesne that was now owned by a man he professed to despise.

"I think, Crispin, that I, too, have grown weary," Beren said simply. With that, he turned away and headed for the narrow stair that led to the upper chambers. He strode forward with purpose and authority, having well learned the advantages of appearances, but he felt neither. Crispin's barb had cut deep. He might be the foremost knight in Britain and baron of his own great lands, but now he was perilously close to a past very different from his present, and it threatened to drag him back down to places he did not care to go.

Worse yet, he had been married only a few hours and already it seemed he was estranged from his wife. *Guenivere.* Although Beren still found it hard to believe that they were wed, he could all too readily accept the bitter truth of Crispin's words.

'Tis not the usual wedding night . . . when the bride retires alone. . . .

two

꒳꒷

As a knight, Beren had vowed to safeguard all women. Now he wondered bitterly if that included protecting his own wife—from himself. Both anger and pride warred within him, along with lingering remnants of old doubts that urged him not to force the issue of his marital rights, for how could he possibly deserve them?

Tense and uncertain, Beren felt a measure of relief when he reached the top of the stair and saw that the door to the great chamber was open. Perhaps Crispin's attack was as pointless as the dull thud of a bated weapon, and Guenivere was simply expecting him to join her here. The thought brought Beren's body back to life, and, heart hammering in his chest, he dared not imagine what awaited him.

Drawing a deep breath, he sought for control over himself and strode to the threshold only to pause in dismay once more. Although there was a fire in the hearth and his things were laid about the room, there was no trace of his wife, nor any signs of her presence.

Beren stepped inside to look more closely, but no hair-brush or feminine personal items of any kind were to be found, and the pegs and chests were empty of clothing. His gaze settled upon his own gear, undoubtedly delivered by his squire, and his temper returned in full force. Slamming down the lid of the final coffer, he stalked out of the room.

In the narrow passage, he hesitated, wondering if his old nemesis had lied, taunting him, while Guenivere remained below. But there was no denying he had not seen her recently. So Beren continued until he stopped in front of her old chamber. He knew it well, and memories pressed upon him, urging his attention until he pushed them away forcibly. He pushed just as fiercely upon the door, but his efforts had far less effect, for it was barred against him.

Beren told himself that there was some mistake, yet he refused to knock. "Guenivere? Are you in there?" he asked. Her name sounded harsh in the quiet, and he swore under his breath. It was this place. If only they were somewhere else. If only he were someone else . . .

"Beren?" He heard her voice through the wood that separated them, and the sound of his true name, not his title, might have been welcome, but for what followed. "What do you want?" she asked.

"I want to retire," Beren answered, annoyed at her foolish question. He was also acutely aware that he stood in the narrow passage that ran along the upper rooms, having a conversation that anyone might overhear. On his wedding night. Outside his wife's bedchamber. How could she do this to him? Surely, she knew how it would look. Did she deliberately humiliate him?

"I, uh, had your possessions placed in the great chamber," she said, from behind her oaken shield. Was she so cowardly as to hide from him? Or was she feeling too superior in her bloodlines to open the wretched door to such as him?

"That is very thoughtful of you," Beren answered, through gritted teeth. " 'But I would sleep with my wife."

Silence came from the other side of the door, a horribly long, telling silence. "I really don't think that is wise," she said, at last. She paused, while his blood began to boil anew. "I want to assure you that you need feel no obligation here. You are free to go back to your own demesne and take up your most pressing duties."

Right now, the most pressing duty Beren was planning to take up was bedding his bride, his doubts having been driven away by her stark refusal to grant him an audience, let alone his rights. Perhaps another man, with less history here, might have accepted her terms, Beren thought angrily. But, no. One

look at her, and any man who did not want to exercise his hus-
bandly claims would have to be either blind or insane.

"For now, my duty is here with you," Beren said. "Or do
you want your overlord questioning your marriage?"

There came another long pause as she considered that sug-
gestion. "He wouldn't dare," she finally answered. "Acatour
wouldn't deign to question *you,* an intimate of the king himself."

It was true, of course. Acatour was a minor landholder,
with a few small fiefs like this one pledged to him. He would
make no protest at having one of the most famous knights in
the country, with great lands and men to serve him, as an ally.
Guenivere was intelligent and clever and unyielding. The
combination infuriated him.

"Open the door, Guenivere," Beren nearly bellowed, his
patience running thin.

"That was not part of our bargain," she answered back.

"Nor was this!" Beren shouted. He could call for an ax and
break down the door, of course. He had done no less in war,
but he had no wish to do so here, among those who might
remember his roots and nod sagely that blood willed out. Instead, turning on his heel, Beren strode away, along the passage and down the stairs, past whispering servants who had
been drawn by the spectacle of the great knight brought low
by a lady.

It sounded like a poor version of a troubadour's tale, but in
such ballads, the cruel woman taunting the knight who loved
her was always married to someone else. None of those songs
and stories, as far as he knew, had the husband lusting helplessly after his own wife. And this one wasn't going to end
that way, either, Beren decided grimly.

Reining in the feelings that threatened to overwhelm him,
as well as the memories that pressed him for recognition, he
focused instead upon his knight's training and just how to win
the battle that lay before him.

The moon was with him, lighting the bailey enough that
Beren need not carry a torch, which was just as well since he
didn't want to draw attention to himself. Some knights

thought it was enough to be able to wield lance and sword, but he had discovered that his most useful weapon was not a strong arm, but an agile mind.

Guenivere wasn't alone in her cleverness. Nor did the trait appear to be governed by birth, for Beren had cultivated it all of his life. Once he had been eager to listen to stories read by another, then he had learned to read and write himself, as did most knights. But he had not stopped there. He had devoured every treatise on knighthood as well as every book he could get his hands on, and he had exercised his brain, watching battle tactics, learning and formulating his own. And now he felt fully confident as he walked along the east wall of the castle, gauging his steps and locating his wife's chamber with ease.

She had left a candle burning, perhaps to be able to see any attack that came through her barred door or to keep a vigil by it. Instead, she had aided him in finding her window, something he was certain she had not intended. Beren stood beneath it now, smiling grimly as he judged the distance straight up to the softly glowing portal.

He could use a rope, of course, with an ax that would catch neatly upon the stone ledge. But Guenivere would notice such an intrusion, and there was always the chance that she might toss it back down, hopefully without him on it. Although she might not want to kill her new husband, lest she have to take another, Beren did not care to test her resolve or take any injury. Glancing up once more, he thought about using a ladder, another implement in time of siege, but that, too, could be seen and knocked aside.

Dismissing such devices, Beren began to consider the moonlit face of stone with careful deliberation, eyeing each crack and crevice. He soon found himself mentally mapping a route, using that first tiny outcropping for a handhold, then moving across and upward. It would not be that difficult, he decided swiftly with the seasoned judgment that accompanied experience, and so he approached the edifice, knowing that only one way would serve his purpose: to climb.

As a child, he had been fascinated by the cliffs, spending what little time he could spare exploring the jagged outcroppings, the tumbled boulders, and the sheer stone faces, always finding a foothold, always seeking a higher one, always mov-

ing upward. A useless waste of time, most deemed it, but his
passion had proven the source of his good fortune, and later,
the skill many dismissed had served him well when assailing
another's defense.

Beren approached the wall, and in the darkness of the deserted bailey, he sought his first hold, carefully, but with confidence. Just like so much else in life, a man created his own
destiny when climbing. If he thought about falling, he fell.
Beren had learned that as a child and had put that lesson to
good use. He never saw himself failing, only succeeding; and
so, always he had moved onward, upward, ever striving, unas-
sailed by doubts until he came back here. Today.

Beren pushed that thought aside, for he needed all his con-
centration. He had not done this in a long while, his new lands
being bereft of anything more than gentle slopes, and so his
fingers did not have the strength they had had once. But still
they held on to the most minute of crevices, and he found his
way with ease, the sheer joy of the climb returning with each
movement. And when, at last, he reached the window, he felt
a sense of triumph unmatched by even the greatest of battle
victories.

There, Beren paused just below the ledge to listen, though
he heard no sound of Guenivere or her attendants. Hopefully,
she was alone. *But not for long.* Putting more weight on his
fingers, he pushed his body upward until he could see inside.

A candelabra stood at one side of room, but he could not
espy his wife. Was she abed? The thought threatened his will,
so he swiftly drew himself up and over the stone, dropping
noiselessly inside. The chamber was so much smaller than he
remembered that for a moment, Beren wondered if he had the
right place. Surely, the vast, luxurious room of his youth was
not this sparse and simple space?

And yet, recollection tugged at him. He gazed about,
slowly recognizing the settle, the hearth, the heavy hangings
that hid the bed. The sight of it caused a low sound to escape
him, giving himself away, for he caught a movement out of
the corner of his eye and saw that Guenivere, standing at the
foot, had stirred, turning round gracefully to gasp in surprise.
She was not abed, Beren realized, uncertain whether he was
relieved or disappointed by the discovery.

"Beren! How did you come here?" she asked, not bothering to hide her surprise and alarm.

"By the window," Beren answered, his expression neutral. He found himself unable to say much more as memories and feelings long buried pushed to the surface, begging an acknowledgment he would deny. So he stood, unmoving, while she ran past him to put her hands upon the ledge, as if to see for herself a ladder or implement of some kind.

Spying nothing, she turned to stare at him with a mixture of horror and wonder, just as though she thought he had sprouted wings and flown through the opening. There had been a time when she thought him capable of any feat, perhaps even that one, he mused, with bitterness. Apparently, the years had altered her view, and she thought him unable even of being a proper husband to her.

"You might have been killed!" she whispered, her hand at her throat and either accusation or fear in her eyes. Beren decided on the former, for Guenivere could ill afford to lose her new spouse. "Why would you dare such a thing?" she demanded, then she stepped back, frowning. "Why have you come?"

Beren met her gaze directly. "I am here because I intend to sleep with my wife," he answered.

Whatever else she might have felt, her dismay now was obvious. "That was not part of our bargain!" she repeated.

"There was no bargain," Beren said. "I recall only that you ordered me to wed you, and I did. Never did you say that you wanted only a mockery of the holy union."

His words had the desired effect, for Guenivere appeared flustered and bit her lip, an innocent gesture that acted like a kick in his gut, for he remembered it well. It was an old habit of hers, but after all these years Beren viewed it differently. Now the movement drew his attention to her mouth and stirred his body in a way it never had before in the innocence of youth.

"Now, Beren, you cannot expect a typical marriage when I will be here and you will be far away, at court or your estates or wherever you will be," she said. She waved her hand, as if to dismiss his whereabouts. Beren noted an odd tenor of accusation in her voice that he could not comprehend. But what did he understand of this situation? Nothing beyond his own simmering anger and growing frustration, and he had no patience for this sparring of words that could only dredge up things better left buried.

"I expect an heir, Guenivere, and you had better become reconciled to that fact," Beren said, speaking as bluntly as possible. Ignoring both her startled expression and his own misgivings, he stepped toward her.

She held her ground as he approached her, as he knew she would, tilting her head upward in defiance. "What? Would you force yourself upon me, Beren? What happened to your knightly vows, your oath to protect women?" she taunted.

Beren felt like telling her that her vaunted opinions of knights, based upon the romance stories she so loved, had very little to do with reality. In his long years of fighting, he had seen few men who even remotely resembled those paragons of virtue. And although he had taken his vows more seriously than most, they would not prevent him from kissing his own wife.

"What about—"

He cut her off, stopping her words with his mouth, taking her gasp of startled breath as his own, and then his lips touched hers, and he knew nothing, not anger, not disappointment, not the press of old memories, *nothing* except the heady wonder of her taste.

Softer than roses were her lips and fragrant as crushed petals her scent. Leaning close, Beren lifted his hands toward her shoulders, where they hovered inches from their goal as he hesitated, still certain he did not have the right to touch the lady of the manor. But Guenivere was suddenly within his reach. And she was not fighting him, either, he realized, with sudden surprise.

Indeed, for someone who had protested his intent loudly, she seemed most compliant. Her lips moved under his, soft and yielding. Beren lifted his head and saw that her lovely neck was arched backward, her eyes closed, and a becoming flush tinted her beautiful cheeks. The sight of her, so obviously struck by desire, stirred both his mind and his body. The kiss he had given half in anger, to assert himself, now seemed a gift, a precious thing far beyond price.

Watching her face with deliberate regard, Beren very carefully, very slowly set his hands upon her shoulders. Though
his fingers met the fine material that gowned her, he could
feel her supple form beneath, and for a long moment he simply stared at the picture they made: His tanned, rough hands
settled where he never thought them to be, upon the body of
Guenivere St. Leger. The sight was startling in its simplicity,
yet so very moving that Beren wasn't sure what was the
dream, the past few hours when he had taken her to wife or all
the years before, spent in hopeless yearning.

So fierce were the emotions raging through him and so
loath was he to break whatever spell lay upon them that Beren
paused, savoring the heat beneath his palms, perhaps too long.
For while he stood watching her, Guenivere gradually returned to awareness, like a sleeper struggling awake. As she
did, her body stiffened, her lashes lifted to reveal not the
dazed wonder that he felt, but the glint of accusation.

"You give the kiss of greeting very well, my lord," she
said. "'Tis too bad that your farewells are not so sweet."

Beren stepped back, away from the denunciation in her
eyes, away from the past that threatened to engulf him and yet
he felt no better for his retreat, for his hands now held nothing. He stared at them, momentarily struck by the loss, then
dropped them to his sides.

"Or perhaps you have forgotten that you knew me once ere
you won your fame and fortune?" Guenivere asked.

Beren glared at her, willing her not to raise all that he had
put behind him. Could they not just begin their lives now, as
husband and wife, without dragging up all that was before?
Already, he was using most of his strength to avoid the past.
Now she would remind him of it? "You know full well that I
remember you," he said, harshly.

"Do I?" she asked, turning toward him. "'Twould be difficult to know for certain since I have heard no word from you,
not one single message since you left this place! You never
even said good-bye."

Beren glanced up in surprise at hearing the break in her
voice, and he saw that she had turned away, unable to meet his
gaze. With a pang, he realized that try though he might to

avoid it, she was taking him back through the years, back here, to the beginning. "What right had I?" he asked, harshly.

When she spoke, it was with her back to him and her tone low, as though muffled. "If nothing else, the right of any human being to speak to another," she said.

" 'Twas not that simple, and you know it," Beren said. She had never understood. What did she want from him? The truth? Though he willed it not, it came to him: He had been afraid he would not have the strength to leave, if she had bid him stay all those years ago. Yet, why should he let her rouse that old specter? What did he know of her now but a cold, businesslike offer of a marriage that would deny him his rights as husband?

"Perhaps you would explain it to me," she asked. In the ensuing silence, he looked over to see that she had turned to face him directly once more, her pale brows lifted in question.

But Beren had no answer, at least none that he wished to give her. "Then you must leave me to my own assumptions, that you were too eager to leave this place behind and all that it once might have . . . meant to you. And, so you have far surpassed the prestige of this tiny fiefdom and treat now with the king himself. Indeed, I am surprised that you could find your way back to such a small, insignificant plot of land!"

So fierce were her emotions that she was trembling. With rage or scorn? Beren did not know, but his temper rose to the challenge. "I came trotting back at your summons, did I not, my lady, like a trained pup? What else would you have me do?" Beren demanded, though he suspected well the answer. He was not to touch her, not to look at her, not to have anything of his own in this bloodless contract, except humiliation.

At his outburst, her passion seemed to die, her expression growing still and bleak. "I would have had you return without the summons, without my reminding you of your old vow, or did you so forget my father and all that he did for you? Do you know that he died with your name on his lips?" she asked.

Guilt assailed him, as was her intention, no doubt, and Beren ran a rough hand over his face. What could he say, without dredging up all that he kept buried? How to explain such selfishness when it was so far from the knightly ideal she so prized? He looked at her helplessly, but she gave him no quarter.

"He was so proud of you! Like a son, he thought you, though one long parted from his sire. He would have none say a word against you, nor complain that you did not return," she said. But the implication was there: Clement had wished to see him, and Beren had failed his old patron.

"I'm sorry. 'Twas wrong of me not to come," Beren admitted, swallowing hard against a thickness in his throat. He owed more than he could ever repay to Clement, but he had made not even the meanest effort to do so. He walked to the window and looked out upon the night.

"Even Parzival returned, though 'twas too late, or have you forgotten such trivial things?" Guenivere asked.

Beren heard her speech, soft and reproachful, but it was her mention of the character, so prevalent in her romantic tales, that angered him. He swung round to face her.

"How dare you stand here and scold me like one of your errant handmaidens, impuning my honor and fabricating motives for me that suit your own purpose? My reasons for staying away are my own and have nothing to do with ingratitude or false pride," Beren said.

Guenivere held out her hands, palms upward, in supplication. "Then what? Why?" she asked.

Beren was faced with a choice. What could he answer that would not release the floodgates of the past? Yet how could he lie? And so he settled for something of the truth. "I thought you were wed and would not intrude upon your household," he muttered.

"If I were married, I would probably not live here," Guenivere answered. "And what did my marital status matter?"

Was she really that foolish or arrogant or unseeing? Beren stepped forward. "I did not come because I did not care to see you wed to another," he said. Then, he reached out to grasp her shoulders, without hesitation this time. *"When I could not have you myself!"*

Beren took her mouth, more forcefully than before, staking his claim, possessing her in a way that was far different from his earlier attempt. Perhaps he wanted to drive away the old memories that threatened, or his awe and wonder were fading with her close proximity. Or maybe his temper drove him, with a mixture of wounded pride and helpless desire. Whatever the cause, Beren caught her gasp and deepened the kiss, entwining his tongue with hers, invading, exploring, and savoring the joining until his body grew taut and hard. He pulled her to him, and all the fierce, hot yearning of the years washed over him.

Beren lifted his hands to her head, fisting them into her long hair, holding her fast as his hungry mouth ravished her again and again. Finally, he paused for breath, his mouth against her silken locks. "Guenivere, Guenivere!" he whispered. The memories he had locked away for so long rushed over him. *All for her. 'Twas all for her.*

And now she was his wife. Heat rose in his blood, throbbing through him in heady victory. In one swift motion, he lifted her in his arms and carried her to the bed, tugging aside the curtains. The covers were laid back, and he placed her against the pale linen, pausing to stare at the picture she made lying there.

It seemed a dream, for so often had he imagined her thus before he had put aside such fancies. Now he would revel in the sight. Her blond hair, gleaming in the candlelight, lay spread upon the pillow, inviting him to lay his head down beside hers. Her body, slender and womanly, drew his attention, and for the first time in his life he allowed himself to take the measure of her breasts with his gaze, the gentle slopes, the clear skin that rose above her gown. He feasted upon the sight and below, at the indentation of her waist, the curve of her hips, her long legs, more visible now as she lay prone, ending in trim ankles and narrow feet encased in thin slippers.

My wife. Beren trembled at the knowledge. He let his gaze wander at its wont, then slowly he brought it back to her face, pale and beautiful and beloved. And Beren could not divine what he saw there. Sweetness, yes, and a kind of dazed aspect that could be attributed to desire, but paramount was a wariness, a guarded look that had never appeared in his dreams. He held his breath, dreading her protest.

Instead of waiting for it, Beren leaned over her, intending to stop whatever words she would put between them, but he halted at the touch of her hand against his chest. Her slender fingers burned through his tunic like fire, but there was no denying her intention: to ward him off. He stayed where he was, watching as she bit her lip. He nearly groaned, for he wanted to bite her lips himself, soft nibbles that led to a voracious feeding beyond his wildest . . .

"Such was Parzival's regard for his wife that he did not think of making love to her for three nights after the wedding," Guenivere said, referring once more to her favorite tale.

"Too late, for I have already thought of it," Beren replied. Indeed, he had dreamed of it endless nights long ago, forever it seemed, until his blood flamed and his body burned. . . .

"Parzival—"

Beren blew out a breath in exasperation. "I am not Parzival, no matter how you would wish me to be!" he said, rising to his feet as anger claimed him once again. "Nor am I Lancelot nor Gawain nor any legendary figure of the romances!"

And finally, amongst all the anger and accusations and long speeches of the tiring night, twas that one thing that stopped Beren from bedding his own wife: the terrible reminder that she knew what he was—and never would accept him as such.

three
❧

Guenivere busied herself sewing. She had continued
with her usual tasks this morning, meeting with the
cooks while ignoring the surprised glances of the servants and
the tittering of her handmaidens. They dared not question her
directly, of course, but she could hear their whispered specu-
lations concerning her wedding night and cringed.

The household was rife with rumor, of course, about how
the great knight had climbed up the side of the very keep to
enter through her window. The men boasted of their new
lord's boldness and daring, while the women sighed at the romantic feat. Only Guenivere knew that romance had nothing
to do with it.

She took a deep, shaky breath, trying not to think of how
Beren had kissed her, or worse yet, the way he had touched
her, carrying her to bed and eyeing her like a starving villein
would a feast. Apparently, men were more interested in such
things than she had ever imagined. How else could one barge
in and demand intimacies from a virtual stranger?

It was her own fault for summoning him here, Guenivere
knew, yet she had acted out of desperation. After her father's
death, the neighbors had swarmed like a pack of carrion
crows, eager to dine on her small holding. Yet she refused to
hand over her inheritance to any of them. Not many cared for
the windswept crags that made up her lands, and fewer still
could appreciate its raw beauty. It was a feeling bred into your
bones, Guenivere knew, and she wanted no absent lord who

would disdain her heritage, abandoning all responsibilities except to exact payment.

But she was no fool. Guenivere knew she could not have held them off forever, the men who deemed the world their venue and would deny one woman her small holding. Sooner or later, her overlord would have stepped in, awarding both her and the castle to whomever he pleased. She would have been forced to marry someone not of her own choosing, a man who might not have liked her home, who might have taken her away from Brandeth and the people who had so long served her family. That terror, more than any other, had made her swallow her pride and beg for help. And who else to give it to her except Beren—knighted by her father? Had he not sworn allegiance in return?

Still, it had taken all her courage to send for him, and even Guenivere had not been bold enough to specify her need, for fear that he would never consider it. Worse yet, there was always the possibility that he might turn her request over to someone else, another lord or the king himself, leaving her situation just as dire as before.

But Beren had come, and he had agreed, and foolishly, Guenivere had deemed her problems over. She had thought that the great Sir Brewere, having fulfilled his oath, would be eager to go on to more important business and finer accommodations. Why would she have imagined otherwise when he had acted as if he hardly recognized her?

Guenivere swallowed hard for she had known him at once, though he was greatly changed. Indeed, such was the power of his appearance that her knees had nearly given way. He was not the skinny youth who had left Brandeth, but a man, full grown and fleshed out, hard with muscle and strength that she had felt in his touch, and Guenivere's pulse skittered at the memory.

Even as a boy, Beren had never appeared soft, yet his face now held the aspect of a fearsome warrior, and for a moment, Guenivere had quailed before him. She had searched for glimpses of the one she had known in his dark eyes, but found them shuttered and steeled herself accordingly. If she secretly had dreamed of another sort of greeting, it had gone the way of all her other dreams, and she accepted his blunt acknowledgment as a harbinger of what was to come: vows made by duty.

What else did she expect when she had forced this marriage upon him? Guenivere felt a prick of guilt. She had pressed Beren, seizing what she thought was her only chance, though he had appeared loathe to wed her. At the thought Guenivere lifted her chin. Who, then, could blame her for seeking the solace of her chamber? And who would have thought that the solemn, distant knight intended to join her there?

The memory sent a flood of crimson to her cheeks, and Guenivere ducked her head in an attempt to hide her embarrassment. She did not want her handmaidens to notice her blush and comment upon it, and she was glad that she had sent the overly inquisitive Alice to fetch a draught. Unfortunately, just as the thought passed through her mind, the girl was back, breathlessly reporting that Lord Brewere had arisen and was breaking his fast.

Guenivere's hand jerked as her pulse quickened again, but she showed no other outward sign of having heard. Whatever Beren was about, she was not interested. However, Alice, who seemed far younger than fifteen years, would not be discouraged by her mistress' lack of attention. She began to carry on at great length about the "new lord."

"He is not lord here, really, but an overlord who will soon be away," Guenivere corrected.

"Off to far places and magnificent castles to fight for his lady!" Alice said with a sigh, while Guenivere grimaced. She had no idea what battle Alice could imagine being conducted on her behalf!

"Surely there has never been the like of such a man, tall and broad-shouldered and dark of hair and eye," Alice said. "Why, just the sight of him is enough to cause any maiden to swoon. And if that were not enough, he is a knight and a baron and a companion of Edward himself. Why, 'tis almost as if an intimate of King Arthur's round table came to life!"

"I thought I told you to stop reading romances," Guenivere said, snapping her thread sharply. She lifted her head to send both girls a quelling glance, for she had scolded them more than once for their habits, yet they continued to defy her.

Guenivere frowned at the ensuing silence. When would they ever learn? The romance stories were fantasy, as were the ballads sung by the troubadours to willing audiences. Despite the prevalence of such plots, knights didn't really commit adultery with queens and ladies or they would be castrated by their lord. There were no "courts of love," unless they existed in exotic foreign lands, for here, men didn't make vows that were judged by ladies. Most were too busy seeking their own glory to give a thought to any female. And those women who hoped otherwise were only asking for heartache. Guenivere pulled on the thread again—hard.

"But, my lady," Alice protested. "How can you ask us to forgo our only pleasure? The stories give us a glimpse of the excitement, such as is, to be had at court and beyond, of far-off places and handsome princes! You have to admit there is little enough chivalry to be found here."

Or anywhere, Guenivere thought, but before she could speak, Alice sighed deeply. "If only some great knight like Sir Brewere were to come for me!"

"Beren didn't come for me. I sent for him," Guenivere said, exasperated. Although she disliked speaking of her marriage, it was better that the girl know the truth than babble on like a dreamy-eyed maiden fed on fables. Like the girl she had been.

Guenivere drew in a harsh breath. Her father, having loved the Arthurian stories, had dubbed her accordingly and encouraged her interest in her namesake and the heroic legends of the past. In truth, Guenivere had needed little urging, for she had devoured the romances, reading them aloud to others, planning and dreaming and investing all her hopes in nothing but a bit of ink and parchment, a tale told by a fool.

But with age had come wisdom and, thankfully, the ability to tell the difference between fact and fiction. Knights did not fall in love with maidens at first sight, nor become so consumed with that love that they forgot all else. *'Twas the maidens they were more likely to forget.*

"Lest you twist the truth to suit your fancy, Alice, I might remind you that until my summons, Sir Brewere had no intention of returning to Brandeth. And he married me only because I held him to the oath he made to my father," Guenivere said, bitter though the words might be to speak.

"But how can you claim so after last night?" Alice asked.

Guenivere's face flamed, and she ducked her head once more, as if intent upon her handiwork. "What do you mean?" she murmured. Surely, no one knew of the kisses Beren had stolen or the way she had felt when he did so.

"Why, 'tis said that so enamored was he, that he called the very clouds to his bidding and soared through the air to your window to enter your bower!" Alice said.

Guenivere grimaced at the obvious falsehood, yet what did it matter what people said? Whether they claimed he sprouted wings and flew or drifted on the breeze or crawled like a spider up the stone, she knew it was a feat that only Beren could have accomplished. Of course, she had watched him climb before, years ago, her heart in her throat, as he seemed to dangle in nothingness only to emerge at the top of a crag, laughing and triumphant.

The memory seared her, tempting her to revisit others, but Guenivere hardened herself with more recent recollections and bitter truths. Only Beren could turn everything, even a seemingly impenetrable wall, to his advantage. And only Beren would expect to take up just where he had left off. But Guenivere was not so quick to forget the intervening years. Nor did she intend to let this man, whom she no longer knew, into her life—let alone her bed.

Guenivere flushed anew, but remained resolved. Last night she had managed to stay him. He had slept on a fur before the fire, completely clothed, while she had lain atop the bedcoverings, wide-eyed and wary. When she finally had drifted off, it was to awaken with a start, bewildered and angry at his presence in her private chamber. Yet there he had been, and she wondered just how long he intended to stay.

What if he remained this day, as well? What of this night? Guenivere felt her pulse pound in a rhythm born of panic, not excitement. Or so she told herself. Obviously, she could not count upon Beren's disinterest to protect her. Nor could she lock herself away, for it was unseemly to have him shout through her door. *Or break it down.* Guenivere felt a shiver pass through her at the thought of defying the man Beren had become: strong, confident, and lethal looking.

What, then, could she do? Fleeing was out of the question, for travel was too difficult, and she had no safe haven but her own home, a keep that now belonged to *him*. Guenivere swallowed that bitter draught and concentrated. Her recollections of the night were a haze of recriminations, threats, and the overriding fear that he would press her to submit. Fear that she would succumb.

Unbidden, the memory of his kisses returned, and Guenivere shivered, though she felt suffused with heat. For just a moment, she allowed herself the recollection. How different those kisses had been than her girlish imaginings! She had thought such things involved only a touching of lips, not a melding of mouths and tongues, not a fusing of souls . . . But perhaps Beren felt no such connection, Guenivere thought. How could he, for he was as a stranger to her now, who refused even to excuse his long absence?

That knowledge drove away whatever warmth that lingered, and Guenivere hardened herself once more. She had spent many hours of the night angrily wondering why Beren could not simply admit that he had forgotten all who dwelt at Brandeth. Instead, he had blustered and hedged his words and lashed out at her! And as for his claim that he had not wanted to see her married to another, Guenivere would have laughed had she the heart.

If Beren had wanted her for himself, he had only to claim her, at any time since that moment in her youth when she had first set eyes upon him and vowed to herself that this man was the stuff of her dreams, the other half of herself, her destiny. But such a man would never have left her, or else he would have returned, triumphant, to sweep her off her feet.

Guenivere made a low sound of disgust, for now she was lapsing into the ways of the romances, a foolishness she had thought long past. Unfortunately, just the sight of Beren seemed to send her slipping into that old habit, for had she not brought up Parzival in their conversation despite her best intentions not to do so? Guenivere winced as she remembered her final words. *Such was Parzival's regard for his wife that he did not think of making love to her for three nights after the wedding.*

It was nonsense, for surely nothing could be farther from her marriage than that of the legendary hero and his wife. Yet when she had quoted the romance to him, Beren had left her, angry at the comparison between himself and the knight of the tale. Had he been reminded of the lack of chivalry in his behavior, or had something else stayed his hand? Guenivere did not know, but she hoped that the words would work as well again, if she were pressed by him in the future.

And after three nights, then what? Guenivere trembled and told herself that Beren would be gone by then, off again to his adventures, leaving Brandeth behind as before.

Beren, however, was still in residence come supper, and Guenivere felt her nerves stretched taut. She had avoided him all of the day, even going so far as to take the main meal in her chamber. Still, she had hardly been able to swallow a bite, for fear he would search her out, bearding her there, especially after Alice breathlessly reported his absence at the high table.

Where had he eaten, and when? Guenivere found herself wondering and worrying only to chide herself for slipping into old patterns again. What did she care if Beren starved? More than likely, the simple fare at Brandeth no longer appealed to his more sophisticated tastes. And 'twas not only the food that could be so described, Guenivere thought bitterly.

She frowned, pushing aside such thoughts to consider what Beren was about. According to Alice, he had shown little interest in the keep or its outbuildings, preferring to remain closeted with Hubard, the old bailiff, going over the books. The notion of another judging her work here annoyed Guenivere, for what did Beren know of this place anymore? Luckily for him, he had not dared to approach her with any questions or quibbles about her management, lest he receive a tongue-lashing far harsher than last night's.

Guenivere stilled at her place by the hearth, seized by the image, for she now knew other uses for her tongue, and she glanced at the chamber door, fearful she would be tempted to them. Already, twilight was gathering outside her window. Would he come, or not? Guenivere was atremble already, though she knew not which outcome she most dreaded.

And then he was there, opening her door as though he had full use of it, her chamber, and herself. Guenivere drew in a sharp breath and glanced up at him, but his dark eyes were shuttered, and she could read nothing in his expression. Would he suddenly seize her? Scold her for avoiding him? Guenivere set her shoulders and told herself she feared no man, least of all Beren Brewere, lord or no.

"I went over your accounts today," he said. Guenivere did not deign to look at him. "You have done well."

Surprised at his words, she glanced up and tried not to stare at the sight of him. Would she ever be used to it? His dark hair swept back, thick and smooth, nearly to his shoulders, which were now broad and wide and strong, as was the rest of him. He had always been tall, but now his body had grown to match it, not an inch bulging or thick, but all hard with muscle, visible even through the linen of his tunic. Guenivere swallowed hard and tore her gaze away.

"Did you get something to eat?" she asked, carefully neutral.

"Yes," he said, and then he astounded her by laughing, though it was not a lighthearted sound. "You might not be pleased to know that since neither of us were at the high table, all the keep thinks that we were up here, engaged in newly wedded bliss."

Guenivere jerked around, nearly choking on her own breath. "B-but, you—! I—" she sputtered, then turned her head angrily away. "Do you listen at keyholes?"

"Nay. I did not have to," Beren answered. "Brandeth is buzzing with rumors and speculation."

That would die down, if you would but leave, Guenivere thought. Aloud, she said, "Yes, I heard some of it myself, most notably how you sprouted wings and flew through my window."

Beren laughed, and this time the sound was soft and low and so compelling that Guenivere had to use all her will to remain still. "Apparently, over the years, the people here have forgotten your unusual talent for climbing," she added.

Silence met her comment, so long and all encompassing that finally, Guenivere turned to look at him again, only to find that he had wrapped his cloak about him and lay upon the floor, his back to her. Obviously, his brief interest in her charms had faded once more. Guenivere struggled with a sharp sense of disappointment that bordered on pain before convincing herself she ought to be relieved instead.

Then she rose to her feet and sought her own bed, pulling the drapes close around her and shutting Beren out. But it seemed as if the habit of long years returned, for though he might be out of sight, he was never far from her mind.

Beren tried to sleep, but it would not come. He had made his bed on harder, colder spots, but none more painful to both body and spirit. All day, he had spent hiding from his past, closeted with Hubard, concentrating on the management of the demesne and redirecting the old man whenever he started to reminisce. But the place pressed upon him, like a weight against his chest, stifling his thoughts and stealing his breath.

Beren winced as the scent of roses wafted over him, making him dizzy with want, while rousing his blood to a fever pitch. Although he prided himself on his good sense, it appeared to have fled, for why else would he ache and throb for a woman with whom he could not even bear to talk? How had he come to marry the one woman who would not have him? And why was she even here, unmarried after all these years?

Beren seized upon that question, worrying it until he could not let it go. Had he not heard that she was betrothed at one time? Without examining too closely that memory, he wondered what had happened. Had the man died or been found wanting? The more Beren thought about it, the more tense he became. Finally, he rolled over and, staring at the bedcurtains, he spoke aloud into the dimness.

"What happened to your betrothed? Why did you not marry?" Beren asked, his voice harsh and accusing as he rose up on one arm. For a long moment, he thought she was asleep or feigning so and would not answer. Angry, he felt like striding over to rouse her; but, in his current state, he knew that was not a good idea. He shouldn't even be looking at her bed, he thought, even as the drapes fluttered and moved.

Although he had tried to forget everything to do with the lady of Brandeth, Beren knew that no matter how long he lived, he would ever remember the sight of those curtains parting. Whatever he thought, he wasn't expecting that, and he held his breath in tense anticipation, his heart thundering. When at last Guenivere was revealed in the dim light of the fire, he could see she was fully clothed, yet still he felt hot desire run rampant through him, for there she was, kneeling upon the covers, her hair loose and flowing. . . .

" 'Twas broken off," she said simply. As if that marked the end of her comments on the subject, she reached up to draw the curtains once more. Beren's heart lurched, as if it would leap out of his chest in order to stay her hand.

"By whom?" he asked, hoarsely.

"By me," she answered, her eyes downcast.

She looked as if she did not care to speak of it, but suddenly it was imperative to Beren that he know. What had the man done? "Why?" he demanded, ready, despite all, to battle on her behalf.

With a sigh, Guenivere swung her legs round to sit on the edge of the bed. "As I grew older, Father became concerned because I had shown no marked partiality for any who sought my hand," she explained in a flat voice, still without looking at him. "So, he thought to force a decision from me by betrothing me to William of Langbane. I thought that, rather than cause trouble for my sire, I should accept," she said, and though her words rang true, Beren's gut churned.

"I believed that I could do it," she said. And while Beren stared, she took an interest in a decorative cord that dangled from the drape beside her, rubbing it between her fingers as though it would give her comfort or strength before dropping it abruptly. "But I could not," she murmured. "I finally told Father that I could not in all good conscious commit myself to the marriage when I felt I would fail William as a wife."

Beren swallowed a protest, for Guenivere had never failed at anything. And he knew of no man who was worthy of her, *not even himself.*

"Since my father cared very much for my mother, he was

reluctant to compel me into a loveless union, especially when it would take me away from him," she added, finally meeting Beren's gaze with a rather defiant look. "And so, that was the end of my betrothal. William was very gracious about it and married Elizabeth Trowford a few months later."

Beren knew he should have been relieved at her words. Instead, he felt a wild euphoria beyond all reason. He was glad that there had been no love between the two, all too glad! And fast on the heels of his elation came a surge of possessiveness. At that moment, Beren wanted nothing more than to go to her, take her in his arms, and make her forget every other man she had ever known.

"What of you? Why have you not wed?" So lost was he to his emotion that Beren barely heard her voice, but Guenivere's question penetrated his thoughts, staying his rampaging impulses and scattering them all like the fancies they were. He pulled his cloak about himself tightly.

"Mayhap I was a bachelor knight too long to change my ways," Beren muttered. Then he turned over once more, shutting her out and hiding from the past that she would dredge up, lest he be laid bare before her.

four

Beren stood at the doors of the hall, staring out to the sea and wondering what he was doing here when it was the last place he wanted to be. He ought to leave. There were no obstacles to his doing so, certainly not the wishes of his wife. And yet, something held him here—whether the past or the future, he wasn't sure.

Meanwhile, he was accomplishing nothing, reluctant as he was to come to terms with his history, while other duties waited for him at his own demesne. *Back home.* Yet even as he thought the words, it seemed to Beren that his new lands were not his home, that his destiny lay here, with his roots. He shook his head with a grunt of denial.

"Are you still here?" As if his own thoughts were being voiced aloud, Beren heard the question, but he had not spoken. He turned slowly to find Crispin standing behind him, a sneer on his lips.

"This is my keep now, Crispin. Would you try to rout me from it?" Beren asked, in no mood for the older knight's taunts. His patience had already been worn down to nothing by his bride. For a moment, Beren thought Crispin might challenge him, and his own hand moved to the hilt of his sword, but the other man only crossed his arms over his chest.

"Nay, for I'm sure you'll be gone soon enough," he said. "Linger for now, if you must, though for what purpose, I wonder? No one remembers you, and those few who do wish they did not."

Beren might have disputed his claim, for from what he had seen, Crispin was in the minority. The other people of Brandeth treated him with courtesy, if not enthusiasm, he noted, surprising himself with the realization. As if to bear him out, another of the keep's knights strode by, calling a greeting.

"Good day, my lord!" the younger man said, adding a welcoming gesture that would hardly be feigned, and with a nod Beren acknowledged the man's passing. Then, he turned back to Crispin, his dark brows lifted in query.

"Those who don't know you may bow and scrape to Edward's lackey, but no one wants you here," the old knight fairly snarled. "I told you that things have changed, so you might as well be gone! And lest you think the lady of Brandeth still pines for your presence, she came to her senses long ago and curses your name as well as any other!"

With that, Crispin turned on his heel and marched away, though he had not been given leave to go by his lord. Beren stared after him, too stunned to dispute his dismissal. Guenivere pining for him? He shook his head, unable to believe it, but he knew Crispin was not clever enough to spin such a lie. Despite his best judgment, hope leapt to life within his breast, and Beren knew that he must discover the truth ere he left Brandeth.

And there was only one way to find out: by asking Guenivere.

Although he had again avoided dinner, that night Beren took supper in the hall, and he had to wonder just what had kept him away. Besides Crispin, who sent him dark looks, none other there seemed to harbor ill feelings toward him. And if some older resident bid him recall the past, Beren simply changed the subject. Indeed, that was an easier task than trying to explain away the absence of his bride. He suffered a few good-natured, if ribald, comments concerning her condition.

Beren let them go, enduring even more when he left the table early to seek his wife's chamber. And yet, eager though he had been to confront her, his steps lagged as old doubts assailed him. What would he say? Even as he wondered, Beren was well aware that the past he so denied might rise up to smite him.

Still, he could not bring himself to leave Brandeth without knowing this one truth, and so he entered their chamber, finding her seated on the settle before the hearth, staring into the flames as if the weight of the world sat upon her shoulders. And in that moment, Beren realized that he had done her ill. She had asked for his aid, and though nominally providing his name, he had thought of nothing but his own pride, ignoring her woes and worries, the burden she carried of her father's loss and the responsibility of holding her lands together. Even if she cared naught for him, Guenivere deserved more than his petulance.

Slowly, Beren approached her. This time, when he dropped to his knee, it was not a gesture born of duty, but one heartfelt. Memories nudged at him, but he ignored them and drew a deep breath. "How may I serve you, lady?" he asked, bowing his head.

To Beren's astonishment, Guenivere burst into tears. Confused, he watched helplessly, then lifted a hand toward her, though he was not quite certain how to provide comfort. But she moved out of his reach before he could touch her. Rising to her feet, she dashed away her tears, yet there was no hiding her heightened emotions.

"Do not mock me!" she said, turning upon him, and Beren was stunned to see the passion that she usually withheld glowing like a brand. "Would you destroy everything that I once held dear?"

"What is it? What have I done?" Beren asked, bewildered and yet aroused by this woman, alight with an inner flame he had never witnessed before. She was grown now, and not only in body, and Beren's blood heated in acknowledgment.

She glared at him, a flush rising in her cheeks, her fury evident. "You? You have done nothing, of course!" Then, as swiftly as it had come upon her, the rage faded away, leaving her looking so lost and forlorn that Beren felt his chest constrict.

"I am at fault," she whispered. "For I placed all my hopes and dreams and love in the hands of another, who failed me."

She turned away from him then, and hid her face in her hands and wept once more.

Beren stood staring in shock, for until today, he had never seen Guenivere in tears. In her youth, she had been too contented, too composed to cry over slights to her happy existence. And now, as a woman grown, she had seemed too cool and remote to be touched by such fierce emotion, but there was no denying her distress.

Something inside Beren jerked to life, and feelings long buried rose to match her own. Who had done this to her? Moved beyond all caution, he stepped forward and took her by the shoulders, drawing her back against him. But the comfort that he intended was hampered by his own anger and jealousy. "Tell me, who stole your dreams? Who failed you? Who . . ."—Beren nearly choked on the words—"spurned your love?"

To his surprise, she laughed, a low gurgle that sounded more like despair than mirth. "Know you not, Beren? Then you must truly be as ignorant as Parzival."

Beren stiffened automatically at the mention of the legendary hero, then went even more still as the meaning of her words struck him. He drew in a sharp breath of both pain and disbelief. "If you think 'twas I, then I can only beg your forgiveness for any broken faith."

"Broken faith?" she asked, as if amused by his choice of words. "Nay, you made no promise to me, ere you left. 'Twas my own fault for foolishly clinging to hope for far too long." Beren's fingers tightened against her arms as his world shook, destroying not only his recent assumptions, but perceptions born of many long years.

"When I heard of your knighting, I rejoiced in your good fortune," Guenivere said. "At last, you had what you most desired! 'Twas your dream, and mine, too, for I had long held in my heart the hope that once knighted, you would ask for my hand." She gave a brittle little laugh that wrenched Beren's heart, and he bowed his head to touch her own.

"But when Father returned, 'twas without you. You went away, he said, to earn a name for yourself." Beren opened his mouth to protest, for it was money that he went to find, having not one coin to his name. But before he could speak,

Guenivere continued, as if unable to stop the flow of words once begun.

"For a long time, I waited for a message. I knew that you could not read, but still I hoped for some sign, and I plagued each passing minstrel and packman, begging for news of you. And still there came no word, and I knew not where you were. I wrote letters to you nonetheless, waiting to send them once I learned your whereabouts. But the months passed, and then the seasons passed, and my hope grew dim."

She paused to draw a ragged breath that made her slender back shudder against him. " 'Then, at last, we began to hear of your deeds, a knight who had won many tournaments, who journeyed far, gaining great renown. Father was thrilled and proud, but my happiness was tempered by selfishness. Had you forgotten me in your quest? Would you ever return?"

Beren felt her pain, as well as his own, dredged up beyond all hope of reburial. He slid his hands down her arms and around her waist, pulling her in to him as if to deny all that had happened. And still she spoke.

"Although I had never divulged my hopes, my father had been patient with my lack of interest in marriage, until, at last, he began to press me. I understood his concerns for the future, and yet, I balked, unwilling to surrender the last shred of my folly. And though outwardly I had given up waiting alone at night, I dreamed that you would ride up to Brandeth to claim your lady."

Beren's arms tightened around her even as she uttered the accusations he could not deny. "And that is why you broke the betrothal," he said. Although he knew he ought to assume guilt for that, instead he was flooded with a primitive surge of possessiveness. Again, he was glad that she had felt no love for another, and now he rejoiced to know that she had waited for him for so long.

"I didn't intend to stay away," Beren said. He drew in a deep breath, knowing that he couldn't ignore the past any longer, or at least the part of it that was Guenivere, and, oh, how much of it she was. "At first, I only wanted to stay alive in the battles. Then, when the fighting ended, I could think of little except becoming a proper knight."

Beren paused to carefully phrase his words. "But, as I soon

discovered, 'tis not the occupation of a poor man, a small fact that is made little of in the romances." He hesitated again, unwilling by long habit to admit the truth even though he knew she deserved it. "I needed money not only to live, to feed myself, but for mail and weapons, and most expensive of all, a good destrier," he admitted.

"But Father would have—"

Beren interrupted her with a rough sound. "Clement had done enough. 'Twas up to me to make my fortune." He drew another deep breath. "I could not return to you penniless, a beggar at the door of the castle, raised up to knighthood, but with nothing to offer you."

Beren felt Guenivere stir within the circle of his arms, but he held her fast, finding himself loath both to let her go or to face her. "All I wanted was *you*!" she protested.

Beren shook his head sadly. "But I would have been no measure of a knight, or even a man, had I come to you with naught."

"What nonsense males take into their heads," Guenivere muttered. Beren smiled at her outrage, even though he knew he could have done nothing else.

"Clement suggested I make a living by tourneying, and I managed to do well for myself," he said. "I defeated many others, winning the value of their horse and mail in ransom, and I began to hoard a tidy sum."

"And what amount would have been enough?" Guenivere asked him, a trace of bitterness in her voice. "When would you have amassed enough to return?"

Beren didn't reply, for he was not sure of the answer himself. Never for a moment had he forgotten her. Guenivere had been there with him always, his anchor and his talisman, the reason for all he did. And yet, even when Edward chose him, Beren had been no more than a bachelor knight, without lands to call his own. Would he come back and claim Brandeth? By what right? And so, he had always put off his return, thinking that he must do more, have more, *be more*.

He swallowed against the tightening of his throat. "Lords began to notice me and take me into service, until finally Edward himself, who loves the tournaments, bid me join him in his war against Wales. 'Twas then that I heard of your betrothal," Beren said. And his anger had sent him pounding into battle, forging through the ranks of the enemy like a lance, earning him a renown that he no longer sought. And when finally the fighting was over and Edward had gifted him with lands, Beren had imagined her already wed to another. He had buried his hopes, along with a good part of himself.

"And why didn't you come for me then, when you heard of my betrothal?" Guenivere asked.

"We were headed into battle," Beren answered. But there was more to it, as they both knew, and he could not tender that excuse. He blew out a low breath in admission. "What right had I to interfere with your happiness?" he asked.

"And so you left me to a stranger, absolving yourself of any concern, without even wondering if I were well and content?" Guenivere asked, her voice rising.

"And neither did you send any of these letters you claim to have written, to commend me or command me or inform me that you still even remembered my name!" Beren countered.

"I had my pride!" Guenivere said.

"As did I!" Beren answered.

The room fell into silence then, until at last Guenivere spoke again. "So we both suffered for it," she said. "And now it is too late."

"Is it?" Beren asked. How could he believe that when he could rest his chin upon her bright hair, smell the fragrance of her essence, and feel her supple body pressed against his own? As he turned her in his arms, reveling in the miracle of her closeness, all the years fell away. And if any doubts lingered from his long exile, Beren ignored them in the rush of joy that swept through him.

When she was facing him, he lifted her chin and saw that her lashes were sparkling with the moisture of her previous tears. Kissing them away, Beren let his mouth wander over her beloved features, brushing kisses against her finely arched brows, her pale cheeks, her lips . . .

When Guenivere met his mouth with her own, tentative but eager, Beren felt his body jerk to life. He groaned, drawing her closer even as her arms slipped around his neck. And then somehow he was carrying her to the bed, laying her among the linens. This time, when he stood over her, she pulled him down to join her.

He was trembling, Beren realized, as he moved over her, so long had he waited for this moment, dreaming helplessly, hardly daring to hope. He looked down into her face, no longer cool or accusing, but tender and yearning, and the last of the walls he had erected between them came crumbling down.

"Guenivere," he whispered, consumed by awe and desire and the love that he had kept so carefully guarded all these years. And every sight, every sound, every touch was a feast for his starving senses, a wondrous treasure. He hovered over her, drinking in the vision, then he lifted his hand. It hovered for a long moment and then fell to the shining length of her hair. The bright strands were like silk under his fingers, rivaled only by the softness of her skin when he touched her slender throat.

"Beren," she answered low, with an underlying urgency that set his blood thundering. Then she pulled his head down to hers and he kissed her with a mixture of the passion and love that flowed through him, drawing her breath into himself.

It was so much more than he had ever dared hope that Beren might have been content to kiss her all the night long, dwelling on the lips that had haunted his dreams since childhood. But she moved against him, beneath him, setting a fire in his loins that must be quenched by his man's body.

So he touched her, running his hands along the fall of her golden hair, along her side and the hip that pressed to him. He sucked in a harsh breath, lifting her to him, feeling the press of her soft belly against his hardness. He fought against the desire to lift her gown and bury himself inside her, seeking to catch some errant thought that might bring him back under control.

It was his love for her that slowed his pace as, breathing heavily, Beren lifted his head and looked into her face. There he saw wonder and desire, the sweet reflection of his own emotions, whether real or imagined, and his heart pounded with his own exhilaration. Loosing a sigh, Beren took her hand and kissed her fingers, drawing in a deep breath to still the thundering of his blood.

"My lady, will you have me?" he asked. "As your husband in truth?" He watched her, his lips upon her knuckles as he waited a heartbeat for her answer.

"Aye, Sir Knight, I will take you," she said, and she smiled, though her eyes seemed curiously moist, her voice atremble.

And so Beren carefully stripped the gown from her body, each inch of flesh a new wonder, a new precious find that he must worship with his eyes and his fingers and his mouth, until at last she lay before him naked, slender and white, but he had only a moment to feast his gaze upon her, for she tugged at his tunic until he tossed it over his head, then she sat up to press kisses along his chest. Beren groaned, catching her against him, and they both went down upon the linens as he dragged away his braies.

The feel of her skin against his own was almost more than he could bear and he shuddered, seized by both a driving need for completion and a desire to remain thus forever, body to body and heart to heart. But Guenivere was sliding against him, a siren call he could not forbear, and he moved over her, laying claim to the prize he had spent his life trying to win.

When at last he entered her body, Beren felt as if he were home at last, and it had nothing to do with the lands granted him by the king or even with the windswept crags of Brandeth. Here, with this woman, he found both peace and challenge, both beauty and wit, both the past and the future.

Beren wanted to speak, to put some of what he felt into words, but they were beyond him as Guenivere enclosed him, and his only thought was to give them both pleasure even as he strove past her maidenhead. She cried out then, and he did his best to soothe her, plying her with pleasure until, at last, she called out once more, this time in celebration, rather than loss. And Beren joined her.

He was slow to recover his wits, so overwhelmed had he been by the force of his release, but gradually he came to his senses, rolling to his side, so as not to crush her slender form, and pulling her close. Now was the time to unburden himself, to tell her all that was in his heart, yet even as his arm tightened around her, Beren heard her breathing, deep and even, that told him she slept.

As well she should, he thought, tenderly drawing a covering over her. Beren was weary as well, but loath to sleep, lest he wake up and find it all a dream, both his marriage and its consummation. So he held her to him, but even within the confines of his current bliss, he felt the nudge of old doubts, the bane of his existence, and his heart beat feverishly within his chest until his body roused to full awareness.

Beren realized that once was not enough, that he needed Guenivere again, to drive away all uncertainty, to assure himself that she was his, now and forever. His hands began moving over her, exploring every part of her until she awoke, already dazed with desire. And Beren marveled at each gasp of surprise and delight as he learned her pleasure spots even as he fed his own excitement.

And so he continued, unable after his long wait to deprive himself of one moment in her arms, with the force of his passion pushing the darkness far away into the night until at last, exhausted, he slept and dreamed no more.

five

❧

B eren's first hint that all might not be well was waking up alone. To his dismay and disappointment, Guenivere was gone from their bed. For a long moment, he thought his memories of the night before might be only phantoms of some long-ago dream. But the scent of their lovemaking lingered in the air, as did the imprint of her body beside him. Why had she left? To groom herself privately or attend her duties? Beren tried to convince himself such was the case, but it was barely dawn. And strive as he might, he knew he could not account himself a good judge of Guenivere's feelings, else he would have been here long ago.

By what right? Beren wondered, and the doubt he had thought banished assailed him anew. For all the passion that had raged between them, Guenivere had never spoken of her love aloud. Perhaps now she regretted what had happened between them, her absence speaking more eloquently than the words that were so difficult between them. Beren exhaled harshly, all of his pent-up emotions rising up to seek an outlet. He rubbed a rough hand across his face, as if to change his features, *himself.*

Suddenly, all that he had been denying, all the bitter realities of his youth came back to him in painful waves. Things he had thought banished from his memory returned to beset him: the smell of animals and hopelessness, the gnaw of hunger and cold, a weariness of body and mind behind anything he had ever known in battle.

Beren broke out in a sweat, reeling with the knowledge of his own existence, but there was nowhere to go, no place to hide. And he was done taking the coward's way, retreating from his own history, burying it as he had all these years. Instead, he pushed aside the blankets and rose. It was time to face everything.

Dressing swiftly, Beren slipped through the keep whose residents were slowly stirring and stepped out into the brisk cool morning. He took a deep breath and felt the ocean air enter his lungs, tangy and delightful. And instead of pushing aside his pleasure, he reveled in it, for he had missed the scent of sea, just as he had missed Guenivere. How had he come to give up so much of himself? And for what?

He walked through the bailey and out the gate toward the village. He did not shut out the past, but let it swallow him up. His birth was clouded in shadow, as were his first years, a darkness of hunger and want and toil, relieved only by sporadic forays to the cliffs, his only solace.

The thought led Beren there, and his breath caught as he let himself look upon the steep crags of this land, more beautiful to him than the greenest of rolling hills that he might claim as his own. Perilous many called them, and those who did shrank from the jumble of boulders that led to the sharp inclines moving straight up. To be sure, Beren had a healthy respect for the cliffs, especially when they were made all the more deadly by cold and rain, and yet, he had been born with a fascination for the rock, with the look and feel of it and with the conquering of it by force of his own will and skill.

And so Beren had found something of worth in his bleak world, that of a poor orphan boy of unknown parentage taken in by the brewer and his brood. He wrinkled his nose, for he still hated the reek of ale and would drink wine or water when he could. He ought to have been grateful, at least that's what everyone said, for he could have been taken for a villein and a life of mind-numbing, backbreaking toil.

The brewer was not particularly kind, but such was the fate of those not born to the castle. Beren had been beaten often enough for "dallying" on the cliffs instead of working, and yet he could not forsake them. Somehow he had found new energy on the stone, an expansion of mind and spirit that renewed his tired body. And it was this passion that had raised him up from a short and weary life.

One day he had climbed higher than ever before, something inside driving him onward and upward until at last he had reached the top and stood staring out from the dizzying height. From there it seemed that he could see the entire world, the sea stretching out into infinity, the line of the cliffs and the coast, and far off, in the distance, a swarm of men, an army, heading toward Brandeth.

That day, Beren had sounded the alarm and the lord of the castle, Clement himself, had plucked him from the sodden despair of his home with the brewers and made him a squire, altering his destiny forever. Many, openly or not, disapproved of this sudden elevation of a ragged boy, little more than a villein, to the coveted position at the lord's side. But not Clement's daughter.

Guenivere had immediately befriended him, and announcing that a squire must be learned, she saw it as her duty to teach him. Although younger than Beren, she was well versed in an existence far removed from his experience, and he eagerly accepted her advice, her friendship, and her tutoring.

She read to him. And Beren listened, rapt, to things beyond his ken, to tales of kings and knights and brave deeds and beautiful ladies, and he had taken them all as gospel. Beren blew out a breath at his own innocence. But Guenivere, with her artless enthusiasm, had made it hard not to believe, to take to heart each word she spoke.

She had loved the stories of Arthur and his round table. With a name like Guenivere, who could blame her? But now Beren wondered if Clement had indulged his own and his daughter's love of such fanciful tales too freely. For the daughter of the castle had filled Beren's head with dreams he would never otherwise have had: to become a knight. And not only that must he rise to such an honor, but also that he was to accomplish great deeds and win his lady fair. *Just like Parzival.*

The name brought an ache to his chest, for he well remembered the stories that were Guenivere's favorites: those of Parzival. Despite various spellings and interpretations, they all concerned a boy raised in the woods, ignorant of worldly things, who, finally meeting some knights, decides to take up that life himself. There were different adventures and versions of the classic, but most dear to Guenivere were the ones where the hero was discovered to be the lost heir to a kingdom, won his quest for the Grail, and married his true love, Condwiramurs. *A love so deep, so ethereal, that he did not think of making love to her for three nights after their wedding.*

Beren loosed a sigh. The dreams he had had back then! And Guenivere had fed them, nurturing his hopes, egging him on with tales of glory until his vision of knighthood, so fiercely desired, bore very little resemblance to the harsh reality of his life, a difference he soon discovered. For Clement was called to war by his liege and Beren went to serve him. There, on the battlefield, he was girded with a sword and named a knight.

He must have seemed much like Parzival, ignorant and foolish, but at least the tales always gave the hero noble lineage, even when unknown. And in some lands, Beren knew that only those of noble birth were legally allowed to become knights. Unfortunately, he had never miraculously found himself to be anything other than what he was, a poor orphan boy of low birth—unworthy, always reaching for those things that were above him, scaling heights that were beyond his grasp . . . just like these.

When Beren looked up, he saw again the cliffs of his childhood, and his heart pounded out a fierce rhythm that once more dispelled despair. This stone had weathered the tests of time, the continuous onslaught of the waves, yet still rose, fierce and proud, into the sky. Feasting his eyes upon the tall faces, he admired each rise like another man would a lover or a friend, and let himself remember the feel of the climb, both challenge and triumph.

Beren's gaze lit upon his old paths, but he walked on, studying the face of the rock and seeing new routes, where others saw naught but a sheer precipice. He searched and he planned, and then, when at last he had found the perfect spot, he began his climb. As he had discovered the other night, his fingers no longer possessed the strength they once had, but his eye was unerring, charting a route among the faint dips and tiny outcroppings. And all during the long, grueling challenge

to himself, he concentrated on nothing but the move ahead
until at last he reached the summit, weary and triumphant.

Beren gazed down from the same dizzying heights that he
had years before, but he found that his perspective was different now. Long ago, he had stood here and looked out and
seen opportunities, the only ones open to him, the challenges
of the climb. Now he saw accomplishments, and not just the
striving against rock, but his achievements out in the world
that he had once only seen from a distance.

Up here the air seemed more fresh, his mind more clear, as
if all the debris of the years had been blown away by the brisk
breeze off the water. From this vantage point, just as he could
see farther distances than from anywhere else, Beren also was
able to see deeper within himself. And in that moment of clarity, he realized that whatever his antecedents, he was unlike
other men. He had forged a new road for himself, taking the
untrodden path, the perilous one that rose straight upward,
into the clouds.

What did it matter if his father were some forgotten king
or the meanest villein? Beren had made of himself what he
willed. But like a child fearing the specter in the darkness, he
had let the question of his parentage rule his life and control
his actions. If not, he would have returned to claim his bride
long ago. But no more would he bow to the past or hide from
it, or imagine the judgments of others, based upon his own
dread, for he knew who he was.

Was he not Sir Berenger Brewere, lord of great lands?
Beren thought. Then he threw back his head and laughed with
a freedom he had never known before.

Guenivere pressed her hands against her pounding temples,
though it was not the only part of her body that pained her. Secret spots she had considered private ached this morn. Worse
yet, her heart, an organ she had long pronounced dead, was
stirring once more. She moved her palms downward, over her
eyes, where the tears she had thought finished years ago
threatened to erupt, just as they had last night.

Last night. All too well, Guenivere remembered staring
into the fire, wary and uncertain, only to have Beren burst in,

like the stuff of dreams, and kneel at her feet. Who could blame her for losing her composure? But she should not have spoken so freely, should not have admitted the feelings she had kept hidden so long and, most of all, should not have allowed herself to succumb at last to the temptation of his touch.

If only it had not been so beautiful, Guenivere thought. Her throat constricted, adding to her discomfort. She drew a deep breath, frantically grasping for her usual equanimity. She could not let others see her like this, especially Beren. She had already admitted too much weakness to him, which he had exploited easily enough.

Guenivere sighed, a faint despairing sound. She was being unfair, and she knew it. Beren had not taken advantage of her, for at any time during the long night of passion, she could have denied him. But she had not. Instead, she had embraced him, reveling in the fulfillment of all her hopes. *Except one.*

Though he had plied her with sweet words, never had Beren said what she had so yearned to hear. He had explained his absence glibly enough, but what had he really said about his feelings? Although Guenivere racked her mind, the memory of their speech was hazy and dim, overwhelmed by what had followed. And now she found herself belatedly advising caution, an act that resembled throwing water upon the remains of a building that had already burned to the ground.

Guenivere felt her cheeks flame. Burn was right. From the moment he kissed her, she had been lost, a creature of heat and desire. The things he had done to her! Guenivere had never imagined that a man might suckle a woman like a babe and press his mouth to every part of her. And she could not have protested, for it had been Beren who touched her, Beren whose hard body moved over her, Beren who thrust inside her until she cried out in ecstasy.

Guenivere covered her hot cheeks with her palms, moaning softly as memory washed over her. How could she distance her heart from such intimacies? And this morning had been no better, for she had awoken in his arms, feeling safe and warm and blissful for one long, precious moment before she had returned to her senses. Then she had fled the naked male body beside her, the bed where she had lost her maidenhead, and the room that no longer seemed her own.

But there was no escaping the body that had betrayed her, and Guenivere had roamed restlessly until, unwilling to let others see her distress, she had sought out the quiet of the tiny solar, shooing away any who would disturb her. A trencher of uneaten food lay nearby, but Guenivere ignored it, walking to the narrow window to stare out sightlessly.

Last night she had surrendered to pleasure, that she could not deny, but no matter how much her body had enjoyed its initiation, she could not allow herself to feel anything beyond the throes of passion. For, sooner or later, Beren would be gone again, lost forever to his fine estates and royal companions, while her place was here. And she would once again be naught more than a forgotten piece of his past.

Guenivere had lived through that torment once, somehow finding the wisdom and strength to survive, but she would not risk her heart again. In truth, she didn't think she could endure another breakage of that tender organ. But meanwhile, how was she to get on? Guenivere wondered hopelessly. How was she to distance herself from the man who had invaded her world, her mind, and *her bed*?

As if her very thoughts had summoned him to mock them, Guenivere heard Beren's unmistakable strides as he walked into the room. Turning slowly to greet him, she drew in a sharp, painful breath, whether because of the intimacy they had shared or something else, he appeared different today to her eyes. Taller. Broader. Stronger, yet more gentle. And so handsome that she wanted to weep for the sight of him. She swallowed hard.

"My lady," he said, his voice dropping to a low rendering that reminded her of whispers in the dark, and Guenivere heard herself make a soft, helpless noise. Who knows what might have happened next, whether she would have fallen back into his arms, despite all her vows, or fled the chamber like a frightened hare? Luckily for Guenivere, she did not have to make that choice, for Beren's entrance was soon followed by another, a boy who raced into the room like an eager pup.

"My lord, my lord!" he said. Guenivere tried to still her trembling as Beren turned his beautiful face toward the youth.

"Yes, Farman, what is it?" he asked, giving the boy a smile that made Guenivere's knees so weak she sought a seat. She sank down upon a settle, entwining her hands in her lap to keep them still.

"My lord, a messenger has come from your demesne!"

"What? Who is it?" Beren asked, his smile fading into a somber expression.

The youth shook his head. "I knew him not, lord. He did not linger, but bade me give you the message and sped away!"

Beren's dark brows drew together. "And just what was this message?"

"That you are needed at your lands and must return at once," the boy said.

Guenivere quivered as something between a laugh and a sob rose in her throat, quickly choked back. Even though she had warned herself of Beren's departure all morning, still she had never expected it to come so soon. *After one night.* She swallowed and twisted her fingers in her lap in an effort to maintain her composure.

"Did he say what was the problem?" Beren asked. Guenivere heard him, though the conversation no longer interested her. All her thought and will was brought to bear upon herself, upon maintaining her dignity, and she lifted her chin and drew a deep breath.

"Nay. Only that it was urgent that you return immediately. Perhaps the king is there, waiting for you?" the youth suggested.

"I doubt that," Beren said. Guenivere saw him rub a hand over his face and thought she heard him mutter a low curse. "I wish I could discover exactly why I am needed, so that I might judge for myself the necessity of returning."

Personally, it mattered not to Guenivere why Beren had been called away, only that he had. And gradually, as she regained control of her wildly careening emotions, she told herself that it was better this way, for him to go at once, rather than tarry here, tempting her to give her heart to him again.

After another whispered oath, he sighed. "Very well. Tell the men to prepare to leave," Beren said. He stood watching until the youth disappeared through the doorway, then turned to Guenivere, his face somber. What now? Would he pretend regret? She nearly laughed aloud at the notion.

"As you can see, I am urgently needed at my own demesne," he said, with a rather awkward gesture of his hand.

"Yes, though I find it odd that the man delivering this vital request did not tarry long enough to discuss it with you," Guenivere said, suddenly struck by a dark, painful suspicion. Was there really a message? Or had Beren tired of Brandeth so quickly that he must needs invent an excuse to depart?

"I admit 'tis unusual, but thus did the messenger from Brandeth leave his summons," Beren said, with a frown. "I can either send a man or go myself, but if 'tis truly a matter of importance I hesitate to wait." He paused to gaze at her directly. "How soon can you be ready to go?"

Guenivere jerked in surprise. "What?"

"When can you make ready to leave?" Beren asked.

"What on earth do you mean?" Guenivere asked, her heart pounding.

Beren eyed her quizzically. "You are my wife now, so I would have you with me," he said, as if stating the obvious.

"I am not going anywhere!" Guenivere answered. "This is my home, and my people need me." She felt panic seize her, constricting her breath, and she struggled to draw in a deep draught of air. She had sought to wed Beren in order to avoid just such a wrench from Brandeth and all that she loved. How could he think that she would willingly leave it now?

Unlike Beren, Guenivere had no wish to see other places or foreign lands, to wander amidst strangers or live among those she knew not. For one terrifying moment, she envisioned a future of being shuttled from castle to court to manor, forgotten by Beren and yet not free to return to Brandeth. Gripped by fear, she lashed out. "Why would I want to be dragged about like a useless appendage?" she asked.

Beren's eyes narrowed. "I thought—" he began, then he paused, as if to consider his words. "Surely you cannot think yourself useless! I wish for your companionship and advice. And though I have done a lot of traveling, I hope to be able to settle down now that I am married, with lands of my own."

"At your demesne," Guenivere said dully. When Beren

nodded, she lifted her chin. "That was not part of our bargain."

"Neither was last night!" Beren answered. "Yet you cannot deny what happened between us."

"I see," Guenivere said, her voice cool, though her insides seemed to roll and pitch with a hot mixture of shame and loss and anger. "Am I to be so grateful to receive your attentions at this late date that I am willing to be wrested from my home, now and forever?"

Beren blinked, as if she had struck him, and his expression hardened into the threatening knight he had first appeared upon his return. But Guenivere refused to be intimidated. "Perhaps you have forgotten our conversation upon your arrival," she said, as calmly as she could muster. "But I married you so that I could remain here and hold Brandeth for my own."

If he had looked dangerous before, Beren now appeared positively lethal, his dark brows lowered, his beautiful mouth tight, and his strong body taut. "And that is it? That is the only reason?" he demanded.

"Can you think of another?" Guenivere countered.

For a long moment, they stared at each other in silent challenge. Then Beren loosed a harsh breath. "Nay," he said, and he turned on his heel and stalked out.

Beren's rage had taken him as far as he could lead his men during what remained of the daylight hours, but a night spent alone in the cold comfort of a cheerless abbey had tempered his fury and hurt. And now, riding out once more across the hills toward his own lands, Beren had cause to consider his rash departure.

What had happened? Upon waking from the most glorious night of his life, Beren had sensed that all was not well with his wife, but all had not been well with himself either. And he had chosen to struggle with old demons along the cliffs, rather than talk with her. Returning euphoric from that foray, all his past doubts banished, Beren had not stopped to wonder what Guenivere was thinking. Yet all the confidence in the world mattered little if she still thought him unworthy.

The notion angered him, even now, and he urged his mount forward. But was it anger—or pride—that sent him on? Beren slowed his pace as he sought an honest answer, and he well remembered the harsh prick of her words. Yet he could hardly hold himself blameless. Just because he had conquered his fears, did not mean that all in his life, especially his newly minted marriage, would be well. He had not taken the time to discuss anything with Guenivere, let alone the long years of their parting. During their night together, she had accused him of betraying her faith. Did he expect one night of passion to heal all wounds and cure all ills?

Beren shook his head at his own folly. Granted, he had been rushed because of the summons, his mind wandering to his own demesne and potential troubles awaiting him there. But in doing so, he had invested little time in that which had come to mean the most to him: his union with Guenivere. How could he have been so careless?

Not only had he failed to probe her own feelings, but he had neglected to mention his own as well. In their last, bitter meeting, he had not told her of the doubts that had long kept him from her, or of the love that swelled within him now, eager and constant. *Until tested.*

Frowning, Beren admitted that her cool dismissal of his plans had hurt his still-tender pride. But it was that foolish vanity that had kept him away before. Had he learned nothing? She had been cold at their parting, but what of the night before when she had melted in his arms, when she had cried for what might have been between them?

Beren remembered those moments, and his uncertainty grew. Would he abandon his marriage over a few sharp words? Would he return to his own lands and find that pressing business always kept him from going to face his wife? He had sworn not to be ruled by old doubts, so why was he heading away from Brandeth? Was it duty or despair that moved him?

All his life, Guenivere had been the force that drove him onward, the greatest height for which he aspired, the dream that he held close. And now that all was within his reach, would he throw it all away without at least attempting to make things right? His mouth tightening with determination, Beren held up his hand and called to his men. He had no idea what pressing problems called to him from his demesne, but they would have to wait.

He had more important things to do.

six
⋟

Guenivere stood at the window of the solar, looking out into the distance, though she wasn't sure what she sought in the windswept heights. She certainly didn't expect to see Beren. He had been gone already a day and a night and nearly another day, yet Guenivere felt her sense of loss growing, not decreasing.

Drawing a deep breath, she searched for the composure that had stood her so well these last few years, but she no longer seemed able to muster it. Unable to face the people she had always coveted as her own, Guenivere kept to the solar, disdaining all company. Was it any wonder she felt so sad and alone? But even as she would delude herself, Guenivere knew it was not Alice or any other resident of Brandeth for whom she pined.

She could not understand the return of the old, familiar feeling of missing Beren when this time she had wanted him to be gone about his business, leaving her free to run her father's keep. Yet, somehow her heritage no longer seemed as important as it once had. Yes, Brandeth was important to her, but without her father, she had no one here to tend, to love and cherish. If only she had a family of her own! But 'twas too late for that, Guenivere thought bitterly, unless Beren's seed had taken root.

Gingerly, she touched her stomach, hoping against hope that she might carry his child, and a flush rose in her cheeks as a certain joy dispelled her gloom. But then what? Would she raise the babe alone? Guenivere's heart pounded out a denial, but what other choice had she left herself?

And if there was no child?

Suddenly, Guenivere couldn't bear to think of the long, lonely years ahead, so different from what she had planned with cool calculation. She had thought herself independent, needing no one let alone a man to order her about. She had summoned Beren only in a desperate effort to save her lands and the way of life she had known. At least, that is what she had told herself. Now, Guenivere wondered if something else hadn't prompted her decision.

Perhaps, in her grief at her father's passing, she had reached out blindly to the only other person she had ever loved. And he had come, reluctantly at first, but determined to take her to wife in good faith. Yet, instead of embracing this new chance for happiness, Guenivere had turned away, unwilling to risk her heart again.

Or so she had told herself. Lifting a hand to her mouth, Guenivere made a low sound of anguish as she recognized the truth, at last. Despite all her claims to the contrary, her heart was already engaged. It had been since the first time she had seen Beren the boy, and not all the years since or their long separation had diminished her feelings.

"Are you well, lady?" The sound of a voice made her turn in startlement, for so sunk in her gloom had she been that Guenivere had not heard anyone enter the chamber. For one wild moment, she thought to see the subject of her thoughts, Beren, but it was only one of the knights of the keep, eyeing her in question.

Irritated by the intrusion, Guenivere straightened and tried to recover her poise, though she knew her eyes were damp. "What is it, Sir Crispin?" she asked as she recognized the older knight. He had no love of those of ignoble birth who sought to better themselves at his craft, including Beren, and Guenivere wondered if he were celebrating her husband's departure. At the thought, a tear loosed and slipped down her cheek.

"My lady! You are not well," Crispin said, looking alarmed. "Please sit down, I will call one of your handmaidens."

Crispin had good cause to be anxious, Guenivere thought, for ever she had hidden her yearning and her grief from her people, unknowingly distancing herself from them as well. Perhaps it was time to rejoin humanity. "Nay. Do not call the ladies to me, for they can do naught for what ails me. No one can. Have you not heard, Sir Crispin?" Guenivere asked. "My husband has gone away."

Her words seemed to stun him beyond speech. She might have laughed had her heart been less heavy.

"M-my lady, I do not understand. I thought this marriage of yours 'twas simply an alliance born of necessity—and one beneath you, as well," Crispin said, stiffly.

"I forgive your confusion, for I did claim to act for my people, when selfishly, I wanted Beren back and used whatever means necessary to bring him here," Guenivere said. There, she had admitted her hidden purpose aloud, and felt the better for it. Perhaps now she ought to tell Beren himself.

Sir Crispin's look of bewilderment gave way to a fierce expression. "He has dazzled you, lady, with his new title and power, but those are the things he values. He left you behind swiftly enough to increase them!"

Perhaps her plain speaking had encouraged his own, or his feelings for Beren had overcome his judgment, but Guenivere could not understand Crispin's sudden agitation. Nor could she let him continue in his mistaken belief that Beren had abandoned her once more. "And yet, I could have gone with him, as he wished me to," she said.

Sir Crispin appeared even more stunned. "My lady! Your place is here, not off with some upstart urchin who would set you aside for his own advancement."

Guenivere lifted her brows at this open insult of her husband, and more subtly of herself. "You would make my decisions for me now?" she asked.

Crispin looked uncomfortable but determined. "I know only that Berenger Brewere is naught but an orphan of lowly birth, a brewer's brat unfit to kiss the hem of your gown!"

"You forget yourself, Sir Knight!" Guenivere said, coolly. "I will hear no slander against my husband."

Crispin sent her a dark look, his face grim. "A husband

who is gone, never to return, for thus have I proven his
fealty!"

At Crispin's words Guenivere went cold. She had sensed
something was not right in his manner and speech, but had
blamed his old rancor against Beren. Now, she remembered
the strangeness of the summons that Beren received, including her suspicion that the message was not real. And she wondered whether Crispin had been the one to manufacture it.

"And just how did you prove Beren's lack? Did you have
something to do with the urgent call back to his lands?"
Guenivere asked.

Crispin's face grew ruddy, but he did not demure. "I will
not lie to you, lady. I had another feign the message that called
him away. But I did it for you, lest you think he has changed,
for he has not."

"You appear privy to much of my husband's mind. You
know him well then?" Guenivere asked, her tone venomous.
Here was a bitter discovery indeed, for she and Beren had
enough difficulties, without suffering the malicious interfer-
ence of another.

"I know him, yes, for what he is, a nameless riffraff who
sought always to take the place of his betters!"

"And think you I care for your opinion?" Guenivere asked.

Crispin flushed, but made no apology. "Who else would
save you from yourself? Berate me if you will, but I could not
stand to see you debase yourself again for that whoreson, who
so easily forgot you and the lord who raised him up! Your father would—"

Guenivere stopped his speech with her own. "He would
have summoned Beren back long ago, had I allowed him, but
I let my foolish pride stand in the way of happiness. And now
I am suffering for the sake of your ill-placed vanity, as well,
when I should not."

"But—"

Guenivere cut him off with an imperious wave of her hand.
"Bid a train be readied for me, so I might go to my husband
and beg his forgiveness for my behavior and your own!"

Crispin looked as though he would keel over from
apoplexy, but Guenivere tendered him no sympathy. Perhaps,
she and Beren could have worked out their problems had they

been given more time to do so, time they would have had, if this knight had not taken it upon himself to challenge their fate. Now, she could only try to make amends for even more mistakes. For, if Beren returned to his lands only to find the message was false, he would lay the blame at her feet.

"Surely, you cannot mean to leave at this hour?" Crispin asked. "Perhaps, I acted out of hand, but do not endanger yourself, my lady, I beg you." Now, at least, the old knight seemed sincere, and Guenivere stole a glance out the window where the sun was sinking low, making travel unwise.

"Tomorrow then," she said, although she despised the delay. "But send out a messenger at once to tell Sir Brewere of my coming. Unless you cannot be trusted to do my bidding?" Guenivere asked the question coldly, letting the old knight see her displeasure. He deserved far worse for his treachery, but she would leave his fate up to Sir Berenger Brewere, Lord of Brandeth.

"By your command, my lady," Crispin said, bowing low, though stiffly.

"For now," Guenivere said.

𝔍t was late by the time Beren reached Brandeth. He had to rouse a sleepy guard at the gate, who sent them through with both surprise and welcome. Would that he would receive the same, or better, from his lady, Beren thought. But whatever Guenivere's greeting, he was not leaving until all was settled between them, one way or another, and all that needed to be spoken was said, he decided grimly.

Assuming that her door was barred for the night, as well it should be, Beren again walked through the bailey to look up at her window. He had no intention of entreating her through a wooden barrier, so once more, he climbed the stone face, familiar now, and by the time he reached the opening, he was flush with the exhilaration of his ascent. Lifting himself up and over, he dropped to the floor inside her chamber.

This time, she was not expecting him, so she was abed. The memories of the night they had spent there washed over Beren, firing his blood and firming his resolve. Without hesitation, he pulled back the curtains and beheld her lying there, and her name escaped his lips like a prayer.

Although he had practiced his speech all during the ride back to Brandeth, the simple sight of Guenivere robbed Beren of his breath. He stood there, silent and staring, as she opened her eyes. For a long moment, they gazed upon one another. Finally, Beren forced his lips to move, but before he could utter a word, his wife flew into his arms.

Automatically, he drew her close, so startled by this unexpected response that he nearly wept against the silk of her hair. It seemed to Beren that the warmth of her greeting drove away a chill that had been lying on his heart for years beyond count.

"Beren! How came you here? Did you get my message?" she asked, raising her head to look into his face.

Beren shook his head. "Nay, I received no summons, except that of my own desire." He lifted his hands to her shoulders, holding her there as he watched her, willing her to see that he spoke the truth.

"I can't let you go, not after living my dream—if only for a night," Beren admitted. "You are all I ever hoped for, Guenivere, all I ever wanted, the sole reason for my striving and for any success I have had. And if you will accept me as your husband, now and always, I will stay here with you and give up my own lands, if I must, for they are nothing without you. My home is wherever you are."

Guenivere lifted her head to speak, but Beren went on, before he lost his courage. "I'm not good at saying things, else I would have told you all this before. In truth, though I have loved you since our first meeting as children, I was afraid to return for you, for fear that you would refuse me, that my ignoble blood made me unworthy."

Beren paused to take a deep breath, before eyeing her directly. "No matter how much you might wish it, I am not Parzival."

"Oh, Beren," Guenivere whispered. "I always accepted you as you are. 'Twas *you* who would not. 'Twas you who valued knighthood and money and lands, not I. And though I admit to a young girl's fascination with the romances, I did not want to marry any of those heroes. Nor did I seek to make you into one. I only wished you to see that you could do anything with your life that you wished, and you did, succeeding beyond imagining!"

Smiling tenderly, Guenivere lifted her hands to cup his face, as if to make him listen to her, as well. "Forgive me for letting you go away, but I was afraid, too, of risking my heart. 'Twas not until you left that I realized I had never stopped loving you. But then and now, I wanted only you, the real you, the boy I knew and the man he became, not some fanciful hero."

Beren felt as if the weight of the world had slipped from his shoulders, leaving him no longer bound to the earth—like a man who has climbed the highest heights. He nearly threw back his head and laughed with the pure pleasure of this triumph, greater than all others.

" 'Tis glad I am to hear you say so, for I am no hero at all, real or imagined. Although I tried to emulate your ideal, I have fallen sadly short, I am afraid. I never found the Grail or a lost father or even a royal uncle," Beren said, with a crooked smile.

"But I discovered one thing," he added, taking her hands in his. "That all the adventures and achievements in the world are worth little without love. Those long years without you were but half living, and I am thankful to have made my way home at last."

Guenivere kissed him then, a sweet, gentle communion that promised far more. "Despite all your protestations to the contrary, you would have done Parzival proud," she said. "Indeed, there is only one thing missing from this happy ending, my lord."

"What is that?" Beren asked, a bit warily.

"We have no twin sons to awaken and welcome you home," she said, referring once more to her favorite story. But Beren did not mind the comparison, for his heart was too full. He grinned.

"We'll work on that," he promised.

And so they did.

The
Siege

✝

Glynnis Campbell

For
Ma and Pa Campbell,
who always manage
to find a candle in the dark

one

❧

"**H**urry, my lady! This way!"

"God's blood!" Hilaire's feet slipped on the slimy steps as she scrambled down the dark, dank passageway, following the bobbling firebrand her maidservant held aloft.

Even here, deep beneath the keep, she heard the ominous pounding of the battering ram shuddering the wooden gates and ancient stone walls of the castle. Hastily, she made the sign of the cross. What she attempted was perilous, but what would become of her if she remained behind was far more terrifying. This way, God willing, if she didn't trip and break her neck along the way, she'd slip out of the tunnel on the other side of the curtain wall and be halfway through the forest by the time the enemy splintered the door to the inner bailey.

"Please, my lady!" entreated Martha, the servant. "Will you not leave the cursed thing behind? In another moment . . ."

The thudding ceased abruptly, heralding the devastation of the outermost gates of the barbican, the first line of defense, and elicited a fretful squeak from the maid. But Hilaire only clutched her small harp closer. She'd be damned if she'd leave the precious instrument behind. After all, she was abandoning everything else—her father, her home, her pet falcon.

"Just go," she said tightly, shivering in the chill air and prodding the maid forward.

Ahead the passage narrowed and the stone steps ran out, becoming less a corridor and more a burrow. Hilaire's pulse raced, and her legs threatened mutiny. She hated the dark, and close spaces in particular. Even the prospect of the garde-robe's confines at night made her heart flutter so that she'd oft languish in misery till morning. This place, it smelled of mildew and decay, like a grave. She dared not imagine the rats and beetles and worms slithering in the clammy chinks of moldering rock.

Swallowing hard to dislodge the lump of terror in her throat, she forced one foot in front of the other.

In all her seventeen years, no one had had need to make use of the secret passageway excavated more than a century past by her ancestors, who'd lived in times of even more ubiquitous wars.

Even now, the attack raging above them wasn't a true bat-tle. It had started as a negotiation—a simple demand met with a blunt refusal. But their enemy had not accepted that refusal. He'd lost his patience, and now what began as a siege had become an assault severe enough to warrant drastic counter-measures.

"Hist!" Hilaire held up a hand, halting Martha. "Did you hear that?"

The torchlight flickered across the servant's pinched fea-tures as she strained her ears. "What, my lady?"

Hilaire's brow creased in worry. She thought she'd heard . . . But perhaps it was only her bones creaking with cold or her knees rattling with fright. "'Tis naught. Go on."

The tunnel angled sharply downward as it passed under-neath the curtain wall, and Hilaire shuddered. Creeping down the incline was like descending into a cold hell.

"Mind the . . ." Martha warned, too late.

Hilaire's toe caught on a tree root. She stumbled and fell hard, landing on both knees in the soil. Her harp struck a dis-cordant *twang* as she caught herself on one hand, biting her lip as tears filled her eyes.

"Oh, my lady! Are you hurt?"

"Nay," she snapped, and she wasn't, not truly. Her nubby woolen skirts had taken the brunt of the fall, and her palm was only bruised. But all at once, the weight of her circumstances and the depth of her dread hit her like a hard slap across the face. Here she knelt like a frightened wretch in the cold, dank mud, with naught but her harp, the peasant clothes on her back, and a frightened servant, running away from home and a future she couldn't bear to face. How had she come to such a coil?

'Twas her father's fault, she thought sulkily, wiping away a rogue tear. He should have betrothed her to someone sooner, ere the King had the chance to arrange her marriage. She would have wed anyone her father named—bandy-legged Lord Iwain, somber Sir Robert, even Lord Leonis, who stuttered and walked with a limp—anyone but the monster the King had chosen for her.

People spoke of The Black Gryphon in whispers, for fear that uttering his name might call his curse upon them. His countenance was dark with the shadow of damnation, they claimed, hair as black as char, eyes as deep as a chasm. He never smiled, seldom spoke, and when he did, it was in a low growl more akin to an animal than a man.

Once the pennant of the Gryphon had flown proud, its master imbued with the noble qualities of that creature, the lion's strength and the eagle's courage. Once he'd been a warrior of great renown. But that was long ago. Now he need only pierce a man's eyes with his devil's gaze to send him cowering to his knees. And so men said the Gryphon had become the most horrible of beasts, for he was as ferocious as the lion and as ruthless as the eagle.

Still, naught was as terrible as the curse he lay upon women. To them he brought death. Three wives he'd already lain in the grave, one beside her young daughter, one with a babe still in her belly. Three wives, and not one had borne him a son upon whom to bestow his title.

A woman would have to be mad to wed him.

And, by blessed Mary, Hilaire was not mad.

Wiping her sniffles with the back of her hand, she struggled to her feet with Martha's assistance, and set out with renewed determination.

They'd come almost to the lowest point in the passageway, where the curtain wall was anchored and where, thankfully, the tunnel once more ascended, when she heard it again, the sinister creaking of mortar and stone.

"Let me," she said, taking the firebrand in her free hand and squeezing past the servant to investigate.

The sound came from directly above her now. She turned back for an instant to see if Martha could hear it as well.

Then, with an unholy crack, the sky fell.

Ryance wiped his damp brow with the back of his sleeve and stabbed at the earth again with his spade, deepening the tunnel. He wondered for the hundredth time if he was doing the right thing. A bloody siege, for God's sake!

He'd known it was foolish to come. All his instincts told him this wedding was not to be. But the King had insisted. The Black Gryphon must have an heir, he'd said, and he'd handpicked the mother of that heir himself. Ryance heaved a weary sigh. He wished to God the King had chosen another.

He clamped his mouth into a grim line and shoveled the dirt aside. There were no others. No woman in her right mind would wed a man like him.

Clenching his jaw, he gouged another wound into the soil and cast the dirt carelessly over his shoulder—showering the captain of his knights, arriving behind him, with soil.

"God's blood!" Campbell swore, spitting dirt from his mouth. "There ye are! I've been lookin' high and low for ye, m'lord! What the devil d'ye think ye're doin'?"

"Begone!" Ryance snarled. He didn't need the nosy Scotsman interfering in his affairs,

"Why, ye're sappin' the castle," Campbell said in wonder, standing his ground. "Ye can't undermine the wall, m'lord, not by yerself."

"Get out, I said."

"Are ye daft? There's naught to shore it up. Ye haven't got the proper braces," Campbell insisted. "'Tis death to linger here!"

Ryance didn't answer his man, only turned and continued shoveling.

Campbell cursed again. "At least give *me* the spade then. *I* don't have several hundred vassals I'm beholdin' to."

"Nay!" Ryance barked over his shoulder, making the torch flicker. "The lady's to be *my* wife. 'Tis *my* risk."

He kept digging, jabbing at the soil with renewed resolve, punishing the earth for coming between him and his prize.

"But I came to tell ye the barbican's fallen," Campbell said. "Once we penetrate the curtain wall . . ."

"Nay! I want the castle unharmed. Delay the attack. Just maintain the siege, keep his men distracted."

"But, m'lord, we can easily take the castle by force."

"And slay my bride's kin?" He tossed the spade aside, and dug a small boulder from the embankment with his hands. "Nay. 'Tis far easier to repair a breach in the wall."

"Then let me call the sappers here. They'll put up decent props, and the work'll go much faster with . . ."

"Nay!" Ryance snapped, casting the stone away. "'Tis a matter for stealth, not force."

Campbell blew out an exasperated breath. "Ye know, m'lord," he said, his voice as bitter as moldy ale, "if I didna ken ye better, I'd say ye were itchin' to kiss death's arse."

Then, as if his man's words invoked some black doom, the air was suddenly severed by an ominous crack. Silt rained down over Ryance's head, extinguishing the candlelight. An enormous slide of rock and earth pelted him, muting Campbell's shouts and utterly blotting out the night sky behind him.

Devil's thunder split the air. Hilaire screamed, but the sound was lost as a violent, crashing deluge of ragged stone and fetid soil sealed the tunnel. Her maid vanished from sight.

Dust filled her nose and mouth, clogging her throat, choking her, and most horrifying of all, smothering the flame of her torch. A brutal impact knocked her forward and sent her sprawling atop her harp. Shards of rock pummeled her back like sharp-sided hail. Then a heavy chunk of stone smashed her hand, and she shrieked in agony.

The awful clamor seemed to go on forever, at last diminishing from a roar to a rustle as the boulders came to rest and pebbles continued to trickle down all around her. But as horrible as the noise was, it was not half as terrifying as the deadly silence that followed.

She struggled to hear anything, anything at all—her maid, a rat, the echo of the battering ram—but her own frantic whimpers and the loud rushing of her pulse were the only sounds remaining.

The world had turned absolutely black, not the black of a starless night nor the black of the dungeon, not even the black of the close garderobe that set her heart to hammering, but a black so heavy, so tangible, it wrapped like a shroud about her.

She was afraid to get up, afraid she'd find the space around her had shrunk to the size of a coffin. Panic rattled the cage of her mind, and a whimper lodged in her throat. She sucked what breath she could into her lungs, but it was impossibly thin. Lord, she dared not succumb to terror or she'd be lost. She had to get up.

The harp dug painfully into her stomach, and her hand throbbed where it was caught beneath the rock. The slimy warmth of blood oozed between her crushed fingers. She was trapped.

Nay, she thought. *Nay.* Biting her lip to quiet its quivering, she brought her knees up under her. Scrabbling through the rubble, she managed to dig away the debris and finally pried the heavy stone up enough to free her hand. With a sob, she cradled the injured member to her breast.

But there was no time to cry over her hurts. She had to find a way out. *There* must *be a way out,* she told herself, willing her breath to slow. She need only find the other end of the tunnel.

Her pulse pounding in her temples, she groped the walls with her good hand, looking for the exit, praying for a breach. She hobbled around the cave, stumbling, fumbling, searching. But as she frantically circled the tiny enclosure again and again, she discovered the horrible truth. The falling earth had sealed both sides of the tunnel.

Blessed Jesu—she was buried alive!

Breathless with panic, a scream building in the back of her throat, she retrieved her harp, clutching it to her breast like a drowning man clinging to a timber.

Her first cries were weak and thready, hoarse with fear, but desperation soon moved her to screech for help at the top of her lungs.

* * *

Ryance sat stunned. He should be dead. Enough debris had fallen around him to fill a decent-sized moat. But, somehow, God in his infinite mercy, or infinite irony, had spared him a quick death.

Oh, he'd still die. There was no doubt about that. He'd search every crevice of his new dungeon with the thoroughness of a captive plotting escape from The Tower, but it would be of no avail. For when The Black Gryphon set about doing a thing, he did it properly. The undermining had worked brilliantly. The castle's curtain wall had collapsed, if prematurely, just as planned. And now he was imprisoned by his own hand under tons of rock and rubble. It was quite a feat of engineering. By the complete lack of light, he was certain not even a chink remained for the wind to blow through.

Campbell, the only one who knew where he was, had probably been buried in the collapse, God rest his poor soul. Even if by some miracle his captain lived, Ryance would suffocate by the time the man could dig through the massive wall of granite.

Meanwhile, Ryance would have time to dwell on his sins, to relive all the ugly passages of his life.

A small part of him, deep inside, felt a twisted sort of satisfaction. This, after all, was the end he deserved. Now, at long last, he would suffer for his crimes and do penance for the innocent lives he'd destroyed.

And the young woman who waited within the castle walls to be his bride, whose father had stubbornly refused to surrender his maiden daughter in sacrifice to The Black Gryphon, could stop wringing her hands in terror, for the monster who was her betrothed would be dead a few hours hence.

Ryance raised his hand to his forehead. His fingers came back slick with blood. He felt the sting of several scrapes and gashes along his bared forearms. All his bones seemed intact, though he was certain he'd be bruised on the morrow. He chuckled bleakly. Bruised! He'd be *dead* on the morrow.

His laugh turned to coughing as the dust settled invisibly around him in the pitch black. Perhaps Campbell was right about him. Perhaps he *had* been courting death. Forsooth, the idea of dying brought naught but relief. No more would he be haunted by the images of his loved ones' lifeless bodies. No more would men cower as he passed, crossing themselves before him, making the sign of the devil behind his back. Once he paid the debt of his soul, he'd be free.

He gathered dusty saliva in his mouth and spit it onto the ground. The thirst would be the worst of it, he supposed. Aside from that, once the air ran out, he'd likely just drift off to sleep. No more worries, no more responsibilities, no more . . . innocents to harm.

He crossed his battered arms over his chest, closed his eyes against the black oblivion, and gave up the fight, settling back against the jagged rock that would mark his grave.

The repose of eternity lasted exactly five measured breaths. And then he heard it, faint at first, like the chirp of a cricket. He opened one eye, as if it would make any difference in the utter dark. It came again, louder this time, from beyond the inner wall of the tunnel. He opened the other eye. It was probably just a mouse, injured in the collapse. He hoped it would die soon. He wanted his last moments on Earth to be peaceful.

He frowned, squirmed into a more relatively comfortable position, and closed his eyes tighter.

There it came again. His eyes flew open. It was no cricket, no mouse. There was something distinctly . . . human about the cry. And it sounded hopelessly forlorn.

He swallowed. When the pathetic wail came again, it sent a shudder through him like a battering ram pounding at his heart. There was no mistake. That voice belonged to a woman.

two
❧

It hardly seemed fair. Ryance had given up his joust with dogged destiny. He'd resigned himself to dying, slipping away in this quiet tomb with naught but his own thoughts, fading from the wretched world on a serene and silent breath.

But it was not to be. That voice called to him, needed him. And stronger than his desire to escape into oblivion was his cursed sense of honor. He was a knight. He'd taken certain oaths, sworn to live by certain morals. And paramount was the vow to protect and defend those creatures weaker than he.

Muttering a mild oath, he pushed himself up from the rubble and fumbled his way toward the source of the noise. It was here, from the place he'd been digging before, a patch of bare earth clear of stones. He pressed his ear to the dirt, listening. The despondent cry came again.

He pulled his head back in wonder. As unbelievable as it seemed, there was someone beyond the innermost side of the tunnel. For one mad moment, he wondered if it was the voice of some angel of the underworld, calling him to Hades.

He groped about, searching for his spade, till he remembered he'd tossed it aside before the avalanche. He'd have to use something else then. His fingers clambered over the debris until he located a honed shard of rock. Hefting it in his hand, he began jabbing determinedly at the soil. While her cries continued, then hopelessly diminished, his efforts at enlarging the hole in the earth were about as effective as a rat gnawing through iron.

He cast the rock aside. The wailing had ceased. God's breath—had she fainted? Was she dead? His heart in his throat, he hurled his body against the tunnel, cupped his hands around his mouth, and shouted at the top of his lungs.

"Hold on!"

Hilaire sat bolt upright, digging her fingers into the carved wood of her harp, every sense strained. Sweet Mary—was that a voice? Or was it only a delusion, part of the panic that had reduced her to this quivering mass? She bit her lip, trying to still her sobs so she could hear better.

And then, blessedly, it came again. Relief burst out of her in a sound that was half laugh, half cry.

Someone was adjacent to the passageway. It didn't seem possible. She was deep underground, and as far as she knew, only one tunnel led from the castle. But possible or no, the muffled voice on the other side of the dirt embankment was real, and it sounded sweeter to her than the strings of her beloved harp.

"Here!" she cried. "I'm here!"

Still clinging to the harp, she dragged herself toward the source of the voice and pressed her cheek against the damp earthen wall.

He called out again, and she answered. Then she set aside her instrument and with her good hand, clawed at the dirt like a shrewmouse. The task was difficult. The tunnel was sunk deep in the bowels of the earth. The soil was more rock than mud. She scraped the pads of her fingers and snapped off two of her nails.

But he kept calling to her, encouraging her, and she continued to wear away at the wall till she heard digging on the other side and felt it give beneath her hand. Breathless with triumph, she scrabbled at the dirt, enlarging the gap inch by inch. Finally, with a ragged sob of victory, she reached through the makeshift burrow to clasp a miracle. A human hand.

A fresh fount of grateful tears squeezed from her eyes and rolled down her cheeks, and she sobbed shamelessly as warm, strong fingers closed around hers.

He didn't speak for a long while, only held on to her, as if he transferred his strength into her, sustaining her. She neither knew nor cared who he was, only that he was another human being in the darkness.

The maiden's hand felt small in his, like a child's, warm and soft and helpless. He'd forgotten how pleasant the touch of a woman was. His own hand was coarse and calloused, no doubt abrasive to her delicate skin, yet she made no attempt to withdraw. On the contrary, it seemed as if she might never release him. His throat thickened at the thought.

She wouldn't have clung to him so if she'd known who he was. That much was certain. But at the moment, she clutched his hand like her life depended upon it. Or her sanity. From her frenzied sobbing and the sweaty trembling of her fingers, she seemed but a whisper away from complete madness.

He called to her through the gap. "Are you hurt?"

"My ha—" she began, then shakily amended her reply. "I'll be fine. Only please . . . get me out of here."

She said the last in a rush, and he heard the fear beneath her polite request. Her voice was light and sweet, yet never had chivalry called to him quite so powerfully.

Then his heart sank.

Get me out of here, she'd said.

Satan's horns—she must be trapped as well. And if her prison proved half as impenetrable as his, all his knightly vows, all his heroic efforts, and all his noble intentions couldn't save her.

He cursed silently. It was a foolish notion anyway. What made him think he could save the wench? His days of rescuing damsels in distress were long over. Now everything he touched he tainted with death.

The girl's fingers tensed subtly within his palm, as if she sensed his unease.

"You *have* come to rescue me, haven't you?" she ventured.

She sounded so innocent, so vulnerable. He gave her hand a gentle squeeze.

"Of course," he lied, praying he'd not live to regret his words. His mouth curved into a rueful grimace at the thought.

He'd likely not live at all. Even if by some miracle he found a way out, he was the last man on earth she should count upon to save her. Still, he was obliged to try.

It was difficult to extract his fingers from hers. She was very reluctant to let go of him. But giving her hand a final clasp of sustenance, he began scrabbling again at the soil. She scraped at her side of the hole as well until the gap slowly grew enough to allow him snug passage through.

"Back away," he told her. "I'll come through."

His shoulders scraped against the rough walls as he squeezed through and foundered onto the rocky ground like a newborn foal.

"Are you all right?" she asked.

Her fingers brushed across him as she bent near, making accidental contact with his shoulder, his chest, perilously high on his thigh. His breath caught. When was the last time a woman touched him there? His nostrils flared for an instant in pained remembrance before her hand slipped away again.

"I'm fine," he croaked, shuffling into a crouch.

The situation looked bleak. The air seemed just as dense and black on her side of the wall. Still, he felt compelled to search every inch for chinks in the armor of their prison.

"Where is your . . . Do you not have a torch?" she asked. The request was subtly colored by trepidation.

"Nay."

Women always feared the dark. He wondered why. He found the dark to be a great friend—so comforting, so concealing.

He explored the cavern slowly, meticulously, but alas, the walls yielded no promise. Those surfaces that weren't as impenetrable as a cured boar's hide were plated in the rocky refuse of the deluge. He found no weaknesses.

"M-may we go now, sir?"

She sounded young. He wondered how old she was. Too young to die, that was certain. Probably no older than his last wife had been when . . .

"Sir?"

A hint of bewilderment touched her words, and he knew he'd not be able to shield her long from the truth. He only hoped she'd not fall prey to a feminine fit of weeping when he divulged their situation to her.

He carefully groped his way toward her, contacting first her long, soft hair. It hung loose, caressing his questing fingers like a lady's fine silk veil. But by the rough fabric of her kirtle sleeve, he determined the girl must be a commoner. He gripped her gently but firmly by the arms. She felt so small, so fragile in his grasp, like a dove. Lord, such a delicate woman might be easily broken. He ran his tongue uneasily across his lower lip.

"There is no . . ." he began, clearing his throat. "There is no way out."

She stiffened beneath his hands, but to her credit, made not a peep of despair.

"I see." Her voice was scarcely a whisper. A long silence ensued, violated only by her shuddering breath. Finally she found her voice. "Are we . . . are we going to die?"

Her words, so guileless, so brittle, cut him like the edge of a blade. A fierce longing to protect her welled up suddenly inside of him. How could he burden an innocent damsel with such an awful truth? How could he bring such suffering to her?

In good faith, he could not.

So he lied. "Nay," he said, giving her arms a reassuring squeeze and praying she couldn't detect the feigned levity of his voice. "Never fear."

Hilaire bit down on her lip. She wouldn't cry. No matter what happened, she wouldn't cry. This man, whoever he was, was doing his best to comfort her, even if he was a poor liar. She'd not disappoint him by blubbering like a child. She'd be brave.

Still, when she opened her eyes to all that smothering black, it was all she could do not to scream in horror. In her mind's eye, the walls began to shrink, squeezing her lungs until she could draw no breath. She gasped in the stale air, wheezing faster and faster, as she fought the suffocating sensation. Not enough air. Not . . . enough . . . air.

"Easy," the man ordered. "Slow down."

But she couldn't. If she stopped breathing, she'd die. Like a drowning animal, she clawed at him in desperation, twining her fists in the folds of his tabard, hanging on for dear life.

He gave her a little shake. "Slow down. You'll faint. Breathe with me."

"I . . . I . . . can't . . ." The sound was no more than a whispery squeak. No air. No air. She scrabbled at his chest.

He tightened his grip on her, almost to the point of pain, shocking her from her panic, and barked the ferocious command inches from her face. "Breathe with me. In!"

He rasped in a breath, and she battled to match his rhythm.

"Out!" The breath shuddered out of her.

"In!" She sucked in another draught of air.

"Out!" She released her breath.

"In!" They drew in a loud gasp together.

"Out!" Her breath escaped on a long sigh.

Then they were breathing together, deeply, calmly, and Hilaire felt her lungs gradually expand to take in all the air she required. For the moment at least, her fears were eased.

"You see? There's plenty of air," he told her.

Suddenly ashamed of her panic, she slowly untangled her fingers from the man's tabard. "I'm sorry. I . . ."

"Don't be." The man ran his thumb soothingly over her arm, as if to apologize for his harshness. For the first time, she noticed the soft clink of chain mail and felt the rigid contour of his hauberk beneath her hands. She wondered who he was.

"Thank you, Sir . . ."

He didn't enlighten her. Who was he? Who was her savior?

His hands were rough, the hands of a man accustomed to labor or warfare, as coarse and rugged as his voice, and yet, like his voice, possessing gentleness and warmth. He smelled of earth and iron and leather, and though she could discern neither his age nor his bearing, he exuded strength and comfort enough to assuage her fears.

"You *are* a knight?"

"Aye," he grunted.

She wondered if she'd seen him before. Her father had so many knights, she honestly didn't know them all by name. But if this man somehow managed to get her out of this hellish grave, she'd embroider his name on every kirtle she owned and remember him in her every prayer.

The man released her arms, interrupting her thoughts. "What is this place? How came you here?"

She flushed, forgetting her own curiosity. The tunnel was a mild embarrassment to her, having been constructed exclusively for the immediate family's use and no other.

"'Tis an underground passageway," she admitted. "It leads from the keep to beyond the curtain wall."

"You were fleeing the castle?" he asked.

"Mm-hmm." Perhaps it was best not to elaborate. After all, she still traveled in disguise.

"Because of the attack?"

"Aye."

"Were you alone?"

There was no reason to incriminate Martha, God rest her poor soul. "Aye."

"No one knew of your flight?"

She bit her lip.

"Will anyone miss you?" he persisted.

"Nay. That is, I mean, aye!" She could ill afford to stretch the man's patience, but deception came uneasily to her.

"I must know," he said evenly, "if anyone will come looking for you."

"Oh." If he'd brought a torch, he'd have seen her cheeks redden in chagrin. "Oh, aye, I suppose they will. At least, I hope so."

Her father was not especially pleased with her. She'd begged and pleaded with him to resist the siege so she could escape. In the end, he'd buckled in the face of his only daughter's copious tears. But it had been a gruff farewell he'd bid her, replete with reminders of the King's wrath he invoked with his actions and the great risk he invited in countering the forces of The Black Gryphon.

Hilaire shivered. If only the ancient tunnel hadn't crumbled, she'd be safe now beyond the wall, far away from the tempers of unsympathetic men like the King, her father, and The Black Gryphon. Safe from the darkness that kept creeping in at the edges of her mind . . .

Nay, she must not think of that.

The man grunted as he struggled with something among the gravel. His low murmur interrupted her thoughts. "He wouldn't have harmed you, you know."

"Who?"

"The Black Gryphon."

She shuddered. "I fear you're mistaken, sir. I heard the blows he thrust upon the outer gate, even from here."

" 'Tis not his way to slaughter the defenseless."

She gave a nervous, humorless little laugh. "Then pray tell what happened to his last three wives and their children."

Cold silence met her query. Then the dull thud of rock upon earth startled her as the man began to pound away at the wall.

"Besides," she added defensively, " 'tis an easy thing for you to say. *You* are not betrothed to the monster."

The banging stopped as suddenly as it had started, and the man's sharp intake of breath seemed to suck all the air from the tunnel.

Hilaire clapped a hand over her mouth. She hadn't meant to reveal herself to him. If, by God's blessing, they somehow managed to escape, she'd intended to continue her merry way along the tunnel to freedom, just as originally planned. He'd think no more of her, just bid her good fortune and toddle on back to defending her father's castle, none the wiser.

But now—now she'd made a mess of things.

three

❧

"**Y**ou're . . . Hilaire?"

The musty air thickened, choking Ryance like smoke from a quickly doused fire.

She tried to deny it. "Nay, I . . ." Then her resigned sigh blew through his soul. "Aye, I am."

A dozen emotions roiled through his head—pain, relief, anger, joy, fear—like knights battling in a fierce melee.

Hilaire. His betrothed. This maiden with the sweet voice, the fragrant hair, the tender touch. This woman who feared the dark, clinging to him with the trust of a drowning kitten. Lord, what would it be like to wake up each morn to such a wife?

But it was only a fleeting fantasy. They were dying, he reminded himself. There would be no wedding. Besides, he thought bitterly, she did not want him. Forsooth, she'd risked her very life to escape The Black Gryphon.

It was another tragedy in a long line of tragedies. And it was stinging salt in his wounds that though he'd scarcely met the wench, he suspected he might grow to care for her in time.

Yet he was damned to destroy all he held dear. Curse the Fates! He'd probably killed her already. It was his fault they were trapped. It was because of him the tunnel had collapsed.

"You won't tell the others, will you?" she fretted, grabbing at his sleeve.

"The others?"

"My father's knights. Will you tell them I ran away?"

Ryance frowned. The little vixen had sneaked off, leaving

her poor father and his knights to defend the castle while she made her escape. It was a childish thing to do, and yet, she seemed little more than a child.

Not a child perhaps, but barely a woman. She'd probably never had her heart broken, never stolen a kiss, never bedded a man. God's bones—she was too young to die like this.

"Please, I beg you." Her hand fluttered about and came to rest upon the middle of his chest, too near his heart for comfort. "Do not tell them. Let me go in peace."

He closed his eyes, almost feeling the warmth of her hand through his tabard and mail and hauberk, and groaned inwardly. "My lady, if I could let you go, I would, but there is no . . ."

"Please do not say it again! There has to be a way out."

She sounded even younger and more vulnerable, and he suddenly regretted his thoughtless words. The lady still hovered on the brink of panic. The last thing she needed was a push over the edge.

He sighed heavily. Even if by some miracle he happened to find an escape, even if they managed to get out alive, Lady Hilaire was doomed. The King had commanded this union. She couldn't avoid marriage to Sir Ryance Alexander. And once wed, she'd not long avoid the curse of The Black Gryphon.

"There's always a way out," he told her instead, though he'd be damned if he could think of one at the moment. The stone of the fallen castle wall was too dense and tightly wedged to allow escape through the hole he'd originally tunneled out, and the earthen wall of her secret passage might as well be rock, so hardly compacted was it. Given the cramped quarters and the dearth of air, their sole hope was to pray for help.

"Mayhaps we can dig out," she ventured, "as we did before."

Ryance grimaced. They could not possibly dig their way out. He had naught to dig with, no spade, no adze, not even a sword, and their bare fingers would wear down to bloody stumps by the time they tunneled out even a yard of earth. It was impossible. But he hadn't the heart to let her know that.

"Aye, mayhaps," he agreed.

They might as well try. It would pass the time and prevent her from dwelling on the darkness. Certainly, it would keep his mind off his miserable past. And perhaps, after all, it was a stroke of God's mercy upon him that in his final hours he was closeted in shadow with a woman who knew him not and thus had no cause to fear him.

"Shall we try here?" she suggested. The optimism in her voice tugged at his heart.

"Where?"

Her hand wandered along the links of his mail until she grasped his wrist. Her fingers couldn't even close the distance around his forearm, but she tugged him along like an unruly child, finally placing his palm upon a section of damp earth.

He shook his head. If they dug there, they would wind up inside the keep—perhaps forty days hence.

"Do you not wish to escape the castle?" he asked. " 'Tis the opposite wall that leads to freedom."

"But if The Black Gryphon . . ." Her fingers curled atop his hand in fear. "You wouldn't understand." Her troubled whisper brushed his face, perfumed with the faint scent of mint. It was as intoxicating as mead. "If he finds me . . . if he discovers I was fleeing . . ."

He scarcely heard her words. The fragrance coming off of her hair, her skin—what was it? Rose? Lavender?

"I cannot wed him. I cannot. He is a brute. He is cruel and dangerous and evil. Have you not heard? He murdered his first three wives and . . ."

"I have heard!" The words tore from his throat with more force than he'd intended.

With a silent curse, he began jabbing at the soil, using his blunt fingers like daggers. She couldn't know what pain she dealt him with her careless remarks, how she tortured him.

"I'm sorry," she muttered, her voice a shade cooler, misunderstanding his outburst. "Mayhaps I should be stronger. You doubtless believe I should honor my vows as you honor yours. But I'm not a knight. I'm only a woman. I cannot bear the thought of throwing myself as sacrifice to a monster when . . ."

"He is not a mon—" To Ryance's mortification, his voice broke. Damn his weak spirit! He thought he'd become inured to such accusations, thought he'd grown scaly plate like an armored dragon and could no longer be wounded by mere words.

He was wrong. His heart plunged in misery, and his eyes stung, weary of aspersions. God's blood—would even his last moments on Earth be corrupted by his vile past?

"You know him," she whispered with a woman's insight. It was not a question, but an accusation. "You know The Black Gryphon."

"Nay." He clenched his jaw against foolish self-pity.

In a sense, he spoke the truth. Once he'd known him well. Once Ryance had been a noble young knight with a blade in his hand, the wind at his back, and adventure in his heart. Now The Black Gryphon was only a nightmare he was forced to live. Nay, he no longer knew the man who lived in the shell of his body.

"But I've known men like him," he said.

She was quiet for a long while. Then he heard her retreat. He should have expected as much. Even here in the dark, without the benefit of face or name or reputation, he was capable of inspiring fear in a woman.

"Who are you?" she finally asked.

"Nobody." He returned to clawing at the mud.

"Are you one of my father's men?"

"I'm a knight. That is all. I go where I'm called. I fight when I must."

She was stung by his curt answer. Even blind, he could sense her hurt. But it was good. It would keep her away from him, keep her safe from his evil, keep him bastioned from her charms.

"What is your name?" she asked softly.

He cursed under his breath. "Are you going to let me dig or ask questions all night?"

A dissonant *twang* sounded suddenly beside her as she recoiled. The wench must have a gittern or a harp. As the jangling chord faded, he heard the unmistakable sniffle of feminine weeping.

He heaved a silent sigh. If one weapon could lay him low in a single blow, it was a woman's tears.

"Oh, do not weep, lady, I pray you." He turned toward her,

chewing at his lip. "Forgive my coarse manner. I am . . . un-accustomed to the company of women."

But ladies' tears were not easily stopped, and he silently cursed himself for getting them started.

"I am called . . . 'Rag' by some," he admitted at last. It was a name he'd not gone by since he was a boy, one his cousin had stuck him with for the initials of his title, Ryance Alexander, The Gryphon. It was a silly name, and for an instant he regretted divulging such a thing to her. Then he remembered they'd likely die here. She'd never utter the name beyond these walls.

Hilaire sniffed back her tears. "Sir Rag?"

He grunted for answer.

"'Tis a curious name." She couldn't recall him among her father's men. She wondered what he looked like. Perhaps if she could see his face, it would ease her fears, for his quick-silver moods certainly did naught to comfort her.

She approached him warily, crouching beside him to help scratch at the dirt. This close, she could detect the faint scent of his bath beneath the tang of iron and leather and sweat, the scent of bergamot and woodruff.

"Do you . . . have a family?" she asked.

"Nay." His voice was gruff, short, to the point.

A long silence ensued, broken only by the sound of fingers fruitlessly scraping against earth, a silence Hilaire soon felt compelled to fill.

"Mayhaps I have seen you in my father's ranks. Tell me, what are your features like?"

"Plain. Dark. You'd not remember me."

His abrupt tone bruised her, but she refused to give up. If he'd not speak to her, *she* would do the talking.

"You are not the knight who lamed de Lancey at the spring tournament?"

"Nay."

She struggled with a cobblestone lodged fast in the dirt. "The one who plied Lady Anne so diligently with roses last year?"

"Nay."

The stone came loose. She tossed it aside. "Then are you . . ."

"Nay! You'd not know me," he said impatiently. "I serve no man save the King."

She gasped. "You're a knight-errant."

A fevered flush stole up her cheek. No man led such a provocative and fascinating life as a knight-errant, pursuing impossible, noble quests, living by his wits and his sword, staring danger in the eyes, never flinching, traveling a long and solitary road.

She turned impulsively toward him, her cheeks still warm with excitement. "Do you ever get . . . lonely?"

He stopped at his labors and cleared his throat, as if he thought deeply about her question. But he answered as briefly as ever. "Nay."

"I think it must be lonely being a knight-errant," she disagreed. "Perhaps you have a lady love?"

"Nay!" He grunted as he plowed his hands hard into the soil, and she worried that he might break his knuckles on a rock.

"Alas, I have no love either," she told him. "Only this wretched beast they have betrothed me to."

He didn't answer, but she heard his labored breathing as he struggled against the unyielding wall.

Suddenly, the full weight of her situation settled upon her like a millstone. She needn't fret about The Black Gryphon, the brute she was to marry, because she wasn't going to get out of here. Even this strong knight-errant could not carve more than a small niche in their prison. They were going to die.

When she thought about dying, she thought about her father and her pet falcon, the flowers that had just begun to pop up in the meadow below her window, the sky and the people and the seasons she might never see again. Though she continued to scrape in futility at the wall with her one good hand, tears wet her lashes, and her heart ached as if it would break in two.

It was a travesty. She was but seven and ten. She'd scarcely lived. She'd never given her favor to a knight in tournament, never written a rebus to a secret love on St. Valentine's Day, never bestowed her affections upon a man.

Though she tried to stem them, her tears spilled over, and soon she was sniffling softly again.

Yet even as grief wrapped suffocating fingers about her burning throat, angry denial sprouted beneath her sorrow. It couldn't be true, she decided, desperate for the man with her to speak further reassurances, even false ones. She couldn't die now. She was too young, barely a woman.

What reason had God to punish her? She'd done naught so evil. Except perhaps to run away from her betrothed. And defy the King. And leave her entire household in peril.

She swallowed guiltily.

"You play that thing?" Sir Rag asked quietly after she'd been weeping a few minutes. By his gentle voice, he clearly knew she was crying again, but was too chivalrous to mention it.

She blinked back her tears. "The harp?"

He grunted.

"Aye," she said around the hitching in her chest. "My father says . . . I play . . . like an angel."

"An angel." He chuckled low. It was a sad sound. "Well, angel, will you play for me?"

For one instant, her spirits soared. There was naught she loved better than playing her harp. What should she play for him? A roundelay to spring? A madrigal about love? A heroic ballad to inspire him? But all at once she remembered her injured hand, and her heart sank.

"I . . . I cannot," she said on a sob.

Sir Rag stopped digging. She heard him turn to her.

"My hand was smashed in the rock slide," she explained.

He dropped whatever stone he'd hefted and moved toward her. "Let me see."

His command was absurd. There was naught to see in the inky black. Nonetheless, she offered him her hand.

She hadn't noticed the pain before, only a cool numbness. In the midst of deadly peril the injury had seemed the least of her worries. Now, as he tenderly cupped the underside of her hand, she grew aware of a deep throbbing ache underlying the sharp sting of torn flesh.

She sucked her breath between her teeth as he carefully examined her fingers one by one. When he tugged on the fourth one, she gasped in pain.

"'Tis cracked, but I think not broken," he told her. "Have you a linen underskirt?"

She started at his intimate question.

"I'll need to make a bandage," he explained. "I don't intend to claw our way out of here only to have you bleed to death." His words were grim, but his tone was teasing, and she was glad of his gruff care. "If you'll allow me?"

She withdrew her hand and steeled herself as he crouched before her. His fingertips brushed her bare ankle before they found the hem of her underskirt, sending an enticing warm quiver up her leg. Then he shredded the flimsy fabric, and she winced as the loud ripping split the quiet of the cavern.

His hands upon her wrist were massive, but far from clumsy. Forsooth, he handled her with such tenderness that she wondered if he oft performed such tasks. She supposed a knight-errant, traveling alone from tournament to tournament, battle to battle, would have to know how to bandage his own wounds.

He wrapped the linen lightly about her hand, enclosing her fingers in a mitten gauntlet of cloth. His head bent over her hand while he worked, as if he could perform the task better by at least pretending to see. She shivered as his slow, measured breaths crossed the back of her wrist.

She wondered again what he looked like. He'd said he was dark and plain, but forsooth, she couldn't imagine him possessing anything less than godlike features by his rugged, masculine voice and his calming touch.

Where had he come from? And why had he joined her father's forces? She couldn't fathom her father hiring a mercenary. He had ample knights of his own. Then again, Sir Rag hadn't specifically said that he fought for her father. Mayhaps he'd only been passing by when the siege . . .

A strange chill settled upon her shoulders like a blanket of snow. Where *had* he come from? There was only one passageway leading from the castle.

"There, my lady," he said lightly when he'd finished, "as good as new."

Her heart thumped ominously in her chest. "How did . . . how did you come to be . . . next to the passageway?"

He stilled, for a moment seemed to vanish, so quiet was he.

"How did you come to be under the wall?" she asked with bated breath.

He cleared his throat, but her mind raced ahead of his reply. Of course. He wasn't one of her father's men. He'd come from *outside* the castle.

Her breath rasped against her ribs, and her words sounded hollow in her ears. "You . . . you were undermining the castle."

His lack of a response damned him.

Fear tripped bitterly on her tongue, and her words came out on a thin wisp of breath. "God's blood—you fight for *him*. You fight for The Black Gryphon."

four

Hilaire staggered backward, stumbling over the rocky ground, groping behind her with her good hand. She had to get away, get away from him before he . . .

"Fear not, my lady. I—"

"Nay!" she shrieked, blocking blindly before her with her bandaged arm. "Stay back!"

She heard him step toward her, and fright made her throat go dry. Two threats menaced her now—the darkness and her enemy—and she was cornered between them.

"My lady . . ."

"Get away from me!"

"I promise you . . ." He took another pace forward.

"Nay!" she screeched. Her heart hammered against her ribs as the two evils closed in, one promising to swallow her, the other promising . . .

"I won't harm you."

The sharp ledge pricked her back as she retreated to the limits of her prison. "Nay!" she hissed, cringing back against the wall. "Please."

"Fear not," he assured her, continuing his stealthy advance.

"Please," she whispered.

But all at once, he grasped her wrist.

"Nay!" she gasped, struggling wildly in his grip.

"My lady," he said, tightening his hold, "trust me."

"Let me go," she breathed, twisting her fingers in panic.

"I can't do that."

"Then leave me here," she bargained. Fear pitched her voice high, and she raced over the words. "Go on without me. Tell him I've died. I'll pay you. I'll pay you well."

"I made a vow."

"You vowed to see me safe." Lord, he was strong as a bull. Why could she not pry free? "Yet you'll hand me over to him. You'll give me to The Black Gryphon."

"My lady, I give you my word . . ."

"The word of an enemy?" Her voice was brittle with fright.

"My word as a knight. I vow I will not force you to anything against your will."

"But you are vassal to him. You are beholden to that . . . that beast!" she cried.

He released her so abruptly she nearly tumbled backward. Then, with a deep sigh of exasperation, he stepped away from her.

She was free. He'd let her go. She waited for a wave of relief to wash over her. But it never came. He'd loosed her, aye, but she still languished in the dark, trapped, frightened. And now she'd alienated her sole source of comfort. She'd doused her only light against the darkness.

Catching her breath, she wrapped her arms about her. Empty and cool, they were little consolation. She sought and found her harp and hugged it fiercely to her chest. But it, too, gave her no ease. And as she tried in vain to re-create the succor Sir Rag had offered her, the shadows of the night seemed to creep closer and closer.

He didn't seem to notice them. He'd begun to grapple again with the wall, gouging away steadily. But she felt their presence, tangible, menacing. She felt the weight of them, pressing in on her, feeding on her fear. Her heart fluttered, her breathing grew shallow. And as the dark wraiths advanced with their ebony cloaks to smother her, Sir Rag's digging grew distant, muffled, until the sound echoed curiously like the scratching of a rat in a hollow log. The edges of reality blurred into watery waves of black, then disappeared altogether.

She'd fainted. Or died. She wasn't certain which. The

world was tipped askew. She lay flat on her back, and swirls of gray and silver, coal and pewter danced on an ethereal current before her eyes.

"My lady!" His whisper was urgent, anxious.

She moaned as a fierce throbbing in her head suddenly commanded her attention. Nay, she wasn't dead. Unless this was the punishment of hell.

He smacked her lightly now, clapping her cheeks with his rough palms until annoyance shredded the last of the silvery cobwebs from her eyes and she dizzily sat up.

"Are you all right?" he asked, his voice tense.

"I will be if you'll cease beating me," she bit out.

Her complaint evidently spurred great relief in him, for he let out a shuddering sigh that seemed to come from the depths of his being.

"I feared . . ." he began.

She waited, breathless. She knew what he feared. He'd feared she was dead. She prayed he wouldn't say it.

"I feared you'd steal all the air with your snoring," he said, and his words, so unexpected, so knavish, took a moment to register.

"Snoring!" she cried. "I do not . . ."

She shoved in his general direction and successfully toppled him. But the sweetness of triumph was naught compared to the sweetness of his laughter reverberating in the cave. It was a low rumble, deep and rich, like well-ripened mead. And though he offered but a sip of it, she curiously longed to taste more.

But he was the enemy, she reminded herself. He would turn her over to The Black Gryphon as soon as they were free. If they ever got free. She swallowed at the sobering thought.

Yet, until they escaped, they were jailed in this prison together, helpless, fighting for the same liberty. In sooth, for the moment he seemed civil enough. He wouldn't harm her. He had no cause to harm her. At least not yet.

And, she realized with a sudden trip of her heart, Sir Rag was not unpleasant, for a foe. Actually, he was rather congenial, warm, and chivalrous, but for that remark about her snoring. And even that brought a brief smile to her lips. The man was obviously no lack-wit.

Aye, she thought, Sir Rag had given her succor and brought a twinkle to her eye. He had mocked neither her tears nor her fainting, but had gallantly offered her what comfort he could. How could she long despise him?

She could not. They were allies waging a war against a common enemy. So she'd fight beside him. For now.

Ryance still shook like a newborn foal. It was absurd. Aye, for one terrible moment, he'd thought she was dead. The dull thud as she hit the ground and her awful stillness when he flung himself to her side had hammered his heart up into his throat, where it seemed to lodge until he heard her breathe again.

But they were dying anyway. What did it matter if she fainted now? After all, sleep might spare her the unbearable thirst and paralyzing lethargy surely to come.

Yet what he'd almost said to her, what he'd almost admitted aloud was not that he'd feared she was dead. It was that he feared she'd left him.

As hardened as he should be to his own curse, to his own failings, he couldn't bear to lose another woman. Damn the Fates—if he did naught else on Earth ere he died, he'd at least redeem his soul by fulfilling this final vow. If it wracked his body and broke his spirit, he would see her out of this hell.

With renewed vigor, he attacked the wall, pounding and scraping as if demons chased him. To his astonishment, in a moment Hilaire joined the battle, fighting beside him. Soon the sounds of their frayed breathing filled the cave, punctuated by blows of rock on rock and grunts of exertion.

They might have gone on silently, wrapped up in their own thoughts, digging away until they either broke through to freedom or ran out of air. But an overwhelming need to enlighten Hilaire gnawed at Ryance like a rat. For pride or honor, he simply couldn't let her believe what she believed about him.

"He is not a beast," he murmured between blows, before he had the chance to think better of it.

"What? Did you say something?"

"The Gryphon." He continued to dig. "He is only a man. He would not harm you."

She sniffed. "He drowned his first wife and child."

The image came to him unbidden—his darling Mary and their daughter, Katie, frolicking upon the daisy-strewn lap of a May meadow. Katie had been the light of his life, Mary, the first woman he'd ever loved. And the last.

That year, the river had run high, swollen by spring rains till it swept and whirled toward the sea with delirious speed, the grasses and trees grown green and lush on the bounty.

Little Katie had called him a big black bear. He'd growled and stomped after the giggling pair, his wife and his daughter, and they'd dashed off to hide among the thick hedge and saplings along the river's edge. That had been his last happy memory with them. In the next painful moments, the two of them, his precious ladies, simply disappeared.

A crofter found them hours later, pulled them from the river. By then their faces were as pale and lifeless as linen. Their hair, bedecked with bits of twigs and leaves and weeds, wrapped around their drenched bodies like fishing net.

His voice grew husky with the memory. "Aye, they were drowned, but not by his hand. 'Twas an accident. He tried to save them. He did everything he could to . . ." To his horror, a wretched sob stuck in his throat. He swallowed it down like tough venison. "He tried to save them."

Hilaire made no reply. He wondered if she believed him. He wondered if he believed himself. He'd gone over the events a thousand times in his head. He'd chided himself for chasing them that day, for letting them out of his sight, Lord—for even allowing them out of doors. He'd searched wildly for them afterward, diving into the icy water time and time again, bellowing their names till his voice grew hoarse and he could call them no longer. Yet he was still racked with the harrowing obsession that he could have done more.

"You seem to know The Gryphon well," she said quietly.

"Nay. I've only heard what others say, those who knew him . . . before."

"Before?"

He thought of the lad he'd once been, and an ache filled his throat, like the profound longing for a departed loved one. He'd been happy once, full of life, eager and ambitious and brimming with young dreams. He'd made men laugh and maidens sigh. Now he only inspired fear.

"Before . . . he was cursed," he grumbled.

He wrenched a stone from its earthen bed. There was no point in dwelling on the past, on dreams that were long dead.

Hilaire bit her lip. Somehow she'd offended Sir Rag. She could tell by the violence with which he tossed bits of stone aside. He obviously didn't wish to talk about his overlord. He clearly bore some loyalty for his beastly master. Perhaps he was irritated with her for threatening to break her betrothal. or perhaps he was only angry with her for talking when she should have been digging.

She sniffed. She was doing her best, considering the wall was as hard as marble and she could only dig with one hand. As for squirming out of marriage, she supposed it was not very worthy of a lady, but contrary to what Sir Rag believed, there must be a kernel of truth in the gruesome tales about The Black Gryphon, and she had no intention of discovering it at her own peril.

So she redoubled her efforts, using a pointed rock to chip away at the soil; and she kept quiet, neither wishing to disturb her rescuer nor draw undue attention to her own shortcomings.

They worked side by side for what seemed like an hour, the only sounds their driven breathing, the dull thud of rock on earth, and the low rattle of his chain mail.

Earlier she'd shivered in the passageway. Now she was drenched in sweat. Salty drops rolled down her brow and stung her eyes, and her bandaged hand throbbed in pain. The air felt thick, and yet it was hard to draw enough of it into her lungs. She wondered what it felt like to suffocate. She was frightened. She didn't want to die.

Tears came unsought again. It seemed there was no end
to the well of weeping. She tried valiantly to hide them from
him. She didn't wish for him to think her a spineless milk-
sop. He already considered her cowardly in running from
her betrothed. She'd be damned if she'd disappoint him further.

"You need rest," he said, startling her.

"Nay, I'll be . . ." Her voice caught.

He wrapped his fingers around her forearm, and gently
pulled her away from the wall.

"You need rest," he repeated. " 'Twill save the air."

She squeezed her eyes shut tightly. It was as she feared.
Already they were running out of air. Already they were
dying. She reined in her panic only by force of sheer will.
And still a great sobbing gasp escaped her.

Suddenly both of her arms were clasped in his hands, and
she could feel the weight of his blind gaze upon her.

"I'm sorry," she whispered, apologizing for her tears.

He bit out a quiet curse. Then to her astonishment, his
hand crooked around the back of her neck, and he pulled her
to his chest. The foreign scents of iron and leather filled her
nose as he held her against his hauberk, and yet his arms, his
enemy arms, lent her curious comfort.

He wasted no breath in chiding her, nor did he ply her
with words of solace. He only held her, stroking her hair
with one hand while she buried her sobs against his wide
chest.

She should have felt shame, she supposed, blubbering her
salty tears all over the poor man's armor. Yet he chivalrously
made no mention of it. Forsooth, she felt so calmed by his
embrace—the strength of his body, the gentleness of his
hand, the warmth of his ragged breath upon her face—that
she forgot for a short while that he was her foe.

Ryance felt the stone rampart surrounding his heart shudder as the woman nestled closer to him, as if she relied upon
him, as if she belonged there.

What had made him reach for her, he didn't know. It was
no concern of his if she wept. She'd likely weep a pond's

worth of tears before the ordeal was over. And yet taking her in his arms had seemed the right thing to do.

Now he was certain it was a mistake. She brought back too many memories, too much pain. Her soft sobbing snagged at his heart. The sweet scent of her hair insinuated its way into his soul. And the feel of her body against his—warm, innocent, trusting—was almost more than he could bear.

How long had it been since someone, anyone, had given him such trust, such belief? Oh aye, his men believed in him. They believed The Black Gryphon was a fierce and fearless warrior. They wagered daily on that belief with their lives. But no one had trusted *him*, Ryance, for a long time.

Nor should they, he thought bitterly. No woman should welcome his cursed embrace, and if Hilaire knew what was good for her . . .

Yet she felt so perfect in his arms. For one greedy instant he closed his eyes and imagined she was his, all of her—her silken tresses, her soft voice, her pliant body. The sweet vision nearly crumbled the bastion of his heart.

And then he let her go.

If perchance her soft moan was one of protest, he didn't wish to know. He set her gently aside.

"Tell me . . ." he croaked, barely able to speak across the empty space her sudden absence created. "Tell me about your family." If he kept her talking, she'd be less likely to dwell on the troubles at hand. And perhaps her chatter would distract him from his own foolish imaginings.

"My family?" Her whisper was rough, groggy, as if she'd just awakened. He didn't want to think of the sensual image it conjured.

"Aye," he said, turning again to delve at the wall and trying to lighten his tone as he spoke over his shoulder. "What is your father like when he's not a commander of men?"

"Oh. He is a good man," she said dreamily, "honest and fair. Just, but very firm."

"Ah. But I'd wager you have him dining from your fingers."

Her low giggle surprised him. "How could you tell?"

"I had a daughter once."

"But you said you had no family."

"She . . . died, along with her mother."

She gave a little gasp. "How awful for you."

"'Twas a long time ago." Not long enough to erase the pain in his voice.

"I lost my mother when I was a child," she told him. "She fell ill. I remember listening to her, night after night, coughing and coughing. 'Twas a horrible sound."

Ryance remembered that sound. Four years after, he could still recall his second wife's wheezing breaths as she struggled to find air in the fluid drowning her. "But not so horrible as the night it ceased."

"Aye. I blamed myself. For years afterward I thought I'd caused her death by praying she'd stop coughing."

Her words struck a familiar and dissonant chord in him. He, too, had prayed for Elaine's end.

"Did you blame yourself for your wife's death?" Hilaire asked, startling him with her candor.

"Nay," he lied. "The physicians did all they could—bled her, gave her poultices to draw out the sickness." He blew out a tired breath. "I even summoned a healer the chaplain claimed was a handmaiden of the devil."

"I'm so sorry," Hilaire whispered. "You must have loved her well."

"I . . . cared for her." He hadn't dared to love Elaine, not after losing his first wife. She'd simply been the King's choice, a political alliance, and though he'd treated her with respect, he'd stubbornly closed his heart to her.

Until she'd taken ill. Then, forced to watch her face an agonizing death with courage, her sweetness unwavering, her faith undimmed, he grew to care for her deeply. Which was the cruelest blow of all. For when she finally succumbed, it was as if a piece of him had been torn away. Worse, while he knelt, stunned with grief, beside her grave, vicious tongues began to wag. And before long, the rumor grew legs.

The Black Gryphon had struck once more. He'd poisoned his wife.

"Have you never loved again?" Hilaire's voice broke into his thoughts.

"Nay." This time he didn't lie. After losing two wives and a daughter, he'd kept his heart under lock and key. To his third wife, he'd shown courtesy and companionship, no more.

"What of your parents?" she asked. "What is your father like?"

"Dead. My mother as well." It was no great loss in his mind. His father had been a cruel man, killed in a brawl he'd probably instigated, and his mother had been feeble, living under her husband's shadow most of her life.

"I'm sorry," she said.

"That, too, happened long ago."

"Forsooth? How old *are* you?" Hilaire asked.

He smiled humorlessly. "Old as Methuselah." He felt that old at least, despite the fact he'd only passed his thirtieth year. "Old as dust."

"Old as sin?" She laughed, and he thought how incongruous the sound was in this tomb. "And just what have you done to pass all this tedious eternity then, Sir Rag?"

Ryance furrowed his brow, puzzled. Was she flirting with him? It had been so long since he'd heard the lilting music of a woman's jesting that he hardly recognized it. But aye, it seemed she curved her words around a coy smile.

So how could he answer her? He'd done naught but eat, breathe, fight, and mourn for years. But there was a time . . .

"I suppose," she said, filling in the silence, as he found most women were wont to do, this one in particular. "I suppose you haven't much time for pleasure with traveling from place to place, going on your noble quests and so forth."

He raised a brow, a gesture completely wasted in the darkness. The only noble quest he'd ever undertaken was trying to catch a butterfly for his little Katie.

"And how have *you* filled the hours?" he asked her.

"With music," she gushed, and he could feel her passion like a living thing in the dark.

"The harp."

"Aye."

Before she could be reminded of her injury again, he intervened. "When we are out of here then, my lady, and you are healed, will you favor me with a performance?"

"Aye," she softly replied.

"I count upon it." His lip curved up into a wry smile. "You shall sing of the great underworld adventures of Sir Rag and Lady Hilaire."

"Aye, and you shall accompany me on the rock wall."

Her gurgle of laughter washed over him like a healing balm, and he couldn't help but wonder what kind of peace he might have found listening to a lifetime of that delightful sound.

five

There was little enough air in their prison, certainly not enough for idle chatter. But Ryance took pleasure in the sound of Hilaire's voice, and she reveled in conversation. Exchanging pleasantries seemed the best way to keep her demons at bay. So he obliged her as he chafed away at the wall, though he doubted he'd uttered as many words in a month of days heretofore.

"Tell me of your adventures, if we're to immortalize them in song," she entreated playfully, reminding him of his daughter asking for stories by the evening hearth. "What great feats of prowess have you undertaken? What dragons have you slain?"

"No dragons," he said, chuckling. "Dragonflies mayhaps."

"Have you saved a maiden in distress before?"

"Maiden in distress." He paused to think. "Once I rescued a damsel from a swarm of bees."

"And how did you do that? Did you battle them with your sword? Lay siege to their hive? Gallantly let them sting you while she escaped?"

He grinned at the memory. Elaine had been none too grateful for his rescue. "I tossed her into the moat."

"Oh, Sir Rag, you didn't!"

He rather liked the sound of that silly name on her lips. And he liked the way she chided him.

"What of you?" he asked. "Any feats of great renown?"

She sighed. "Alas, nay. I am my father's youngest, his only

girl, and he guards me like a mastiff. My brothers have seen the world," she said enviously, "but I've not set foot outside England."

"Never?" Ryance asked, incredulous. A wealth of images suddenly riffled through his mind like pages of a book—scenes of the stark Syrian desert and the steamy Tunisian coast, of crumbling Roman temples and lush Greek olive groves, Flemish towns crowded with craftsmen and fishmongers, and Paris, where velvet-clad nobles encrusted with jewels shared the streets with waifs and mice skittering through alleyways. To take her there, to see it all again through her unworldly eyes . . .

But it would never be. She feared The Black Gryphon. Even if, by some incredible quirk of fate, they got out alive, it would be on another man's arm that she'd discover the world.

"I wager you've traveled far and wide," she marveled.

"Some."

"Tell me the places you've seen." He could almost hear the sparkle in her eyes.

He paused to lean against the rock wall and think. "My father took me to Spain when I was four." Odd, but he hadn't thought of that journey in years. "'Twas the first time I'd seen the sea." He smiled. "I waded in the waves near the dock, and my mother scolded me for ruining my new boots."

"Is it as vast as they say?"

"What—Spain?"

"The sea."

He blinked. "You've never seen . . ." Sweet Mary— she *was* young. He wiped the sweat from his careworn brow with the back of his hand. He'd always loved the sea, but how could one describe it? "'Tis magnificent. The water stretches as far as you can see, like an enormous coverlet, till it meets the edges of the sky. Its hue is always changing—blue, green, silver—and sometimes the wind whips the peaks of the waves to white froth. You can taste salt in the breeze, and when you're far from shore, the only sounds you hear are the lapping of waves against the ship, the creak of the hull, the slap of the sails, the screech of the gulls circling above the open sea."

"The open sea," she sighed. "I should like to sail there."

And he should like to take her, to share the ecstasy of wild ocean breezes caressing their arms, salt spray bedewing their faces, to point out the sleek silver dolphins that followed, leaping and frolicking and chattering like playful children.

"Where else have you ventured?" she demanded, her appetite for his travels only whetted.

He should be tunneling at the wall. Time was slipping away, and their discourse wasted precious air. But it was so long since he'd engaged in agreeable patter with such a charming companion. Her words were like sweet mulled wine to his parched spirit.

"I earned my spurs at Havenleigh and went on campaign in Scotland."

"Scotland," she repeated reverently.

"The country is rugged there. The mountains weep with waterfalls. In the fall, the heather turns, and 'tis like the hills wear a plaid of purple and gold."

"Oh," she breathed. Then she hungrily asked, "Where else?"

"After Scotland? The Holy Land."

"On Crusade?"

"Aye." Those images were not so joyous. But despite grim memories of poverty and bloodshed, he recalled other things—the warmth of the desert wind, the magnificence of the walled cities.

"Tell me about it."

"The fighting was ugly, but the country . . . The air is scented everywhere with exotic spices—myrrh and cinnamon and frankincense," he remembered, "and the people dress in layers of cloth as sheer as mist and in every color of the rainbow."

"Was . . . he . . . with you then? The Black Gryphon?"

Her question caught him off guard. "Nay. I . . . came after the death of his first wife." In a sense, it was true. Ryance, the man he once was, had been buried by The Black Gryphon, sunk into the grave beside his wife and daughter.

"Were you not afraid of him, of his curse?"

Aye, Ryance thought, that curse was the *only* thing he feared. Instead he said, "I'd not judge a man by the misfortune that plagues him."

"Some say 'tis more than misfortune. Some say he's," she murmured, ending in a whisper, "the servant of Lucifer."

"God's blood." Ryance didn't mean to swear, but it was just such gossip that had made his life a living hell. Just because he'd lost faith in a God who would tear away all the beauty in his life did not mean he was the devil's minion. "The Black Gryphon is a man, no more, no less, and anyone who . . ."

Her hand made awkward contact with his chest. "I'm so sorry, Sir Rag. 'Twas wicked of me, speaking thus of your lord. Please forgive me."

It was not her words, but rather her proximity, her warm breath upon his cheek and the womanly scent of her, that instantly cooled his wrath. He wanted to take her in his arms again, to feel the slender nape of her neck and the playful caress of her hair. Forgive her? He wanted to envelop her.

But when he didn't respond, she withdrew her hand.

"Forsooth," he sighed with a twinge of disappointment, "you say naught that hasn't been said a thousand times."

"But you clearly care for him to leap so quickly to his defense. He must count himself fortunate to have such a loyal vassal."

Ryance didn't know how to answer her.

She didn't seem to require an answer. "Tell me, what is it about him you admire?"

He puzzled over the question. Was there anything left of Sir Ryance in The Black Gryphon? Anything he could be proud of? He supposed his stoic suffering counted for something. And there was still his sense of justice. He was generally a man of peace, preferring diplomacy to the sword. And he was unflinchingly loyal to the King. But Hilaire was probably too young to understand any of that. She still believed in shining knights who saved damsels from dragons.

Quietly, she added, "Tell me why a woman should desire to marry him."

His heart skipped a beat. Was she reconsidering her escape? Was she asking him to persuade her to stay?

He could not. Not in good conscience. He might convince her that The Black Gryphon was not an ogre, that he was undeserving of the taunts that dogged him. Indeed, he longed to purge that poison from his soul. But naught would lift the curse destiny laid upon his wretched name.

"He is . . . fair," he decided, "in trade and in battle."

She muttered low, "Yet he lays siege to my father's keep."

"Only to claim what is his by rights."

She mulled that over. "What else? How else is he worthy?"

He thought for a moment. "He works hard. He trains hard. His hospitality he gives freely. His coin he spends frugally." Upon reflection, that last might not seem a virtue to a young lady. His own daughter had begged him endlessly to spend his coin on ribbons or cloth dolls or a jeweled trinket every time a peddler came to the gate.

"Does he play music?" Was that hope he heard in her voice?

"Nay."

"Oh." She sounded discouraged.

He added quickly, "But he likes to hear it. At least he used to."

"You mean, before he started ki— Before his wives started dying?"

Ryance bristled. She still doubted him. Pointedly, he told her, "Aye, before his wife and daughter fell in the river and were drowned."

"What about his second wife? Was she not poisoned?"

"She died from sickness," he said wearily.

"Ah. Like *your* wife."

"What?"

"Like *your* wife. You said *she* died of sickness."

"Oh, aye."

"And what about his last wife, the one they say he beat?"

His blood began to simmer. He bit out a reply between his teeth. "He'd sooner cut off his arm than lift it against a woman."

"But he pushed her from a tower and . . ."

"Nay!" he shouted, startling even himself with the vehemence of his denial. After that, against his better judgment and against his will, his thoughts poured from him like ale from a cracked barrel, and there was naught he could do to stop them. "She flung *herself* from that tower. He had no part in it." Ryance wondered at the verity of his words. Was he truly blameless? Could he have stopped her? Could he have reached her in time?

"Why would she do that?" Hilaire pressed.

He blew out a quick breath. "She was afraid . . . very, very afraid."

"Of him?"

"Of herself." He swallowed hard. He'd never spoken to anyone about the horrible agonies Bess had endured.

"Herself?"

He rested his head back against the rock wall. "It started as voices she heard whispering in her head, telling her evil things. She tried to ignore them, but they wouldn't go away. Then she began speaking to them, yelling at them, cursing . . ." That had been the most painful, listening to gentle Bess shriek in a voice that no longer belonged to her. "But they wouldn't leave her alone. Soon she could see demons. She imagined they were attacking her. She'd beat herself purple with a poker trying to pry their hands free. Her arms were laced with cuts from her own dagger and then, when I took that from her, her fingernails. She shunned her clothing, claiming they'd only steal it from her, and oft wandered naked through the halls of the castle. She tore out her hair, and once she lit her veil on fire." He took a shuddering breath. "One night, her mind cleared long enough for her to see what had happened to her, how mad she'd become, and she couldn't bear to live with the fear any longer. Before I . . . before anyone could stop her, she leaped from the tower ledge . . . and broke on the stones below."

Hilaire could scarcely breathe. It was a horrifying story. But it wasn't the story itself that paralyzed her. It was the telling of it.

The truth was too amazing to believe, but it had to be.

Sir Rag.

The Black Gryphon.

They were one and the same. Ryance was his given name, but no matter what he called himself, he was The Black Gryphon. His slip of the tongue had betrayed him, but she would have discovered his secret anyway.

Who but a husband could speak so intimately of a woman's mind? Who else would know her so well? The ragged timbre of pain in his voice described not the distant suffering of a vassal, but the agony of a loved one.

This was him. This was The Black Gryphon.

A frisson of cold panic raced along her spine. She was trapped with him. Alone. In the dark. He knew who she was. He knew she feared him. Merciful God—what would he do to her?

He *was* cursed. It was certain now, for though they'd not yet spoken the vows of marriage, already he brought her death.

Her heart stuttered, and she felt the walls closing in again. But before she raced into headlong anxiety, he spoke.

"Forgive me. 'Twas not my intent to sadden you."

The words stuck in her dry throat. "'Tis . . . 'tis . . . it must have been dreadful for y-your lord."

He grunted in agreement. "He has lived with much sorrow."

They were only a few words, but he spoke them simply and from the heart. And suddenly their truth rang out like a hollow bell in the melancholy dark. Her fear evaporated. The Black Gryphon was no ogre with a diabolical plot for revenge. He was but a man, a sad and lonely man. Suddenly, inexplicably, she yearned not to cower from him, but to console him, this lost soul with the broken spirit.

"Mayhaps," she allowed, "I have been too hasty in my judgment. Mayhaps he is not cursed so much as . . ."

"Nay, you have it aright," he snapped. "He *is* cursed. But by Fate, not by his own deeds."

She could hear it now—the bitterness, the anguish—hidden appreciably by his gruff voice, but there nonetheless.

"Well, then," she murmured in all humility, "as you say, I should not judge him by his misfortune."

A weighty silence ensued. If she hoped he'd reveal himself now, she was disappointed. Instead, he returned to his labors. She, too, scraped at the wall, but her mind flitted about so wildly she scarcely heeded her own progress.

After a long while, he rested, and his weary panting filled the cave. "Pity 'tis a harp you play and not a clarion," he said in a rare moment of wry humor. "Else we might be able to fell the walls as Joshua did."

She giggled at his unexpected wit, which threw her into an even more complex melee of thoughts.

Who was he? Who was The Black Gryphon? All she knew of him was what she'd heard, largely improbable tales about his vicious nature, his dark moods, and the curse that followed him. Certainly this was not the man with her now.

This man spoke kindly, nobly. He offered her comfort. He'd dug his way to her when she cried out for help. He'd breathed with her, bandaged her injured hand. He'd held her when her fears got the best of her and anxiously seen to her when she'd fainted. He'd even promised to get her out, even though he must know . . .

He must know they would never escape.

She tried to swallow the knot of dread choking her, but it lodged like a gallows noose against her throat.

He knew. He knew, because he was cursed. The pall of misery hung over him. All his wives had died tragically. She was doomed to be another victim of The Black Gryphon.

Yet he'd hidden it from her. Why?

Because she was frightened, and he didn't wish to frighten her more. It was no matter to him that she'd tried to flee their marriage, that she'd said terrible, hurtful things about him, that she'd poked and prodded at his painful history as if it were fiction lived by some hapless character in a fable. Still he protected her. Still he did all in his power to save her.

She had sadly misjudged the man who was to have been her husband. And now, because of her childish flight, she had doomed the both of them. She wished to God she could turn back time's plow and unfurrow the ruts she'd gouged in their lives. But it was too late, too late.

Sir Ryance resumed working with scarcely a moment's repose, toiling away at his Herculean task with nary a complaint. She ought to let him stop. It was clear he only dug at the wall to assuage her despair. He'd been right at the beginning. There was no escaping this grievous tomb.

She bit her lip to quell its trembling. She wouldn't cry, and she refused to panic. The Black Gryphon, Ryance, had carried a heavy enough burden in his life for three men. She would not add herself to the weight he bore. Nay, she thought, she would suffer in silence, and if she could do anything to ease his spirit, say anything to atone for the harsh words she'd spoken . . .

A trickle of pebbles rattled along the wall to Hilaire's right. It was an innocent sound, truly, and yet it prickled the tiny hairs along the back of her neck.

"What was—" she began.

"Hist!"

Tense as the highest string on her harp, Hilaire waited, her ears pricked up for the slightest noise. But none followed.

After a long moment, Ryance turned back to the wall. "Must have been a . . ."

Before he could finish his sentence, a deep growl like thunder shook the ground, and suddenly Hilaire relived the nightmare of the rockslide all over again.

Rocks rumbled and pounded and shrieked. Metallic dust tainted the air, smothering her. She was knocked to her knees or fell, she wasn't sure, and a barrage of cobbles battered her arms as she crossed them protectively over her head.

This time, in a few moments, it was over. And, miraculously, she was mostly unhurt. She gagged on mildewy dust and coughed it free of her lungs, flaring her nostrils to seek breatheable air.

Perhaps, she dared to hope, groping about her, the stones had shifted in their favor. Perhaps the passageway was clear now. Or his sapping tunnel had reopened.

"Can you . . . see anything?" she asked, unable to conceal the excitement in her voice. "Can you see light?" She patted the rocks around her and ventured forth at a crouch. "Sir Rag?" The taste of metal grew suddenly strong in her mouth. "Sir Rag?" It was the taste of fear.

She scrabbled about more urgently now, running even her injured hand along the uneven ground. "Sir . . ." Her fingers contacted chain mail, then the buckle of a greave behind his knee, and she sighed in relief. He was here. He was here. He'd probably dived facefirst onto the ground at the first rumblings, protecting himself from the collapse, and was too stunned to move. "Sir Rag, I was so worried. Are you . . ."

Her fingers shrunk atop his mailed calf. "Sir Rag?" There

was no reply, no movement. Her heart thrumming furiously, she traced her fingers up along the back of his leg, past the poleyn to his thigh, but there she was forced to stop.

An enormous boulder straddled his motionless body, pinning him to the ground, crushing him like grain beneath a millstone.

six

❧

"**N**ay!" she cried, scraping her throat raw with the scream. "Nay!" She tugged hard on his leg, terrified, desperate, but he didn't respond. The word rasped from her over and over like a metal file on an iron pot. "Nay! Nay!"

He couldn't be dead. She'd just been talking to him. He couldn't be. He wouldn't have left her. Not when she needed him. Sweet Jesu—she couldn't bear to die alone. Horror seeped out of her on that one piercing syllable. "Nay!"

Her own labored breathing grated on her ears, and she knew it would turn to whimpers if she didn't seize command of her wits. It was no time to indulge in selfish panic. Despite her fears, there was a chance Ryance still lived, and she might be his only hope. With a determined sob, she clenched her fists and gradually willed her terror to subside.

When she'd regained a modicum of control, she set about examining him more thoroughly. She could feel naught through his mail leggings save the thickness of muscle with which he was endowed. But she discovered if she lay flat against the tunnel floor, she could slip her good arm into the crevice beneath the boulder, along the length of him, and find his hand.

As she clasped the limp fingers, tears started in her eyes. His hand was slippery with blood, not from the avalanche, but from the pointless digging he had done for her sake. Sweet Mary—his knuckles were raw, and she could feel the jagged edges of broken fingernails. And she knew he'd done it for her.

Then, as she traced questing fingers over the pads of his callused hand, she found a miracle. A pulse beat in his wrist. He was yet alive.

A wordless cry of joy escaped her, unfettered for a brief moment by the fact that her situation was no less hopeless. He was still trapped beneath the boulder. They were still prisoner within the earth. And the shadows still pressed in upon her.

Reluctantly, she let go of his hand and knelt by the boulder. She made the sign of the cross, clasped her fingers before her, and squeezed her eyes tightly shut.

"Heavenly Father, blessed Mary, please forgive your wayward servant her trespasses." She blushed to think how many of them stained her soul, now that she'd caused so much trouble. "I have sinned much against this man who was to be my husband. But I beseech you, do not take him to your bosom, not yet." She shifted, and a sharp rock bit into the bare skin of her knee, but she tolerated it like a penitent monk enduring the lash. "He is a good man, a kind man, and I have done him much wrong. But if you will save him, if you will seize him from death's arms . . ."

She opened her eyes, nonplussed. What? What would she promise? What could she bargain with? She gulped.

He *was* a good man. He was a *wonderful* man. Aye, he'd had his share of misfortune, and there was an air of gloom about him. But wasn't it her maid who was always saying the love of a good woman could transform a man from a beast to a prince?

"If you let him live, God, I vow . . . I vow I will marry The Black Gryphon willingly." Her voice shook under the weight of her promise. "I will care for him and honor him and love him as a wife must love her husband." For a moment, she felt dizzy. What was she promising? She hadn't even seen his face. She didn't truly know him. And yet she knew him better than most brides knew their betrothed. "In the name of Jesu, this I pray," she added for good measure.

Then she waited.

No light suddenly appeared before her. No sound disturbed

the silence. She reached her hand out for Ryance's calf and gave it a jiggle, but he didn't respond.

Now she grew angry. Satan's ballocks! She'd just promised away the most valuable thing she had to offer. What more could God want? Did He not hear her plea? Did He not understand her sacrifice? Or perhaps, she thought, lifting her chin against the painful insult, God considered her beyond redemption.

A tear squeezed out between her lashes, but she vexedly swiped it from her cheek. She would show Him. She would show God. If He wouldn't help her, she'd do it without Him. She'd bring Ryance back to the living, even if she had to wrestle the devil to do it.

Pushing up her sleeves, she started jostling the dozing knight wholeheartedly.

"Wake up! Wake up, damn you! We're never going to get out of here if you don't wake up. Do you hear me?" She poked at his calf. "I know who you are. But know this: I'm not afraid of you. And I don't believe in your damned curse." She shook his leg like a mastiff shaking a rabbit. "Wake up, you . . . you selfish knave! What kind of knight are you to desert a lady in her hour of need?" She raised her fist and pummeled the back of his leg until her knuckles were scraped from the chain mail and tears rolled down her face. "Wake up, Gryphon! Wake up, you son of a harlot! Wake . . ."

It was no use. His heart might beat, but he was as dead to her as wood.

She rocked back onto her heels and then slumped onto her hindquarters, defeated. Her hand struck the low strings of her harp, which had somehow survived the rockslide, and out of habit, she gathered the instrument to her bosom for comfort.

No sooner had she surrendered to despair than the shadows of her mind began to creep in. They'd been there all along, she realized, waiting for her, waiting while she played her silly little game, waiting for her to succumb to their embrace. She felt them coming for her, promising peace, delivering death. She shuddered and clung to the harp like a magic amulet.

"You're not real," she murmured, but her voice was reedy and uncertain.

The shadows answered her, pressing closer, brushing their

chill fingers atop her shoulder, against her cheek, over her eyes. She gasped and felt a cold rush of air enter her lungs, as if one of them had dived down her throat to claim her from the inside. She closed her lips against a scream and dug her fingers into her harp, engraving the wood with crescents from her nails.

She had to think of something else, anything but the ominous shapes surrounding her. Her harp. Her maid. The flowers outside her window. The sea.

The sea . . . He had told her about the sea. She closed her eyes and imagined it lay before her—an enormous coverlet stretching as far as the horizon, the fabric shifting from gray to green to blue, white frothy caps bobbing up toward the vast sky—the vast, open, bright, cloudless sky.

She saw it clearly now. The sun sparkled on the waves. Seabirds circled overhead. And she stood on the deck of a grand ship, slicing through the sea like shears through silk. She took a long, deep breath, and she swore she could almost taste the crisp brine air.

They were gone now. The shadows were gone, fled to the corners, vanquished by the vision Ryance had given her.

Ryance. She had to save him. Somehow she had to get him from beneath that boulder. She set her harp aside and groped her way toward his legs again. She crouched, seized his ankles, and tugged backward, wincing as needles of pain shot through her injured hand. The gravel skidded beneath her heels, but his body didn't budge. He was imprisoned by the rock.

Gingerly, aware she was touching him in a most inappropriate manner, she ran her hand up along the back of his thigh and over the curve of his buttock. It was there the edge of the rock met his armor, wedging him against the floor. She wondered if she could drag his hips sideways into the crevice and pull him out that way.

Clenching his tabard in her fist, she pulled as hard as she could, cursing foully under her breath, but only succeeded in twisting the garment. He was stuck fast.

She sat back, panting. The only way she'd get him out was if she lifted the boulder off of him. Refusing to be daunted, she set about measuring her adversary.

The rock was large, as big as the oak chest at the foot of her bed. Its left side nested in the bed of gravel, but at the right, it angled up and perched on a shelf of stone. If she could somehow get her shoulder beneath that side and lift it up a few inches . . .

But it was too low to the ground and too heavy. An ox couldn't have lifted the thing. Even if she did manage to raise it, how would she move Ryance from beneath? Lord—what was she to do?

If she only had a lever of some sort . . .

She remembered watching her father's masons rebuilding the chapel. They'd transported and overturned scores of heavy granite blocks with a system of ropes and winches and pulleys, but the cornerstones they'd levered into place using nothing more complex than a wooden plank.

A wooden plank . . . a wooden . . .

Her harp. Of course. If she could slip her harp diagonally through the crevice, anchor it against the floor, and rock it back onto its seat, it would lift the boulder. Then, if she shoved the harp forward, the rock would wedge itself into the dip at the top of the harp, and she could pull Ryance out.

She plucked the instrument quickly from the floor, but as soon as her fingers contacted the curved wood, her throat closed. She'd had her harp as long as she could remember. Her mother had taught her to play as a little girl. Her musical talent was a source of great pride to her father. Whenever she grew melancholy, she had only to pluck out a madrigal, and soon the harmony would dispel the mists of sorrow.

She caught one string upon her fingertip and released it, letting its pure, light tone resonate in the cave. Using the instrument so roughly would irreversibly damage it. The stone would abrade the wood finish and possibly crack the sounding box. Yet, she thought, giving the harp a teary hug of farewell, it was without a doubt the instrument's noblest calling.

With only a slight grimace of remorse at the atrocious grating noise, she slid the instrument across the gravel into the crevice until it lodged under the boulder. Then she straddled the harp, gripping the top edge along the highest strings. With a few preparatory breaths, she tipped in counterbalance, and gradually, slowly, she felt the rock give. When the boulder raised a fraction of an inch, she became so ecstatic she nearly dropped it through the floor.

But it wasn't enough. She eased the harp back into place. The base wanted to skid against the uneven floor. If she was going to do this at all, she'd have to be quick. Summoning up all her strength, she dug her heels into the earth at either side of the instrument, joined her hands atop the apex of the harp, and groaning with the effort, leaned back with all her weight. This time the boulder lifted at least an inch, and using one foot, she kicked the base of the harp forward to wedge it beneath the elevated rock.

The wood creaked in protest at the tremendous weight, and Hilaire gasped. Had she made things worse? Would the rock drop even further? She dove for Ryance's feet and attempted to haul him backward. There was still little clearance, and she struggled to twist him free, wincing as his chain mail scraped betwixt the boulder and the gravel floor, afraid of what she might be doing to his exposed skin.

The harp groaned again. Hilaire tugged hard.

"God's bones!"

He was stuck. His breastplate must be caught. Damn his broad knight's chest! She groped with one hand along the underside of the rock, seeking the snag. It was the edge of his epaulet. She skinned her knuckles holding it down while she struggled to wrench him backward.

One of the harp strings popped under the strain.

"Come on!" she panted. "Come on!"

She struggled back, her heels skidding in the dirt. A second string popped. The wood screeched in slowly rising complaint.

"Come . . . on!"

She scrambled to her feet as several more strings broke, portending the fatal cracking of the harp's spine. Then, just as the instrument gasped out its final splintering word, she managed to pull him clear.

She didn't know if the boulder simply came to rest back where it was or fell further and sealed the crevice, and she didn't want to know. Either way, her harp was gone, and if she hadn't moved swiftly, he, too, would have been lost.

But she'd saved him. She'd saved Ryance. She mopped her forehead with the back of her sleeve and paused for a moment in silent victory.

There was still much to do. His heart beat, aye, but was his body sound? Curse the dark—she couldn't even see if he bled. She'd have to assess his injuries by touch then. And to do that, she'd have to remove his coat of mail.

She took a deep, steadying breath. Then, with her sense of propriety strained to the limits, she began undressing the near stranger.

Someone was disarming him. Perhaps his squire. But the lout fumbled with the rivets as if he'd never done the task before. Ryance would have upbraided the lad, but he couldn't move, couldn't speak.

Then he remembered the accident. There had been another rockfall. He'd been knocked forward and . . .

And now he was dead. That was it. That was the reason he couldn't move. It was an angel taking his armor from him, for what need did a knight have for chain mail in heaven?

But nay. The Black Gryphon was not destined for heaven. More likely it was one of Satan's minions stealing his plate.

He lay helpless while the wretch unbuckled his greaves and cuisses and epaulets, then struggled with his chain mail and hauberk.

Then the poking began. First his arms, then his chest, then along the length of one leg. Someone seemed intent on finding each and every one of his bruises.

But it was the hand pressed with sudden and alarming candor upon his loins that roused him from his stupor. Demons might lay claim to his mail, but . . .

"What the devil do you . . ." he slurred.

"My lord!"

Much to his amazement, it was Hilaire. With a startled gasp, she removed her hand.

"I . . . I cannot see in the darkness," she explained, "and I . . ." She'd clearly not meant to touch him *there*. And Ryance couldn't help but wish she would again. Already that neglected part of him roused to her brief caress. "But you're all right?" she asked.

"So it would seem." He groaned, sitting up dizzily. "What happened? Are you hurt?" It rankled at him, knowing he'd lain helpless while she ministered to him, unable to come to her defense.

"I'm fine. There was another collapse. You were knocked breathless by a great boulder, and I used my harp to pry . . ." She sighed shakily. "It doesn't matter. You're safe now, and you seem whole. You've a nasty gash on your forehead, but as for the rest, I felt no broken bones." She gasped again softly. She obviously didn't want him to know how extensively she'd examined him.

He found her feminine modesty rather charming. "I'm grateful for your tender care, my lady," he murmured, though it was more desire than gratitude his body expressed to him now. He slicked his fingers briefly across his brow. Indeed, it was swollen and wet with blood, but the cut was insignificant. He'd wear but a mottled bruise on the morrow.

The morrow . . .

Would there be another morrow for them? Was it possible the second rockslide had brought them closer to escape? Or did God mock them by doubly sealing their fate?

He had to find out.

He discovered at once, cracking the back of his head as he stood up, that the ground above the place he'd been digging had collapsed, lowering the ceiling considerably. He had to sidle halfway around the cavern before he could stand aright. And rather than opening the passage above, it seemed a fresh spill of earth and pebbles had filled in every possible crevice. Considering the wealth of debris and the fact he'd been standing directly under the slide, he was lucky indeed to be alive. He ran blistered fingers over the rubble and pricked his thumb on a long sliver of wood.

Her harp. Or what was left of it.

The thing lay in splinters, smashed beneath a great boulder . . . He frowned. What was it she'd said? A rock had knocked him senseless, and she'd used her harp to pry . . .

Dear God—she'd levered this enormous rock off of him. He shuddered as he realized by the size of the boulder how close he'd come to getting his skull crushed. But, however she'd managed it, Hilaire had sacrificed her most precious possession to save him. And a new longing swelled in him, a desire he'd little hope of realizing, a desire to cherish her.

Which made it all the much harder to admit the truth: The fresh slide had successfully blocked their most likely avenue of escape.

seven

S he would not cry. She would *not*. He'd done everything in his power to save them. She'd not demean his efforts with tears. But he'd circled the chamber thrice now, and she knew he only stalled at telling her the inevitable bad news.

"I've heard," she said, swallowing hard, forcing her voice to remain steady, "'tis not an unpleasant way to die." The last word cracked, and her eyes filled with moisture, but she bit her lip to halt its quivering.

"What's this?" he said, and she could hear the forced levity. "Have you given up on me so soon?"

She groped forward and contacted his upper arm. It was a good arm, a strong arm, warm now without its steel plate. It was an arm a wife could have depended upon.

"Kind sir, I pray you won't think me too selfish," she said, summoning up all the dignity and grace her station had taught her, "but I'd rather have you here when I draw my last breath than dead from exhaustion hours before."

"My lady, I . . ."

"You've worn your fingers ragged."

"I would gladly wear them to the bone for you," he answered, startling her with his fierce promise.

Nonetheless, she squeezed his arm. "Nay. Stay with me. Please." She hoped she didn't sound as desperate as she felt. "I cannot bear the thought of dying alone."

He said naught, but when he cleared his throat a moment later, she could tell he'd taken her words to heart.

"Forsooth," he murmured at last, "'tis said to be no more fearsome than drifting off to sleep."

Tears brimmed in her eyes. Though she'd known the truth, hearing it from his lips gave it brutal substance.

"And one so young and sweet," he added, "shall doubtless be conveyed to heaven ere your flesh feels the chill of death."

"And you'll come with me, won't you?" She clasped his arm tightly now, afraid to let go.

"I?" His chuckle was melancholy. "I fear not, my lady. A man such as I was not made to dwell amongst angels."

"Nay! Say not so!" she cried, stepping close to him. "You are a good man!" She clenched her fists upon his gambeson, over his heart. "You gave me comfort in the dark. You told me about the sea and . . . and bandaged my hand. You bloodied your fingers digging at the wall for me. And not once did you lift your voice in scorn, though you knew I fled my betrothed. God's truth, you've been as virtuous as . . . as a saint!"

He laughed in sincere amusement this time, which only fueled her righteous rage.

"Sirrah, I will *drag* you to heaven if I have to," she insisted, "else I will join you in hell."

He seized her wrists lightly in his battered hands, and she could feel the bittersweet warmth of his smile.

"I believe you would," he said.

He ran his thumb along the palm of her good hand, and she marveled at the way such a well-muscled fighter could gentle his warrior touch. Perhaps it was as her maid said, that a woman brought out the mildness in a man.

But she would never know. For she would never marry.

And that realization, more than any other, planted the seed of yearning brutally in her throat and opened the floodgates for her tears, tears she shamefully spilled all over the fabric of his gambeson.

Ryance melted at the sound of her weeping. Taking Hilaire in his arms was as natural as gathering his cloak about him on a winter's eve. She fit into his embrace as if she were forged for it. Her head tucked perfectly into the hollow of his shoulder, and he could smell the womanly scent of her upon the

soft cloud of hair beneath his chin. She felt so tiny, so fragile
within his brawny arms that he feared to crush her, and yet she
cleaved to him with amazing strength. Her body hitched as
she tried to cease her sobbing, but when he brushed the back
of his finger across the delicate line of her jaw, it came away
wet.

She thought him a hero. The idea was dizzying. He'd done
naught to help her. Forsooth, by his very name, he'd sentenced her to this fate. And yet she looked to him for comfort.

Would God he could save her! But what meager hopes
they'd had of escaping were dashed now by the avalanche.
More digging would only increase the risk of a deadly slide.
Running out of air was a merciful passing, but to be crushed
under a deluge of rock . . . Nay, the best he could do was to try
to make her last moments on Earth as painless as possible.

He slowly traced her backbone with his palm. She was
slender, this betrothed of his, with the subtle curves of a
young woman. It was a travesty she'd not see the other side of
twenty.

He gathered her hair in his other hand, brushing it back
from her damp cheek. It was soft as rose petals, thick and possessed of a sleek curl that was wont to curve about his hand.
How odd, he thought—he'd no notion of its color.

"I'm sorry." She said it so quietly he thought he imagined
the words. "For my weeping."

He cradled the back of her head. "No need to be."

She sniffled against his chest. "I don't mean to be such a
burden."

"Nay." He gave her a little shake. "Think naught of it."

" 'Tis only that there were so . . . so many things I'd yet to
do . . . and now . . ." She stifled her sobs as best she could
against the thick padding of his gambeson.

He tried to remember what it was like to be so young, like
an arrow nocked for the firing, to have a lifetime of adventure
stretching out its hand and the bright blue promise of the open
sky above. Sir Ryance had had his adventure. The Black
Gryphon had fought for his King, traveled abroad, won a castle, wed not once, but thrice, served his fellow man as best he
could, and if he lacked that one elusive hallmark of achieve-

ment, an heir to carry on his title, still it couldn't be said he would die before he'd tasted life. But Hilaire . . .

He enfolded his arms more tightly about her, enveloping her in all the solace he could extend. She didn't deserve to die. Curse Fate—she didn't deserve this.

Hilaire rested her head against him. His arms felt wonderful around her. Which made her all the more miserable.

Without chain mail, his embrace this time was far more intimate. She felt the flex of his muscles as he tautened his hold, the warmth of his skin where her forehead touched his collarbone. He smelled like iron and sweat and leather and spice, utterly masculine and irresistibly intriguing.

She closed her eyes, soaking in the scent of him, the feel of him, memorizing his essence, longing to carry the impressions with her into eternity. For it was all she'd ever have of him, all she'd ever know of any man.

She wept anew, but silently this time. His knuckles grazed her cheek, collecting her tears, and yet he neither shrank from nor hushed her. How noble he was, she thought, how chivalrous and honorable and kind. She rubbed her cheek against his hand. His fingers were ragged but warm with life, and on impulse, she turned her head to rest her open lips against them. Without thought, without invitation, she kissed the back of his hand, closing her lips tenderly over each skinned knuckle. A curious addiction came over her, and she found, like dining on sweetmeats, she could not stop. Again and again she pressed her mouth to his flesh, until she heard him groan.

Sweet Mary—she hadn't meant to injure him.

He didn't pull away. But he turned his hand over and stopped her, crossing his palm over her parted mouth.

"Did I hurt you?" she whispered against his hand.

He sighed. "Nay." His low chuckle confused her. "Nay. Not with those soft lips." He brushed his thumb across her mouth, and she felt a peculiar tingling go through her body, as if he'd touched her soul.

It left her feeling reckless and brazen and strangely giddy.

There was naught left now, she realized, no one to answer to, no one to judge her. Why not cast caution to the wind?

"Kiss me," she murmured.

"What?"

"Kiss me." Even the heat that rose in her cheeks couldn't prevent her rash plea. "I've never been kissed. Please . . . kiss me."

His breath collapsed out of him, blowing tendrils of her hair back. "You want me to . . . you want *me* to . . ."

"Aye, kiss me." He was stone silent, and a shiver of worry rocked her. "Unless you find the thought distastef—"

His hand slipped aside, replaced so quickly by his mouth she hadn't time to draw breath. And suddenly she floated on a wave of sensation the like she'd never felt before.

His chin was rough and foreign to the tender skin of her face, but so distracted was she by the startling softness of his mouth, she scarcely noticed. He tasted of earth and ale and desire, and the way his lips clung to hers, tugging, drawing, calling to her, she cared for naught but responding in kind. It was heaven, this kissing, and she wished it would never end.

Then he opened her lips with his, and the liquid heat of his tongue teased at the edges of her mouth before sliding in to brand her own tongue. As if she bore his scorching mark, she writhed against him, and a hot bolt of lust shot through her, sizzling her very bones.

His hands cupped her face then, steadying her, thank God, for she feared she might well collapse under his onslaught. He tasted like fiery nectar, and she longed to drink and drink until she grew besotted upon his kiss.

Her ears were still thrumming, her body vibrating like a harp string, her heart racing when he slowed his kisses and drew gradually away from her.

She should have been sated. She knew that. He'd given her what she'd asked. Why then did she hunger for more? Why did she crave him as keenly as a starving man craved meat? Why did every nerve in her body sing with current, as if the west wind whipped up a storm in her soul?

She had no answer, nor was it her intent to wonder long. Casting off modesty like a stifling cloak, she snagged her fingers in his gambeson and hauled him back to her.

She behaved like a wanton. She knew she did. But it didn't matter. It was her last day on Earth. Her last chance for love. And she refused to succumb to death's sleep until she'd wrung every last drop she could from life.

He'd never felt so clumsy in all his years. It wasn't the dark that crippled him, but rather the maelstrom of emotions coursing through his mind. Here he was, buried under tons of earth, both feet in the grave, no hope in sight, his miserable life near its end. Yet his spirit soared with ecstasy.

Blood long tepid now simmered and pulsed through his veins. Desires long dormant awakened. His mouth still tingled from her kiss, the kiss he'd found nearly impossible to end. But he'd let her go, the way a falconer must let his prize tiercel fly. And, miraculous as it seemed, she'd returned to him. Now his senses centered on the delicate woman who seized him with all the strength of a knight reining in his warhorse.

She kissed him fiercely, hungrily, and the pressure of her sweet lips sent a frisson of desire straight to his loins. Lord— she knew not in what perilous sport she engaged. It had been months since he'd lain with a woman. With the slightest bit of encouragement, he might burst like a keg of overripe ale. But the way she urged him on him now—it was akin to hefting a battle-ax at the barrel.

Still, somewhere within his lust-fuddled brain he remembered he was a knight, a gentleman, a noble sworn to protect ladies, not seduce them. And if it killed him, he'd not violate this woman's trust.

She explored his face now, sliding a fingertip along the crest of his brow, sweeping the bristled hollow of his cheek with her thumb, smoothing the flesh across his jaw, then plunging her hands into the curls at the base of his neck. She sighed against his lips, and her breath was the breath of life, of spring, of sunlight in the dark.

She couldn't know how exalted she made him feel. In the blinding black, she embraced him, accepted him as if he were that man he'd thought lost so long ago. She neither shrank from him in horror nor shook her head in pity, and for once, he reveled in blessed anonymity.

Her fingers coursed along the strained cords of his neck, over the vein pulsing madly in his throat, and he swallowed hard beneath her touch. She nuzzled his ear, her lips nibbling at the lobe, her breath tickling the whiskers along his jaw, and he sucked a tight breath between his teeth.

He wanted her. Urgently. Needed her. He hardened like a molten sword plunged into snow. Surely she felt him stiffen against her, felt the blatant proof of his desire. And yet she didn't retreat. Nay, she pressed even closer, torturing him with her tender woman's shape, letting her hands roam at will over his shoulders, his arms, his chest, so close to his heart.

Hilaire knew not this brazen woman inside her. She was wanton, wild, and unbridled, like a mare quartered with a rutting stallion. She knew no shame, only greed. For what, she was uncertain. But she couldn't keep her hands from roving over the masculine curves and hollows before her. And if lips followed where hands led, it was with an overwhelming thirst that found no quenching.

He swiftly hardened against her belly like a dagger, and though her cheeks burned at the sensation, for she knew well the significance of his swelling, she felt no desire to withdraw. In truth, she longed to press even nearer his man's body, to lose herself in his arms, in his lust, in his power.

A vibration sang along her spine like the sounding of a harp string, humming in her ears, reverberating low in her belly, until it emerged on a moan from her throat.

He answered at once, a groan edged with animal heat, and her passion flared like dry boughs tossed onto flame, turning her to a burning pillar of longing. She needed . . . needed . . .

Him. His arms. His mouth. Closer.

With a stranger's hands, she clawed at his garments, willing them gone, whimpering against his mouth when they'd not obey her.

And then he caught her fists against his heaving chest, halting them, gasping as he grunted a warning. "Nay . . . you must not."

"But I want . . . I need . . ."

His hot breath seared her fingers. "Go now. Get away. Before I forget I am a gentleman."

But she was beyond caring. "Nay. I want . . . I want . . ." She knew what she wanted, but mere words could not express her desire. So she pulled her hands from his and rapidly began loosening the laces of her kirtle. It was a wicked thing, displaying her lust like a common tart, and yet no pang of regret afflicted her. When she had loosed her garment, she took his hand in both of hers and, kissing his palm, placed it where she wanted it most, upon the tingling curve of her bosom.

He gasped as if burned, but she held his hand there, thrilling to the sensation of the rough pads of his fingers upon her untried flesh.

"Lady, you know not what you do . . . what you . . ."

She slipped his hand further inside her bodice, sighing in pleasure at the way his fingers curved perfectly about her breast, as if they were made for such a thing.

"Ah, God . . ." he cried, and the hunger in his voice incited her to a fever pitch of longing.

She lunged against him, and his hand moved fully over her, his fingers brushing the sensitive peak. She drew in a sharp breath, catching her bottom lip between her teeth, so aching sweet was the sensation. Naught could possibly feel more divine, she thought.

Until he lowered his head, tickling the flesh of her bared shoulder with his thick mane, and closed his lips over the crest of her nipple.

Ryance knew better. He knew if he dared to taste her, if he dared slake his thirst, it would be his undoing. Yet her own reckless abandon, her wantonness, her encouragement, compelled him onward. So, despite dire misgivings, he knelt to take tender suckle from her, savoring her ambrosia on his starving tongue.

"Aye. Oh, aye," she groaned, firing his blood till he shook with an ecstasy of longing.

Her breast's twin was just as succulent, and she moaned

softly as he took his pleasure there as well, laving the supple flesh and teasing the nipple to a stiff peak.

She tangled her fingers in his unruly locks, holding him to her, accepting him, and his heart soared even as his braies swelled to bursting.

"Oh, God . . ." Her sigh ruffled his hair. "Please . . ."

It was as if she spoke directly to that appendage rising betwixt his legs, for it responded as if it knew for what she begged. But here he had to intervene. Here he had to curb his animal desires and muster strength to prevent them both.

"We mustn't . . ."

"Please," she whispered.

"But my lady, I fear . . ."

Her fingers found his lips. "Do not fear. Do not speak. Only . . . please . . ."

His groan was somewhere between a laugh and a sob. Lord, Hilaire hadn't even the words to ask for what she desired. She didn't even know her passion's name.

But that didn't stop her from demanding satisfaction. Or begging for it. She dropped to her knees before him and caught his gambeson in her fists. "Please."

He had to drag the words from the depths of his moral soul, from the heart of his chivalry, and they came from him as harshly as an arrow from a wound. "I . . . cannot."

"Why?" she whispered.

"Because you are an innocent," he murmured. "And I am a knight, under a vow to protect . . ."

"Damn your vow."

He desired nothing more. But Hilaire spoke from that innocence. She knew not what she demanded of him.

"What have we to lose?" she asked. "What more horrible Fate awaits us if we act on our desires rather than denying them?"

He felt her gaze in the dark, and he knew, for all her youth and innocence, she was right. They were bound to die anyway. And no act could further stain his already scarred soul.

"Please," she entreated, reaching up one hand to stroke his cheek. "I would taste love just once before I die."

His heart melted at that, and he swallowed hard. Then he nodded, and she collapsed gratefully into his arms.

"It may not be as you expect," he murmured against her hair.

"It doesn't matter."

"I don't wish to hurt you."

She toyed with the quilting on his gambeson. "Does not a new-made knight endure the accolade of his lord's fist?" Her fingertip traced the outline of his mouth. "What is a rite of passage without pain?"

He nipped at her finger, calmed the beast in his braies, and considered carefully what he was about to do. Hilaire was his betrothed. She was to have been his. Their wedding would not, it appeared, come to pass. They had no lifetime together then, not years or months or even days. But they had this moment, now. And perhaps in this small sliver of time, he could grant her just one precious gift—the gift of his body, the gift of his love.

Hilaire would have been lying if she said she was not apprehensive, but as soon as Ryance gently began removing her garments, setting each aside with care, assuring her with constant touches that he was there for her, her fears vanished like mist. Soon she stood naked before him in the dark, listening while he disrobed as well.

He lay her tenderly atop the hard earth floor, cushioned by their garments. For a long while he did naught but run his hands over her, like a potter molding clay, and by the quickening of his breath, she could tell he approved of her form. She explored his contours as well, the magnificent breadth of his shoulders, the hard ridges of his stomach, the powerful cut of his arms. He was beautiful, this man who was to be her husband, who *was* her husband, and she let her hands roam lower, eager to know everything about him.

He grunted as she enclosed the warm, firm length of him in her palm. For all the crisp nest of curls at his base, his skin was amazingly soft, and he stiffened in her hand like a steel sword sheathed in velvet.

"Lady," he rasped, guiding her hand away, "you will undo me. Have patience."

She lay back then, surrendering to his pace, and he brought

her a feast of delights. He left little of her untouched, stroking her reverently from the crown of her head to the sensitive soles of her feet. He kissed her belly, and she arched to meet his mouth. He ran his tongue along the back of her knee, and she squirmed in pleasure. He sucked on her fingers, licking the delicate webbing between, and she gasped in unexpected delight.

But all the while an ache grew deep inside her, a carnal hunger between her thighs, and this was the one spot he would not touch, no matter how her body silently begged. She moaned for him, rocking her head to and fro, lost in dreamy languor as he tormented her.

"Shh," he admonished. "Hush. 'Twill come."

At long last he slung one heavy thigh over hers, pinning her, and slipped one stealthy hand down between her breasts, over her belly, and into the thick of her woman's curls. She arched upward, mewling, willing him to touch her . . . there. And when he finally did, when the moist tips of his fingers parted the petals of her maiden's flower and touched the treasure within, she had to bite her lip to still her cry of relief.

He circled over her flesh then, sliding his hand across her again and again. And he kissed her—on the mouth, on her eyelids, beneath her ear, atop her breast—branding her with his lips till it seemed he possessed every inch of her. For a long while she languished in an agony of ecstasy, and then he murmured in her ear.

"Are you ready for me?"

His rough voice tugged at her passions, and she answered him breathlessly. "Aye. Oh aye."

Then she felt him move over her, felt the weight of him above her, and she stiffened, but he did not press down upon her yet. Instead, he moved his fingers with more purpose over and over the aching nubbin at her core. With his other hand, he plucked gently at her nipples, awakening such pleasure that she felt afire with it. And then, when she thought she could feel no higher joy, a curious current began to build within her, amassing emotion and sensation into one swirling cloud of pure rapture. For one glorious moment, she floated high above the ground, free of care, free of fate, free of her body. Then with a brilliant flash like a thousand bolts of lightning, she cried out her passion on his name and plummeted earthward on the wings of a comet.

Ryance pressed into her as swiftly and mercifully as he could, but his focus had been irrevocably shattered by her victorious cry.

Ryance. She'd called him Ryance. She knew.

She couldn't possibly understand what redemption she offered him when she spoke his name, but he felt suddenly as if he could burst through walls of solid rock for her.

He filled her completely now, and he sighed at the utter bliss of womanflesh surrounding him. She made not a murmur of protest while he waited for her burning to ease and her muscles to relax.

"Oh, Hilaire." He wanted to say a hundred things to her, to apologize, to thank her, to vow his undying devotion. But she moved against him, and all his thoughts were lost as desire surged in his veins like a swollen river.

A score of thrusts, and his long-idle member nigh exploded with relief, spilling its bounty into her hot womb. He shuddered, torn apart mentally and physically by the wondrous woman beneath him. Moved past speech, grateful beyond expression, he simply groaned her name over and over, kissing her face, her hair, her mouth until she giggled with delight.

Hilaire had never felt anything so wondrous. His breaching of her maidenhead had been like the splitting of a chrysalis, birthing a new and brilliant butterfly. She felt beautiful and precious and alive.

This was the magic of lovemaking, she realized. Not only the heady desire and the fierce explosion of passion, but this enveloping glow afterward. He still filled her, and it seemed he belonged there, deep inside, as if she'd always been waiting for him, as if he were a part of her.

She nuzzled his neck, where his pulse yet throbbed warm against her cheek, and for one miraculous moment, forgot about everything but the two of them.

"I love you," she whispered recklessly, blushing at her own confession, but knowing she'd follow him anywhere now, whether he journeyed to heaven or hell.

He squeezed her tighter, and his chuckle sounded almost like a sob. "God curse me for a fool, but I love you as well."

And then, laughing together in the somber face of despair, they slowly drifted to sleep, their limbs entwined, their hearts entangled, The Black Gryphon and Lady Hilaire.

A trickle of dust awakened Ryance, and he opened his eyes. How much time had passed? An hour? A day? Two? The air was so stale he could scarcely breathe, his mind so confused he couldn't comprehend the bright white line that appeared to cut the world in half.

He heard voices. Faint, growing stronger. Campbell. A woman. Somebody else. And he realized the line was a beam of sunlight. The captain had found them at long last! His men and hers, from the sound of it, were breaking through!

His heart leaped in his breast, and he turned to jostle Hilaire awake, to tell her the good news.

"Hilaire!" he croaked, his throat as dry as dust. He shook her by the shoulder. "Hilaire!"

The light was dim, yet bright enough now to make out her features. Her hair was dark and lush, and her face, though smudged with dirt, as lovely as an angel's. Her lashes fell thick upon her pale cheek, and her mouth possessed a natural upward curve, even in sleep, as if she dreamt only of happy things. Lord—his betrothed was beautiful.

"Hilaire! Wake up!" He shook her more roughly. "Hilaire!" But she would not budge. "Hil—"

Mother of God.

Nay.

It couldn't be.

His face crumpled, and his heart knifed painfully in his chest. It *couldn't* be. God could not be so cruel, could He? She couldn't be . . . dead. Not now. Not after all they'd been through.

And yet how else had it ever been for The Black Gryphon?

Had he really believed he could break the curse? Had he truly expected salvation?

Anguish seeped into his veins like bitter poison. He smoothed the tresses back from his angel's forehead and clasped her limp hand. Her image blurred in his tearing eyes, and he cursed the Fates that had let her die without taking him as well.

A warm, wet drop fell upon Hilaire's cheek, and her eyes fluttered open. Where was she? The light was gray, and a man was bent over her, his face concealed by a fall of dark, unruly hair. She frowned. The poor man was weeping. Horrible sobs racked his chest. Her heart went out to him instantly.

Though her throat felt thick with sleep, she managed a whisper. "Don't cry."

His gaze flew to her with such intensity that for an instant she was petrified. But in the next heartbeat, she remembered everything—the siege, The Gryphon, the passion they'd shared.

It was Ryance. It was her betrothed, the man she'd vowed to marry, this—dear God—devastatingly handsome man with sad eyes and a tousled mane, an expressive mouth and a bristled jaw. She could see him. Every bit of his watery gaze and battered face and dazzling smile. Which meant there was light in the tunnel.

"Blessed Virgin!" she croaked, struggling to her elbows. "We're going to get out, aren't we?"

The curse of The Black Gryphon was broken at last.

And she was going to be the wife of . . . Lord—he was beautiful when he looked at her like that.

She flashed him a shy smile, and his eyes twinkled in return. But it was all the exchange they had time for, for—sweet Mary—there they sat, naked as newborns, and already Hilaire heard her father commanding The Black Gryphon's men to make haste with the tunnel.

Epilogue

❦

Ryance tucked his tiny son deeper into the crook of his arm, shielding the infant from the icy spray drenching the deck of the ship. Hilaire laughed again in delight, reveling in the mist, shivering as the sea rose up to spit playfully at the small vessel rollicking across its bosom.

"You'll be soaked by the time we reach port!" he warned.

"I don't care!" she cried, grinning with excitement just before a wayward splash careened off the bow and doused her, plastering her hair to her head. She shrieked in alarm, but refused to give ground. Instead, she raked her hair back from her face, gripped the rail, and braced herself for another onslaught. Riding the sea was the most exhilarating, thrilling, heart-tripping sensation she'd ever . . .

Nay, she thought. There was one thing more rousing. She glanced sideways at her husband, who stared at her with an expression of such adoration that it took her breath away. Abandoning her play, she swallowed hard and ambled toward him.

"You know," she murmured, running a finger along his arm, "if you don't stop looking at me like that, I might have to pleasure you here on the deck in plain view of the other passengers."

His reply was part chuckle, part groan.

She took the babe from him, careful not to drip on little Alden's sweet, slumbering face, and nestled back into her husband's protective arms. He made no protest as she rested her wet head against his broad shoulder.

The ocean was just as he'd described, wide and open and endless. It shimmered azure under the cloudless sky, shifting and folding like liquid samite, winking at her where the sun tickled its crests. The crisp breeze whipped at the ship's sails and left its briny flavor in her hair and on her lips.

Wood and ropes and chains creaked in complaint as the ship rocked with the current, but Ryance assured her they'd make the short journey to France in one piece. And from there, who could say where they'd go? After their harrowing escape from beneath the earth, neither of them desired to be confined again. As soon as she could travel, Ryance vowed to show Hilaire London and the world and all the open sea she could endure.

It sounded marvelous, voyaging to exotic places, breathing the air of foreign climes, sailing at the whim of the wind. But in truth, Hilaire had all of the world she desired beside her.

The babe fussed in his sleep, and she bent to him, hushing him with a tender promise. Then she pressed her chilled ear against her husband's warm chest, listening for his steady, strong heartbeat. He sighed in pleasure, and his contentment rumbled all through her.

This—this was all she needed. All she'd ever need. Her Ryance. Once cursed, now blessed. The Black Gryphon. And the precious child born of their love.

She turned her back on the ocean and burrowed into Ryance's welcome embrace, her love for him as free and enormous and eternal as the sea.

Turn the page for a preview of . . .

My Warrior

the exciting new novel by
Glynnis Campbell
coming soon from Jove Books!

Cambria saw her father in the dream, walking toward her with his arms outstretched. She smiled as he crossed the sunny meadow toward her. But suddenly a great gray wolf appeared between them, its paws massive, its eyes penetrating. The beast opened its jaws in a mournful howl, and a great black shadow fell across the Laird.

She woke with a scream stuck in her throat. Her heart raced like a sparrow's as she tried to break the threads of the nightmare. She rested her damp head in trembling hands. They came more frequently now, the prophetic dreams that haunted her sleep, forcing her to glimpse the future. This one was a warning, she was certain. The wolf boded ill for her father.

Shaken, she rose on wobbly legs, dragging the fur coverlet with her, and peered out the window. Damnation! The sun was in the sky already. Katie had let her oversleep, probably out of kindness—Cambria had been up past midnight polishing armor—but she couldn't afford to be late, not today. She let out a string of curses and tossed the fur back onto the pallet.

A loud crash echoed through the stone corridors and shook the oak floor, bringing her instantly alert.

The shouting of unfamiliar voices rumbled up from below the stairs, and then she heard the frenzied barking of the hounds. Her heart began to pound in her chest like an armorer's mallet. She scrambled over the bed, snatching her broadsword from the wall. With frantic haste, she struggled into a simple gown, cursing as her tangled hair caught in the sleeve. The crash of hurled crockery and women's terrified shrieks pierced the air as Cambria finally pulled open her chamber door and rushed out.

She was fairly flying down the long hallway when she heard the unmistakable clang of blades colliding. She hurtled forward, descending the spiraling steps that opened onto the gallery above the great hall.

At the top of the landing, she froze.

The scene before her took shape as a series of gruesome paintings, none of which she could connect to make any sense: brightly colored tabards flecked with gore; servants huddled in the corners, sobbing and holding each other in terror; hounds yapping and scrambling on the rush-covered stone floor; lifeless, twisted bodies of Gavin knights sprawled in puddles of their own blood; Malcolm and the rest of the men chained together like animals. For a moment, a numbing cold seemed to enclose her heart like a great helm warding off the attack of a blade.

But as her eyes moved from the overturned trestle tables to the slaughtered knights and cowering servants, trying to make reason out of the confusion before her, that armor shattered into a million fragments.

The Laird. Where was the Laird?

Panic began to clutch at her with desperate claws. She shifted her death grip on the pommel of her sword, her eyes frantically seeking out her father. If she could only find him, she thought, everything would be all right. The Laird would explain everything. He always took care of the clan.

She ran trembling fingers over her lips. Dear God, where was the Laird?

As if she'd willed it, two lads came forth from the side chamber, struggling with the weight of the grisly burden they carried between them.

Dear God, no! Cambria silently screamed as she recognized the tabard of her father. Not the Laird!

Even as her heart clenched in her breast, she dared to hope he yet lived. But his body was limp, drenched with blood, far too much blood, and when his head flopped back, the glazed eyes stared sightlessly toward the heavens, where, 'twas clear, his spirit already resided.

The shrill keening initiated in her soul pierced through her heart and escaped her lips. "Nay!" she screamed, hurtling down the steps, her gown floating behind her like a wraith. "Nay!"

Cambria dropped her sword and shook the pale body, unwilling to accept the Laird's impossible stillness. He had to wake up. The clan needed him.

She stroked his forehead, but there was no response. She took his big hand in hers, but 'twas as heavy and slack as a slain rabbit. Blood soaked her linen gown, smearing across her breast as she embraced his silent form.

"Nay," she whispered, "nay."

He couldn't be dead. He couldn't. He wouldn't have left her alone. She'd already lost her mother. He wouldn't have made her endure that pain again.

And yet there he lay, as silent as stone.

A wretched sob tore from her throat, choking her. Dagger-sharp pain lanced through the empty place in her chest.

The Laird was lost to her forever.

Hot tears spilled down her cheeks onto her father, mingling with the blood of the Gavin who was no more. She wept as all around her the nameless invaders murmured on, calmly wiping the blood from their blades, blood of the brave Gavin men who'd not live to fight again. She peered at them through the wild strands of her hair, the obscene enemy who had massacred her people.

Who were they? Who were these bastards who had in one bloody moment destroyed the Gavins?

The pain in her heart twisted into a bitter knot of hatred. Nay. She refused to believe it. These strangers hadn't destroyed the Gavins. No one could destroy the Gavins. Gavins had lived for hundreds of years. They would never die. They lived in her. She was the life's blood of the clan now.

Wiping the tears from her face with the back of one hand, she reached down to clasp the pommel of her fallen sword with the other. She kicked her gown out of her ankles' way and tossed her hair over her shoulder. Whirling, she came up with the blade and faced her foe. Several of the servants

crossed themselves as she turned toward the knights with all
the fury of a madwoman.

"You bastards!" she shouted. "You have slain my father!"

The knights scattered, dodging her slashing broadsword,
and her steel flashed wildly as Cambria attempted to take on
the entire company. She slashed forward and back, using both
hands on the pommel to strengthen her blows. Two men who
underestimated her sincerity received serious wounds.

But the element of surprise couldn't remain long on her
side. Though Cambria kept them at bay briefly, the enemy far
outnumbered her. Two of the knights finally caught her from
behind, squeezing her wrists until she dropped the sword,
which clattered heavily to the floor.

One of the knights yanked her head back by the hair. She
bared her teeth, and her eyes narrowed like a cornered animal's.

Suddenly the unguarded doors of the great hall burst open.
An enormous black destrier galloped like thunder across the
hard floor, bearing a helmed knight. He was flanked by several other riders who hauled their horses to a skidding stop on
the stones. Rushes scattered everywhere, and the knights
fought to control their mounts in the close quarters.

Cambria was forced to her knees by the hulking dark captor beside her, and she squinted against the rising dust.

"My l-lord," the golden knight stammered in surprise, in-
clining his head toward the newcomer.

Tension hung in the air as he awaited a reply, but the silence was only broached by the snorting of the horses, the
squeak of leather tack, and the sniffling of maidservants.

Cambria sucked in great gulps of air through her open
mouth and tried to center her mind. She could feel her body
drifting toward unconsciousness, toward the place where
nothing could harm her, but she resisted its lure, clinging desperately to reality by reminding herself over and over that she
was the Gavin. She clenched her nails into the palms of her
hands to keep from fainting and focused intently on the rider
at the fore, who was nudging his mount closer.

The knight set his huge destrier into motion, Cambria
noted, using only the slightest pressure of one of his armor-
plated knees. The steed tossed its head proudly and ambled

forward. Man and beast no doubt made a formidable foe in battle, their carriage that of champions.

With bullying arrogance, the rider let the steed come to within a foot of the golden knight till it huffed its breath into the man's eyes.

Cambria scowled up at the helmed rider. This had to be the monster responsible for the Laird's murder. She swayed momentarily with nausea, recalling too clearly her father's bloody surcoat and his dead, glassy eyes. She swallowed to control her rising gorge. She prayed God would give her the strength to hold out until help came, until de Ware's knights arrived. The English lord was bound by his word, after all, to protect Blackhaugh from enemies such as these. He'd be obliged to capture and punish these murderers. She hoped The Wolf would tear them limb from limb.

She watched, unable to move, unable to speak, as the knight before her removed his helm, eased the mail coif from his head and ran a hand through his dark curls.

Then her heart stilled as well.

A heavy weight seemed to press on her chest, making it nigh impossible to breathe as she looked upon his face.

He wasn't at all the villain she'd expected. In fact, he was the most striking man she'd ever beheld. His face was evenly chiseled, so perfect it might have been pretty were it not for his furrowed brow and the scars that told of many seasons of battle. His hair, damp with sweat, reminded her of the rich shade of roasted walnuts, and it fell recklessly about his corded neck. His jaw was firm, resolute, but something about the generous curve of his lips marked him as far from heartless.

Most startling, however, were his eyes. They were the color of the pines in a Highland forest, deep and almost sad, eyes that had seen violence and suffering, and had endured. Those eyes caused her heart to beat unsteadily, and she wasn't entirely certain 'twas from fear.

He angled his mount with another nudge of his knee and cocked a brow at the golden knight. "Have you finished here, Roger?" His voice was low, powerful, and laced with irony.

The golden knight regarded him with ill-concealed hostility. "Aye, my lord. They resisted, as you see, but . . ." He shrugged.

The lord shifted in his saddle, tossed his helm to his squire, and blew out a long breath.

The carnage before him was inexcusable. As he'd suspected when he set out this morning to intercept Roger's advance, something here was amiss. He should never have trusted Roger Fitzroi. The man obviously didn't understand the proper use of violence. Judging by the age of the shields of the conquered lining the great hall and the frayed edges of the Gavin knights' garments, this poor clan could have hardly posed a threat. Good Lord, there weren't even that many of them, he thought as he let his gaze roam over the broken bodies.

And then he saw her, kneeling at his knights' feet, in the midst of all the slaughter. The breath caught in his throat. For a moment he forgot where he was.

It was an angel. Nay, he corrected as he continued to stare at the eyes that were too fierce, the jaw too square, the hair too dark. Not an angel. Something more fey—a sprite. Accustomed to the fleshy, languorous women at Court, this lass's exotic looks were as refreshing as the dip he'd had yesterday in the cool loch.

He couldn't take his eyes from her. She looked the way he'd made women look many a time in his bed—hair spilled carelessly, lips a-quiver, cheeks flushed—and all at once, he wished to caress that fine-boned cheek, run his fingers through those too dark, tangled tresses, kiss that spot on her neck where her pulse visibly raced.

The wench was glaring at him with those cut crystal eyes, and he was amazed to see her defiance falter only infinitesimally beneath his regard, a thorough scrutiny that usually made his foes tremble.

She reminded him of a wildcat he'd seen once on his travels through the moors, one caught in an abandoned snare. Before he'd cut the animal free, it had looked at him just this way—frightened, hateful, suspicious. He suddenly had an absurd longing to remove the pain from the liquid pools of her eyes as he'd done for the wildcat.

Ariel nickered softly beneath him and stamped an impatient hoof, jarring him back to reality. Damn, he thought, shaking off his insipid dreaming with a toss of his head. This new life of lordly leisure was making him soft.

He frowned into the girl's face. Then his gaze dropped lower. Her body strained against the thin linen of her gown, and he could clearly see a perverse crimson streak across her fair breast.

Desire fled. He grew instantly livid. "Have we taken to wounding innocents?" he demanded.

Roger answered belligerently. " 'Tis not her blood, my lord. 'Tis that of her traitor father, Laird Gavin. Though this *innocent* wounded two of my men!"

He snorted in disbelief. A wee Borders lass was hardly capable of fighting off the formidable de Ware knights. He looked dubiously down at her again to see if he'd overlooked something. He was sorry it was the sprite's father who had died, but if the Laird was indeed a traitor, it would only have been a matter of time before he was executed for his treachery. Perhaps it was better he'd died nobly, with a sword in his hand.

"Who is your father's successor, lass?" he asked her quietly.

The girl lifted her chin bravely and replied, "I am."

He should have guessed. "And your husband?"

"I have no husband."

"Your betrothed?"

"I have no betrothed. I am . . . the Gavin." Her voice broke as she said it. He could see she was fighting back tears.

Several of his countrymen smirked at the idea of a young woman claiming a castle, but he knew there was nothing odd about it for the Scots. He stared at the girl with a mixture of pity and disgust at the Laird's foolishness in leaving his daughter unmarried and, therefore, unprotected. He swore he'd never understand the Scots' ways.

"I'll spare your life if you swear fealty to me."

To his amazement, the girl fixed him with a jewel-hard stare and shook her head firmly once. "Even now the castle is being surrounded by an army of the King," she proclaimed. "You'll not escape alive."

"Lass . . ." a burly old Gavin man called from the corner, but his captor jerked his chain, ordering him to silence.

He scowled down at the girl and held up a hand to quiet his men's snickering. "The King . . . Edward's army?"

"Aye!" she hissed, her eyes sparking like sapphires. "Lord Holden de Ware will slay you for the murder you've committed! He is a powerful warrior, known to all as The Wolf for his savagery, and he has sworn to protect this keep!"

He stared at her, stunned. Her eyes gleamed with victory, and the thrust of her chin was confident and proud. He almost hated to dash her hopes.

But he had to.

He held her gaze with his own and explained softly, "I am The Wolf. I am Lord Holden de Ware."